O|

LEFT

BEHIND

BOOKS BY CARLA KOVACH

ONE

LEFT

BEHIND

CARLA KOVACH

bookouture

Published by Bookouture in 2021

An imprint of Storyfire Ltd.
Carmelite House
50 Victoria Embankment
London EC4Y 0DZ

www.bookouture.com

ISBN: 978-1-80019-396-3
eBook ISBN: 978-1-80019-395-6

This book is a work of fiction. Names, characters, businesses,
organizations, places and events other than those clearly in the
public domain, are either the product of the author's imagination
or are used fictitiously. Any resemblance to actual persons, living or
dead, events or locales is entirely coincidental.

To teenagers and parents of teenagers. As a teen, you're probably battling your hormones and itching to reach for your adult freedom that is now in sight. As a parent, you may feel that you're losing your child and you fear the dangers that you know exist in the world. You have the wisdom to advise, they are looking to explore this world in readiness of looming adulthood. This is both a difficult and exciting time for you both. I hope the transition runs as seamlessly as possible.

PROLOGUE

Then

The librarian's head disappears through the door marked *Staff Only*. That's the moment you take your opportunity. That librarian has a bobbing head and she reminds me of one of those nodding dogs that people put on shelves in cars. It's like her head isn't properly attached to her shoulders.

My attention goes back to you. You think that no one can see what you're up to but there's little me, peering between Roald Dahl's *BFG* and *Fantastic Mr Fox* on a shelf, watching in silence. I stand so still, I can't even hear my own breath.

Then, you come to life. Charlotte leaves her pencil case and books on the table to go to the toilet. As soon as she's left the library, your trembling fingers root through her pencil case until you come across her gel pens. You like shiny things: stationery, stickers, fluorescent pens. It's all that art you do. This isn't the first time I've seen you taking other people's stuff. I hold back a laugh, not wanting you to see me.

As you walk around pretending to look at books, I glance out of the window. It's a gloomy February. There's a fog on the horizon and a frost glitters on the ground with no sign or promise of spring. A smell of strawberry gum hangs in the air. I think that was Charlotte's but it soon fades, only to be replaced with the damp smell that follows you around. I know your family are poor like mine and you sleep on a sofa bed in the living room. I've heard the other kids call you names. We have a lot in common really. Both outcasts, definitely unpopular and we both look a bit scruffy.

You pat down your clothes and glance around one more time before leaving just as Charlotte is coming back through the door. I run after you, almost tripping over my own feet to catch you up outside. 'Hey. I saw what you did.' With a downturned mouth, you look like you might cry. You go to hand the pens to me but I smile and push your hand away. 'I won't tell. I'll never tell. We're friends.' That's how it started. I don't think you'd noticed me up until that point.

You tell me about your brother and your family. I tell you that Mum and my sister and I live with my nan at the moment. I feel we know each other better and I don't want you to go and ignore me next time we see each other at school. I like being with you. It's fun. 'Do you want to come to mine for tea tomorrow?' I know my mum won't mind, she's always telling me to make friends.

'I'd love to. Sounds good. I'll tell my mum tonight and maybe I can walk home with you after school.' She bites her bottom lip. 'Please promise me you won't say anything to Charlotte. She's so popular, if anyone finds out the whole school will be out to get me.'

'Never.' I make a zip motion with my finger across my lips. 'Best friend's pinkie promise.' I beam a smile as we hold our little fingers up, link them and shake them. Now we're bound together forever and I like that. It makes me feel all fuzzy. I've never had a proper best friend, one that I can tell everything to.

The other kids can be nasty, especially about my hand-me-downs but I like you a lot, and I don't want to lose you, ever. You're my new best friend and you'll always be my best friend. I want someone to play games with, someone who'll come over for tea and maybe sleepovers. I've never had a slumber party before. Maybe I'll get to draw with your new gel pens.

'Why didn't you tell Charlotte about me?' She scrunches up her nose.

'Because you're my best friend and if anyone finds out they won't talk to me either for being your best friend. The other kids hate me. They wouldn't care that I didn't do it, they'd blame me anyway. It's not just that though, friends don't tell on each other and they look out for each other. I won't tell on you ever but you can't tell on me either.' I find myself staring hard at her, then I look away quickly. 'Say it. I will never tell on you.'

She presses her lips together before speaking in her sweet voice that now shakes a little. 'I won't tell.'

'Say promise.' I stand even closer to her.

'Okay, I do.'

'Say it.' Why has she gone quiet on me now?

She swallows. 'I promise.'

I smile. 'See, that was easy, now you have to be my best friend forever.'

CHAPTER ONE

Sunday, 1 August

The gentle sound of chirping birds sent a sharp stabbing pain through Naomi's skull. Already it was sweltering hot and lying in a sealed canvas tent was making her stickier. She almost heaved as she inhaled the smell of vomit on the tissue that she still clutched from the night before. Never again. It had been fun at the time – so much fun. *We're going to have the best party ever*, Oscar had exclaimed as he'd emptied the shopping bag of several bottles of cider. Some he'd stolen from his father's stash and the rest had been bought from a small shop on the estate, a shop they all knew would serve them without question. They'd pooled their funds, determined to have the best night ever.

As her stomach turned, Naomi reached for her phone in an attempt to try to push the nausea from her mind but the sour taste in her mouth wouldn't let her forget too easily. She reached into the tight pocket of her jeans and smiled as she pulled out a packet of mints and popped one into her mouth. The relief was instant. Her heart hummed as she swallowed. That crack on her phone screen wasn't there last night. She pressed the button on the side of the phone to turn it on. Great. Not only had she broken her new iPhone, she'd used all the battery up too. Her mum was going to freak like never before. That present was only a week old and it was a reward for all her study in the run up to taking her GCSEs.

Reaching for the tent zip with shaky hands, she peered out at the ashen grass where they'd lit a small fire last night and she wondered if the others were awake. She spotted Jordan scratching his bottom, hand down the back of his trousers before he peed up a tree. She needed to pee and it was getting more urgent by the second. As she swallowed again, the roof of her mouth almost stuck to her dry tongue. Reaching for her water bottle, she shook it and threw it. Empty was no good to her. She reached into her yellow handbag, no water in there either. A glint of sunshine reflected from one of their empty bottles, almost blinding her. She knew she needed water but her bladder told her she needed to pee more. Maybe one of the others had something to drink.

'Good morning, lazy ass.' Jordan zipped up his fly as he headed back towards the tents.

'What time is it? My phone has run out of charge.' She didn't mention that it was damaged too, opting to have it out with everyone when they were all awake. Someone must know how it happened.

'About nine. The others are still out of it.' He grinned. 'You were so wasted last night, it was hilarious, especially when you tried to strip off. Elsa had to fight you to keep your clothes on.' He scratched the ginger stubble on his chin.

She had no memory of stripping off and her clothes were intact now. As the sun beamed through a broken cloud, she winced and covered her eyes with her arm, resisting the urge to heave. Rolling the mint around her tongue, she spread its flavour all over.

'Hangover?' Jordan bent down and laughed as he pretended to vomit in a comedic way. 'That was you last night. It was like that scene in *The Exorcist*.' He burst into laughter. 'So embarrassing. You kept begging Elsa to not let you get it in your hair. She was trying to hold it back as you ran around in circles like some deranged headless chicken. I filmed it. Do you want to see?'

'Shut up and no, I don't. Delete it now.' She felt her face flush. A flash of recollection came back to her. Had she been crying at one point? There had been an argument and then there were the eyes in the bushes. A shiver ran through her body. She forced her fingers through her long tangled blonde hair but it didn't make her feel more human, they simply got tangled in the lugs.

'Soz, I didn't mean to upset you.'

'I'm not upset and you're not sorry.'

'So are.' He wasn't, she could tell. Then he laughed and continued to make mocking vomit noises.

Naomi shook her head and shoved past him, knocking into his firm arm as she hurried towards the bushes. 'And don't follow me. I'm going for a piss. If I see you lurking, I'll…' She held up her fist and scrunched her nose. 'I'll break your face and that's a promise.' She wouldn't have a hope in hell of hurting her rugby-playing friend but he knew she was serious. How dare he film her when she'd been suffering? That was the biggest breach of trust going. What happened at the parties was meant to stay at the parties. They weren't meant to collect evidence of what had gone on.

His smiling eyes creased at the side. 'Why would I want to watch you taking a piss? I already saw that last night when you pissed just there,' he said, nodding towards her tent. He shrugged and winked before turning back to where they'd lit the fire. It was nothing more than a charred hole in the ground where they'd attempted to toast marshmallows.

Although the sun had come out bright and early, the ground was slightly dewy, or was it a little bit cold? Her flip-flop cladded feet were chilly and she felt a shiver under her vest top. Crows cawed just beyond the line of trees that surrounded them, obviously disturbed by her movement into denser woodland. She stepped over a line of ants that were disappearing into a crack in the earth below and glanced around one more time, making sure that no one was lurking. She'd already put on enough of a show last night.

This was where she'd take a pee, a few steps away from the ants. Backing into the bush a little, she took one last glance. The coast was clear.

Pulling her jeans down, she squatted and felt instant relief as the remains of last night's cider drained out of her body. Crack – that was a branch. She stiffened. It had come from just behind a mass of foliage to her left. 'Jordan. Shove off will you!' Fuming, she pulled up her jeans and parted the leaves and branches but he was nowhere to be seen. 'This isn't funny. Come out now.'

Pushing through the branches, Naomi took another step and all she could see were close-knitted trees and bushes. Maybe she didn't hear anything.

Another crack. Her heart battered against her ribcage. Someone had been watching her and now they were running away. Her head jolted to the left, then to the right as she swiftly sobered up. That's when she saw something fleshy in the undergrowth. 'Leah.' She recognised the pink and black trainers and ran over. 'What the hell are you doing here? Did you sleep here all night?' Her freezing cold friend felt stiff and heavy as Naomi tried to pull her by the legs from in the dip, under the bush. Giving up, she dropped the girl's legs and swallowed. 'Leah?' Kneeling down, the branches shredded her bare arms as she pushed through, then she let out a scream when she saw the blank pale face of her friend. Eyes open and protruding, a pallor to her skin and her tongue lolling and swollen. Leah wasn't breathing.

Bile spurted from her mouth as she quickly turned to the side, then she began screaming as loud as she could. No one was coming, then there was that cracking sound again. Stumbling back, she fell onto her bottom and tried to peer through gaps in the leaves. 'Please don't hurt me.' Tears began to spill down her face. She wished she hadn't come to the party. Someone had killed Leah and now they were watching her.

Digging her nails into the hard earth, she managed to stand on her jellied legs then she ran as fast as she could, entering their makeshift camp where she screamed at the top of her voice. Oscar had now woken up. He threw his stub end to the ground and puffed the last of the smoke from his mouth and then she spotted Jordan's ginger hair emerging through the bushes.

'What's up with you? I bet she saw a spider.' Oscar burst into laughter. A clump of his brown hair was kinked from where he'd slept. 'Want a smoke?' He offered her one of his roll-ups.

Naomi pushed the packet away. 'I need a phone, now. It's Leah, she's dead.'

CHAPTER TWO

Gina jolted awake from a deep sleep, heart pounding in time with her buzzing mobile phone that was about to fall from her bedside table. It was Sunday and she wasn't scheduled in at work. Saving it just in time, she snatched it up and placed it to her ear. 'DI Harte.' Flinching at the booming of the voice, she moved it away from her ear a little.

'Guv, a body has been discovered in the woods that run alongside the river, not too far from the Waterside Café where the truckers stop for food.' DS Jacob Driscoll sounded perky, like he'd already had plenty of caffeine that morning.

'Do we know anything?' She wiped the thin film of perspiration from her forehead and noted the fact that today was set to be a hot one. Bodies and high temperatures were not the best mix. Her curtains blew a little in the warm morning breeze as she threw the sheet off her body and her cat, Ebony, darted from under it and hurried down the stairs.

'All I know is what was reported in the emergency call. Sixteen-year-old girl and she has been named as Leah Fenmore. Her friend, Naomi Carpenter, called it in after finding her in the bushes. They were all camping out together last night. Having a party apparently.'

'Damn. Have forensics been notified?'

She could hear Jacob clicking his mouse. 'Yes, they are about to arrive and uniform are there cordoning off and taking statements.'

'I'm on my way.'

After ending the call, she hurried out of bed, quick shower and brushing of her teeth, then she spotted DCI Chris Briggs at the bottom of the stairs sipping his coffee. Against her better judgement, he'd come over last night. What should have been a pleasurable evening had turned sour when he received that anonymous message on his phone. Someone knew about her past and they knew what she'd done and they were making sure that Briggs knew too. She'd left him asleep on the couch about two in the morning before creeping up to bed and having the most atrocious nightmares. Her skinny black cat, Ebony, began to wind its body around his legs, pining for food. He held up his phone. 'I just got the call too. Murder by the Waterside Café.'

Gina wished that a girl's murder was the main thing on her mind, but it wasn't. Gina's secrets were coming back to haunt her. Their mystery messenger knew things that could end her career and take away her freedom, and they were making sure that Gina and Briggs got the message. 'What are we going to do about the message?'

He ran his fingers through his floppy uncombed hair, some still half stuck to his head from sleep. 'I seriously don't know. Just sit on it for now.'

'Why are you protecting a murderer?' Gina blinked as tears formed in the corners of her eyes. 'How does this person know what I did and why are you helping me? You could just turn me in for what I've done. I wouldn't even deny it and this whole mess that is my life would be over for you.'

'You are not a murderer. Terry was no husband to you. He was an abuser who got what was coming to him.' Briggs pulled her in and kissed her on the head, both of them knowing that they were slowly drowning in Gina's murky past.

She took his coffee from the ledge and finished what was left. 'I don't think a jury would see it that way.' She frowned and wiped her eyes.

He reached out and stroked her cheek. 'This message could be nothing. It might not even be about you. We're jumping to conclusions. I'll head to the station straight after you and see you there in a bit. Got to work out how we tackle the press. I can guarantee that because a bunch of teenagers are involved, this poor girl's murder will already be all over social media.'

'I just love it when our job is made harder.' Her phone beeped again and she froze.

'It's a message, isn't it?'

Gina gulped down her panic, unsure of how she was going to get through the day. 'It just says, *murderer*.'

'Let me see.' Briggs glanced over her shoulder.

'I have to get to work.' She left him standing in the hallway as she slammed the door and got into her car. A sick feeling began to whirl. She'd struggled to get hold of her daughter, Hannah, lately and their relationship had never been good. Gina pressed her number again, hoping just to hear a friendly voice, but her call was immediately cut off. All she'd needed was some reassurance that it couldn't be anything to do with her daughter. There wasn't a reason that could be the case but there was no one else that could delve into her home life. Then, her mind whirled as she began driving through the lanes. The press had tried to mess with her head before. Were they trying it on, hoping that she'd crack and tell her story? They knew of her past. Her drunken ex-husband, dead after a so-called fall down the stairs. She'd got the message loud and clear from whoever was sending them. How many other murderers was Briggs protecting? Involving him had been strategic.

Focus – she had to get her mind on the case. There was someone dangerous on the loose, capable of killing a teenager and she had to find them and quick. Whatever was happening in her personal life was going to have to wait.

CHAPTER THREE

Leaving her jacket in the car, Gina stepped out onto the torn-up tarmac road at the far end of the Waterside Café's car park, next to the three police cars, an ambulance and the forensics van. A red articulated lorry was the only other vehicle parked up. She undid the top button of her blouse and fanned her face with her hand. Not only was it hot, the occasional hot flush gave her trouble. Bloody menopause.

A man in an apron ran towards her. 'Hey, wait.'

She checked her watch, not having time to stop and chat but it was possible that this man knew something so she did as he asked and waited.

'Are you police?' He wiped his hand on the tea towel that dangled from his pocket.

'I'm Detective Inspector Harte. You are?'

'John. Sorry, John Tallis. I own the café. What's going on here, only I saw on Facebook that someone has been murdered?'

Briggs had been right about social media blowing up. 'I can't comment right now but do you know anything that might help?' The smell of bacon oozed from his pores.

He shrugged. His peppered fair hair looked as though it was stuck to his forehead and he scratched his stubby nose. 'I only know that there are always kids lurking around here. They come from the estates and party the night away. I sometimes open up to urine in the doorway if they venture out of the woods and

I keep finding things like these gas canisters around. They're a nuisance but they do give me a bit of business here and there.'

'Business?'

'They come in for chips and cans of pop, things like that. I open fairly late to capitalise on truckers passing through.'

Gina pulled out her notebook. 'What time do you close?'

'Ten every evening, even Sundays.'

'Did you see anything last night?'

'I heard music thumping. It sounded like it was coming from over there.' He pointed into the woodland. 'They were listening to some sort of modern stuff that I didn't recognise, then I heard the odd shout or laugh. That was it. I don't really take much notice as this happens all the time.'

'Do you have CCTV out here?'

He shook his head. 'Wish I did. I can't afford such extravagances.'

'Thank you, Mr Tallis. We'll take a statement from you in a while—'

'I have to give a statement?'

'It's routine.'

'Of course.' He linked his hands together and began fidgeting. 'I guess I'll wait until someone comes by. Is there anything I can do?'

He seemed eager to help in a strange way. Maybe too eager. Gina looked into his eyes for a moment longer than was comfortable, then he broke their eye contact by looking down. 'Yes.'

'Okay.'

She pulled her wallet from her pocket, removing a twenty-pound note. 'Can you bring us a lot of coffee? Make it strong. If you just hand it all to the PC on a tray, whoever's guarding the cordon, that would be great.' She knew everyone would need a little bit of perking up. She could feel a tremor in her hands and wondered if caffeine was the best thing on a day like this. Handling a murder and those damn messages was a double burden she could do without. It was a Sunday morning and quite a few of the officers that had been called in would probably have been working last night. They would definitely appreciate coffee.

He nudged her hand. 'It's on the house. I want to do my bit so I'm glad to help.'

'Thank you. That's very kind of you. I must get on.' She took a couple of steps back, hoping that he'd turn to go but his gaze remained on her until she left his car park.

As she approached the PC at the edge of the woods, she smiled and filled in her details on the log sheet. She checked again and John Tallis was now jogging back to his café. A wash of unease came over her as she shoved the twenty pounds and her notebook back into her pocket before following the marked-out route. She gulped, knowing that at the end of the trail would be a body.

CHAPTER FOUR

'Guv, over here,' Jacob called her, and she caught sight of him waving his arms from behind the trees while jumping in his puffy forensics suit that hid his hair that always looked shiny and stuck to his head. It was still morning, but already the temperature was rising. PC Smith was placing cordon tape around one of the trees. She slipped through before he closed off her entrance to the crime scene.

'Are all the other kids still close by?' It would make her job easier if they were.

'Yes, PC Kapoor is with them now and some of the parents have turned up too. O'Connor has just arrived and he's headed over there to speak to everyone.' She peered over and could just about make out DC Harry O'Connor's shiny bald head and PC Jhanvi Kapoor's uniform. Despite her injuries from the last case, she was recovering well and had even begun to study for her sergeant's exam. PC Kapoor waved and hurried over. Jacob stepped aside and began checking out the area.

'Hi, guv. We're just speaking with all the kids now. You okay? It's a hot one.'

Regardless of the circumstances, Jhanvi Kapoor looked as perky as ever. It never ceased to amaze Gina how such a small woman with a loud Brummie accent could be so tough. The last case they worked on could break anyone but the PC had taken a week off at most after leaving hospital and vowed to come back stronger, putting in straight away to study to be a sergeant. 'It'll be great to have you on the team again on this one, and PC Smith too. Only the best!' And Gina meant it. PCs Smith and Kapoor had helped them with many murders and were always a welcome and useful part of the team.

'I wouldn't miss it for the world, guv. As long as I don't get kidnapped by any killers this time, we'll be okay.'

Again, Gina wondered if Kapoor was so perky inside. She worried that the trauma would come back to haunt her or maybe it would eat away at her, manifest itself as post-traumatic stress disorder but she'd been released from her counselling sessions. 'I know that this is the first big case since what happened.'

Kapoor looked at her with large chocolate eyes, smiling, which emphasised her youthful dimples. 'Guv, I really am okay. I'll always have a few scars on my body, but up here,' she pointed to her head, 'I'm tip-top.'

'Well, you know if you ever need to talk, my door is always open, day or night.'

'I know and thanks, guv. If I need it, I'll be the first to barge through and ask for help. Promise.'

Gina knew that was the time to shut up. She'd tried to look after Kapoor a little since but now she needed setting free from being asked if she was okay all the time.

'Right, I best get back to it.' Kapoor hurried back to the camp area.

'Great. Let's head further in.' Gina smiled at Jacob and pulled a bobble from her pocket and tied her own wild hair up before it dampened with the heat.

'I don't know how she keeps it together.' Jacob frowned.

'Me neither. I'm in total admiration of her.' Gina grabbed a forensics suit and pulled it on over her black trousers and cream shirt. Then came the shoe covers, followed by the stifling gloves and mask. Already she felt sluggish and the day had barely begun. 'Is Bernard on duty?' Bernard Small was the crime scene manager and she'd worked most of her big cases with him in charge of forensics.

'Yes, he's already there, assessing the scene. The CSIs have put down the stepping plates as you've noticed. They're videoing and photographing at the moment.'

Gina led the way down a dried mud slope and along a trampled out path with thick bushes and tree stumps on either side. This is where the stepping plates began. They both clip-clopped, trying not to slip on their boot covers.

Beyond the lined path, she could see that there were little clearings where the big trees splayed out above. Perfect pockets for camping and partying teenagers. The telltale signs were everywhere. Bags of rubbish, empty alcohol bottles. She spotted a used condom ahead, then another. What should be a beautiful nature spot to be enjoyed by walkers and families really was the pits.

The sound of the camera clicking and the CSIs stepping back and forth over the plates alerted Gina to where they were. Bernard Small's tall wiry frame emerged from behind a shrub as he stood up straight, blocking the sun from her eyes.

'Ahh, Bernard. I would say nice to see you but given the circumstances.'

He nodded. 'I know. We always meet up over a murder. Come through.' He parted the branches for her and Jacob, and they followed him to the evidence boxes, where samples were laid out and tagged. 'We're still documenting all we can but you might be able to see from here. It's probably going to be a while before you can go through as the body is in an awkward position. We don't want to lose any trace evidence, however minute, so as always, we're being careful and methodical. However, we have managed to pull the foliage back to take photos and examine what we have so far.'

Standing on tiptoes and peering over a clump of leaves, Gina spotted the team at work. She tried to ignore her stomach clenching because of the vomit next to the body. Jacob held his hand up and waved at CSI Jennifer and she smiled back. They'd been in a relationship for ages and they always did this little wave and smile when they met on the job. Gina peered down and could see the girl's legs but that was all. Most of her body was still in the bushes. 'Can you fill me in on what you've seen?'

'Yes. Teenage girl between fourteen and eighteen,' Bernard replied.

From what the girl's friend had said when calling in, this matched so far. Naomi Carpenter had identified the girl as Leah Fenmore – aged sixteen. A slight knot formed in Gina's throat, having a daughter made looking at this young girl tough. She couldn't imagine how the parents were going to take the news. If it were Hannah dead in the bushes, Gina would feel as though her world had collapsed.

'She's approximately five feet three inches tall, of slight build. Shoulder-length brown hair and a lip piercing, but I guess you want me to get to the nitty-gritty.'

Jacob scrawled a few notes with his gloved hands.

'Yes, please.'

'The cause of death looks to be strangulation as there are what look to be fingermarks around her neck.' Bernard nodded to a CSI who responded by pulling the branches back. 'See the bruising that is starting to come up?'

Gina nodded. 'Just about.'

'The eyes are protruding and you can see that the blood vessels have burst. Time of death – between one and two in the morning. Determined by the temperature and stage of rigor mortis.'

'Any sign of sexual assault?'

Bernard took a step back and transferred his weight from one foot to the other. 'I can't be sure just yet but there is a bite mark on the top of her right breast. It hasn't pierced the skin deeply, but there's a red scratch and a little bruising. We will know more when we get her out of here and examine the body thoroughly.'

The thought of someone biting that girl's skin hard enough to leave bruising made Gina shudder. Her dead ex, Terry, used to bite her sometimes when they had sex and the more she'd tell him it would hurt, the more pain he would inflict. She shook those thoughts out of her head. Maybe their victim had been assaulted or maybe those marks were made in the heat of passion. She didn't have those answers yet and jumping to conclusions based on her own grim experiences wasn't going to help the situation.

'Oh, you can just about see the edge of her denim shorts. They're undone at the button, as is the zip.'

Gina looked away from the body. 'Any semen present?'

'Not that we've been able to tell, but, as I said, we'll know more when we examine the cadaver further.'

The cadaver was a young, healthy, breathing, living girl only a few hours ago. A shiver ran through Gina's body. 'Any further signs of a struggle?'

'So far, we haven't spotted any more bruising or defence wounds at all.'

This was telling Gina that the girl didn't fight. Was she frozen with fear or did something start out as consensual then turn out badly? Or maybe she was drugged. 'Can you arrange for toxicology to test for anything that might have incapacitated her? Rohypnol, anything that can make a person drowsy or disorientated. I guess they were all drinking too.'

'You know that the tox report won't come back for ages?' Bernard reached into his beard covering and scratched his chin.

'Yes, always a shame but we will eventually need to know if there was something else at play. If she didn't make any effort whatsoever to fight back while she was being strangled to death, there has to be a reason and I want this case to be watertight.

Cross everything and dot everything.' She paused. 'The moment you know more, please let me know.'

Jacob stepped onto another plate and continued to make a few notes as they spoke, wiping his brow every now and again.

Bernard nodded. 'I will do.' He glanced over at the others and smiled. 'You can take a closer look now if you like. Just make sure you stay on the plates. I don't think you'll see as much as you hope to. She's been dragged out of the bushes slightly. The girl who found her pulled her by her feet, thinking she was asleep.'

Bernard was right. All Jacob and Gina could properly see was the girl's legs and a glimpse of her lolling tongue. To get a better look would mean pulling back the branches. She spotted what looked like a bit of dried blood. 'What's this on the thorny branch?'

Bernard looked over. 'Blood. The girl who pulled her out from the bushes cut her arm on those thorns.'

Jennifer bent over and placed a yellow evidence marker next to a cigarette and another next to a crisp packet. The whole of the woodland was dotted with yellow and most of those markers were next to litter.

'Hi, Jen,' Jacob said as he placed his pad in his pocket.

'You okay?' Even though Jennifer was wearing a face mask, Gina could tell from her eyes that she was smiling back at Jacob.

He nodded and smiled. 'I'll catch you later.' She carried on working.

'So, any further thoughts for now?' Gina turned to Jacob, now speaking louder to be heard over the chorus of birdsong. The lovely morning, flooded with golden sunlight and with lush foliage spreading across the land, was now tainted by the death of a young girl and Gina clenched her hands. Whoever strangled her had to be caught and they had no time to waste.

He shook his head. 'She had to be really drunk or even drugged not to have any form of defence wounds. I mean, if I were being strangled to death, I'd be going mad.' He wiped his brow.

Although the crime scene suits were light, Gina's was literally sticking to her neck and she knew Jacob was feeling sticky and uncomfortable too. 'Let's head to the camp and see where they all stayed last night, then we can get these suits off and speak to Kapoor and O'Connor, see if the witness statements have come up with anything. I also want all the kids down the station with their parents to give a formal statement. It's going to be a long day but we need to record everything. I want to know exactly what those kids were up to last night.' She glanced across the landscape. 'Those cottages over there, I guess you could walk to them in several minutes.' She pointed to the chimney tops that reached towards the sky.

'That's Oak Tree Walk. Nice little road, sought after as far as cutesy terraced cottages go.'

'I want to know if the residents heard or saw anything. They're close enough to be disturbed by noisy kids having parties. Maybe one of them walked a dog or was sitting in their garden last night. We also need to know if anyone has made any complaints in the past. I can't rule out someone flipping after being regularly disturbed by parties. Can you give Wyre a call at the station? She can take a look before we get back?'

As they reached the cordon, Gina removed her face mask. She nodded at PC Smith who was keeping guard to make sure that no locals passed with their dogs or decided to jog over any evidence. Jacob pulled out his phone and began speaking to DC Paula Wyre. Gina glanced around. There was often a crowd at a crime scene but here the cordon was just billowing in the breeze. No reporters were yet trying to lean over for photos or statements. It would only be a matter of minutes before they turned up. The news had already hit social media and the media were always hot on that.

Jacob ended his call. 'She's getting onto it now, guv.'

'Right, let's check out this camp and see if the bigger picture will help us to find our murderer.'

CHAPTER FIVE

Caro yawned and prised an eye open. The sound of her mother clattering downstairs had woken her. She turned on her phone and glanced at the time. It was way past eleven. Maybe she could get out of going to Grandad's for Sunday dinner. The food was normally pants. Some horrible fatty meat covered in thin gravy with a huge portion of mushed up veg. Maybe she could claim to be coming down with a cold. No one would want to risk Grandad catching it, not with his asthma. The family all go on about his chest and his wheeziness.

Her bedroom door burst open and her little brother, Jake, leaped onto her bed and began jumping and screaming. The mattress squeaked and dipped with every jump, threatening to cave in. 'Dad said, get up you lazy arse and you've got ten minutes.'

She grabbed a pillow and threw it at him. His eight-year-old onesie-clad body dodged her fluff-filled torpedo with ease. Her knuckles whitened as she clenched another pillow and held it above her head, ready to strike again.

Jake stuck his tongue out and laughed.

'Get out of my room, Jake. You know you can't just come in without knocking. Turd face.'

Sticking his tongue out, he blew a raspberry, dotting his spit on her cheek. He jumped off the bed with a thud so heavy the window frames and lightshade rattled, then he helped himself to a couple of her chocolates that sat in a bowl on her chest of drawers. Stuffing them in, she saw the mulching chocolate churning around in his cavernous mouth, then a string of brown dribble pooled at his chin before landing on her carpet – yuck. He went to grab another.

She hurried over and fought it from his tight fist, his face reddening. He tried to cling on until it squelched underneath the wrapper. 'Let go, you little weasel shit. They're mine and you're disgusting. Go clean your ugly face.'

'Not fair. I want some and you're the ugly face.'

She picked him up kicking and screaming then dropped him on the landing before slamming her door shut. She'd tried arguing with him many times but he always won as he'd just hurl a load of insults and laugh.

He banged and banged to come back in. 'Caro, let me in. I love you, big sis. I was joking. You're only a bit ugly.'

'Just go away.'

'Spotty face.'

Some days she hated Jake, she hated him a lot; and today was one of them. She rubbed her throbbing temples and stared into the mirror on her dressing table. A film of face powder covered it so she rubbed it away with the sleeve of her pyjama top for a clearer view. There was no way she'd be able to get dressed in ten minutes. Her almond-shaped brown eyes were a little puffy from being woken so abruptly and spots, so many spots to cover up. They always came out worse when she was stressed. Nothing whatsoever had cured her acne and the scarring was getting unsightly. All she wanted to do was cry and have a shower, but she didn't even have time for that. Great – not only was she going out looking a mess, she'd smell too.

'Caro – five minutes.' Her dad's booming voice travelled up the stairs.

Her phone lit up again, then again. Then several messages flashed up in her WhatsApp groups. There was one for school friends, one for the friends she hung out with outside school and then Facebook flashed, followed by Twitter. It was all happening at once. Something big was going down and she had to see what it was. She opened Twitter and looked at the local groups that she and her friends followed.

BellaBoo89xx
OMG! Girl murdered in woods. #CleevesfordMurder

AJJ1loveheart
@BellaBoo89xx Who? Do we no her. #CleevesfordMurder

OrElsa_
Here now. Gruesome. Police everywhere. 😭 RIP @Fenny_Leah_
#CleevesfordMurder

AJJ1
@Fenny_Leah_ RIP Will B sadly missed. I had PE with her.
#CleevesfordMurder

AllyKayBenson
OMG Not @Fenny_Leah_
She was my bestie in primary. #MrsSmithClass
@OrElsa_ What's happening? No who killed her?

OrElsa_
@AllyKayBenson So traumatised and no. #KillerOnTheLoose

TheMeeganMrs
I mean, those kids were out partying and only 16. What kind of parent allows this? They're a bloody nuisance too.
#OakTreeWalk antisocial behaviour.

JimBerryATW

@TheMeeganMrs too true. Bloody nuisance kids. Probably drugs or gangs or something. The sooner they all shoot each other the better. #OakTreeWalk

OrElsa_
@TheMeeganMrs @JimBerryATW
She was my friend and her parents are lovely. Hate people sometimes. #TwitterBitches

JimBerryATW
@OrElsa_ Grow up #GenerationSnowflake

OrElsa_
@JimBerryATW up urs!!!!

WarwickshireHerald
Murder reported in Cleevesford last night by @Waterside-CafeCleevesford Witnesses urged to call police immediately.

WatersideCafeCleevesford
@WarwickshireHerald Thanks for mentioning us – not. It was more like the back of #OakTreeWalk
We are still open for business.
RIP @Fenny_Leah_ Thoughts with Ur fam. X

The tweets went on and on, some blaming Leah's parents, others blaming Leah but most were condolences and RIP messages. Caro gulped and choked on her tears, then a knock at the door broke her sobs. 'Go away, Jake.' She didn't need him teasing and annoying her right now.

'It's Mum. One of the parents from school just called me. Can I come in?' Her mother didn't wait to be asked, she gently nudged the door open and hurried across the room, embracing her daughter and wiping the tears from her cheeks. 'I'm so sorry, honey. I hope whoever did this is sent to hell.'

Little did her mother know that Caro had been invited to the party but she had turned down the invite. Another stream of tears fell down her cheeks. She couldn't catch her breaths between sobs and her chest heaved with sorrow. A flash of a memory stopped her sobbing, something suffocating and crushing, then darkness – that was all she saw and all she kept seeing. Now wasn't the time to delve into that dark memory of the last party she went to. There were things she could remember and others she couldn't. It was the things that she couldn't remember that worried her the most. 'Can I have a moment alone, Mum? Please?' She pulled away from her mother's floral-scented embrace and stared at her with glassy wet eyes.

'Okay, honey. Come down when you're ready. I'll give Grandad a call, tell him we'll be over later instead.'

'Thanks, Mum.' Her mum made a downturned mouth sad face and left, pulling the bedroom door closed behind her. Caro ran to her bedside table and pulled the bottom drawer open. She scribbled down the tiny bit of information that she remembered – a flicker of light coming from the darkness. Glancing at her other notes, there were still so many blanks. She had to fill those blanks and quick. Her phone beeped. It was a Snapchat.

Say a word and you'll be next to die!

It disappeared off the screen and an uncontrollable shiver flashed through Caro's body. She dropped the pen and notebook and wiped the tears away. Who wanted her dead?

CHAPTER SIX

Gina led the way to the camp where all the action had taken place the night before. PC Kapoor was sitting with the four teens on the grass away from the fire pit and tents. The parents were passing tissues to the distraught teens and words of comfort were being whispered. PC Kapoor ran over, leaving them consoling each other while O'Connor remained with them.

'We have just about taken all the initial statements. Parents have turned up so all of them have an appropriate adult with them. I have to head back to the station in a moment. Forensics have also said that we all need to get out of the way soon as they are widening the search. The kids are in shock so not much is coming out clearly which means that DC O'Connor and I don't have much to share with you. As you can see, we've moved away from the camp area but we really need to get them all out of here.' Kapoor held up her notebook.

'Have any of them been checked over by a paramedic?'

'Yes, they're shocked and upset but they were all cleared to be able to give a statement. The girl over there sitting to the right, Naomi, had cuts to her arm but those have been treated and cleaned.'

'Great. Before we head over and check in with O'Connor, can you give us a quick overview on what has been said so far? I can relay that to the team before formal interviews get underway?' Gina led Kapoor even further away from the group so that they could talk freely. Jacob followed and they stood in a small huddle.

'Yes, guv. Naomi Carpenter found the body. She's the one with the white blonde hair. They were the same age, in a lot of the same classes at school and close friends. She said that Leah, the victim, decided to go home last night but didn't give a reason. I pressed her on it a little but she just kept saying she couldn't remember anything as they were all drunk.' Gina glanced over Kapoor's shoulder and her gaze met Naomi's. The stony-faced girl quickly looked down at her flip-flops and began nervously tapping her feet on the earth below.

'Was there anything other than alcohol in play?'

Kapoor shook her head and Jacob removed his notebook from his pocket. 'They are saying no, but I get the feeling we're not getting the whole story from them. DC O'Connor is still talking to them now as you can see. Maybe he's finding out more as we speak.'

'How about the others?'

'The other girl is Elsa James. She was still in her tent when the body was discovered. She too says that she can barely remember the night before.'

'Hmm, how about the boys?'

Kapoor shifted a little in her uniform. 'Again, guv, they had nothing to add. It's like they've all agreed to say absolutely nothing to us apart from that they were all drunk.'

'I get a feeling you're right. Very odd that they're all saying that they remember nothing at all. We need to know what they're hiding. As it stands, they were all within the vicinity at the right time and something may have gone down. An argument, a fall out. Maybe it was enough for one of them to kill Leah. Obviously we need far more evidence but keep it in mind that they had opportunity. Let's look for motive and leave forensics to work their magic.' Gina paused and glanced back at the camp. The circle of charcoal in the dug-out earth was surrounded on the one side by three two-person tents and the grass was littered with cigarette butts, empty bottles and cans. 'Any evidence of drug use, maybe nub ends that could be weed, etcetera?'

Kapoor bit her lip. 'Keith in forensics has had a preliminary walk through and found a few but can't confirm anything yet. I've kept away as he's coming back to secure the site in a moment. He said the tents and everything in them have to stay how they were left. Some of the teens whinged about wanting their bags but we explained that the whole of the camp is a crime scene and nothing must be moved or tampered with.' Gina watched as another PC began to tape up the area.

'Are you okay getting them and their parents to the station for further questioning? We need them there ASAP, especially if we need to clear the area for forensics. I'm going to speak to John Tallis who owns the truck stop before heading back. Keep each of the kids apart from now on, especially when you or O'Connor aren't there with them. I want to speak to them all in turn and I don't want them to have any further opportunities to work on a story. We need the truth.'

'I'll sort that now.'

'Oh, Keith has probably mentioned this, but we'll need their clothes, some swabs and footwear. Hopefully everyone will cooperate with us taking those.'

'He did and we're on it, guv. Already got agreement from the teens and the parents. They are claiming that they want to help and seem genuinely upset by what has happened.'

'Thank you. Great job, Jhanvi.' Gina wanted to walk over and offer her condolences to the teens but something was amiss and she needed to keep her game face intact. She was the authority here and she would be interviewing them. If there was an inconsistency to be found, she'd find it. The stocky red-haired lad stared over, then he looked away quickly. He nudged the boy next to him and then he looked up, his stare a little worrisome as if he was trying to suss Gina out. The second boy broke away before Gina did and the pair went back to talking quietly between them.

'I've been discreetly watching those two. There have been a few looks between them. Did you see how the red-haired lad looked over then nudged the other girl, Elsa, is it?' Jacob whispered in her ear.

'I did. They know a lot more than they're letting on but we have to tread carefully. A close friend of theirs has been strangled to death and they were the last people to see her alive. I wish I didn't suspect them, but I do. What they may have done is another question entirely. Do one or all of them have a hand in Leah Fenmore's murder, or are they hiding something minor that they would class as major? We're going to have to be gentle for now if we're to get them to talk.'

Kapoor began to address the group and explain what would happen next, then O'Connor took over with them all as Gina and Jacob left the scene.

'Do you think the café owner,' he clicked his fingers as if trying to remember the man's name, 'Tallis, that's it, do you think he knows something?' Jacob trod down a few fallen branches as they headed back to the outer cordon. PC Smith was coming their way with a tray of coffees in polystyrene cups.

'I don't know but we're going to speak to him now. I know he sounded casual about the kids camping up and causing a nuisance but who knows? Maybe it all got too much and he lost it. By the time we've finished there, the kids should be at the station and hopefully ready to speak.' As PC Smith passed them, Gina grabbed a coffee. 'Thank you.'

PC Smith murmured something about needing caffeine and continued down to distribute them to everyone.

As Gina stepped off the trodden path onto the corner of the car park, she glanced along the row of recently parked up trucks, including the red one that was there when they arrived.

'I wonder how many trucks stayed overnight. That's something else we need to find out.'

A stocky man carrying a washbag began to pull himself into the huge red cab.

'Excuse me.' Gina ran over to him.

'Yes.' He sat in the driver's seat, looking down at Gina with his door open.

'Did you stay here overnight? Your lorry was here when I arrived a while back.'

'Yes, got here about nine last night and tacho rules said I had to park up and rest, so I stayed.'

'We'll need to speak to you before you leave.'

His brown eyes were a little crinkly around the edges and his greying beard splayed out in an unruly manner. 'But I can't stay. My company will get hit with a huge penalty if I don't get this load delivered before two and I have to get it to Oxford.'

Gina checked her watch. 'A young girl was murdered last night. I'm happy for an officer to call your depot and explain what has happened.'

His shoulders dropped. 'But I was asleep. I don't know anything.'

'We need to speak to you regardless. If you could come down and talk that would be great.' Gina's neck was aching from looking up.

The lorry driver muttered a few expletives and stepped down. He pulled his loose jeans up a little.

Gina glanced at his articulated vehicle and knew immediately that there would be nowhere for him to park near the station. 'One of the PCs will take you to the station and drop you back to your lorry after you've given us a statement.'

'Bloody hell! I could do without this.'

'So could we but, as I said, a girl was murdered and we really need your cooperation. Could you please go and wait over there with the PC?' The lorry driver slammed his cab door shut and locked it up. Gina nodded to the PC that was standing in the corner of the car park, who then radioed for assistance and came to stand with the driver while his lift was on the way. Glancing back, she spotted a used condom under the front of his cab and pointed at it. 'Jacob, call forensics now and tell them to bag this up. He too had opportunity.'

Jacob made the call and they waited a few moments until one of the CSIs hurried across to take over. Gina braced herself as she checked her phone again, then she sighed. No more messages yet. The word murderer filled her head. *Murderer, murderer, murderer.*

She shook those thoughts away as they continued towards the truck stop café and there was John Tallis talking on the phone, red-faced with a clenched fist like he was having an argument. As he saw them approach, he ended the call and dropped his phone into his pocket before wiping his brow.

'Ah, come in.' His overcompensating smile had an air of unease.

Gina and Jacob followed him into the Waterside Café where she took a sip of the cold coffee in her hand. It was time to find out what John Tallis knew.

CHAPTER SEVEN

Red plastic chairs surrounded several cheap-looking metal fold-up tables and a television was pinned to the back wall, directly opposite to the kitchen and serving area. Fans blasted cool air around the large open room. Truckers were dotted around tables, some reading newspapers and some watching morning television. 'Shall we sit here, out of the way?' John Tallis pointed to the table at the far end next to the door marked 'Private'.

Gina and Jacob followed him over. She placed her coffee down and pulled out the plastic chair before sitting. Jacob took his notebook out and placed it on the table, just missing the stream of dried-up ketchup.

'Tell me a bit about your business.' Gina wondered if his circumstances might tell her a bit more about him, ease him in gently.

'As I said before, I own and run this café pretty-much single-handedly. I do the usual, meals with chips, breakfasts and hot drinks. We have a shower and wash block outside that the drivers who pay to stay overnight can use. I also live here in the studio flat above this café.'

'How many drivers stayed over last night and do you keep a record of their details?'

'Only the one last night and, yes, I take their name and registration number for the receipt.' He stood and reached over by the till where he pulled out a receipt book. 'Last night only a driver named Rodney Hackett stayed. He's the one in the biggest lorry out there now, the red cab. The others that are in here now have arrived since I've been open.'

Jacob scribbled a few notes.

'When you closed up at…'

'Ten o'clock.'

'Ten last night. What could you hear?'

'As I said, there was a party with music coming from the woods. I couldn't see it, only hear it.'

'Did you hear anyone saying anything or maybe shouting?'

'No. I'm too far away to hear them talking. I caught wind of the occasional scream, playful scream, I mean. It didn't sound like anyone was in pain or danger. As far as I was concerned, it was a few teens getting plastered in the woods. Happens all the time around here so I don't think anything of it. Like I said before, they don't bother me and sometimes they come here to buy snacks so it's a win for me really.'

'Did anyone come to buy snacks last night?' Jacob paused. 'Mr Tallis.'

'Oh sorry. Yes. A girl with brown hair and a pierced lip. She bought some chocolate, maybe crisps too and left. I didn't talk to her at all as I was talking to Rod, the lorry driver.'

'Is Mr Hackett a regular user of your facilities?'

'Not really. I guess I've seen him here two or three times before. Anyway, we got into some heavy talk about how Brexit is affecting the haulage industry, that's when the girl came in. She's the one who got killed, isn't she? I saw on Twitter.'

So the news really had broken out on Twitter. Gina felt her hands tense up. She knew that an officer would have been dispatched immediately to speak to Leah's parents but still, it would be awful for them seeing all the gossip surrounding their daughter's murder before they may have even been told themselves. 'Yes, I'm afraid it was her.' There was no point denying his question if the answer had already been announced for the world to read.

'Poor girl. I mean she seemed polite enough when she came in. I try not to judge the kids too harshly. We were all kids once and I know I got hammered at a few parties. It's part of growing up.'

'Did the noise from the kids affect your business though? I mean truckers would come here for a peaceful night's sleep. They pay to stay here. These kids come along and disrupt the peace.' Gina wondered if that would be enough to push a business owner over the edge.

'No, it's a part of growing up and no they don't affect my business. I've already told you, they give me business.'

'You looked a little tense as we walked up, when you were on the phone.' Another angle was needed and she saw Tallis was slightly shaken.

His eyes widened and he clenched his jaw. 'I was on the phone to a supplier who was late delivering my bacon. Do I need a solicitor for that?'

'No, Mr Tallis, but what I will need is for you to come down to the station today and make a formal statement. I will also need the name of that supplier?'

'So that you can check that I was discussing bacon?' He shrugged. 'I'm not saying any more to you lot. Right, please leave, I have work to do.'

Gina stood, scraping the plastic chair across the hard floor. A couple of the truckers looked across, noticing their host's change in mood. Another stood up and walked to the counter.

'I have customers to tend to so if you would kindly leave.'

Gina smiled. 'Of course. We'll see you at the station this afternoon, after your lunch rush. A PC will be in touch shortly.' As Gina stepped out she noticed that the tarmac was shimmering with the soaring temperature. 'That got a little tense.'

'Yeah, as soon as you asked him about his phone call it was like a switch had been flicked.' Jacob closed his notebook and squinted as he gazed across the car park.

'Yes, both he and Rodney Hackett saw Leah Fenmore come in. Did one of them decide to head to the party later that night for their own personal reasons? Did one of them kill her?' She glanced back and saw John Tallis step back as she caught him watching out of the window, nervously biting his bottom lip. 'Tallis definitely knows more than he's letting on and I don't believe him about the bacon conversation. He looked too... I don't know, overstressed. There's something off about both of them and I want to know what that is.'

CHAPTER EIGHT

'Sandy, for heaven's sake. Hurry up in there!' Frank calls.

After a half an hour struggle, I'm finally washed. I stare at myself in the mirror, sitting in my clunky mechanical wheelchair. I'd love an electric one but we don't have the money, not yet, but Frank keeps promising that we will have enough soon. I hate relying on him for everything but he says he doesn't mind every time I get upset. But I know he does and his mood changes like the wind. One minute he loves me and everything will be okay, the next, I've taken his freedom and he's seething and throwing things. Then, he might take a swipe at me, which always catches me off guard. I have no idea what today will bring. He rushes in, looking flustered as he lifts up his top and begins to rub cream on the scratches on his abdomen. 'How did you do that?'

'Gardening. You know I was out there yesterday morning chopping the shrubs back.'

I know that much but I don't remember him mentioning having those scratches across his gut yesterday and I didn't see any blood seeping through his T-shirt.

'Stop looking at me like that.'

'Sorry.' I look away.

He says ouch a couple of times and then covers the scratches back up. 'Right, Sandy. Let's get you to the lounge and I can start making lunch.'

'Thanks.' I do as he says and smile sweetly, not wanting to annoy him. My smile normally reassures him that I won't be troubling him today. He can quickly lose his patience with me and I don't want that to happen. I already feel rotten enough that he does everything for me. I grab my phone just as he's about to wheel me through the hall and into the lounge where, as always, he'll leave me positioned in front of the television with a stack of books for most of the day. I can get around on my own but it's awkward. We have too much stuff but Frank won't get rid of anything. The place looks like a bit of a junkyard but if I mention it, he gets angry.

Here I am, TV on. He drops the remote control into my lap and then he's gone. Moments later, I hear the clattering of pans as he rummages through the cupboards. He swears as they all fall out. A crash follows. He has a terrible temper. He's taking it out on the pans now and I'm just glad it's not me. Maybe I shouldn't have mentioned his scratches. With Frank occupied in the kitchen, I know it's safe to get my phone out. I need to delete that comment I made on Twitter.

TheMeeganMrs
I mean, those kids were out partying and only 16. What kind of parent allows this? They're a bloody nuisance too. #OakTreeWalk antisocial behaviour.

I, Sandra Meegan, should have been more sensitive but instead I made a bitchy comment and I was wrong. That's what I tell myself. The girl who answered me back on Twitter was right. That was a totally nasty thing to say given the circumstances but I let my bad mood get the better of me. After spending hours lying in bed listening to their racket all night, I hated them and I should have stepped away from Twitter and thought things through properly.

Last night's party wasn't the first time. Since the run of good weather and the start of the summer school break, they were coming all the time. I've called the council, the police, and no one does a thing. I let my anger win and I've let myself down with this post. I hit delete, hoping that I can just forget what I've done and move on but then I think of the parents. I cast judgement on them and one of them has woken up to find that their child is dead. Frank and I never did have children, we decided not to. I suppose I didn't feel like I wanted children with him given his short temper but I do like children and I'm sure that if I'd personally spoken to the teens or met them, I'd like them too.

'You frigging idiot.'

I feel a hard slap across the back of my head as he strikes me, the sting bringing tears to my eyes. I'd hoped that today was going to be okay but now I'm sure it's going to be yet another challenge, just like all the others. Another day of me trying to placate Frank and being overly nice. I can change his mood if I work at it. I will make him happy. I have to because I need him.

'Whatever it is, I'm sorry.' The side of my head feels hot from his slap but I'm used to it. He slaps me a lot. He's even kicked me when he's really angry but I try not to think about that. Deep down, I know that he wishes I was dead so that he could be free of me.

'You should stay off Twitter. How could you say that and bring attention to our door?'

Tears begin to fall down my cheeks. I want to stop them but I can't. He doesn't care about the dead girl, he cares that the police will come knocking here, and with good reason. I won't bring that up again or I'll get another slap.

'Oh, for heaven's sake. Stop with the crying, woman.'

Easy to say but I can't. I don't want to be here and be Frank's burden but I am. The family I had deserted me a long time ago when I chose Frank over them and now, I'm lying in that bed I made, just like they said I had to. 'I deleted it.'

'Too late. Every man and his dog has replied and it makes us look bad.'

'It makes me look bad, not you and I'll tweet again and apologise.'

'No, you won't. It's deleted now and you'll just make it worse. Just stay off Twitter. I tell you what, I'll make sure you stay off Twitter.' He snatches my phone. That's my punishment for doing something he doesn't approve of and he's right. I tweeted that comment and I was wrong. He's taking it away from me for my own good.

'You're right and I'm sorry. Do you forgive me?' Sucking up to him normally works and I hope it will this time. He remains silent and I scrunch up my eyes, bracing myself for another blow but it doesn't come.

'I'm deleting Twitter from your phone, and Facebook. You're going to bring trouble to this house one day and I don't want it.'

We both know that Frank is the only one to have brought trouble to our door but I don't want to think about that now or ever again. I have to ask him a question and I know it'll upset him but my stomach is skipping like a broken record. 'Frank?'

'What now?'

'I heard our back patio door sliding open in the night.'

'What are you saying?' He walks in front of me, kneeling so that his eyes are level with mine. I see the sleep crud in the corners and his chapped lips look sore. They're always chapped. His greying hair sticks up on his head. He still has plenty of it and he's quite a distinguished looking fifty-year-old, a little George Clooney like. At least if he looked after himself, that's who he'd look like.

'I just wondered where you went, that's all.'

'Frank. Went. Nowhere. Last. Night. You will never speak of it. Repeat that back to me.'

I feel a tremble running through my body as I repeat what he said. I know he's capable of violence, but murder? He can say what he likes but I know what I heard. I tried to dismiss it as he sometimes goes into the garden to smoke, but it was late, really late and he doesn't normally need to smoke in the early hours. He'd been gone ages too. I'd been in bed since ten and he normally falls asleep in front of the television, which is why I'm usually alone. 'I just thought I heard something.'

He slams his hand on the arm of my wheelchair. 'Say it again.' His stare is stark and he's seething so harshly that spittle hits my arm.

'Frank went nowhere last night,' I blurt out through my sobs.

'Good, at least we got that sorted. You say anything to the contrary, I'll do more than take your phone away. And stop blarting. It's bloody annoying and boy it makes you look ugly.'

I hold my breath and close my eyes. Whatever he said, I must hold on to the fact that I know what I heard. I am not losing my mind, *my* mind has never been in question.

'That's better.' He swipes his thumb across my face a few times, wiping away my tears, then he kisses me on the nose before heading back to the kitchen. My body immediately relaxes now that he's left the room. Only now can I rub the sore on my head. I flinch, knowing that there will be a bruise underneath my straggly hair. I wonder if it can be seen along the edges of my hairline but I'm nowhere near a mirror to check.

The rummaging continues, then I hear him slamming something down on the worktop. It sounds like he's removing the lid from a tin, a sound I've heard a few times and I always wonder what he's up to. Then the radio goes on and a blast of seventies music fills the cottage.

Where did you go last night, Frank? And why are you telling lies?

CHAPTER NINE

Gina smiled at Naomi Carpenter in an attempt to put her at ease but the sixteen-year-old continued to suck the ends of her dust-filled hair. The blotchiness on her face had died down a little. Jacob shifted in his seat and pulled his chair under the table. They'd introduced everyone in the room for the tape; that was herself, Jacob, Naomi and Naomi's mother, Dina Carpenter; the appropriate adult. Both mother and daughter looked alike, both pale, possibly having Nordic ancestry. The standard issue track bottoms and T-shirt that Naomi was wearing was shapeless but she'd willingly given her clothes over and had swabs taken on arrival.

'I know this is hard for you, Naomi, so thank you for coming here to give a full statement. We want to find out who did this to your friend as much as you do. You're being very brave.' Gina tilted her head. 'I know you already gave a brief statement to DC O'Connor and PC Kapoor at the scene, but I'd like you to tell me in as much detail what happened last night. If you could start with your arrival, we can take it from there.'

The girl glanced at her mother just as a ray of sunlight pointed directly into her eyes through the tiny window, causing her to squint a little.

'Come on, sweetheart, just say what happened.' Dina rubbed her daughter's back.

'You're going to be angry with me, Mum.' Naomi's bottom lip began to tremble. The sun's rays had dipped a little.

'Look at me.'

The girl turned to her mother, her blue eyes damp and red at the corners.

'What you were all doing… having a party… maybe drinking. Whatever it was, it doesn't matter. Do you hear me?'

'Yes.' Naomi swallowed.

'We need to find out who killed Leah. That's what's important right now.' Mrs Carpenter held her daughter's hand and squeezed.

'Thanks, Mum, and I'm sorry I lied to you about sleeping over at Leah's house. I'll never do anything like that again.' Naomi took a couple of breaths and wiped the tears that meandered down her cheeks. 'We planned this party about a week ago, well, it was Oscar's idea. It was just meant to be a bit of fun, that's all.' She paused in thought. 'We met Oscar in the car park of the corner shop on the new estate. He borrowed what he calls his dad's battered car, a cheap run-around his dad uses when he doesn't want his posh car dinked. Because Oscar hasn't been driving long, his dad tells him to take it out and practise. I think the street the shop is on is called Herringbone Close. We all got into the car and parked up near Oak Tree Walk, which is where we walked from with all our camping gear. It was either park there or on the truck stop car park, but he charges to park which is why we parked on the street.' She paused and scrunched her brow. 'A couple of the people living in the cottages gave us the evils through their kitchen windows as we passed. I think they knew what we were up to, I guess all the camping gear and bags gave us away. Or maybe we'd nicked their parking space. Who knows? Oscar said the car was taxed and they were a bunch of losers who needed to get a life. I know a lot of kids come to party over here so I guess they were annoyed. I don't know.' She shrugged.

'What happened after that?' Gina leaned forward slightly and placed a clump of stray hair behind her ear.

'Oscar led us to the clearing and we pitched up.'

'What time was that?'

'I'd say about six that evening. I was really rubbish at putting up my tent so it took a while and Oscar and Jordan began trying to light a fire. Leah had brought marshmallows with her. We were going to toast them on the fire when it got dark. We set up and sat around talking for a bit, then we started drinking and the music went on. Oscar and Elsa had managed to get some bottles of cider and beer. I think Oscar brought a bottle of vodka from his dad's drinks cabinet so we had that too.'

'Did any of you take anything else?'

'You mean drugs?'

Gina nodded. 'Yes.'

Naomi glanced at her mother who swallowed as if not wanting to hear the answer to that question.

'I'm sorry, Mum. We had some weed, which we lit and passed around. It was just the one and we shared it.'

Dina Carpenter inhaled and squeezed her daughter's hand. 'That's okay, just tell the truth.'

Naomi turned her attention back to Gina. 'Yeah, we had weed. Just one spliff, that's all. I had one puff and it made me feel sick so I didn't have another.'

Jacob scribbled a few notes.

'You're doing really well, Naomi, and I thank you for your honesty. With what happened, I know all this isn't easy. Could you please continue telling me about what happened after?' Gina noticed the tremble in the girl's hand. She began to tap her fingers on the table. The sixteen-year-old seemed a lot younger. Messy hair, no make-up and her tiny frame made her look more like a thirteen-year-old. Her skin was almost translucent and a blue vein pulsed at her temple. Gina had to remind herself that Naomi was potentially a suspect though and drilling down on her relationship with Leah was essential. Leah was killed in such a way that it wouldn't take much strength, which made each one of them physically capable.

The girl bit her lip and flinched as it bled before continuing. She dabbed it with a tissue. 'Leah said she was really hungry after a few puffs on the spliff so she went to the Waterside Café, that's the truck stop. It's not too far from the river. We all put our orders in and she left.'

'What time did she leave?'

The girl shrugged. 'I have no idea. It shuts at ten so it must have been before then.'

'How long was she gone?'

'That was the weird thing. She should have been back after about twenty minutes at the most but she was gone nearly an hour and she looked a bit more drunk than she should have. She seemed a little sleepy and was slurring her words too.'

'Did she say why she'd been gone so long?'

'No, but she came back with a four-pack of lager to add to our stash and she said someone on the truck stop car park gave it to her.'

Gina felt her heart rate picking up. 'Did she say who it was or what this person looked like?'

'No, just some man.'

'Did you ask why she was gone for so long?'

'No. I was just happy to get my crisps and I'd had a few shots while she'd been gone. We all had. After that it gets blurrier. We basically drunk everything we had. At one point I saw Oscar snogging Elsa, then a while later it was Leah. We were all just messing around and wasted. The music was turned up loud by then. I got caught up in the night and spent most of the evening dancing like an idiot with whoever wanted to dance, that was until much later. Then…' Naomi scrunched her brow.

'Then, what?'

'There was some sort of bust up, an argument, and Leah wasn't very happy. I think it was the drink and weed. It sent her into a funny mood. She wanted to go home but Oscar couldn't drive as he was drunk. She stormed off and said if he wouldn't drive her, she'd walk. I remember grabbing her as she pushed past and she told me to let go or she'd make me. She sounded angry but I could tell she was more upset and teary. Her eyes were red. She left and we all just carried on partying. We thought she'd just walk home even though it would have taken about an hour. It wasn't impossible and none of us could stop her. Besides, we were all in a state by then. I remember Oscar doing a staggering pacing walk while swearing, then we were back to the party. I fell asleep a couple of times after Leah had left, only for a few minutes each time. But saying that, I could have that wrong.'

'As far as you're aware, did anyone else leave the camp at any time after that?'

'They might have but like I said, I drifted off a couple of times. I think everyone was there though, I could still hear them laughing and dancing around the fire.'

'Did anyone else come to the camp? Someone who wasn't a part of your party.'

She shook her head and ran her fingers through her matted hair, raking a few strands out as she teased the lugs with her skinny fingers. 'No, it was just us. But...'

'But what?' Gina gently urged the girl to carry on speaking.

'I went to pee in the bushes a little while later and I'm sure I heard rustling. I don't know if it was one of the others or someone else. They all denied it but then laughed as if they were playing a joke on me. I told them they were being dicks—'

'Watch your language.' Dina Carpenter placed her hand over her daughter's hand.

Naomi picked at the scratches on her arms. 'Sorry, Mum. And that's when I went to my tent to sleep. I woke up the next morning and walked a bit further away to pee, that's when I discovered Leah's body.' A flood of tears ran down the girl's cheek and she buried her head into her mother's chest. 'Leah was dead.'

'I know this is hard, but can you tell me a little about how you knew Leah? Tell me about your friendship.'

The crying girl blurted out words between sobs. 'We were in most of the same classes at school. We have been since starting senior school. We went to the same junior school but we weren't in the same class there. She was the person who spoke to me on the first day and we soon became really good friends, I'd say best friends. Sometimes, she'd stay over at mine and I'd stay over at hers.'

'Do you know if she had any problems with anyone?'

Naomi took a tissue from the box and blew her nose. 'Everyone liked her. She wouldn't hurt a fly.'

As Naomi sought comfort in her mother and took a moment, Gina wondered how the other interviews were going. DC Harry O'Connor and DC Wyre were currently interviewing Jordan Rolph. She needed to wrap this interview up. It was becoming distressing for Naomi and she really wanted to be the one who interviewed Oscar Spalding as he seemed to be the organiser of the party. As it stood, she had no evidence to suspect Naomi but all that could change depending on what forensics came back with and what was said in the other interviews.

'Look, my daughter is in distress. Her friend has just been murdered and she needs a break.'

Gina nodded not wanting to overstep the mark with the sixteen-year-old. 'Of course. Naomi, thank you for being so helpful. Just one last question. Did anyone else attend the party at any time during the evening, or did anyone call, or maybe someone else who was invited didn't turn up?'

The girl took a few sniffs. 'No one visited, but there were two others that were invited but they said they weren't coming.'

'And what are their names?'

'Caro Blakely and Anthony Truss.'

'Did they say why they weren't going to attend the party?'

She shook her head and shrugged her shoulders. 'I don't know.' Naomi's shoulders went rigid and she looked down while biting her lip again. What wasn't she telling them?

'If you can give us their addresses before you leave, that would really help us.' It would be quicker to get that information now than to wait for the school administrator to get back to them during the summer holidays.

'I'm going to insist that my daughter has a break now. She's upset.'

Gina smiled sympathetically. 'Thank you again. We may well be in touch again but in the meantime, if you think of anything that might help us, you can call me on this number.' Gina passed a card to Dina Carpenter. 'Also, I will ask that you please don't discuss this on social media. It can hamper the case and we really want to catch whoever did this.'

'I won't. There is something else but it might be nothing. It's probably me being silly. I didn't like peeing in the bushes and I'd probably scared myself a bit.'

'You're not being silly. It may be something that can help us.' Gina tilted her head to the side.

'Just before I found Leah in the bushes this morning, I was having a wee. I heard a rustling, like someone was close by, then it stopped as if they'd gone. I didn't see anyone and it might have been an animal. That's it. That's all I know.'

'Thank you, Naomi. Interview terminated at twelve forty-five on Sunday the first of August.' Jacob stopped the tape.

Gina opened the door to the interview room and spotted PC Smith walking by. 'Hey, could you please show Mrs Carpenter and her daughter out, then take the details of a Caro Blakely and Anthony Truss before they go?'

'Will do, guv.' PC Smith finished eating the bit of sandwich he was carrying and smiled.

'Thank you.' As she listened to their footsteps leaving the corridor she turned to Jacob. 'I suspect more went down than she's saying and we've been fed a few breadcrumbs. Question is, was it just innocent but embarrassing teenage antics, or is there more at play? I also want to know why the other two chose not to attend the party. They knew where it was and when it was so we definitely have to look into their whereabouts. What's really making me concerned is that Leah Fenmore came back from the truck stop with a four-pack of lager that was apparently given to her by a man in the car park. I know we have Rodney Hackett the truck driver waiting to be interviewed. We also know that he was the only driver to stay there overnight. We need to speak to him next.'

'Why would he give a teenager he doesn't know alcohol?'

Gina's mind flitted to the condom that she spotted under the truck. 'I wouldn't like to think but we're going to find out.'

CHAPTER TEN

'Sorry, lass. Your mum told me about what happened to your friend.'

Caro couldn't look at Grandad, instead she stared at her mother. 'Why did you make me come out, Mum? I've just found out that my friend has been murdered.' Not only that, she'd been sent a threatening message and all she wanted to do was hide in her room. *Say a word and you'll be next to die!* Those words were making her feel sick.

'I'm sorry, honey, but I didn't want to leave you on your own in the house, not after what's happened. Besides, I called Grandad and he'd already put dinner on.'

'Eat your sprouts, sis.' Jake flicked a pea at her and it landed on the tiled kitchen floor. Grandad's yapping terrier raced over and ate it.

'Jake, stop it. Your sister has had some really bad news and winding her up like that is only going to upset her more.'

'I was only—'

'Say you're sorry.'

Jake shook his head and half smiled as if testing his mother's patience.

'Enough.' Her dad slammed down his paper napkin and the plates jumped on the flimsy table. 'Jake, get on those stairs now. You will stay there, staring at the front door for a ten-minute timeout. You can have a long hard think about what your sister is going through before you come back to join us. Understand?'

His bottom lip began to quiver as he left the room. Caro was now staring at his empty chair across the table. She stabbed one of the sprouts and it turned to mush. She couldn't face the dinner, she couldn't face talking and she couldn't face her past. If her family knew the half of it, they'd hate her, she knew they would. The smell of grease that was ingrained into Grandad's house made her stomach turn. The closing in surroundings reminded her of a part of her family's past that she'd rather forget.

Her mind went back to the last party where she'd run through the woods naked for a dare, hyped up on adrenalin and alcohol. They'd all laughed and her friends had completed equally embarrassing dares too. She remembered the dancing and Jordan's lips pressed on hers, his hand reaching under her shorts before she pushed him away. Then there was the scuffle followed by more drinking. She never knew that Anthony had a thing for her up until the moment he punched Jordan. The whole night had kicked off into a drunken brawl, leading to Anthony stomping off into the night. That's when the memories blur until much later.

'Caro?' Her mother gave her a nudge.

'Sorry, Mum. I just can't stop thinking about what happened. I can't eat this. Sorry, Grandad. I know you worked hard on the dinner.' She began to choke up. Her cheeks began to burn with the cooking heat and her top had stuck to her chest as the midday temperatures soared. 'I have to get some air.' Darting past her little brother, she flung open the front door and ran into the front garden, sitting on Grandad's weather-beaten wooden bench with her head between her legs and eyes pressed shut.

A memory of someone's nose touching hers as she drifted in and out of what felt like an uncontrollably heavy tiredness made her shiver. At that party, there was laughing and things were being done to her but it was still such a blur. It was dark where her tent had been pitched. Her own sweaty damp hair was all she remembered feeling when it went quiet.

Anthony had fought for her. She'd kissed Jordan and Oscar had been laughing. He never gave his feelings away with ease and that was the worst thing about him.

'Caro.' Her mother sat beside her on the bench and placed an arm around her. 'Come here.' She slowly pulled Caro close to her and gave her a gentle hug.

'It's so scary, Mum. I—' She paused and stuttered the word I several times but the rest of the sentence would not come. The last thing she wanted her mother and family to know were her shameful secrets. She wished she'd never gone to the previous party and now Leah was dead.

'What is it, love? Do you know something?'

Caro shook her head. 'No, Mum. I wasn't there. Why would I know anything?' There were things she never wanted to discuss with her mother, especially that message.

Jake came padding across the front lawn in his sandals. 'I'm sorry, Caro.' He joined in their group hug, the hug that was doing nothing to take the pain away. That still lay in the pit of her stomach like a brick, turning and taunting; scratching her from the inside.

Her phone beeped. She broke up the embrace. 'Can I just have a couple of minutes? I'm feeling a little better. I just need a minute to myself.'

'Of course, love. Come on, Jakey-boy. No more upsetting your sister, do you hear me?'

'Yes, Mummy.' She ruffled his hair and led him back into the house, his little hand gripping their mother's, leaving Caro sitting alone on the bench.

She pulled her phone out and glanced at the message from Anthony.

WTF! U heard what happened? Need to call you now. A

She pressed his number immediately and he answered just as quick.

'Damn it, Caro. You can't tell anyone what happened at the last party. The cops will ask us, I know it. As soon as they know we were meant to be at that party it's gonna dredge up the last party and I did things I wish I hadn't. Promise me.'

She paused and wiped her eyes. 'What happened to me at the last party?'

'Nothing. The fight, the dares. That's all.'

'After, later?'

He went silent.

'Anthony, I need to know.'

'Caro, are you okay?' It was her mum, fussing again. She wouldn't leave her alone for five minutes.

'Look, my heads a mess. Just don't say anything about the fight or about anything else. You know how strict my parents are and with losing my grandma that week, they'll hate me. My mum will kill me if she knew what we were all up to. Besides, we didn't kill her so the police would be looking in the wrong place anyway. There's no need for everyone to know our business.'

She went to tell Anthony about the message but then stopped. Would the messenger know she'd told and would she then die? Instead, she cleared her throat.

'Caro.' Her mother's shadow spread across the grass, eventually covering Caro's feet.

'Got to go. I'll call you later.'

Anthony went to reply but she cut him off and stood. 'I was just coming back in, Mum.' She wondered how much of that conversation her mother had heard.

CHAPTER ELEVEN

'For the tape, your full name is Rodney Brett Hackett, date of birth, twentieth of September 1961. DI Harte and DS Driscoll interviewing and the time is thirteen hundred hours.'

'I can't be staying here too long. I told you, my load is overdue and I really need to get to Oxford and, what's more, you've kept me waiting ages. I've been sitting in reception twiddling my thumbs for over an hour like I've got nothing to do. Get a friggin' move on, please.' His cheeks and nose reddened like he was wearing a mask. His Meat Loaf T-shirt swamped his skinny frame. A tattoo of a snake wound around his right arm, escaping beneath his sleeve.

'Mr Hackett, a young girl was murdered last night and all we want to do is find who did this, so your cooperation is much appreciated.' Gina felt her collar getting damp as the temperature crept up. Jacob leaned over and turned the desk fan on and its gentle whirring began to fill the room. 'Did you see this girl while you were parked up last night?'

Gina pulled out the photo that Leah Fenmore's parents had given to them from the paper file and slid it across the table.

'Never seen her in my life.' He leaned back in the chair, legs wide open, arms crossed.

'You didn't see her when she came into the café to buy some food last night?'

He shrugged.

'Only the café owner, Mr Tallis, said that she came in while you were both having a discussion about the impact of Brexit on the haulage industry. He said he had to stop your discussion to serve her.'

'I guess I didn't take any notice. I think I went for a piss.' The man grinned.

'And where are the toilets for the Waterside Café?'

'In the toilet and shower block that's next to the main building.'

'So to access the toilets, you had to go outside. She would have left just after.' Gina felt adrenalin working its way through her body. He'd left the café while Leah was being served which would definitely give him opportunity to wait for and speak to Leah, maybe take her back to his cab and give her the lager. Then maybe, she'd told him that she and her friends were camped up in the woods for the night.

His stare felt as though it was boring into Gina. 'I did not see her.'

'Her friends tell us that she came back with a four-pack of lager and they stated that this was given to her by a man in the car park. The Waterside Café doesn't sell alcohol. You were the only person with a cab who was parked up for the night. No one can park there free of charge so there would be a record of anyone else present. The only man she could have taken the lager from is you.'

He sighed.

'A used condom was found under your cab.'

'I. Did. Not. Touch. That. Girl. So I gave her a few beers to have with her buddies—'

'So you did give them to her?'

'Okay, okay – yes! She was being a little jokey and laughy, saying that she and her friends were having a party and how guilty she felt for not bringing any drinks, which is partly why she'd gone to get food. I felt sorry for her and she looked a bit spaced out. We were all young once. I made a joke about her not getting too off her face, then I gave her the cans. She thanked me and went trundling off back to her party.'

'You can see how this now looks. You have obstructed us in our investigation and that puts you firmly in the picture.' Gina paused. 'Did you head over there, later that night?'

'No way. I didn't head anywhere. I was asleep.'

'Going back to the condom. What explanation can you give me for that?'

He shrugged. 'Other people parked up that day. It must have been left there by someone else.'

'So, when the lab results come back your DNA won't match the DNA that we find in the condom. The forensics team are working the area as we speak.'

He sat up rigid in the plastic chair and shuffled around a little, nervously brushing down his jeans. 'I want a solicitor.'

'And that is your right. Do you have a solicitor in mind or is it the duty solicitor?'

'Duty.'

'We will need to take swabs and your clothing as you are at present a person of interest. These tests may also eliminate you.'

He shrugged and began biting his thumbnail.

'Can I get back to work soon?' He checked his watch.

'We need to continue the interview. As soon as your solicitor arrives, we will do so.'

'What if I just leave, walk out?'

'We're looking at placing you under arrest for the murder of Leah Fenmore while we investigate further. At the moment, Mr Hackett, you had opportunity, you spoke to the victim when you told us you didn't, and you lied when we asked if you recognised her. That gives us ample grounds to keep you here while we investigate further.'

The man kicked the leg of the table and swore under his breath.

Gina glanced at Jacob. There was no way Hackett was leaving the station until they'd checked his cab for evidence relating to Leah's murder. 'Interview terminated at thirteen hundred hours and seven minutes.'

As they packed away, she noticed Rodney Hackett glancing up at her when he thought she wasn't looking. As always, everyone had something to hide, she just wondered if he was trying to hide the fact that he'd murdered a sixteen-year-old, Leah Fenmore.

The image of the fingermarks around the victim's neck made her feel like throwing up the breakfast and lunch she never had. The nauseating emptiness was making her feel worse and her own flashbacks to the past were worming their way to the forefront of her mind. Feeling like someone else is holding your life in their hands, that they get to choose at the moment of strangulation whether you live or die can be thrilling for some, she was aware that people played such dangerous sex games, but it was never thrilling for her. It was terrifying. Gina's throat began to constrict. That message Briggs had received meant her secret was known. It had to be about her. She grabbed the paperwork off the desk and left Jacob to finish up. She needed to get out so that she could breathe. In her mind, she kept telling herself to forget the past, to move on, but trauma is trauma and it won't let you forget. And when you manage to put it aside, some harbinger of doom comes into your life. Her past would always hold her hostage.

'You okay?' Briggs pushed the door open while holding a drink.

'Yes, sir. All good.'

He opened the door for her to go through first. 'We'll have a briefing when the interviews are finished. I know you said you wanted to interview Oscar Spalding but you were tied up with Hackett so I took that one. Oscar's father was making a bit of a fuss and kept saying that his son had been through enough. As we don't have anything to keep him on, we had to let him go for now.'

She placed her hand on her neck and rubbed a little. 'Where are we with Leah Fenmore's parents?'

'Obviously distraught. They want to see the body but given that it's so soon, the mortuary isn't even remotely ready for them yet. We've sent them home with a family liaison officer.'

'Great.'

'Briefing at, say… four this afternoon?'

'I'll be ready. I think I'm going to pop back to the Waterside Café. Since speaking with Rodney Hackett, a few more things have come to light. We also need to discuss Mr Hackett's arrest before his solicitor arrives. I'll update you before I go but he's definitely a suspect and he started off in the interview by lying. Also, interviewing him threw up a few things that don't match John Tallis's story and I don't want him to have too long to think about things.'

'What are you thinking?' Briggs leaned on the door frame.

'Tallis said that he and Hackett were having a conversation when Leah entered the café for some food but he didn't mention that Hackett had left by the time he'd finished serving Leah. I want to know why. We've also confirmed that Hackett spent time with Leah in the car park and gave her a pack of lager.'

'Yes, stay on it. I agree, putting it back to Tallis is the best thing to do. I read up on the notes so far, a condom was found under Hackett's cab, is that right?' Briggs sipped his coffee, holding the delicate polystyrene cup with his thick fingers, looking like he might crush it.

'Yes, Keith collected it and I believe it's now at the lab being fast-tracked but, as we know, the analysis won't come back for at least twenty-four hours. I'm hoping that we can get Rodney Hackett's swabs to the lab ASAP, then we'll be able to see if there's a match. In the meantime, it would be great if Tallis could tell us more. Hackett claims that the condom must have already been in the car park before he pulled up. Maybe he's telling the truth.'

'Does he have any previous?'

Gina frowned. 'Only for throwing a bottle of urine out of his cab window on the M5. It was just his bad luck that there was an unmarked police car behind him in a traffic jam that day.'

'So, one minor offence.'

'Yep. Right, if I'm to get back before the briefing, I need to go now.'

'We'll catch up later. Oh, before I forget, you might want to grab a slice of fruit flan before it all goes.'

'Mrs O's latest bake?'

'Yep.'

'She's a lifesaver.' If she was to cull the queasiness, that sounded like a good plan. She saw Briggs looking nervously at his phone. 'Any more messages?'

His shoulders dropped. 'I didn't want to worry you.'

'I need to know and I'm worried already. I've been worried all morning.' She swallowed.

He held his phone up and she read the message.

You're as guilty as she is!

'We could do without this.'

'I tried to call the number but all I got was a dead tone. I'd say it's a burner phone.'

'You know or you're guessing?' She knew that Briggs could maybe have researched that much.

'It's a burner.'

'Dammit!'

Jacob burst out of the interview room with all the paperwork under his arm. 'I've explained to Mr Hackett what happens next.'

Gina cleared her throat and Briggs smiled. 'Are you okay to head back to the Waterside Café with me in the meantime. I have a few questions for John Tallis and they can't wait.'

Jacob nodded. 'Yes, definitely. I'll grab my things. Everything okay?' Jacob scrunched his brow.

'Just tickety boo.' Gina hurried past, not wanting Jacob to see through her. Her phone buzzed and she shook as she stopped in the corridor to check it.

GUILTY!

CHAPTER TWELVE

The afternoon sun was beating down on the shimmering tarmac in the packed car park. Trees rustled as a hot breeze caught them. The blue cloudless sky went on forever.

'Right, let's find out what Tallis has to say,' Gina said to Jacob. She inhaled and her lungs felt a little hot. Her flat shoes clonked on the ground until they entered the café and her trousers were sticking to her legs.

The hum of voices filled the room. One man laughed raucously and another told him to shut up as he was trying to hear the news. The smell of fried food was dense. A woman in a checked shirt bit into a sandwich and a stream of egg spurted from the other side. Gina knew it wasn't a good time as John Tallis caught sight of her through the queue, while trying to flip a burger at the same time.

A young woman came out from around the back with a huge block of cheese and a tray of eggs.

'Mr Tallis, may we speak with you?'

He raised his brows and mouthed, 'Really?'

Gina nodded and sat at the only free table with Jacob.

'Hally, can you manage for five?'

The girl nodded and took the burger flipper from him before he joined them at the table with a bottle of cola. As he unscrewed it, it almost fizzed over. He took a long swig and used a napkin to wipe the sweat off his brow before belching. 'This is not a good time. I'm run off my feet.'

'Apologies for that but we really need to ask you a couple of questions and it can't wait.'

'Okay.' He screwed the lid back onto his drink then removed his white cap before ruffling through his sweaty hair. 'Make it quick, if you can. Hally only backs me up, she doesn't usually cook out front so she's bound to get flustered in a minute.'

Gina glanced up at the girl who looked to be between sixteen and twenty. She smiled and served with one hand as she used the flipper to place a burger on a bun with the other. 'She looks like she's coping amazingly.'

'So she is. What do you want? I told you everything I know earlier.'

'We need to check something with you. Can you please go through the night before again when Rodney Hackett was in here talking to you? You said that Leah Fenmore came in for some snack food. Tell me about that.'

'This is ridiculous.'

'It would be really helpful.'

He rolled his shoulders and rubbed the back of his neck before sliding his chair closer to the table. 'I was sitting talking to Rod when the girl came in. I served her and she went, then I went back to my conversation. It's as simple as that. There is nothing else to add.'

'Except that when you were serving Leah Fenmore, Mr Hackett claims that he left to go to the toilet and then he spoke to the victim outside for a while, so you didn't carry on your conversation as soon as you'd served Leah.'

He scrunched his brow as Jacob began making a few notes. 'Okay, I just checked a few things, you know, tidied up a bit so that I could leave dead on ten. I loaded the dishwasher, wiped the surfaces down and then I talked on the phone for a few minutes, then Rod was back. That was when we carried on with our conversation.'

Gina glanced between all the people lined up at the counter. The queue was getting longer. 'Did you wipe the whole counter down?'

'Yes. Why would I only wipe some of it down? Believe it or not, I have a four-star hygiene rating and I pride myself on keeping everything clean. Admittedly, it's not an upmarket eatery but it's mine and I keep it pristine.'

Gina turned her chair a little. 'So, when you wiped that end of the counter, you would have had a full view of the car park through that huge window.' Gina pointed at the glass that almost covered the top half of the whole wall. 'And, as you say, it's a very clean place. Those windows are gleaming.' She wasn't about to pull him up on the ketchup that Jacob nearly put his hands in earlier. The state of his tables wasn't much to boast about. 'You would have seen Mr Hackett talking to Leah in the car park.'

He shrugged his shoulders. 'Well, I might have seen them.'

'Why didn't you tell me that when we spoke earlier?'

'Well, I know he didn't do anything and a trucker is probably an easy target. He's an alright bloke and, yes, he spoke to the girl but that was it.'

'Did you see him passing anything to her?'

John scrunched his nose up. 'No. He just looked like he was being friendly, you know, saying hello as she passed. I remember loading the dishwasher after that and that's out the back. I didn't see a thing after that.'

'John, can I get some help here?' Hally called.

'Duty calls.' The man stood and pushed his chair under the table. 'I really have to get back to my kitchen.'

'As soon as this crowd dies down, I want you to head to the station to make a formal statement. Potentially perverting the course of justice by not telling the truth about what you saw is a very serious offence, so next time a police officer asks you what happened, be honest, or it makes you look like you have something to hide.'

John Tallis's Adam's apple bobbed as he swallowed. 'I am so sorry. I will come and make a statement in a bit. I promise. Can I get you a drink in the meantime?'

Gina stood. 'No, thank you. Just come down the station before your evening meal rush.' Jacob closed his notebook and popped his pen in his pocket.

'Will do. I'll ask Hally to stick around for a bit longer.' The man scurried back behind the counter and took the spatula from his flustered-looking assistant.

Gina's phone beeped and she read the message.

'We best get back. One of the residents on Oak Tree Walk has a past record and after an officer went around to ask if anyone had seen anything, he got short-tempered with her.'

'What past record?' Jacob asked.

'Voyeurism. Specifically, installing equipment with the purpose of obtaining sexual gratification.'

CHAPTER THIRTEEN

Four in the afternoon soon came. Gina quickly followed Jacob through to the incident room. The smell of sweat and food along with the thought of someone sending her sinister messages made her recoil. Wyre and O'Connor were fanning themselves with their notepads and Briggs had loosened his tie. PCs Kapoor and Smith sat at the far end and were sharing a pack of chewy sweets that were giving off a strong smell. 'No Bernard or Keith?'

Briggs stood to the side of the board. 'They're still processing everything from the crime scene, trying to fast-track as much as possible. Bernard has just this minute emailed his initial findings and there is something.'

'Great. Let's get started and you can tell us all. Hey, can I have your attention?' Gina hushed the chatter in the room and stood at the front of the long table. 'We have an update from forensics.'

Briggs stepped forward. 'Leah Fenmore had recently had sex. Bernard couldn't confirm whether it was that evening or a little earlier but we're hoping for more details tomorrow.'

'Any sign of a struggle? Any injuries?'

'No. The only thing that was actually found was condom lubricant inside Leah.'

Gina headed over and glanced at the board. A photo of Leah Fenmore had been stuck in the middle, then the crime scene photos had been pinned underneath. She couldn't believe that the girl they found in the woodland was the smiling girl with the braces in the school photo. The body had a bluish tinge, the type of colouring that is left when all life has gone. 'Tell me that we still have Rodney Hackett here?'

Briggs nodded. 'He's with his solicitor at the moment.'

She glanced down at the team. 'We can't let him go, not without the forensics results from the condom. We can keep him for twenty-four hours and press Bernard and his team to work as fast and hard as they can. After we've finished up here, I'll re-interview him with his solicitor present, then we'll make an arrest under suspicion of murder while we investigate. Wyre?'

'Yes, guv.' She clipped a strand of her shiny black hair back up into the bun on her head.

'Find out as much as you can about him. We need to see if he has family and call them. Speak to his employer. They may have something to add about his character. Something they say might help.'

Wyre nodded and made a note.

'O'Connor?'

'Yes.' He sipped from a can of fizzy orange.

'Continue going through the statements that have come in from the cottages and surrounding houses in the area?'

'Will do.'

'Right, onto the interviews. We'll talk about our teenagers and what we have so far. I managed to glance at the updates quickly before the briefing so I'm hoping if I've missed something, you can all fill me in. I'll start. I interviewed Naomi Carpenter. She claimed that they had all had a drink and smoked weed before Leah left for the Waterside Café. That short walk should have taken twenty minutes for the round trip but she was gone an hour. We have Rodney Hackett admitting that he saw Leah in the car park where he gave her a four-pack of lager. She arrived back at the camp where the party really kicked off and the group drank even more. We all know that she had recently had sex with someone. Bernard's estimated time of death is between one and two in the morning. The next day, she is found dead by Naomi Carpenter. What happened between the party and the next morning when Naomi found her? There are several possibilities.'

The sound of pens scribbling on paper filled the room. Gina's shirt was beginning to stick to her upper torso so she turned on the fan. The open windows were letting dandelion seeds drift through and they were gathering in a strip against the far wall.

'Possibilities include: there was an issue between one of the teens and Leah, then one of them killed her. Each partygoer is on the table as having opportunity at the moment. She was described as drunk and even slurring a little. That would make her an easy target, especially a few hours on. Then we have Rodney Hackett. He knew where she was. After having sex with her, consensual or not, we don't know yet, maybe he deposited the condom under his truck. We need to look at the possibilities that she may have been drugged or had even feared him and went with what was happening – not struggling but not giving consent, either. We must also take into consideration that maybe she slept with him for the lager. These are just working possibilities at the moment. Or, maybe he headed to their camp later, when Leah was really drunk and high, where he waited and watched them all as they partied until he saw her alone. Naomi claimed that Leah got upset over something and had wanted to go home. Hackett could have seen her walking off and seized his opportunity. Maybe he followed her, raped her and then killed her, taking the condom away with him. Again, we come back to the fact that there is no evidence of a struggle. Then there is our resident on Oak Tree Walk. O'Connor, you processed this statement. Can you tell us more?'

O'Connor wiped the sweat from his shiny head with a tissue and exhaled. 'A Frank Meegan was charged in 2016 with voyeurism. He'd been caught in a supermarket's toilets with a hidden camera on the floor of the toilets where he'd film and watch women. There were also other reports that couldn't be proven at the time so were dropped by the CPS.'

'What reports were they?'

'Two women accused him of watching them through their bedroom windows two years earlier. When the case went to court others came forward. He'd also been accused of watching a teenage couple having sex in a wooden house on a play park one night. It took a lot for those kids to come forward but again they didn't have any evidence. He soon became known as Pervy Frank.'

'Where did this all take place?'

'In the Croydon area.'

'He's definitely a person of interest. What do we know about him?'

O'Connor flicked through a few pages. 'He's fifty and is a carer for his disabled wife. He used to be a joiner and he still works when he can.'

'So, to sum up, we have a man charged with voyeurism who lives close by to where the murder of Leah Fenmore took place. Let's add him to our list of possibilities. Maybe he spies on the teens when they have their parties. He watches them from the periphery, drinking, smoking drugs, then they pee in the bushes or maybe they have sex, but he's there lurking. Had lurking not been enough? Does someone who gets their kicks from spying on people suddenly stop or do they move to somewhere new where they're not known as Pervy Frank? Do they then just start again with a clean slate in the community where no one knows them? We have a lot to consider but, as always, theories are no good without evidence. I've taken a brief look at the statements of all the teens that were at the party.'

Wyre stood up and turned another fan on, blowing a few sheets of paper across the table.

Gina spoke a little louder but welcomed the addition of more cool air. 'So far, all their statements match. That in itself is suspicious. It's like they're telling us what we already know. We could deduce that they were having a party, drinking and maybe smoking weed. They all said exactly the same things in what looked like the same order, both at the scene and in the follow-up interviews. The only one who veered off course was Naomi Carpenter who told me that she heard a rustling in the bushes while she was peeing this morning. Given what we know of Frank Meegan's past, we need to investigate him fully. We need to speak to his wife, check to see if he has an alibi. In the meantime, I'm going back into the interview room with Rodney Hackett. Jacob, can you also organise a search warrant for his cab. From the notes I have, the load that was destined for Oxford is sealed, so the cab, not the trailer is our prime place to search. We are looking for evidence that Leah Fenmore went into his cab. Any clothes that might later match fibres at the scene of the murder should be seized. This could make or break the case so it needs handling with care.'

'I'll sort that as soon as we wrap up this meeting.' Jacob bit the end of his pen and closed his pad.

'Hackett is at present our hottest lead but that doesn't mean we can drop the others. I want Leah's killer found and I want him or her found fast. How are things going with the media?'

Briggs stepped forward from the board and addressed the table. 'I've put out a holding statement for now but as always they're constantly onto Annie in corporate communications. They've already latched onto social media where people are speculating all sorts on Twitter and Facebook. It wasn't helped that one of the teens tweeted from the scene just before we arrived. That would be...' he glanced at the list of names on the board, '... Elsa James. There have been numerous responses which I know we're monitoring.'

Wyre interrupted. 'I've been monitoring them from the go. One thing I did see this morning was a tweet that was made by a tweeter calling themselves TheMeeganMrs, basically blaming the parents. It was deleted soon after and she'd also hashtagged Oak Tree Walk. Maybe it's Frank Meegan's wife. I'll continue to monitor her account.'

'Great work, Wyre.' Briggs smiled.

Gina glanced across the board and to her notes, checking whether she'd missed anything. 'We have the names and addresses of two other teens that were invited to the party. They knew about the party. They knew where it would be and they'd chosen not to attend. We need to speak to them. Wyre, could you check where we are with them? In an ideal world, I'd like to speak to both of them tomorrow. One last thing, we know Leah was upset when she left but no one we interviewed could shed any light as to why. I don't buy the fact that Leah just upped and left late at night after a petty argument while faced with an hour's walk, alone in the dark. Something else happened, and I want to know what. Keep pressing on. Keep the system updated at every turn so that we all have full access to the case. That's it for now.'

As the room began to empty and the sound of chatter picked up, a PC walked up to Briggs and Gina. 'We've been monitoring Mr Hackett and I thought I'd let you know, he agreed to the swabs being taken. They're on their way to the lab.'

Gina smiled at the woman. 'Thank you.' As she left, Gina turned to Briggs. 'That was easy enough. His solicitor must have told him that there was no way he's getting out of having them taken. We'll have twenty-four hours to get those results back before we have to release him.'

'Let's get this done.' Briggs went to leave. 'Do you want to work on the case later, at mine or yours?' He paused. 'I don't think you should be alone and I don't want to be alone either.'

'Can I call you in a bit?'

She left Briggs standing by the board as she headed to the kitchen to make a quick drink. If Briggs came over, all they'd talk about was the messages and she couldn't handle it, not tonight. She needed to wallow alone. Finding Leah's murderer had to come first.

The photo of the young girl's body, legs jutting out of the bushes sent a shiver through her. The fingermarks on her neck. Hackett, Meegan, the party of teens. Her mind flitted between the three. All seemed possible at the moment but there was something about the lies told between Rodney Hackett and John Tallis, like some little pact had been made. There was more to their stories and they were both hiding the same thing.

Gina tried to call Hannah again. Her mind working overtime but there was no answer, in fact, her daughter cut her off, then sent a text.

I'm working. We need to talk and soon. I'll message you when I can.

That was all. Hannah knew something about the messages. It was obvious she was being more evasive than ever.

She tried to call her daughter again but there was no answer. Gina wanted to throw the phone on the floor and stamp on it. Instead, she smashed her fist down onto the worktop. Why was this happening now? What did Hannah know?

CHAPTER FOURTEEN

Gina leaned over the interview table still reeling from her message exchange with Hannah. She clenched her teeth. Wyre sat beside her taking notes. Rodney Hackett and his solicitor were answering no comment to every question she and Wyre asked. They'd arrested him and had only a few hours to prove their case against him before they had to let him go. He'd be spending the night in a cell while they waited for the forensics results to come through. She checked the small window at the top of the door, hoping that Jacob would hurry with the authorised warrant to search his cab. The tape had been rolling for over fifteen minutes and not one useful word had come from Hackett's lips.

The solicitor mopped a film of perspiration from his glistening head for the third time in as many minutes. 'My client doesn't have anything to add other than what he's already told you.'

Gina glanced at her watch and movement caught her eye. She spotted Jacob through the window and all he did was give her a quick thumbs up. They were in a position to go. 'It's DI Harte. I'm opening the interview room door to let DS Driscoll in.' As she stood and opened the door, Hackett swallowed. His solicitor remained steely faced.

'Here it is, guv.' Jacob placed the warrant into her hands and left.

Gina remained silent for about half a minute as she placed the sheet of paper face down. Hackett uncomfortably squirmed in his chair as he stared at it. His face had reddened.

'Mr Hackett, this is a warrant to search your cab. We are searching for any evidence that Leah Fenmore was in there or any evidence that you followed her to the camp later that night and murdered her. Do you understand?'

He glanced at his solicitor and the solicitor held out his hand. Gina passed him the warrant where he peered at it for a few minutes and whispered in his client's ear. 'My client doesn't wish to say any more at this time.'

'Except I never touched her.' Hackett slammed his hand on the table. 'I gave her some beers, that's all.'

'But you originally lied to us about that, Mr Hackett.'

'I knew how it would look.'

Hackett's solicitor gave him a nudge. 'My client isn't saying any more.' The words were loud, clear and over-pronounced for the sake of Hackett getting the hint.

'Okay. Interview ended at eighteen twenty-one.' Gina gathered up her papers and nodded to Wyre to finish up. The clock was ticking and she had so much to do. Speaking to Bernard about the post-mortem was on the top of her agenda. Hopefully that would shed more light on Leah Fenmore's murder.

As she headed back to her office she grabbed a drink, then she went in and closed her door. Pushing the window wide open, she let out the musty smell that always seemed to linger. Her in tray was full, her inbox was heaving and she had several answerphone messages. Three of them were asking for callbacks which she did earlier, then there was one from O'Connor asking her to check the system for his latest updates.

She skimmed through the updates. Not only was Frank Meegan's full record attached, there was also the list of complaints from all the neighbours to the council and the press over the past couple of years; all about the kids partying in the woods and by the river. Nearly every person living in Oak Tree Lane had put in a complaint about antisocial behaviour. There were so many complainants, which gave so many motives. Graffiti, breaking into sheds, damage to cars, noise and litter. There were comments on social media stating that they wished all the kids would die, that they are a plague to the area. She glanced at the comments.

If they were my kids, I'd kill them myself!
Bloody self-entitled brats need a good kicking!
Parents need stringing up!
They are a disgrace and need dealing with. If the police or council won't, we will!

The list went on and on. Some posts on social media sounded more like a call to arms. Basically the whole community had issues with the kids that came to their blissful quiet location for a party. They thought the police and the council were doing nothing and Gina knew that they'd failed the community too. With cuts, it had become impossible to keep on top of these problems. One thing that did surprise her was that none of these comments came from Frank Meegan, but a couple of the tamer ones had come from his wife. Sometimes the people that didn't speak were the ones who stood out and in his case, and given his past conviction, he stood out. Every person living there had something to say, everyone but him.

She called Wyre. 'Are we ready to search the cab?'

'Yes, guv. I've just signed the keys out from Hackett's belongings. Okay to leave in ten minutes?'

'Definitely.' She wanted to be there for this one. They were about to discover if Leah got into Rodney Hackett's cab.

CHAPTER FIFTEEN

Caro sat on the garden swing and began playing a game on her iPad as the sun went down. It wasn't working as a distraction; she couldn't think about anything else but that message. Her stomach began to turn as she replayed those words in her head. Someone wanted to kill her.

She glanced at the house. Her mum and dad were in the kitchen, clearing up after the sandwiches that they'd eaten since coming back home. Caro had binned hers when her mother looked away but the onset of a rumble in her stomach was making her nauseous. She bit a chunk out of her thumbnail.

Her mum peered across and waved. Caro forced a smile and waved back, not wanting her mum to come over and make a fuss again. Placing her finger over the Twitter app, she closed her eyes, willing herself not to press. She would resist for now. Staring into the black hole that was social media would make things worse.

'We're having some ice cream. Do you want some?' Jake ran towards her with his gappy smile. Since his timeout at Grandad's he'd been a little nicer to her.

'Yes, I'd love some.' She turned her iPad off and took his hand, glancing around as she led him back to the house where Caro's mother was starting to dish up her favourite cookies and cream flavour. She wondered if someone was watching her every move, lurking outside the gate and looking through holes in the fence.

'Get this down you.' Her mother had filled a bowl.

'Thanks, Mum.' She didn't have the heart to tell her mum that she'd never eat it all but her mother was doing all she knew how to do and that was to fuss and protect.

Her mother placed the scoop down and hugged her. 'I can't imagine how awful you're feeling right now, but we're a family and we're going to get through what has happened together. The whole community is devastated.'

No they weren't. The whole community hated us. 'That's not what I read on Twitter earlier. Some people say that we should all die because we make them miserable.'

'Well, those people don't have a heart. Your friend was murdered and we're all devastated, they should be banned from Twitter for saying things like that. Look. Put that away,' her mother pointed to her iPad, 'and don't read their spiteful comments. They are nothing and nobody. Just a bunch of trolls.'

Caro placed her iPad on the sideboard. 'Okay.' For once she agreed with her mother.

'I'm just glad you weren't at that party.'

'And me.' She had attended the last party but she wasn't going to tell her mum that. Without warning, she remembered a smell. A pungent smell, maybe body odour, really strong. Her mind was giving her another link to what happened during her black out. Her dad left the room, taking Jake to set up a game in the living room. Sunday night board games had been a tradition in their family for as long as she could remember.

'Do I need to worry about you?'

She looked at her feet, then back up. 'No.'

'Oscar was at that party, wasn't he?'

Caro nodded.

'You two don't see each other much anymore, not like you used to.'

Shrugging, Caro took the bowl of ice cream that her mother pushed towards her. 'I guess we've grown apart a little.' She couldn't tell her mother the truth about what she did at the last party. Since then she hadn't wanted any of her friends over. She wouldn't normally snog all three boys there, in front of everyone, but that had been her dare, and who had come up with it? Naomi Carpenter. Caro had a drink, that was a fact but something hadn't felt right. In her mind, she drifted back to that night.

The fire's smoke had seeped through her clothes, giving them an acrid stench. Marshmallows and cider; that was what they had to drink and eat. The feeling of wooziness and then unsteadiness. She'd had one measly can of cider. She'd kissed Anthony; soft and slowly. While kissing him, she'd glanced over her shoulder at Oscar. Then she kissed Jordan, which had almost made her heave. He'd tried to press his tongue too invasively into her mouth and his lips were so wet. Lastly, she'd kissed Oscar and their friendship somehow felt compromised but it was also daring. A step into the unknown. Then Leah. That's it, she kissed Leah. She wasn't meant to as a part of the dare but Leah just got in line and leaned in. It happened without thought. Then she laughed and accepted another drink. Think, think! Who gave her that drink? After that drink, it was as if her mind blanked a little, like the darkness of the woods was closing in. Her eyelids had drooped and her limbs had felt heavy, like she was wading through mud that turned to stone. Then the world went black. She was sure someone helped her into her tent. The smell of body odour. The party sounded like a skewered record and the laughing scared her. Were they all in her tent, staring at her incapable body? Was it another dare?

Early the next morning, just as the birds had begun to tweet, Oscar had called her from outside her tent and she'd managed to mumble for him to come in. Was it Oscar? With one eye open, she saw the canvas roof of the tent and some of the evening was racing through her thoughts. With the world spinning, she'd remained closed eyed, hoping that another couple of hours of sleep might help. Oscar had fallen asleep a few minutes later with his head in her lap and he was still completely wasted. His snoring filled the tent. Then a flash of a memory from the early hours filled her head. Grunting noises along with that smell of body odour. She nudged Oscar away before allowing herself to fall asleep. Then came the nightmares. She'd kissed Jordan and he changed into a huge red-eyed beast, then Leah had sliced him open with a sword. She was startled awake when she heard voices outside and what came next was the worst hangover she'd ever had. It was like lightning pulsing through her head and her vision was fuzzy. It hurt to focus on anything.

Something was ringing as true. One whole can of cider does not equal even a mild hangover. She'd had up to four on a normal session and not felt that bad the next day. Her friends had found her shaking and sweating while vomiting in the bushes. She'd never felt so ill. In fact, she thought she was dying. Stabs of pain to her head and stomach almost floored her. What made it worse was that she had to make the biggest effort to hurry home while feeling like death and try to look well enough to have dinner at Grandad's. What had happened between entering her tent and Oscar coming into her tent and falling asleep on her? There was one thing she knew for certain but the rest was like cotton wool.

'Caro?'

She flinched as her mother's voice brought her back to the present. 'Sorry. I was just thinking about Leah.' Her heart began to bang in her chest.

The home phone began to ring. Her mother snatched it up and placed it to her ear. 'Hello.'

Her brow scrunched. 'Yes, I'm her mother.'

A tremble went through Caro, uncontrollable and fierce. She couldn't hide it. Her mother's gaze met hers.

'Yes, we can come in tomorrow. I'll put it in my diary. What's this about?' A pause. 'I see.' Her mother nodded and smiled at Caro. 'Just routine.'

Caro knew the police would want to speak to her. One of her friends had said that she was meant to be at the party. Anthony would get called too. Everything they got up to was going to come out, including that night; the night she couldn't fully remember. She knew what her dare was but what was everyone else's? *Pull yourself together, Caro.* The police weren't asking about that party, they were asking about the one last night. If they do mention other parties, just don't mention the dares and keep to the basics. That's what everyone else would do. 'Thanks for the ice cream, Mum.' There's no way she'd tell anyone about that message and that included the police.

'Come on. Let's go and play games. It'll take your mind off things.'

She doubted that very much. A Snapchat message flashed on her phone.

Say anything and u r next! I will break you if you speak.

The message disappeared. Forever gone.

Gulping, she followed her mother through to the lounge, bowl of ice cream in hand and she saw her dad and little brother setting up Pictionary. Her heart banged like a thundering train and the thought of eating was making her sick. In fact, she was going to be sick. She dropped the bowl and ran to the downstairs loo and keeled over the bowl.

'Caro, are you okay?' Her mother pushed the half-open door.

Shaking, Caro waited but nothing was happening. Nothing but her speeding heart and some sort of feverish flush that was subsiding a little. Her face burning red and knuckles white as she gripped the bowl. 'I just felt… sorry.'

Her mother kneeled down and hugged her and they stayed like that for a few seconds until the panic had subsided a little.

'Do you want to talk?'

Caro shook her head. 'I need to lie down.'

Her mother kissed her on the head. 'Call me if you need me, promise?'

'Promise, Mum.' It was the shock of the message. Who wanted to kill her? She had to be alone while she got her story straight for the police.

CHAPTER SIXTEEN

Jacob hurried over to Jennifer as she began to set up and pull her forensics suit up. They had been a couple for quite a while and given the circumstances in which they always met up at work, he was always happy to see her.

Gina stood outside the cab all gloved up, still shook up from the messages that wouldn't leave her head. Had she slipped up in a subtle way like one of the murderers she'd investigated in the past? Maybe she'd made a slight movement as someone said a word. A word out of place or an omission so subtle that only a highly observant person could see. *Murderer!* She pulled a forensics suit over her clothes and put her hair in a cover, swallowing the lump in her throat down.

Several lorries, some rigid and some articulated, were parked at the other end of the car park. The Waterside Café appeared to be filling up. She knew that John Tallis had come in earlier to give a statement and she'd even had a chance to quickly check the details that had been entered into the system. He'd pretty much stuck to his script, repeating the same things he'd told her earlier.

'Right, let's open up.' Gina couldn't wait to get in there but it was going to be tight.

Jacob stood behind her and PC Kapoor was maintaining the cordon that had been placed around the lorry. A couple of drivers who were standing outside the café were smoking and staring across at them.

Gina climbed up the steps to the cab and slotted the key in the lock. As she pulled the door open, a musky smell escaped. A combination of sweat and the heavy smell of sex that she could recognise instantly. A crumpled tissue and a pack of opened baby wipes sat on the dashboard along with the paperwork pertaining to Rodney Hackett's delivery that was meant to reach Oxford earlier that day. The company had been understanding about the delay once they'd explained why their delivery had been held up. Once forensics had looked in the cab and seized what they needed to seize, one of Hackett's colleagues would come and attach the trailer to another cab and take the load to its destination. The pressure was on to get this search done quickly and thoroughly.

'Can you shout down, telling me what you see?' Jennifer called up, mask dangling under her chin.

'Will do.' Gina entered the cab and leaned over. Jacob got into the passenger side, door open, standing on the top step as he peered through. After Gina had taken a first look, Jennifer could get in there and go through everything thoroughly, taking samples and fingerprints. 'Fingerprints in dust on both the passenger side and the driver's side. Crumpled tissue on dashboard. Lots of half-eaten packets of sandwiches. Empty drinks cans.' She glanced at the bed behind the seats. A crumpled quilt covered the bed and a flat pillow had been placed at one end. 'Hair that looks to be the same colour as our victim's. Definitely not Hackett's hair. It's long. A pair of what looks like yellow socks with red watermelons printed on them. I'm guessing they're not Hackett's socks. They also look small.'

Gina stared at the space for a short while longer. Attached to the sun visor was a photo of two teenage girls and Hackett. It looked like they were on holiday somewhere in the Mediterranean. Gina had read Hackett's notes. He was divorced and had two daughters that were in their early twenties now. She could see the resemblance, they all had the same shaped nose and broad forehead. 'Open box of condoms. Same brand as the one we saw under the cab.' She paused. 'I'm getting out now so that you can take photos and bag everything up. There's not much else here. A pile of clothes and a few packets of biscuits.' She stepped back as Jacob did. The lorry rocked a little as they both climbed down.

Gina headed to the end of the lorry with Jacob. 'Everything is pointing to him having had sex in his cab last night, at some point. The socks with the watermelon print, they could be Leah's. We need to ask her friends if she owned a pair like that. They are quite distinctive and as she was wearing shorts when we found her, the socks would have been visible for all to see if she had them on before she headed to the café. Leah was sixteen. I know she was at the age of consent, but seriously, do I think she could have willingly slept with Hackett? I can't see it.'

'Me neither, but stranger things have happened.'

'Agreed. What the hell happened here and back at the camp? Roll on tomorrow. We need those results. Get a good night's sleep as we have a pig of a day coming up tomorrow. I'm going to head home and continue working there. If you hear anything, call me straight away.'

'Will do, guv.' Jacob flashed her a smile before heading back over to Jennifer. The one good thing about them being in a relationship was that Jennifer would discuss the case with him in real time if he stuck around. They'd talk about it when they got home and work through what they knew, together, so she left him to it.

Gina glanced over at the café where she saw John Tallis staring at the cab with his phone pressed to his ear. He had no CCTV but he did have a clear view of the whole car park. She knew he wasn't sharing everything. In fact, she was sure he was purposely holding something back and it was something to do with Hackett and last night. His phone conversation looked like it was becoming fraught. He pressed hard on the screen and his shoulders slumped. His gaze met hers. He ran his fingers through his hair to neaten it, then he smiled and waved.

CHAPTER SEVENTEEN

It was only seven that evening but Frank has insisted that I go to bed, so I lie here with light still coming through my bedroom curtains. I heard him making pained noises at one point and I wonder if those scratches are sore as he dabs them down. He's not likely to tell me if I ask and I'd probably make him angry again. I don't want that.

The TV volume is so low that I can't hear what is being said by the actors in some sitcom I've never heard of. All I want to do is tune out from Frank and lose myself in something to pass the time. The remote control is on my chest of drawers and they are positioned at the other side of the room – impossible for me to get to right now. I know he does this to control me and he's getting worse by the day; I'm not stupid. We argue about this all the time but it gets me nowhere. I rub my head. His slap still stings a little.

Children still play on the green outside our row of cottages, kicking a football back and forth; shouting goal every so often. 'I want to get back up, Frank! Get me out of bed now.' I'm not a child and this is driving me crazy. Only a few minutes ago, he abruptly wheeled me from the lounge, manhandled me into bed and removed my wheelchair from the bedroom. There was no way I could get out of this bed without a major struggle and injury, and Frank knows that. If my wheelchair is next to the bed with the brakes on, I can wiggle my way into it, but my upper body strength isn't good enough for me to scuttle across the room, somehow reach up to open the door while I'm in front of it, then find my wheelchair – all before Frank sees me. That would enrage him and I know what his anger will do to me.

'Shut up and go to sleep.' I listen as he bursts around the downstairs of the cottage and lastly, he's in the kitchen. Again, he's rooting through the cupboards.

'Frank, get me my wheelchair.'

He ignores me. My life is hopeless. I wish I'd never gone on that holiday. I wish I'd never jumped into the sea from that rock, shattering my spine. I flinch as I remember the jolt of pain before the world went black. Waking up a week later in a Greek hospital had been the worst day of my life. I still think I have feeling in my legs sometimes; strange but true. I was warned of this by the hospital staff but nothing could prepare me for the weirdness of that feeling. I feel my legs twitch as if they want me to walk; to touch and stroke them, but the plain reality is always there to see. They are phantom sensations and I am still paralysed both physically and by Frank.

'Frank! I want my phone.' I haven't seen any news all day. I'm sick of everything and being in solitary confinement most of the time is sending me out of my mind. I also want to know if anyone else had seen my tweet earlier. Maybe someone has said something or sent me an angry message. A pang of guilt washes through me and not for the first time today. I want to yell and cry. I, of all people, should know what it's like to be silly and impulsive, just like those kids are with their parties and drinking. I stupidly jumped from a cliff into the sea when warned that it was a bad idea. The locals did it but they also knew where the rocks underneath were and how to avoid them. Stupid, stupid, stupid. Frank is still angry with me. Not only did that stupid act cost me my independence, it took Frank's too. Maybe I deserve all the hatred I get from him.

I hear him tipping a box of something that thuds onto the table and I wonder what it is he hides and why he spends time going through it every day. I can't go into the kitchen anymore, the door is not one of the doors we had widened so the kitchen is all his. His mood is changing for the worse and I know it's something to do with what he's hiding in that cupboard and what he did to gain those scratches. I need to get in there somehow. If I know what's bothering him, maybe I can help to make things better. If I don't make things better, things will get worse here. Much worse.

Shaking my bed frame, I scream out again. It bangs against the back of the wall over and over again, chipping away at the plaster just a little more each time. 'Frank, get me up. I think I need help with my catheter.' No answer. 'I hate you!' And I do. I hate him. Especially today.

He bursts through the door, scowling and seething as he stomps towards my bed. Grabbing my hair, he wrenches my neck back to the point I feel it might snap if I breathe. 'If you don't shut up, I will kill you and that's a promise.' There's rage in his wide-eyed stare.

He's never said that before. Things must be bad, but I can't take it. I slap him across the face, again and again, missing most of the time and he slaps me back. I don't care if it hurts and I don't care if it provokes him. I got one in, that's all that matters. I have to show him that I'm prepared to hit out too. He doesn't get a monopoly on this household's violence but he wins all the battles. The odds are stacked in his favour. He lets go of my hair and pushes me down, the back of my head sinking into the pillow and he places a hand around my neck, not hard enough to leave a mark but hard enough to make me take heed of his warning. I feel my vision prickling as I fight for breath and I want to cry hard. He could take me out with ease and there's nothing I could do about it. I just want him to love me like he used to before I became his burden. I'm so confused. Do I want him to love me or hate me? I don't know. All I know is I don't want to be stuck in this rut. They say love and hate are closely related. I never understood that until now. At this moment though, I want to get out of bed. I want to go and sit in the garden or watch the telly in the living room. I don't show him my fear, my stare remaining on his until I begin to go red. This isn't how I want to die…

He releases me then sits on the edge of my bed in silence as he stares into thin air.

There's definitely something up with him and it's not only my demands causing this outburst. Things have never got that bad. He's never tried to choke me to death. He turns slightly and I see sadness washing over his face. The aggression is going as he snaps out of his rage. 'What's going on?' My voice is more of a broken-up crackle.

He shrugs. 'It's everything.'

I know it's the burden of me so I don't push any further. I'll stay in bed and shut up, just like he wants me to. He needs some alone time and I need to give him that. 'I'm sorry too. Can I just have the remote so I can watch Netflix?' Swallowing, I'm hoping he says yes. I'm not sorry though.

Walking across the room, he passes it to me before kissing me on the head and smiling, this is why I'm always confused. He pulls my blanket up to my chin and I'm immediately too hot but I don't say anything. I'm going to be good and do what he wants. I will be quiet. I'll watch a film and I'll go to sleep. All I do is force a smile. The last thing I want to risk is another outburst like the one I've just seen.

For a second, I see the Frank I used to know and I feel a knot in my stomach. I did love that man. I don't anymore, I need him; but that doesn't stop me trying to hang on to the good times before everything went wrong. They're all I have. 'Can I come shopping with you in the morning?'

He nods. 'Yes, I suppose. We'll go together after breakfast.' He leaves, closing my bedroom door once again. Going out is a huge win for me. I throw the blanket off me, instantly releasing the heat as I exhale slowly. I'm going out tomorrow. It doesn't happen often but I'm going out. I peel the curtains back slightly and grab the two heavy figurines. When I hear that he's gone, I begin my repetitions. Slowly lifting them as high as I can reach, then gradually bringing them down. I repeat this fifty times. I used to only be able to do about ten when I started but I'm improving every day. My lack of strength is keeping me a prisoner. Time to stop moping around, bathing in self-pity and fight the weakness.

CHAPTER EIGHTEEN

Monday, 2 August

Gina passed Jacob a coffee and they both watched the pathologist at work as Bernard examined the body of Leah Fenmore. It was never a joy to be present while the Y-incision was being made, especially with what followed. Leah Fenmore's ribcage would be lifted off, then her organs would be removed one by one before being weighed. The saw would whirr through her skull before her brain was lifted out. Slices of this and samples of that would be taken. As far as Gina was concerned, it didn't pay to overthink what was happening.

The light of the stainless steel and white clinical room glinted off the scalpel that scored Leah's chest. The pathologist finished the incision and dropped it with a clang into the metal dish.

The greying girl's body lay naked on the slab, all evidence of life long gone. Only a couple of days ago, she was a living, breathing girl with so much ahead of her. She'd finished her GCSEs and was probably looking forward to sixth form, college, or starting an apprenticeship like all her friends were. But someone had other plans and they took her life. Gina sipped her coffee as the scales bounced.

Jacob looked away. 'This part of the job is the pits.'

'I know, but this is where we get to find out more, hopefully. I'm pretty sure she died of strangulation. Did you manage to contact Leah's party friends again? I wondered if any of them were happy to speak further so that we could ask about her socks.'

'Oh yes. I got onto that straight away after going through Hackett's cab last night. Oscar Spalding's father said we can go to theirs anytime today but he wasn't making his son come back to the station.'

'I can understand that. It's scary to be questioned in a police station at that age. As we have the two teens that didn't make the party coming in this afternoon, we should head there straight after here so that we make it back on time. I'm intrigued as to why they didn't go.'

'Great. I have the photo of the socks amongst others. Jennifer brought me a print from work when she finally came home last night, oh and they were emailed to you too. Three in the morning. Can you believe it?'

'Sadly I can. We see three in the morning a lot more than everyone else. That hour is hell. It's not night and it definitely doesn't feel like morning. How is Jennifer, by the way?'

'Good. She's started cycling, which means I have too. My thighs are burning and I have a touch of saddle sore and sweaty—'

'Good for you. I don't need the details.'

He shrugged and laughed. 'It was better than the alternative.'

'Alternative?'

'Swimming. Nothing would get me into the public baths. I have childhood nightmares about ear infections and verrucas. I was a sickly child.'

Gina chuckled before gazing back through the window. She gulped down the rest of her drink before dropping the paper cup into the waste bin. She noticed it wasn't a mesh bin and she knew why. It wouldn't be the first time someone had used the viewing room bin to throw up in while watching a post-mortem through the glass. The clean CSI took a burst of photos and someone else was filming each stage while the pathologist provided an intensely scientific voiceover, citing the Latin names for body parts and bones; shouting out weights and measurements.

An hour passed, then another. The last of the samples were neatly lined up on the far side and the pathologist began to sew Leah back up. Now devoid of her lip piercing and clothing, she looked so young and tiny. Gina looked away. Her daughter was grown up now and even had a daughter of her own, little Gracie who was now at primary school. In these circumstances, she always used to think of Hannah but the worry never ended even though they were always falling out. Before she knew it Gracie would be a teenager and those worries would start all over again. She felt her throat dry when she tried to swallow. The circle of worry never ends. Whatever Hannah wanted to discuss couldn't be good. After all this time, speaking about her father would not do either of them any good. She glanced back as the pathologist stood back to check his work. 'Looks like they're finishing up.'

'I think you're right.' Jacob stretched and shifted his weight from one foot to the other.

The pathologist left the assistants to tidy up and catalogue everything then he waved, calling Gina and Jacob over to the door. He snapped his gloves off, removed his apron and scrubbed his arms to his elbows in the hand basin.

'That's our cue. Let's find out what he has to say.'

They hurried along the corridor and the pathologist came out. The smell of faeces, and death mixed with disinfectant spilled out, almost catching the back of Gina's throat as she inhaled. She took a step back, trying to escape it then the pathologist closed the door on the corpse. 'Follow me.'

He led them to a little room with a table and chairs, and a two-seater couch where they all sat. An artificial plant and a seascape picture were the only things that brightened up the room. The tall man pushed his glasses up his nose further and loosened his tie. Gina noticed the cartoon body parts that covered it. They reminded her of the board game, Operation. 'Okay, we're just finishing up. I will begin working on my report later today but it will take a while as we have so many samples to get through and I need lunch first.' He chuckled slightly, not put off at all by the job he'd been doing for years. 'As for the toxicology report that you requested, that will take weeks but I'm sure that's not a surprise.' He gave a slightly goofy grin.

'Definitely not a surprise.' Gina wished there was a quicker way but there wasn't. Toxicology always came late, quite often after they'd solved the case but it was good for the court cases that followed. She just hoped it wouldn't be weeks before she could take Leah's murderer off the street.

'We'll be examining her blood, urine and even hair in this process.'

'Thank you. Can you tell us anything about the injuries that might have led up to her death? Anything that might help with our investigation.'

'I can confirm that the cause of death was strangulation but I already told you that was the most likely cause at the scene. There was very little evidence of a struggle, in fact there was none. There was a trace of semen found on her leg that was picked up in the swabs at the scene.'

'That could have got there when the condom was removed?'

The pathologist nodded. 'Yes. I also know that several used condoms have been found in the area and they haven't all as yet been tested against the semen sample.'

'How about the one found in the Waterside Café car park.'

He flicked through his file. 'Still waiting. You asked for a comparison between that and a swab that arrived at the lab late yesterday.'

'That's right.' Gina's stomach muscles clenched at the stale odour coming from the man. He may have scrubbed himself clean and wore protective clothing but the smell of death knew how to get into everything and now it was lining the wall of her nostrils. 'Any indication of when they will come through?'

The pathologist flicked through a few pages in his file. 'I'm certain you will get your answer by this afternoon.' He began to play with the end of his tie.

'That's good. Hopefully before we have to let our suspect go.'

'I'll chase it up for you if that's any help.'

'Thank you. It's already marked priority but anything you can do to hurry it would be much appreciated. Is there anything else?'

He read his notes and scrunched his nose as he concentrated. 'As I said, no signs of a struggle during intercourse or during strangulation which, as you mentioned before, could point to drugs in her system. Being strangled is an extreme act of violence where death is imminent if the victim can't get free. I would have expected a huge struggle. There is nothing at all on her body to suggest that she made any attempt to get away. Stomach contents look to contain sugary food. I'd say sweets. Of course there is the faint bite mark on her right breast. I will be able to provide you with all the measurements. Because of the bruising, that bite mark looks like it was done recently, possibly the same night.'

'Meaning, it could belong to the murderer. Getting the bite details emailed to me would be a great help. We might get a dental record match. Is there any evidence to show that the person Leah had sex with and the person who killed her are the same person?'

'At the moment, the person who left the bite mark might be different from the person who had sex with her and they both might not be the person who killed her. We will go through all of the samples thoroughly, test everything and hopefully my full report will help more but as you can appreciate there is so much work to be done still.'

Gina slumped back a little, deflated at having nothing new to work with right now. She'd have to wait for the dental measurements and bite photos.

'Oh, there is one more thing. The bite mark suggests that the biter has a missing tooth. Top row, right-hand side of the mouth, third after the incisor so you might not see the missing tooth even if the person smiled at you. It was a wide-open mouth bite. Very bizarre.'

'That's really helpful. Thank you.'

As they wrapped up the meeting, Gina checked her watch. It was time to head to Oscar Spalding's house to ask about the watermelon socks. She also wanted to see him for herself as she didn't get to interview him at the station.

She smiled as they left the building. The person who was missing a tooth had a lot to explain and she wanted them found, fast. 'Right, to the Spalding residence.' She checked her messages and Hannah's name lit up the screen.

I want the truth. No more lies.

Gina allowed Jacob to continue ahead as she tried to call Hannah. Again, she rejected the call. Her knuckles were white as she gripped the phone. She could feel the blood draining from her face. What truth was Hannah seeking? The word murderer flashed up in her mind like a slap and she breathed out the anxiety.

'You coming, guv?'

'Yes, course.' She turned away from him as she gasped. Hands trembling, she knew the truth was fighting to get out and there was nothing she could do to prevent it.

CHAPTER NINETEEN

Gina tried to put all thoughts of her own problems into a compartment in her mind as she tried to recall everything she'd read in Oscar Spalding's notes. He was seventeen and gave the same story as everyone else. He was also a driver. As she drove along the carriageway, Jacob chomped away on a chocolate bar.

Jacob screwed up his wrapper and shoved it in his pocket. 'That's better. My stomach was starting to rumble.'

'I know how you feel.'

'Sorry, guv. I should have offered you a bite.'

'I'm off chocolate, at least until the smell of death no longer coats my nostrils. Okay, about Oscar. He's a school friend of all the others that were at the party. All of them were in some classes together and I'm sure I read in the file that they all went to junior school together; so we have a lot of shared history between the teens. He lives with his father who is a war veteran, Iraq from what I read about him. Mother died when he was about nine. We managed to obtain some information from his last form teacher after the school administrator asked her to get in contact with us. Oscar got into some minor troubles there; a scuffle in PE; drawing a pair of breasts with a Sharpie on his locker; answering teachers back. He'd received a fair few detentions for not doing homework or study but he surprised his teachers with all A and B grades in his GCSEs.'

'Imagine what a kid with that potential could achieve if only he applied himself better? Seems naturally gifted.'

'Totally. He's also still a suspect, we just have nothing to bring him in on. I'm hoping when forensics have analysed everything from the camp that we might have something concrete. Those kids are all covering for each other, I know it. What we need is something tangible to bring them in again.' The satnav told Gina to take the next left. 'Right, Oscar's father left the army after his wife died. He doesn't actually work now.'

'So how can he afford to live here?'

As they pulled into the road, the large double-fronted houses with huge detached garage blocks and electric-gated drives took them to another world, one that could never be achieved on a detective's salary. 'When I saw the address, I thought the same so I read up on them. Mr Spalding's wife was a songwriter and her estate still pays out royalties.'

'Anything I know?'

'Not unless you're into nineties hip-hop.'

'I guess not, then. I was more into Britpop. Give me a bit of Oasis any day.'

The satnav reminded them that they had arrived at their destination. Gina pulled up on the kerb and they got out and stood outside the intercom at the gate of 7 Nightingale Avenue and pressed the buzzer.

'Hello.' The man at the other end cleared his throat.

'DI Harte and DS Driscoll. You're expecting us. Is that Mr Spalding?'

The buzzer sounded and the gate began to smoothly open. They walked down the tree-lined drive and came face to face with the mock Georgian mini mansion. Potted palm trees greeted them, framing the door, which was opened by Mr Spalding.

'Right,' the man spoke slowly and calmly, 'before I take you in to see my son, I want you to know that this has all been distressing for him so keep the conversation easy or I will ask you to leave. Do you get that?' His temples twitched as he stood straight and still, his stare bouncing between Gina and Jacob. He didn't blink once.

'Of course, Mr Spalding. Our aim isn't to upset your son. We just need to ask a couple of questions that will help us with our investigation. Your son is a witness and we will treat him like so.'

The man pushed the door open and stepped aside. Gina stepped on the pale slate tiles and she was instantly bedazzled by the rainbow the crystal chandelier cast on the large hall's pale grey walls. The whirr of air conditioning was a welcome relief from the sticky heat outside. 'If you both take a seat in the snug, I'll get Oscar for you.' Mr Spalding pointed to the open door of a room.

No offer of a drink? Gina was parched. 'Thank you.'

They followed Mr Spalding to the room he had called the snug but it was more like a huge television room cum cinema. When the man left to get his son, Gina felt the tension seeping from her shoulders as they relaxed. The largest TV she'd ever seen was fixed to the wall. This was surrounded by built-in units containing loads of books, computer games, DVDs and even a mini fridge full of cans of pop. The window to her left was bigger than the far wall in Gina's living room. She sat next to Jacob, sinking back. 'This is a comfy sofa. I think I feel wood pushing through mine,' Gina joked.

'I could stay here all day.'

She glanced around looking for photos, something that would tell her a little more about Oscar and his father, but there weren't any. It was as if the home, although beautiful and grand, was devoid of a family. Some of the computer games still had cellophane wrappers on them.

Footsteps padded down the hallway before Oscar entered, closely followed by Mr Spalding. 'I've told him, if he feels uncomfortable at any time, this chat or whatever it is, is over. My son would never have had anything to do with hurting that girl in any way. I've brought him up to show respect.' The vein on the side of the man's head stood out as he clenched his mouth shut.

Gina glanced at Jacob before smiling at Oscar.

The boy ruffled his messy, shiny, chestnut coloured fringe. Underneath the floppy top, his hair was shaved almost to the skin. His pointed chin made him look quite delicate but she could see his muscles due to the vest top he was wearing. This delicate boy was as strong as an ox. Average height and a light tan. 'How can I help you, ma'am; sir?'

Gina wondered if he called his father sir. 'Thank you for coming to the station yesterday and making a statement. Once again, we're so sorry for your loss. I know that you and Leah were close friends so this must be distressing for you.'

The boy clenched his teeth and pulled a chair up, placing it opposite the settee with such a precise motion, it landed exactly where he wanted it to. 'We were all good friends. When you've been through both schools together, you develop a close bond, ma'am. So what can I help you with?'

Ma'am again. Gina pulled the file from her bag and fumbled for the photo that Jacob had given to her. 'Please take a look at this photo. Do you recognise these socks?'

His brow furrowed and his father walked over from the door for a look. The boy glanced up at his father. 'Sir?'

'It's okay, son. Just answer the detective.'

'Yes, I think so. They belong to Leah. She was wearing them on Saturday.' Each word he spoke was clear, precise and without any hint of an accent; not like the other teens in the group.

A whoosh of adrenaline flushed through Gina and she felt a buzz from her stomach to her fingertips. Leah had been in Rodney Hackett's cab. How else could her socks being on his bed be explained? Maybe the kids were innocent as Hackett had lied again. 'Thank you. You've been really helpful. Is there anything else you'd like to add? Maybe we can talk more about how Leah seemed.'

'No. My son told you everything he had to say yesterday so if you have nothing new to discuss, no evidence to share, that will be all.'

Gina wished the floor would swallow Mr Spalding up. She turned her attention back to Oscar. 'If either of you think of anything else in the meantime, I'll leave you with my card.' Gina stood.

'I'll see you both out.' Mr Spalding waved an arm and pointed to the door.

'Thank you again, Oscar. You've been most helpful.'

The boy nervously nodded, his hair flopping back and forth as he did. His father glanced back and the boy sat back down while waiting to be told he could go. As Mr Spalding walked them back to the hall and out of the door, he smiled. 'I hope that will be all. Have a good day.'

As Gina and Jacob stepped out, the door was already shut. 'He couldn't wait to get rid of us but that's a positive ID on the socks. Another nail in Hackett's coffin. I hope my suspicion about the kids being involved will be quelled. An arrest of Hackett and a confession would close that line of investigation and solve the case. We're on a roll today. Oh, is that the time, we best hurry; I need to find out if Bernard is close to getting us those results. With those and the socks, we'll be ready to nail Hackett.'

Gina popped the key in the ignition, firing the car up. 'That whole interview didn't feel right. Not one bit. From what his teacher said, he was disruptive and got into minor scuffles. It looks like he behaves in his father's presence but people see the real Oscar when he's out and about. He hides his true self well and I don't like that.' Gina almost shuddered knowing how well she'd hidden her true self for all these years. Not any more though. Someone knew everything.

Jacob popped a stick of gum in his mouth. 'Agreed. Over polite with a plummy use of language. He's putting an act on, but why?'

'Hmm. Is he scared of his father or just laying it on thick to hide something?'

'It's looking like Hackett is our prime suspect though.'

'Hmm.' Gina nodded.

The smell of minty gum spread around the car as Jacob chewed. 'Let's go nail him.'

CHAPTER TWENTY

When you leave the house as seldomly as I do, a trip to Tesco is exciting. It's a reason to put some make-up on, to wear that perfume I save for special occasions that never materialise. This is a special occasion. Frank normally comes here alone, citing that my luggage is too much work for him. He hates taking me out in the car and today was no exception. As he pushed my wheelchair into the back of the van, he huffed and puffed and then managed to trap his finger somehow. Then it was my fault he hurt himself; me that fuelled his anger and frustration. I wonder if he really trapped his finger, I sometimes think he says things to make me feel bad. But I made it to Tesco and it feels epic. I never would have said that in the past. Shopping had been boring; a task to rush in order to hurry home. Not now. It's an outing to be savoured. 'Can we stop for coffee and cake while we're here?' It might just be my lucky day.

'Who'd want to spend any more time in a supermarket than needed? Besides, I want to get back.' He clenches his jaw as he wheels me down the tinned food aisle, then he places some beans into the basket on my lap.

'What for?' I lean back, bending my neck until it hurts but at least I caught sight of his face.

'Look, I just do, now stop asking questions.' He glances up the next aisle as if he's worried. No one else is walking around so he hurries forward towards the tuna. The strip lights are bright and the sound of staff being called on the tannoy system is so loud it makes me jump slightly. This is life. It's what I miss and crave so badly, and he wants to rush my enjoyment of feeling like I'm a part of society, not just something to be hidden in the house. 'Damn, I forgot the tomatoes. Wait here.' Before I know it, he's gone leaving the basket on my lap so that I can't move.

A woman leans over me, trying to reach for a four-pack of tuna. My brakes are on too and I'm squashed in by the basket. 'Sorry, my husband has left me here. Forgot something as usual.' I roll my eyes and smile, then something draws me to her face. I know her but I can't think of her name. If I say something but I don't use her name, I might come across as rude.

She smiles back and winces in thought. 'Sandy. I knew I recognised you. It's been a few years.' Her smile drops a little as she looks at my wheelchair and then back at me. That's what people do. They don't see me anymore. They see a wheelchair. Don't they know that I'm a living, breathing person with thoughts, opinions and desires? I'm more than what they see. Far more. Before this chair I had a job, I had hobbies. I helped at the food bank for a while but since the accident, I guess I alienated people. Depression took a tight hold and they stopped calling. Only I can turn this around and rebuild my life. Only I can get them to see me, not just the chair. Then it clicks. I remember her name – I think. 'Lara?' I'm sure it's the girl I used to hang out with when I was a kid. Or was it Lana. I know I'm close.

'Yes. Oh my goodness. We used to be so close. I can't believe I haven't seen you around for all these years but then again, I normally shop online. Coming here is a bit of a one-off.'

I smile, warming to her and the fond memories that I recall. She is a part of my past, a lovely part. We lost touch when she went to a different secondary school to me. Her light coppery hair falls in wisps over her well-structured neck and shoulders. She always did have perfect bone structure. 'Would you like a coffee with me, in the café here? I'd love to catch up.' I hope I'm not setting myself up for rejection here but I can't let her go. She's the first friendly face I've come across for ages and I need someone. I need people around me other than Frank. I need a friend who I can talk to and confide in.

She glances at her phone as if checking the time. 'A coffee would have been lovely but I really have to get on.'

I tense up and the basket I'm balancing on my lap begins to rattle as I shake slightly. I want to cry.

'But, I would love to speak to you again soon.' She fishes in her bag and pulls out a card. 'My phone number is on here. Call me soon. Maybe we can do something together.' I take the card. *Lara Blakely – interior designer.* 'It's my new business.' She smiles.

'I will.' My heart is racing. As soon as I have my phone I will call or text her. I know we can be good friends again. I push the card deep into my pocket, knowing that Frank wouldn't really like me trying to arrange something with an old friend. I'd get the spiel about how anything I arranged would be all put on him as he would have to get me there but I'm past caring. I need people in my life and they're not going to come to me while I sit in front of the television back at home. I'll book an adapted taxi if I have to. Sod Frank.

'I must go. I really would have loved to have a drink with you but my daughter's waiting in the car. We knew the poor girl who was murdered in the woods on Saturday night and we have to get to the police station to give a statement. She was a good friend of Caro's. So sad. Whoever killed that girl should die for what they did.'

A pang of guilt flashes through me. What I published for all to see on Twitter was unforgivable. I hope she didn't see it. 'I'm so sorry for your loss. We live on Oak Tree Walk, so we've had police everywhere for the past couple of days. Your poor daughter. She must be so upset.'

Lara paused. 'I'm glad it wasn't her. Sounds selfish, doesn't it?'

'Not at all. It's natural to want to protect those we love. How old is she?'

'Sixteen. She's just finished her GCSEs.'

'Wow, you have a sixteen-year-old daughter. That's so lovely.'

'I have a son too. He's eight and can be a little terror when he wants to be.' She titters a little. 'How about you? Any children?'

I wanted a child more than anything but Frank never did. 'No, not by choice. The time was never right and then my accident happened.' He kept promising me that the right time would come. The right time would never come now. I'd already left it late in life and now, it really was too late. Besides, Frank never touched me anymore and I doubt he ever would again.

'I'm sorry.'

'Don't be. I was stupid and now I'm paying a hefty price.' We pause but now I've started, I'm going to finish. 'I jumped from a cliff into the sea on holiday and this happened. There's a lesson to be learned. One to share with your kids.' My eyes begin to well up. Talking to someone about what happened, other than Frank who no longer cared, was like a huge burden had been lifted.

'I'm so sorry, Sandy.'

'I'm getting used to it now. Anyway, I hope your daughter's okay. Well not okay, how can someone feel okay when that has just happened to a friend.' I think of Frank, the scratches and the fact that he did leave our house in the night and I swallow hard.

'I think we'll all feel better when they catch the bastard. I hope he dies.' Lara gripped the tin of tuna like she was trying to strangle it and my heart began to bang in my chest as I thought about Frank and wondered if he knew more about the murdered girl.

I hear the sound of Frank's heavy feet getting louder before he comes to a stop. 'Right, let's get this shopping done and get the hell out of here. Hello?' He glances at Lara.

'Hello.'

Frank didn't have a way at putting people at ease. He stares, intensely. 'I'm Sandy's husband, Frank.'

They shake hands. 'I'm Lara, Sandy and I went to primary school together. Anyway, I best get going.'

Lara smiles at me as she leaves for the tills. Frank's gaze stays with her. As she disappears into the distance his brow furrows. A tear slides from the corner of my eye.

'I guess you just gave her the woe-is-me sob story. People don't want to hear it. Seriously. You bring them down.'

They do. I know my friend, Lara, was happy for me to share the details of my accident with her. Frank can be horrible sometimes and I hate him for it.

'Look at her. She couldn't wait to get away.'

She was getting away from you, arsehole.

'People hate misery. They don't want it in their happy lives. But me, I'm here for you. Always am, always will be.' He kneels down and wipes my tear away before taking the basket from my lap.

'She was happy listening to me.'

He laughs as he throws the tomatoes into the basket and starts to walk ahead of me. I wheel myself towards him. 'You might think she was happy listening to you.'

'She's having a hard time too. We were talking, you know? Having a conversation. Her poor daughter was friends with the girl who got murdered by us.' I stare at him, looking for him to give something away but he doesn't.

He huffs out another laugh from his nose. 'Did you tell her what you wrote on Twitter? You're glad one of those pain in the arse kids was murdered. I think you should stay away from her. You'll only get hurt.' That was a threat. He'd make sure I got hurt.

He was right. I'm not a good person and I have no right injecting myself into Lara's life. As we approach the tills, I spot Lara in the self-service checkout, several along. Frank can't stop gazing over at her to the point I'll be embarrassed if she looks back. 'Stop staring at her.'

'I wasn't. Don't be such a jealous mare.'

He is staring and I'm not jealous. Lara wouldn't look at him twice. He's still staring and I feel he knows who Lara is. It's the way he's scrunching his brow and biting the inside of his cheek. Again, I wonder if all the clues to what he's hiding are hidden in the kitchen. As soon as I get my chance, I'm going to find out what he's hiding in there.

Reaching into my pocket, I feel for the card. I watch as Lara leaves the store, her wavy hair bouncing as she walks away, and I wonder if Frank is right. Should I or shouldn't I make contact? Either could lead to disastrous consequences.

CHAPTER TWENTY-ONE

Gina headed out to the reception area and smiled at Nick, the desk sergeant, as she entered. That's when she spotted the girl with her mother, both nervously playing with hair and biting their nails. It was obvious that neither of them had ever been into a police station before.

'Caro and Mrs Blakely are here to see you, guv.'

'Thanks, Nick.'

She walked over and smiled at the girl. 'Hello, Caro, I'm DI Harte but you can call me Gina. Thank you for coming in to speak to me. I'm sorry about your friend too and what you're going through.'

Caro smiled and stood. Her mother placed her hand on her shoulder.

'We'll talk in the family room. This is an informal chat so please don't worry.' Gina led them along the corridor and into the room that was a little nicer than the interview rooms. It had comfier chairs that were designed to put people at ease. 'Please take a seat.'

Jacob knocked and entered.

'This is DI Driscoll, or Jacob. He will sit in too. If you need to stop at any time, just let us know.' Mrs Blakely and her daughter sat on the couch and Gina pulled a couple of chairs from the corner of the room for her and Jacob. 'I know it's hot in here and I apologise. We don't have air con and the window is jammed.' That window had been another thing on the list of ignored repairs that needed doing at the station. The result of all the cuts was that nothing ever got done, so now they were all stifling in this tiny box while still working murder cases on what felt like a skeleton crew. Mrs Blakely began waving her tiny handbag in front of her face to create a draft. The edge of her hair was slightly damp with perspiration. 'I'll leave the door open. Can we get you a cold drink?'

Both mother and daughter shook their heads.

Jacob passed the paper case file across to Gina and he flipped his notebook open to a clean page in readiness to take a few notes.

'How well did you know Leah?'

Caro glanced at her mother. Her long lashes glinting in the sunshine through the window.

'She was a good friend of my daughter's.'

'Could Caro please answer.' Gina smiled.

'Of course. I'm so sorry. We're really nervous, that's all.'

'And that's perfectly normal. I understand it's not every day something like this happens and thank goodness it doesn't. Caro?'

The girl shifted slightly and pulled her tiny shorts down a little. 'We were friends at school.' Her lightly bronzed freckles glistened on her nose. 'I've known her since we started junior school. We've been friends since.' Caro paused. 'Had been.' She swallowed and placed her hands under her legs so that she was now sitting on them. Gina spotted a slight sweat patch forming under the girl's arms, her dark T-shirt showing the dampness up.

She reached over and plugged the fan in and pointed it towards Caro and her mother. She and Jacob could suffer a while longer. 'What was she like at school?'

'Leah was lovely. We were good friends and I really liked her. She'd always share her things and help people with homework. She was clever, really good at science, not like me. She loved netball and played for the school team.'

'Do you know if she'd fallen out with anyone lately?'

Caro scrunched her nose and shook her head. 'No. We all liked her and she was friendly. She wasn't being bullied as far as I know. She and Naomi had a little tiff a year or so ago because they both liked the same boy but that was nothing and it was over the minute it started.'

'Moving on to Saturday night. Your friends have told us that you were invited to the party but you turned down the invite. Can you tell me a little more about this?'

'You didn't say you were invited!' Lara Blakely said.

'Sorry, Mum. I didn't think it mattered because I told them I wasn't going.'

Gina pushed on. 'Why didn't you go?'

Caro shrugged her shoulders. Her face was beginning to redden.

'My daughter probably didn't want all the trouble that comes with drinking in the woods and staying out all night. She's a good girl.' Mrs Blakely seemed to be a little frustrated now.

'If you could let your daughter answer.'

'Sorry.' Mrs Blakely leaned back in the chair and looked down at her feet.

A tear ran down Caro's cheek.

'What is it, sweetie?'

She shook her head as she started to sob.

'Look, this is too much. My daughter has just lost a close friend. I don't think she's up to it.'

'I'm okay, Mum. It's going to come out anyway.'

Gina paused, waiting for the girl to open up.

'There was another party two weeks ago and I went, Mum. I'm so, so, sorry. I told you I was staying at Naomi's house. I lied. I went to the party.'

Mrs Blakely grabbed her daughter into a hug. 'You silly girl. You should have told me.' She kissed her daughter's head. 'But it was stupid, very stupid. You could have got into trouble. It could have been you who was murdered.'

'Can you confirm the date of the previous party?'

Caro began counting on her fingers while looking up. 'Saturday the seventeenth of July.'

'And what happened at that party? The one you went to.' Gina needed some answers. Caro and her mother could talk through this later, together.

'We had some drinks, mostly cider and we danced for a bit, then we slept in our tents. We woke up with a bit of a hangover and then went home.'

'Why didn't you go to the party this past Saturday?'

'I felt really ill the last time and I didn't want to go through that again. I've never felt so rough. That's the only reason.'

'Did you stay at home?'

'Of course she stayed at home. We were in all night on Saturday.' Mrs Blakely couldn't help but chip in. She elongated the words *all night* with a smile.

'Yes, like Mum said. We had a pizza at teatime, watched a film on Netflix and went to bed.'

'What time did you go to bed?'

Caro shrugged. 'I can't remember. Probably about eleven, then I watched TV in my room.'

'Did you receive any phone calls or messages from anyone at the party that night?'

'No. We do message each other a lot but I thought they were probably having too much fun. I didn't expect any of them to message me.'

'Is there anything else you can tell me that might help?'

Caro pulled her hands from under her thighs and placed them in her lap. 'At the last party, someone was hanging around watching us. I told the others and I think Oscar went to check but he said that there was no one there. I couldn't focus, but I did see the outline of a man. There was only a bit of moonlight, which barely helped. It was quick and before I knew it, he ran away.'

'You're doing really well, Caro.'

Mrs Blakely scrunched her brow and bit her bottom lip. 'It really could have been my daughter who was murdered, couldn't it? Whoever did this deserves to die after what they put Leah through. I don't know what I'd have done if you were—'

'I'm okay, Mum. Nothing happened to me and the boys said there was no one there when they checked and he didn't come back.'

'Where were you when this happened?'

'Just a short walk away from the camp. I went to have a wee in the bushes.'

'So, let me get this straight. A man was watching you whilst you were urinating in the bushes?' Gina said.

Caro nodded. 'Yes. Then he ran off.'

'Are you sure there is nothing you can tell me about this person?'

'No, it was too dark. As I said all I got was an outline. I knew it wasn't the boys we were camping with. He was stockier.'

'Is there anything else you can add? Did you hear anything?'

'No, nothing. It all happened in a few seconds. I almost doubted myself it was that quick.'

'What you've told us has really helped. In the meantime, if there's anything else you remember, please call me.' Gina passed a card to Mrs Blakely.

Caro went to speak but then stopped.

'Is there something else?'

'Erm, no.'

Gina detected a slight air of worry in the teen's demeanour. Her fingernail went back into her mouth as she glanced at her mum for reassurance.

'Right, we best go. I have to go pick her brother up from my neighbour before she has to go to work. I can't believe what happened, I'm absolutely stunned. If someone hurt my daughter, I'd kill them. I hope you find them and quick.' Mrs Blakely shook her head and stood, lifted her sticky top from her chest and waited by the open door. Caro left first. That was all Gina was getting from them today.

As she stood alone, the fan wafted some air at Gina's face. Lara's words as she left made her shiver but she understood the primal instinct that was protecting your child. She shivered at the thought of a grown man watching that poor young girl with her underwear down. Had their voyeur heard the party in full swing again and come back to spy on them all again, waiting for his opportunity to strike. Seeing Leah leave the pack, looking drunk and vulnerable, had he then seized his opportunity to kill her?

Jacob came back for his notes after seeing the pair back to reception. 'That girl is worried sick about something. She wanted to talk but her mother virtually pushed her out the door.'

'I know, I could tell, but I suppose being spied on by some weirdo a couple of weeks before your friend was killed could do that to a person. I know what you mean, though. There's more to it. Again, she stuck rigidly to the story of a few drinks, dancing, then into their tents for sleep. Everyone telling the same story should ring true so why does it feel so fake?'

Jacob exhaled and grabbed his paperwork. 'That's what we need to find out.'

Gina heard heavy feet clopping down the corridor and O'Connor reached them with a frown. 'Tallis has just called; the Waterside Café owner. He wanted to share something with us but it wasn't what we hoped for. Also, Hackett's results have just come in. I'll bring everyone up to speed now in the incident room.'

Gina hurried out, following Jacob and O'Connor. Was this news the breakthrough in the case that they needed?

CHAPTER TWENTY-TWO

Gina sat at the head of the table and Jacob and O'Connor sat either side. Wyre hurried in with an apple in her mouth. Teeth clenching it as she gripped a pile of files.

'What have we got?' Gina sat rigid, waiting for O'Connor to fill them in.

'I'm going to get the biggie out of the way first. Bernard called and said that the semen sample we found on Leah does not match up to Hackett's. The used condom was his but we have no evidence that he had sex with Leah. He had sex, but with someone else.'

Gina slumped back. 'I still want to know why he had Leah's socks in his cab but that's a blow. I really thought we had him.'

'And me.' Wyre crunched on her apple.

Jacob opened a can of cola and took a sip before it fizzed over.

'It weakens our case, but the fact that he didn't have sex with her doesn't mean he didn't kill her. There was no sign of force so we can't pre-empt that she was sexually assaulted or raped. She may have been drugged then raped. There are still too many ifs.' Gina allowed her thoughts to settle. 'What did Tallis have to say?'

O'Connor took a tissue from the box and patted his bald head while Jacob reached over and turned the fan on. 'He said he was sorry to have wasted our time in not telling the full truth when asked but he didn't want to get into trouble. Tallis claims to know of a sex worker called Betsy who he calls for the truckers if they request her services. He claims that he does this for no financial gain and that Betsy is a friend.'

'So, it's looking like Hackett asked Tallis to call him a sex worker and they had sex and deposited the condom under his cab when they'd finished.'

O'Connor nodded.

'We need to check out this sex worker called Betsy, to at least get a statement. It's possible that she saw or heard something that might help the case.'

'Tallis gave me her number,' O'Connor replied.

'I wonder if she was the person Tallis was on the phone to when we saw him at the Waterside Café, talking away and looking a bit shifty. He was obviously tipping her off as to what had happened.'

'Stands a chance, guv.' Jacob nodded.

'And I thought we were onto something. We may be able to have him charged with procuring a sex worker. It's probably best to look at what we have and call the CPS.' She paused. 'I still want to know why Hackett had Leah's socks. There's no reason he should have them and I'm still classing his possession of them as suspicious. Wyre?'

'Yes, guv.'

'Can you get Hackett into interview room one for another interview? I need to speak to him before we have to let him go. I'm aware that his time in custody is almost up and I doubt we'd have grounds for an extension.'

'I'll get him now.' Wyre threw her apple core into the bin and left the room.

'Dammit! No forensics, possibly an alibi. Having Leah's socks will not be strong enough to make a case unless I can get something out of him in interview. Where next?' She glanced at a blue tit sitting on the window ledge. 'The residents of Oak Tree Walk. Lay focus on the locals, go through the door-to-door statements and get me more information on our voyeur. What was his name again?'

O'Connor glanced at his notebook. 'Frank Meegan.'

'Maybe he went beyond voyeurism this time. Maybe looking and recording wasn't enough and he's escalating. Both Naomi and Caro claim to have seen someone watching them in the woods.' Gina's mind whirled with possibility. He was definitely a strong suspect and she was going to personally pay him a visit.

'Oh, guv?'

'What?'

'The other teen, Anthony Truss, is due in soon. He's the other one who couldn't make the Saturday night party. He was in Devon apparently with his parents. His grandmother's funeral was Friday and the family spent the weekend with the grandfather so that rules him out.'

'Great. While Jacob and I interview Hackett again, could you take Anthony? See what you can get out of him about the others in the group. And, I know I'm rushing you, but please get the system updated quickly so that we're all working off the same sheet. Also, can you and Wyre arrange to speak to Betsy while Jacob and I head to Meegan's house? As long as we all keep updating in real time, we can all access up-to-date information. I'll do the same. Are we sorted with a plan for the rest of the afternoon? Let's do this.'

CHAPTER TWENTY-THREE

Rodney Hackett leaned back, the chair creaking with his weight. He clapped his hands and pointed at Jacob. 'I told you I didn't do it!' His finger moved to Gina next. 'You lot just wanted to fit me up with a murder.'

Jacob placed his pen on the table.

Gina took a deep breath. She glanced into his open mouth. He had a full set of crooked and chipped teeth, including the one on the top right, third from the incisor. She could rule him out as the person who bit Leah.

It wasn't going to be easy to get any more information out of Hackett but there was one loose end that needed tackling. He had been in possession of Leah's socks and he still possibly had opportunity. Until they had spoken to Betsy, they didn't have his timeline fixed for that evening. 'Mr Hackett, we were following leads and evidence of which there is still something you need to explain.'

'Do I need my solicitor?'

Gina shrugged. 'That's your choice and he has been called. From what I've heard, he's on his way so if you do want your solicitor, we can hold this interview and wait but if you're innocent, as you claim, I'm sure that you just want this to get cleared up so that you can call up your employer and be on your way.'

'What do you need from me?' She could tell he'd had enough. The standard issue track bottoms he was wearing had ridden down a little and the T-shirt was two sizes too large.

'We found a pair of socks in your cab. They look like women's yellow socks with watermelon slices printed on them. Where did you get them from?'

'The prostitute left them behind. They were hers.'

'Are you sure that when we speak to her, she will back up your story?'

He shrugged and let his arms drop by his sides as he sighed.

'On Saturday, the victim, Leah Fenmore was wearing a pair of watermelon print socks. When we found her body, she wasn't wearing them anymore. They weren't found amongst her possessions or at their camp or in the vicinity, which means their absence is unaccounted for. It's a bit of a coincidence that a pair matching that exact description turn up in your cab.'

His brow furrowed. 'This is stupid.'

Gina shrugged and stared right at him. 'You need to explain yourself. The truth, please?'

Hackett stood and walked over to the far wall, where he stared at it for a few seconds before sitting back down. 'I don't know why I kept them.'

'Go on. How did they come to be in your possession?'

'When the girl, Leah, was walking across the car park to go back to her friends, she stopped to ask me the time and we got talking. She seemed like she'd already had a couple of drinks, you know; she spoke loud and laughed a lot about nothing. She saw me opening a beer and asked for some so I gave her a swig. It was then I noticed she was limping slightly. She sat on the grass in front of my cab and removed her pumps and socks before rubbing her feet. Betsy was coming soon so really, I was hoping that the girl was going to hurry up and go. I had bigger plans of my own that evening.' He paused.

'Then what happened?'

'I saw Betsy's car pull in. She went in the café to talk to Johnny Tallis for a few minutes. I met up with her when I stopped at the

Waterside last time. She's really nice, just a young mother trying to make ends meet.'

Gina imagined the poor woman having to sleep with men like Hackett to feed her children and it made her cringe inside.

'Leah was just gibbering away about her stupid party and friends, saying nothing in particular. She was just an annoying kid to me. I was losing patience so I offered her a four-pack to scrat. She seemed thrilled at taking my lager. She put her shoes on, weirdly kissed me on the cheek as she said thank you. Then, she kept going on about how bad she'd felt as she hadn't contributed to their booze pile and now she had something to offer. After that, she headed back towards her camp looking happier than ever with all her sweets, crisps and lager. That was the last I saw of her. As Betsy walked towards my cab, I grabbed the socks and hid them amongst my things. After she left, I went to bed. It was then I pulled them out and threw them down by my feet. I didn't think any more about the socks after that.'

'You could have saved us all a lot of time and hassle if you'd told the truth in the first place.'

He shrugged. 'I didn't want to get Betsy into any trouble but it seems I need her now. Only she can help me out here. I was with her for ages.'

'What time did she arrive?'

'I think it was about ten. Johnny was just cleaning up for the night, I could see him through the large window. She stayed for hours and left at about two in the morning.'

'She stayed that long?'

He puffed out a breath. 'It's not just about sex. It's lonely; life on the road. We listened to some music and talked. She talked about her kids, I talked about mine, even though they're grown up. I actually really like her and I didn't want her to go but she has another job. She cleans in the mornings and she needed to get home to catch some zees before work. She gave me her number and we planned to meet up again for a date; a proper date, I mean. Betsy isn't really a regular prostitute, she's just desperate. Her benefit top-ups don't even cover the basics.'

Gina knew for now that this line of questioning was over. As soon as they'd managed to speak to Betsy, he'd be free to go as long as his story stacked up.

'Can I go back to the cell for now? And, I'm hungry. I could also murder a cuppa.'

Jacob nodded. 'Interview terminated at fifteen forty-five.'

As Jacob led Hackett out, Briggs hurried down the corridor and came into the tiny room. 'O'Connor asked me to pass an urgent message on as he and Wyre are now interviewing Anthony Truss. He managed to contact a woman called Betsy. She is coming in to make a formal statement but she's adamant she was with Hackett until gone two on Sunday morning.'

'Thanks, sir.' Disappointed wasn't the word. Gina watched as Jacob left through the door with Hackett. 'Any more messages since we last spoke?' She swallowed.

He shook his head and she checked her phone.

'Why is this happening now? I don't know how much more I can take.' Gina popped her phone back into her pocket.

'Gina, look at me.' She glanced up. 'We have to carry on as normal. We can't fall apart.'

That was easier said than done. She nodded and hurried after Jacob. They had to carry on. What else could they do?

It was time to let Hackett go. For now, she had to concentrate on the next solid lead, which was Frank Meegan.

CHAPTER TWENTY-FOUR

'I can't believe you went to a party. One with booze and boys and staying out all night, in a tent! Do you know how dangerous all that was?' Lara Blakely placed her handbag on the worktop and pushed the back door open, allowing a flow of fresh air to enter. 'You could have been raped... or killed, like Leah was. I am so upset that you went behind my back like that.' Lara stared at her daughter and stroked her hair. 'Has anyone hurt you? Is there something you want to tell me because I'll help you in any way I can. If anyone has hurt you...' Lara shook her head.

Caro caught her little brother sticking his tongue out behind their mother's back. 'Get lost, Jake.'

Lara turned and sighed. 'Jake, get to your room and have a long hard think about what your sister's going through right now.'

'But I didn't do anything.' The boy huffed and folded his arms.

'Room now, Jakey.'

'Don't want to.'

Jake grinned, knowing he was pushing their mother too far. She grabbed his hand and led him to the bottom of the stairs before giving him a slight nudge forward. 'Get up those stairs now until I tell you to come back down. Your sister doesn't need your teasing right now.'

'But, Mum—'

'Don't but me. One more word and you won't be going to play football tomorrow.'

Caro felt the jitters building up as Jake stomped up the stairs then slammed his bedroom door.

'Right, talk to me. Go.' A beam of sunshine caught her mother's coppery locks, making her hair look almost orange at the ends.

'What?' Caro shrugged, getting defensive. She didn't want to talk to her mother about it. 'It was just a stupid party, that's all.'

'Do I look like I was born yesterday? If I could tell there was more to the story then I'm sure those detectives could. They're not idiots. What's going on?' Lara tilted her head.

Caro shrugged. To satisfy her mother she'd have to say something. She could tell her mother about the weed but that was all. 'Okay, there were drugs. I didn't want to get anyone in trouble and I didn't take any.'

'What drugs?'

'Weed.'

'Weed?'

'Yes. One roll-up that was passed around. I swear I didn't smoke it and I hated being there which is why I didn't want to go ever again. I just wanted to come home.' She felt tears welling up in her eyes.

'Who brought the weed?'

She paused and looked up at her mother. 'Oscar.'

Lara rolled her eyes. 'I should have known. That boy is trouble so I want you to stay away from him in future. He's no good for you. He's trouble.'

'Mum, that's not fair.'

'It is. He was always in detention. That little act he puts on for his dad, everyone can see through it apart from him.'

'Can I go to my room too?' Caro needed this conversation to end, now.

'Okay. When your father gets home, we're going to have a family talk.'

She hated the family talk. Her mother always thought that airing out their problems as a family was a good thing. It made Caro cringe every time they did it. 'But—'

'Don't but me. That's how we get through things in this household.'

Caro sighed as she hurried out of the kitchen and up to her room. She grabbed a stuffed dolphin cushion from her bed and threw it at the window. If she played up over the so-called family talk, she'd end up grounded. She was sixteen, not six; that made her almost an adult. She could join the army at this age but still she had a mother who treated her like she was a little kid with groundings and stupid family meetings. No, she wasn't being grounded. She crept back down the stairs and as she reached the bottom, she glanced at the front door and took a deep breath. She opened it as quietly as possible then slammed it closed as she darted down the path, heading to the playing field two streets away. As she approached she spotted Anthony sitting on the grass, puffing away on his vape. The air smelled of toffee. Her phone rang. It was her mother. She turned it off and sat next to him, taking his vape and having a puff. She exhaled and felt the calmness of the nicotine work its way through her body. 'I'm sorry to hear about your grandma, by the way.'

'Thanks. She'd been sick for a long time but I'm glad the funeral is over. Poor Gramps. We had to leave him alone to come back home for this. I wasn't with the police long. As soon as they knew I was in Devon, that was it, then I messaged you.'

Caro paused, giving him a moment. 'How did it go with the police?'

Anthony took his vape back. 'Hated every minute of it.'

'You didn't tell them what I did?'

Anthony laughed. 'No, your naked arse running through the woods is safe with me, innit?' He removed his cap and ran a hand over his extremely short shaven brown hair that covered his head.

'Only my mum would freak. She's already freaking about me just being there. I'm not meant to be out now so I'll probably get grounded later.'

'She grounds you?' He shook his head.

'She tries. I friggin' hate living there. My little brother is annoying and I hate this shitty town.'

'Did you tell 'em that I punched Jordan?'

'No way.' She made a zip motion with her fingers against her lips. He placed a friendly arm around her.

'I got a weird message. Say anything and you're next.'

'What?' Anthony's eyebrows went up as his eyes widened.

'I know, sinister, isn't it?'

'Who sent it?'

'Durr, if I knew that I'd be having it out with them and giving you the goss!'

'Be careful and if you need anything, let me know and I'll sort it.'

Caro knew that Anthony would struggle to pair socks from a laundry basket. She had no idea how he could help her get to the bottom of who sent her the anonymous messages that could no longer be seen anymore. 'There is something you can help me with and no lies, okay?'

'Okay.'

'Where did you go at the last party, when you stomped off after the fight?'

He nudged her away and began to grind his back teeth. 'What you tryin' to say?'

'Nothing. I just remember you leaving and I don't remember you coming back.'

'That's because you were pissed. I just went to cool down, then I went back to my tent. Went to sleep. That was it.'

'You said you wanted to help me and I'm just trying to piece the night together. I have such vague memories after the fight. Tell me what happened.'

'I feel really bad havin' to tell you this but that was the roofie.'

'What?'

'Look, you deserve to know and before you think anything. I. Was. Not. On. Board. Jordan and Oscar and even the girls are prize pricks, which is partly why I ended up scrapping. Their dare was to get a roofie into you.'

'What did they do to me? That's used for date rape. I'm not stupid.'

'It's not like that. It was just for a joke, no one touched you. I made sure of it.'

'What? Like you watched me all night? Seriously?'

'It was just a stupid dare. They thought you might do more stupid things for a laugh, that's all. The girls were there so you were safe. They just knew you were game to make a fool of yourself.'

She swallowed a sob back. 'And did I?'

'Nah. They dared you to do naked dancing around the fire so that they could film it for a laugh but you told them where to go. You managed to fall into your tent and that was it. I think they thought you'd be game as you'd already got your kit off once.'

'That's why I felt so ill. How could you of all people let them do that to me?' Her bottom lip began to quiver. 'I thought we were friends.'

'We are and you know how much I like you, that's why I punched Jordan. What they did was stupid and I didn't agree to it. They got carried away and I did try to stop them. Hello.' He pointed to his ribs. 'I think one of 'em cracked my rib.'

'They drew all over my arms.'

'Just pretend tattoos, innit? That's what I mean. It was just immature shit. That was all. They were going to shave your eyebrows but I stopped them.'

'How do I know I can trust what you say?'

'What? You serious?'

She nodded.

'I stuck up for you at that party. Got myself punched up by Oscar and Jordan. I wouldn't go to another of those stupid parties if you paid me.'

Over this past two weeks, that evening had been a blur, but something flashed to the front of her mind, then it went as quick as it came. She hit the grass with her closed fist and roared.

'What's up?'

She scrunched her brow and stared at a beetle crawling over a blade of grass before flicking it into the bushes. What was her memory trying to unlock and how much could she trust of what Anthony was saying?

A flashback to the party came again. A sound, more like a sex groan. She knew who was doing the groaning and the sound was haunting her.

'Oh, I saw Oscar put a roofie in your drink. While Jordan wasn't looking, he poured some of the powder into his pocket, maybe even more and he just gave you a bit. I didn't think it would do anything, if I'm honest.'

'Thanks for stuff all.' She stood and kicked his leg before running off. He'd let her down.

'Hey, Caro. I'm sorry.'

It was all too much to take in. They drugged her and now someone was threatening her. For now, it was time to go back home and face her mother, which she was dreading.

As the sun began to fall, she thought one more time about Leah and she sobbed until she couldn't sob any more. So many tears. Tears she never thought she had in her. That groaning she had heard while in her half-drugged state had been Leah's. Leah had been having sex. That's what she'd heard but then, she knew that Oscar and Leah were flirting so it shouldn't have been a surprise. It had to be them.

Knowing that she'd been drugged had changed everything for Caro. Perhaps Leah had been drugged that night too. Maybe she had read the whole situation wrongly. She kicked a tree stump until she felt a hot pain spreading through her foot. She thought about the Snapchat message again. Who was threatening her if she went to the police? She glanced around, searching for that very threat. Suddenly, it felt like the whole world was closing in on her, like they were watching from the houses surrounding the field.

Between two houses on a path that led to the bus route, she spotted someone wearing a cap and track bottoms. The low sun shone a fraction above her eyes, making her squint to see. Before she could get a good look, this person turned and went. She half-hopped away as fast as she could trying not to put any more pressure on her small toe.

Her mum's anger was the lesser of her fears right now. The person who had sent that message might have been the person who was watching her, knowing full well that she'd been talking to Anthony. Did talking to Anthony count or was it the police they didn't want her to talk to? She had to get home. For now, all the secrets from the party would remain within the party group and no one else could know. Not her mum and not the police. The dares were stupid, that's all. Leah's murder would blow over and no one would want to know about their party then. If they all held their nerve, it would all be over soon.

Not speaking equals staying safe. *Say a word and you'll be next to die.* She gulped.

CHAPTER TWENTY-FIVE

I've been placed in front of the TV watching *Pointless* and my whole life feels pointless. At least Frank gave me my phone back under the provision that I don't publish anything on social media. He just got home from one of his walks and now he's upstairs having a sleep. He says that I wear him out and I know I do. This afternoon has been a challenge, what with his shouting at me and the tension he's filling the house with. Before he popped out, he paced around, agitated, and he didn't eat the lunch that he prepared for us both. His sandwich still sits on the coffee table, the corners of the bread now dried up. I wave my hand at the fly that lands on it. I don't know, maybe he'll want to eat it later. The tuna is starting to stink, so maybe not.

Since seeing Lara in the supermarket this morning, he hasn't been himself. She didn't appear to know him but I'm sure that he recognised her from somewhere.

I pull out my phone and Lara's card. My finger quivers as I unlock it. Maybe she gave me her contact details out of politeness and if I call, I'll feel stupid as she makes her excuses to get me off the phone. Or if Frank doesn't want me to be friends with her, he might just tell her what I wrote in that tweet if ever we were to meet up. Given the circumstances, that might be enough to ruin a friendship that has just been rekindled. And Frank would do that. He doesn't want me to have anyone else, which is bizarre as he doesn't seem thrilled to spend time with me, ever. I don't know what he wants. And I don't trust him. If he hurt that girl,

Lara will hate me too. Gosh, I don't even know what I want. I'm stuck in the unknown with no way out.

I think back to our old house only a few years ago. Frank and I grew up in Cleevesford but moved away together in our twenties. For a better life. For an adventure. We both settled into good jobs south of London and had a lovely home in Croydon. I worked as a finance manager for an engineering company and him as a self-employed kitchen fitter. We made money on our house. He improved it, the value went up and we were able to come back to Cleevesford and buy this cottage outright. I loved our old life but Frank ruined all that. So, here we were. Back living in our hometown. I shake my head, trying to banish thoughts of the reason for our move back. I can't let the past swamp me anymore. This house was our new start and I still need to find mine. Maybe I'll start doing accounts from home.

A tinge of sadness washes over me. Our house down south was spacious and open plan, not like here. If we still lived there, I'd be able to wheel myself around without bumping into everything but we chose the simple life when it came to our finances. That's a lie and I know it. I can't get the past out of my mind, not today. This is what I do all the time now, I dwell on things. We were forced out of our home. However hard I try to forget, the memories sit there, festering like the stinking sandwich on the coffee table. Slowly it will turn to rot just like our lives. It can't get worse and I suppose that's something to be happy about. Right now as that same pesky fly lands on the bread again, I sense that the sandwich is about to become so full of life, it'll start crawling. That thought makes me shiver.

First came the crime back then in 2016. Then the reporters followed, and then the angry mob; then came Frank's conviction. He got off lightly really. I didn't, even though I committed no crime. People thought I knew what he was doing, that maybe I got kicks out of it too. I lost my job, which was down to the abuse my company got because of Frank. After two months in prison, Frank was released early for good behaviour. I lived in a rental lodge during that time, hiding from the angry mob who seemed to want to blame me for Frank's perversions. He promised me he'd changed and I loved and craved him so deeply; obsessively even. I couldn't lose him. I mean, doesn't everyone deserve a second chance? It's not as if he touched or killed anyone. Now, I'm not so sure I made the right choice. I really think he's capable of killing a girl. He's become more violent and I see a turbulence within him that I fear more than anything. Whatever he's hiding in that kitchen is about to ruin our lives again. I just know it. If he goes to prison, we are over. I can't go through all that hate and I don't want to have to leave the town I grew up in because of his mistakes which means I will stand against him if he's done wrong.

My body begins to shake and I can't stop it. Rapid breaths escape me, rendering me a little woozy as oxygen becomes scarce. Without him, I can't do everything I need to do. I need him. Shaking those thoughts away, I put Lara's number in my phone under 'the council' and start typing out a text message. I don't want Frank to see that I've texted her so as soon as it's sent, I will delete it from my outbox. Lara was my friend. She can be my friend again and if Frank has committed the unspeakable, I'm sure she wouldn't blame me. She knows me from years ago and she knows that I would never harm anyone.

Hi Lara. It was really nice to see you today after all these years. Thought I'd text you so that we have each other's numbers. Be lovely to catch up soon. Sandy. X

Too much? Not enough? Am I about to humiliate myself? For heaven's sake! It's not a date. She's just an old friend. Before the accident I wouldn't have a problem with sending a text to an old friend. I need that Sandy back and only I can dig her out of her rut.

I hit send. That's it; done. The text has gone and now I wait. Staring at the phone for a few minutes, I hope she'll answer quick but nothing. My phone is silent. *Pointless* is now coming to an end and the news is about to start.

I'm startled by a loud knock at the door so I turn off the TV. Listening for Frank, I soon realise that he hasn't stirred.

Struggling to manoeuvre my wheelchair around the cramped living room, I eventually steer it in the right direction. I wheel past the staircase, the kitchen to my right and then past my bedroom to the left and I almost crash into the door. It's no good, I can't reach the bolt which seems to be in the highest position possible. I wish Frank wouldn't use it. 'Who is it?'

'Cleevesford Police. I'm DI Harte and I'm with DS Driscoll.'

My stomach drops. I knew it. Frank is in trouble again and the police have come for him. 'Can you come round the back?' I call out. 'I'm wheelchair bound and I can't reach the top bolt.' I don't want them to think I'm trying to keep them out which might make them slam the door down. I've seen that happen in films.

'Of course. Is that Mrs Meegan?'

'Yes.'

'We're heading around the back,' DI Harte says.

I listen as they leave. The gate hinges screech as the detectives leave the front garden. We are the cottage on the end of a terrace so it won't take them long to follow the fence around the building. I back into my bedroom, calling up the stairs to Frank as I pass through, then I wait by the back sliding doors at the one end of the living room. I can't get to them properly so I'm banging everything in the way. The dining table takes up too much room. I can just about reach the key. I turn it just as they come in through the back gate so I beckon them in. As the glass slides open, Frank enters the living room, rubbing his eyes. 'What the hell did you wake me for?' It's like he's instantly awake as he sees the two detectives entering and I want the ground to swallow me up. My phone rings. It's Lara. I kill the call and pocket my phone.

'Mr and Mrs Meegan, we need to talk to you both about the murder of Leah Fenmore.' I wish I could just vanish. The pain, hate and humiliation. I can't go through that again but deep down I know I don't have a choice. I didn't have a choice last time and I certainly don't now.

CHAPTER TWENTY-SIX

Gina shifted her body through the narrow gap between the dining table and the sliding doors. She left them open allowing a warm breeze to carry away the smell of fish, then she spotted the sweaty looking sandwich on the coffee table. Jacob almost bumped Gina into Mrs Meegan as she stopped. 'Apologies for interrupting your evening, but we're speaking to everyone in the area.'

'We've already spoken to uniform. Someone came around here asking questions on Sunday morning. We ain't got anything to add to what we've already said, have we, love?' Frank Meegan rubbed his glassy eyes and yawned.

Mrs Meegan shook her head and wheeled her chair back a little, allowing Gina and Jacob to fully step into the room.

'That may be so, Mr Meegan, and we thank you both for your cooperation, but there are further questions that we need to follow up on. May we sit?'

'No.' His stare hardened. 'Just get to the point.' The man stood with his arms folded, his T-shirt not quite covering his round belly. His forehead shone with beads of sweat and he looked sick, like he drank too much which gave his skin and eyes a yellowish tinge. He reached down and picked up an open can of cider from the dining table. After flicking the fly away, he began sipping.

'Where were you between ten in the evening on Saturday the thirty-first of July and three in the morning on Sunday?' Gina leaned on the wall between the window and the patio doors and Jacob pulled out the case notes.

'I've already been through this. The other copper asked. Why don't you just read what the copper wrote down?'

'Because I want to hear it directly from you, Mr Meegan?'

'Am I under arrest?'

'No, should you be?'

He stared at Gina for a moment too long. She felt the weight of the moment between them but she refused to break eye contact.

'What? No.' He sat on the leather settee and leaned back. 'I just don't know why you're asking me the same question again.'

'Mr Meegan, a sixteen-year-old girl was murdered in the woodland that I can see from your back garden. If I didn't question everyone thoroughly, I wouldn't be doing my job.'

'You lot are picking on me. I have a record and you know it. That's why you're here. Why aren't you next door, or maybe three doors down giving them a second go over? You came here because I've done something that I bitterly regret which is now in my past. I've done porridge and I even got out early because I was a good boy. Besides, I never touched anyone. I don't go around murdering girls.'

'It is true that you're a person of interest which is why I will ask again, where were you between Saturday night and the early hours of Sunday morning?'

He slammed the can of cider onto the table and folded his arms. 'I was here all night, with Sandy, weren't I, love?'

Sandy nodded.

'Look at my wife. She needs constant care. I couldn't just leave her to go and commit a murder. Besides, she'd know if I went out. We were together all night. I watched a series on Netflix and Sandy was reading her book.'

'What were you watching?'

'What?'

'It's a simple question. What were you watching?'

He paused. '*Breaking Bad.*'

Gina knew that series was on Netflix, she'd watched it herself.

'You won't catch me out because I didn't do anything.'

'Right, if you head into the kitchen, Mr Meegan, DS Driscoll would like to speak to you separately. I'll speak to Mrs Meegan here.'

'Oh, bleeding hell. We haven't done anything. It feels like you're interrogating us.'

'We're doing no such thing. This is routine questioning and it would look good if you cooperated fully. We can do it here or down the station.' Gina clenched her right hand.

The man stood and headed out of the room. Jacob followed, leaving Gina alone with Mrs Meegan. 'I'm sorry that you and your husband are being asked all these questions again but I need to make sure I've done my job properly by following up on the initial statements. May I sit?'

'Yes, please do.' The woman forced a worried smile. Gina could see the tremor in Mrs Meegan's arms that she was trying to hide.

'Could you please describe your Saturday evening up until you went to bed, in your own words and your own time?'

Mrs Meegan nodded and bit her bottom lip before speaking. 'Frank was telling the truth. He watched several episodes of *Breaking Bad* that evening while I read.' She pointed to the book on the coffee table. 'I think I got through half of my book that night. At about eleven, he started helping me to get ready for bed. This takes a while. He doesn't need to do everything for me but he's always a shout away in case I need him. I wheeled myself into the downstairs bathroom. Washed and did my teeth and changed into my nightie, then I went into the bedroom. I can get into bed on my own but I remember being tired, I mean physically tired. It really helps me out if Frank gives me a bit of a lift. I then lay in bed watching TV for a couple of hours while Frank was in the living room still watching the TV.'

'How would you know if he was there all night?'

'I can hear the sliding doors opening if he went out the back way and I'd hear the front door locks if he went out the front. The bedroom door was left ajar and I even spoke to him here and there. I heard him making drinks in the kitchen and flushing the chain. Everything sounded like it normally did. He was in the house, I know it.'

'Where is the bedroom that you sleep in?' Gina couldn't imagine that Mrs Meegan could hear all this from upstairs.

'Just by the front door. We haven't got a stair lift, so we sleep downstairs.' Mrs Meegan scrunched her brow slightly.

'I see.'

'Can you remember what time Mr Meegan joined you in bed?'

'Yes. It was about one in the morning and he fell asleep soon after.' The woman's temple twitched slightly and she looked away.

'So, let me get this straight. At eleven you got ready for bed. Then soon after you were in bed and Mr Meegan joined you about one in the morning, then you both went to sleep?'

She smiled and shrugged. 'That's exactly it.' Mrs Meegan ran her fingers through her hair and flinched a little. 'I'm scared but I don't want to say anything to Frank.'

Gina leaned in, feeling her heart rate pick up a little. That flinch was subtle but Gina had made a mental note of it.

'The press. If they link Frank's past to what happened to that girl, they're going to hound us out of our home. It happened in Croydon. Once he was arrested my life was hell. I know what he did was wrong. Spying on young women in the way he did was unforgivable but we were both stressed and he knows what he did was wrong. We came back to Cleevesford for a new start.'

Gina doubted that Frank Meegan's urges would go away that easily and the reports from Caro Blakely and some of the other teens about hearing and seeing someone spying on them would put Mr Meegan firmly in the picture. If he wasn't involved in Leah's murder, then it was quite possible he was up to no good spying on the teens and saw something. Gina really wondered if he was capable of taking that next step. He'd got his kicks from secretly filming women in public toilets or through their windows, then he'd replay the footage over and over again. It's possible that a very drugged or drunken Leah confronted him and he took her down with ease, strangling her to death so that she couldn't report him.

The woman swallowed and touched her head again.

'Are you okay?' Gina leaned in a little, providing a little bit of intimate space between her and Mrs Meegan, hoping that she might say more. She could sense fear in the woman. Gina remembered looking that meek and hunched, with a constant nervous tremor when Terry was at his abusive peak. She'd never have said a word against him, in fear of her life or her sanity. He tried to take both during the course of their marriage but she'd finally taken his life. Gina gulped, hoping that the woman in front of her couldn't see that she too had been abused. It was like this unspoken code was bouncing between them. She also hoped that she wasn't giving more away. Her anonymous messenger had seen through her. No, maybe this person just knew something about her past or was having a stab at guessing. There was still hope in that department. Gina swiftly took a breath in and exhaled through her nose.

Mrs Meegan shook her head and her eyes glassed over with tears that she was trying to hold back. At least she'd been more consumed with her own thoughts than what Gina was thinking. 'He was in all night but he gets so angry with me. If the press hound us, then the community all gang up, he'll take it out on me… I can't go through it all again. I'm scared.'

'Are you safe here? I can arrange something for you straight away if not.'

Mrs Meegan sniffed and wiped her eyes with her hands. 'Of course I am. Frank was with me all night. I will swear that on my life.

There's no way he could have hurt that girl or have seen anything. If either of us knew something, we'd report it straight away.'

'Is your head okay? You keep touching it.'

'Yes, I just hit it on a shelf earlier. Nothing to worry about.'

Gina had lost her. Maybe talking about the parties in general might at the very least bring the interview back on track. She caught up with her notes and looked up again at Mrs Meegan, tilting her head with a smile to put her at ease. 'I'm sorry that this is distressing for you. May I ask about the parties that happen in the woodland? Can you hear the music from your cottage?'

'If I'm honest, those parties are an absolute menace to our community. It's not just Frank and I that get upset, the whole of Oak Tree Walk does. We've put in numerous complaints and petitions at the council, we've called the police in the past but no one does a thing. The parties keep on happening.'

'Sorry to hear that. I'll look into those complaints further when I get back to the station. It's not something I work on but I'll follow it up.'

'The kids… they often park up here and we see them passing with all their booze and camping gear. Some of us have got a little angry and shouted the odd insult out of the window, not me though. The noise is horrendous. It's not too loud from here but when you're in bed and all you can hear is constant beats in the background until about four in the morning, it gets tiresome. We came to live in the country, not next door to a nightclub. Then there's the mess. They get drunk and play pranks, like spray rude pictures on our back fences. There was a penis on ours over Easter and someone had sprayed the word wanker on the neighbour's fence. Sometimes people have mentioned that their cars have been scratched or the wing mirrors have been pulled off. Things like that happen at the same time these parties are on.'

Gina thought back to what Oscar's teacher had said about him defacing his locker with a Sharpie.

'Frank spent all day scrubbing that mess off our fence but it didn't help. He had to paint it in the end. Then there's the litter and the vomit on the pavements. It's just disgusting. They have no respect for anything and I'm not happy about the parties but neither I, nor Frank, would take the law into our own hands. We do things properly. Frank attends neighbourhood meetings where petitions are organised. That's what we do.'

'Do you have any CCTV?' Gina was sure that uniform would have asked this question of everyone on the row.

'No but we were talking about getting some. Frank is super wary that if his past came to light and we had CCTV, people would accuse us of spying on them. That's how we live now.'

'Is there anything else you can add? In the night, maybe while lying in bed, did you hear anything or anyone outside? Or did anything seem out of place or odd?'

Mrs Meegan shook her head. 'I rarely leave this house and no, I didn't hear anything unusual, just music.'

'If you think of anything or you need to call me, here's my card. If you're scared, worried, or feel under threat in any way at all, don't hesitate to pick up the phone.'

'I can't see why I'd be under threat. I suppose if the press get wind of Frank's past, I'll need all the help I can get.' The woman took the card and pushed it deeply into her pocket. Her brow furrowed and she went silent. 'I'm really tired now. Will they be long as Frank has normally put dinner on by now.'

'I don't think they'll be much longer.'

The kitchen door burst open and Jacob came in alone. 'Right, all done, guv.'

'Well, thank you for your time.' Gina gave one last smile to Mrs Meegan before they left through the patio doors and out the back. She would have asked if they could leave out the front but it seemed that the Meegans had had enough of being questioned.

'What are your thoughts, guv?'

'I'll tell you when we get back to the car.'

As Gina placed her hand on the door handle a man ran out. 'Are you the police?' He glanced up at the Meegans' cottage and in a low voice continued. 'I'm Jim, Frank and Sandy's neighbour. I have something to tell you.'

CHAPTER TWENTY-SEVEN

'Thoughts, then?' Jacob popped a sweet into his mouth and the smell of orange filled the car as Gina pulled out of Oak Tree Walk.

'That neighbour, Jim Berry, is going to start some trouble now that Frank Meegan's past is out of the bag; I just know it. I guess all he had to do was put Meegan's name into Google and search. It was as easy as that.' Gina took a left onto a country road. The sun had all but gone as they drove under the trees that arched over the tarmac.

'I saw that he's quite prolific on Twitter when I was searching for comments on Leah's murder.'

'And?'

Jacob pulled his phone from his pocket and began tapping and scrolling. 'Dammit. He's already put something on Twitter about Meegan's past despite us telling him not to for the time being. Now Mr Meegan will really be on the defensive.'

Gina slammed a hand on the steering wheel. 'What the hell? Go on.'

'It's a link to an old article about Frank Meegan's charge for recording a woman in a public toilet. He's hashtagged Oak Tree Walk and there are already thirty comments and twelve shares. It's been up less than ten minutes.'

Swallowing, Gina thought of Mrs Meegan. She was so close to saying something about her relationship with her husband but she'd clammed up. This would only make things worse for the woman. 'We'll get an officer to do regular drive-bys overnight and I suppose if things get really bad, we may need to see if the Meegans want a panic alarm installed. I'm actually worried for Mrs Meegan's safety and well-being.'

'I'll arrange that as soon as we get back to the station.'

Gina's phone flashed in its hands-free cradle. It was a message from Hannah that she'd read as soon as they stopped. Her stomach dropped. With every day that passed, she was getting ever closer to having this talk with Hannah, a talk she was dreading. She stared at the road ahead as they turned onto Cleevesford High Street, passing through to take the road off to the station.

The pain of not knowing exactly what Hannah knew was worse than being totally rumbled. The way her daughter had messaged was so clinical, lacking emotion and expression; not even Hannah's usual angry tones came out. She thought of Leah and Mrs Meegan and it struck her. This could be her very last case if her own past was brought out into the open.

'I can tell there's something on your mind. Are you okay?' Jacob crunched the last of his sweet.

Gina grimaced. 'Hannah wants to visit soon. I just hope it's not in the middle of this case but whenever it is, I can't put her off.'

'You'll get to see Gracie which will be nice. I know you miss her.' Jacob smiled.

Gina forced a smile back as she pulled into the station car park. If only she was getting to see Gracie. Hannah was probably coming alone for the talk; the talk that Gina didn't want to have. 'I'm heading in to just do a quick update then I'm going home. I'll be on duty so if you hear anything, if Jennifer mentions anything useful, whatever it is, call me or message straight away. I really want to plough through the Oak Tree Walk neighbour statements tonight. Am I right in saying that no one had CCTV on that row or close by?'

'Actually, two people had CCTV but the cameras only pointed directly into their back gardens. Uniform have looked but there is nothing of any use. Right, I'm popping in to arrange the drive-bys past the Meegans' cottage, then I'm heading home for a nice hot shower. I'll catch you tomorrow unless something big comes up in the meantime.'

'Great and thanks. Oh, tomorrow, first thing, I want to speak to Leah's parents and catch up with the family liaison officer. I know we haven't spoken to them yet, but I want to delve in a bit deeper, see if the parents can help us get to know Leah a little better.'

'Shall we meet at theirs?'

'Yes, I'll call them. See if nine in the morning is good. Unless you hear from me, see you then.'

'Great.' Jacob got out of the car and slammed her door shut.

Gina grabbed her phone, her stomach doing a sickening dance as she read Hannah's message.

Hi, I'll be with you about lunchtime on Sunday. No distractions. We need to talk.

Not even a, hi, Mum; how are you doing, Mum? Take care; love you. Every element of that message was cold. After their talk was their relationship set to be even frostier or over? Gina stared up at the station. She could see through the incident room window. Jacob walked past and was talking to O'Connor. That place was her life. Those people had become her family. It was all she had and now the fear of losing it was worse than anything she'd ever experienced. An image flashed through her mind. One of her standing in court telling every truth she could, then that was followed by her sitting in a cell, counting the days and years away, wondering if she'd ever see her granddaughter again. They say time heals but when you're carrying the burden of guilt, every moment that passes is a moment closer to the truth escaping. Gina stared at the message again and struggled to swallow, almost choking as she did. A loud knock on the car window made her heart jump.

'Alright, guv. I'll catch you in the morning.' Wyre smiled. 'Are you okay?'

Gina turned off the engine and the air conditioning stopped. As she opened the window, warm air seeped in. 'I'm all good. I'll be heading home myself in a short while.'

'We could go for a drink if you're up for it?'

Gina scrunched her nose. 'Thanks for the offer but I really need to get home for a shower. I feel as though I've been trapped in a sauna all day and then there was the post-mortem. I feel as dirty as hell.'

'No worries, another time. Catch you tomorrow.'

Was tomorrow a day closer to the end of her life as she knew it?

CHAPTER TWENTY-EIGHT

'No,' I yell as Frank forces me into bed. He slams me onto the mattress, not even stopping to make sure my pillows are comfortable. The violent throw has taken my breath away. I gasp as he speaks.

'Shut up and stop fighting with me, Sandy. You know you can't win.' After grappling with me for a few minutes, he punches me in the side, knocking the wind out of me, then he turns the television on at almost full volume before slamming the bedroom door as he leaves. I hear the sliding doors in the living room opening, just like I did on the night of the murder. I should have told the detective when she questioned me. If I had, I wouldn't be here now, waiting for a mob to form outside my front door. Like before, he's deserting me and leaving me to face them alone.

A call from the station had alerted Frank that his secret was out and that we were officially now in danger. As if driving by once or twice an hour could offer any protection and, if Frank was guilty of a murder, did we deserve any? Then there was the reply on my phone from Lara. The rage in Frank's face when he read it had told me everything. Lara had seen the link on Twitter too. Her reply made me shiver as much as it hurt me.

You people sicken me. Murderers! We need to take action.

Maybe it's good that Frank took my phone from me. Seeing those comments now would make everything worse. I shake my head. Frank is not a good person but he can't be a murderer, which is why I lied. I need him. But now he's gone, leaving me alone, once again friendless and stuck like this, I wonder how well I really know him.

A car engine starts and I know it's our car. Frank is going somewhere and leaving me to deal with all the trouble that is coming our way, just like he did before. I don't know where he's going or when he's coming back. Soon, there will be bricks through the window, red paint on the door, hate, chanting and shouting; and I'll be alone. I'm so confused. My heart pounds and a sick feeling hits me.

When Frank saw Jim's tweet, his face had tensed up. His stark-eyed stare and the spittle coming through his seething teeth made me cower. Our secret past was out for all to see and the mob was coming.

Awkwardly, I use my arms to shuffle into a sitting position until my back is against the headboard. No phone, no remote control and no idea of what is going on outside. I'm almost too scared to look but I can't lie here in ignorance. I lift the curtain and see that there's no one around; not yet. A young woman from the next row of cottages walks past with her dog, then she stops and stares at our cottage. She hurls an egg at my window as she shouts *paedos*. I drop the curtain, gasping for breath as I move my head back from the window, too scared to try that again.

I'm trapped, well and truly stuck and if someone attacks the cottage, there is no way I can call for help. Tears spill down my cheeks. My face burns as I clutch the sheet underneath. I've never hurt anyone and I'm not a paedo. That word burns through me like no other pain.

I reach over and grab the half empty glass of water from my bedside and throw it at the TV, hoping to shut it up but the glass smashes against the wall just above it. 'I hate you, Frank,' I yell. 'I hate you.'

CHAPTER TWENTY-NINE

Caro stared at the new message on her phone for just long enough, then it was gone. Shaking, she went to place a pillow over her head as she tried to drown out her parents arguing in the kitchen. They'd started off quietly but now each time they went for it, the house shook with slamming doors. At first, she had been the one in trouble for storming out of the house earlier. Both her parents had scolded her when she'd returned home but that had been the least of her worries. Someone had been watching her when she left Anthony earlier that day.

She glanced at her digital clock, five to midnight.

'That bastard could have killed our daughter and what do you do? A big fat nothing. As always, it's me who takes the action. I will go out there and protect our children from these disgusting vultures.' Her mother slammed her hand down on the worktop. That's a sound Caro could easily recognise. It was her mother's go to temper move.

Another message lit up. She placed the pillow over her ears and lay on her side, staring at the Snapchat message.

I know your secret.

This time the number wasn't hidden. She knew exactly who had sent that message and she knew why he was terrorising her. But that wasn't the last message. They kept coming, then disappearing. She managed to snap one of them, preserving it forever.

Soon, everyone will know. You're dead meat.

Another message. They were coming for her. Caro felt her own knuckles tense through the trembling. That last party was her downfall, the one she can barely remember. The one in which Oscar drugged her and they all did who-knows-what to her. She hoped Anthony was telling the truth about keeping an eye on her but then she remembered Oscar coming into her tent and falling asleep. Where was Anthony then? She released the pillow from her ear and the arguing had stopped. The house was silent. Her father slammed the front door and her mother was now crying in their bedroom. She had to know which secret her so-called friend was referring to and it couldn't wait. Caro hadn't hurt anyone or drugged anyone that night. They all did things to her, things that were still buried deep in her subconscious and she was going to get to the bottom of it all. Another message flashed up. This time it was from the unknown contact.

What I said about not talking. I meant it. You're dead!

CHAPTER THIRTY

Tuesday, 3 August

Jacob was already waiting outside Leah Fenmore's house when Gina pulled up. The morning sun was just coming over the terrace of houses that were built in the late fifties. Gina reversed into the tight space between Jacob's car and the car in front and a woman opened the door and left. Gina recognised her instantly, it was Ellyn, the family liaison officer.

'Any updates?' Gina asked as she got out of her car and stepped onto the path.

Ellyn shrugged, her loose bun bobbing on the top of her head. 'I arrived about half an hour ago but they've just asked me to leave. They want to be alone. I sense there's a lot of tension between them but that's nothing unusual when a couple have lost a child. Various members of the family have popped by and so have friends. Nothing out of the ordinary to report on that front.'

Gina walked a little way from the house and the FLO followed. 'Can you fill me in on how things were yesterday? I would have come earlier to speak to Leah's parents but there have been so many leads to follow up on that we've barely been able to touch base.'

'That sounds promising, about the leads.'

'I wish. Dead ends mostly, which is why we're going over initial statements. We have a possible person of interest but he appears to have an alibi but that's it. I also know the kids have been holding something back about their party nights and I aim to find out what that is. It could very well be the information we need to break it and I don't trust any of them. They are still firmly in the frame. So, what are your thoughts after spending a couple of days with the Fenmores?'

Jacob finished tapping on his phone and joined them.

Ellyn let her hair down, re-twisted it and clipped it back up into an even messier bun. A few stray brown hairs stuck to her T-shirt. 'Parents are distraught. Leah was their only child and from what they're saying, they had no idea that she'd been to any party, ever. They seem fairly strict. Leah told them that she was staying at Naomi's house and they believed her.'

'Ooh, trusting. I know first-hand how convincing teenagers can be. Been there and got the T-shirt.' Hannah had lied to her on many occasions when she was in her teens. There were times she'd sneaked into nightclubs while underage, gone to drinking parties in the great outdoors – similar to what Leah had attended – and then there were the pubs and the boys. The deceit and the need for independence was all part of growing up but then most teens didn't end up murdered and their parents don't always find out what they were up to.

'Yes, that's for sure.' Ellyn smiled. 'I did pretty much the same. Different party every weekend and I looked like butter wouldn't melt. My parents are still clueless as to all that I got up to and I'm thirty. As for Leah's parents, they hate her friends, thinking that most of them were a bad influence on her, particularly Oscar. Leah got caught shoplifting but the Fenmores seem convinced that Oscar put her up to it. They don't seem to like Naomi, Elsa, or Jordan. Over the past year, Leah's academic performance suffered a little and the Fenmores think it's because of this group of friends. They say she was set for grade As but now it's Bs and Cs.'

'That's great to know. It gives me a starting point. How about them? Anything not stacking up?'

The FLO shook her head. 'I'll update the system in a short while. You've probably read their initial statement. They were at a dinner party in Bromsgrove with friends and they were there until about two in the morning, drinking. The taxi company confirmed their drop-off time, which was approximately two thirty. Mrs Fenmore was paralytic from what the taxi driver said and Mr Fenmore was also in a state. Apparently he had to help them to the door. Their alibis were tight.'

'Thank you for that. No opportunity and no motive. I suppose we best go in and I'll check out your updates later.' Ellyn waved at them as she got into her old red Fiesta and drove off.

Jacob knocked on the door and a few seconds later, a woman answered. Her tangled brown hair was twisted into an elastic band. She looked up at Gina through her red-ringed green eyes. 'Mrs Fenmore? I'm DI Harte and this is DS Driscoll. We're so sorry about what happened to your daughter. Could we please come in and talk to you? It would be good for our investigation if we got to know a little more about Leah.'

The woman nodded and let the door creak open. It led straight into a tiny dark lounge with a fireplace on the main wall. She followed Mrs Fenmore into a small windowless dining room with stairs behind the table. 'Take a seat.'

The stairs creaked and Mr Fenmore appeared, his gingery beard covering his whole chin. 'Have you found the person who killed my daughter?' His broad Scottish accent boomed through the room.

'I'm sorry, Mr Fenmore, but we're still investigating.'

'I heard that you had someone in custody. Don't tell me you let him go?'

'We can conclusively say that it wasn't him.'

Mr Fenmore slammed his fists on the wooden table and the empty fruit bowl bounced, making Gina flinch. 'What about that disgusting nonce on Oak Tree Walk? The whole town is talking about him. Have you arrested him?'

'There's no evidence to suggest—'

'No evidence. He's been done for perving on young women. My guess is he was perving on those kids and my Leah was a vulnerable young woman when she left the pack for whatever reason. He saw her and he wanted her. Not just content with filming like he did in the past he decided to attack her. My daughter being my daughter would have fought him like mad so he killed her. You need to arrest that bastard before I kill him!'

Gina stepped back a little. She could see Mrs Fenmore quivering and her eyes were watering up. 'I know you're upset but we're doing all we can, I promise you that.'

'Bollocks. You're here talking to us and there's nothing that we can add that will lead you to our daughter's killer. Waste of bloody time. Arrest the nonce.'

'May we sit?' If Gina could get the couple to sit and stop Mr Fenmore getting even angrier before they'd even spoken, that would help.

He pulled out a chair, scraping it on the tiles beneath and Mrs Fenmore sat beside him. With them all seated, Gina cleared her throat and started again. 'We'd just like to know a little more about Leah. We feel that knowing Leah a bit better may give us more avenues to investigate and we were hoping that you won't mind talking to us for a few minutes.'

'Okay, what do you want to know?' he asked.

'Can I get you a drink?' Mrs Fenmore went to stand but her husband's hand came out and pulled her back into her seat.

'Karina, they won't be here that long. The nice detectives know that there is nothing more we can add and they're going to hurry up and get the killer, isn't that right?'

Gina nodded. 'I promise, it won't take long. Can you tell us how Leah got on at school?'

Karina Fenmore's voice cracked as she began to speak. 'She was so bright and good at sports but I suppose this last year, she hadn't applied herself as well as we'd hoped. I think that was down to the company she kept.'

'Can you elaborate on that?'

'Really? We've been through all this with an officer and bloody FLO!' The man folded his arms and tutted.

'Hamish, please.' The man huffed and stopped talking as his wife placed a gentle hand on his arm.

'Sorry, as you can see, Hamish and I are struggling to cope. We loved her so much, she was everything to us and we've lost her. Knowing that she lied to us and put herself in such danger, it came as a shock. Losing her…' Mrs Fenmore sniffed and blew her nose. 'It hasn't sunk in yet. People have brought us food, cards, and family keep calling and it's hard. Nothing prepares anyone for losing a child. Her friends…'

Gina loosened the buttons at the top of her shirt. The heat was making her slightly light-headed, that and the three coffees she'd had to perk her up before setting off. After not sleeping most of the night, she'd finally nodded off about five in the morning only to have her alarm go off at six.

'Elsa and Naomi seemed to be nice enough girls but she went out with them at Easter and came back with a lip piercing. I mean, we didn't even get to talk about it. It was things like that and Leah's attitude changed. She knew how to push our buttons but she'd only do this when she'd been hanging around with them. There was another girl, Caro. She came by sometimes but not often. A bit of an outsider, she was. Nice, quiet girl. We liked her.'

'What about the boys?'

'I don't know them well. Oscar had been a long-standing friend of Leah's but they'd had a bit of a falling out not long ago. He was waiting outside on the street when Leah came out with that phone charger from the shop on Cleevesford High Street. I forget the name of the shop. It sells phone cases and things like that.'

'Came out with?'

'Shoplifted. You lot called me to come and get her. The man who owned the shop detained her until the police got there, then I was called. Leah said that Oscar had been waiting outside. The worst of it was, the charger she tried to steal wasn't even for her phone. I know he put her up to it but he speaks like a posh boy and no one thinks that Oscar could be behind something like that, but that boy is trouble, I'm telling you that. Aren't friends meant to protect each other? If they'd have looked out for her, she'd still be alive. I blame them too. She was in a state and they let her leave, all alone, in the middle of the night.' Mrs Fenmore sobbed and buried herself in Hamish Fenmore's chest.

'I know this is hard but it's really helping us. Do you know if Leah had a boyfriend?'

'No way. She would have told me if she was seeing someone.'

Gina knew that she probably wouldn't have said anything to her parents. 'May I take a look at her bedroom?' Gina clenched her hands under the table, hoping that Mrs Fenmore would say yes.

Her husband held her tightly and kissed her head. 'It's the first room on the right at the top of the stairs.'

Gina exhaled. They left Mr Fenmore comforting his wife and headed up. Maybe there would be a clue, a diary, something that told her who wanted to kill Leah.

CHAPTER THIRTY-ONE

'Hurry up, Mildred,' Gillian called as she started to make her way down the steep stony steps. She could hear the river thrashing below and about halfway down, the most amazing view would appear. Sunken low and surrounded by the wildest of trees, it was a delight to see. Maybe today they would spot some interesting birds. She pushed the overgrown stingers away with her arm and continued down. It was as if nature was closing in on the path and at the same time, concealing its dangers, but Gillian had taken this route many times and knew where it was safe to walk. It didn't make it any less scary though. One wrong move and she knew she'd be in trouble and with her fall a month ago, she wasn't about to risk another. Take it slowly, that's what she'd do.

'Is this where the spotters saw the kingfisher?' Mildred undid her cardigan as she took another step.

'Yes. I've got my binoculars and camera ready and I just hope I can get a photo. My new macro lens is the business.'

'I can't wait to see the photos but I'm also looking forward to getting back and eating those scones.' Mildred took one step at a time and Gillian waited for her. She was, after all, waiting for a knee replacement and things were tough on her joints.

Gillian felt her vision shimmer a little as she stared down at the uneven steps. Mild vertigo when it came to even the tamest of heights did this to her. With each one she took, a flurry of gravel trickled down onto the next step and beyond. Flinching, she pushed the image of her head hitting the rocks and earth below if she fell. She wasn't going to fall. As she took the bend, she stared at the view in front of her. A gathering of ducks and moorhens swam downstream and the sunbeams landing on the rippled water was a magical sight. Mildred caught up, laying a hand on Gillian's arm as she reached her, causing them both to have a little wobble. Only about another thirty of these pesky steps to go. Her legs went a little jelly-like now as the descent got steeper and muddier. With Mildred now holding her arm, getting down was going to be even harder.

Foliage had grown over half of the path and the sections that remained in the shade were mossy and damp. All the easier to slip on.

'What's that?' Mildred squinted and pointed at the base of the steps where a burnt orange hoodie caught her attention.

Gillian stared at it for a moment then carried on walking down the steps. 'I don't know, looks like someone lost their clothing.'

'Looks like more than just clothing to me.' Mildred's brow furrowed.

Hurrying, Gillian reached the bottom. Mildred was right. She groaned as she kneeled on the earth below and took the person's wrist; feeling for a pulse. As a first aider she'd done it many a time. She followed the red dots of blood to the pool beside the rock and her stomach half lurched. She'd never seen a skull crack like that. 'Call the police. He's dead.'

CHAPTER THIRTY-TWO

Leah's bedroom was typical of a teenage girl's room. Clothes were strewn over furniture, across her desk and make-up appeared everywhere. Foundation smeared the carpet and a lipstick kiss stood out on her wardrobe mirror. Posters filled the walls, mostly of fashion models and a couple of singers. Gina recognised Cardi B but not the others.

A collage of photos filled a whole board at the back of the bed. Gina stepped in for a closer look. Leah and Elsa, then with Caro and Naomi; all of them duck pouting. Then there were a few with Oscar. Group pictures of them in school uniforms. So many photos and some covered up by other photos. Gina lifted a couple to see what was beneath. That's when she saw the photo of a camp out, nicely hidden beneath the others. Maybe it was the previous one or maybe it was a camp out that was before that. Gina pulled out her phone and snapped them all to look at later. There were too many to observe in detail.

'Interesting collection.' Jacob stepped behind her and squinted as he focused on the photo of the camp.

'Yes. Look at the kids here.'

He leaned in a little closer.

'There's this photo and then another just underneath the school picture. In the first one, it looks like they're all with it but the second one, it looks like some of the kids are drawing on Caro – the girl we interviewed? The one who didn't take up the invite last Saturday.'

'She looks out of it, I mean they've drawn what looks like a skull and cross bones on her arms. There's dribble running down the side of her mouth.'

'I'm getting a real feeling that there's more to her not going to the latest camping party. To look that out of it while so many people are around you and drawing on your body might suggest she's had something stronger than alcohol. We know they had a bit of weed. I think I saw that Bernard had found a nub end at the scene too. We know that Leah didn't fight back. Can you hold that?' Gina removed the photo that was covering the one of Caro and passed it to Jacob while she took a close-up photo on her phone. 'There.'

He passed the photo back to her and pinned it back into place.

Gina slid open a bedside drawer and reached right to the back. Something rattled. She pulled out a strip of contraceptive pills and then popped them back. Riffling through a pile of paper, some of it containing study notes, she stopped on a printout of a blurred photo. Darkness in the bushes showed the outline of a head but nothing more. Gina recognised the place though. 'Look at the way the shrubs and trees curve around in this arc shape. That's the clearing that some of the teens were using to go to the loo, just a short walk from the camp. Who is that?'

Jacob took it from her and rubbed his chin as he closed one eye, then the other. 'It's nothing more than a shaded head. It could be anyone, including one of the kids.'

'What did we get from her phone? I did have a look on the system but I don't remember this photo.'

'No, it seems Leah was good at taking her photos off her phone. There were some of earlier that day, a few selfies. Some of her sitting in the garden but that was it. This photo wasn't on her phone.'

Gina glanced around the room. She remembered seeing a family computer in the corner of the living room as they came in and there was also a printer. She lifted the curtains and looked on the floor and on all the surfaces, then she kneeled down and riffled amongst the board games under the bed. 'There's a laptop here.'

'Will you be long?' Hamish Fenmore made Gina hit her head on the bed frame. 'What are you doing under my daughter's bed?'

'Mr Fenmore, did Leah ever use your computer downstairs?' Gina pulled the laptop out and placed it on the bed.

'No, she plugged it in to use the printer sometimes but she used that.' He pointed to the laptop.

'May we take it to look at? Only we found a photo amongst Leah's things and there's a person in it that we can't identify. We might be able to enhance the digital image to get a clearer view.' Gina knew she was clutching at straws but there might be much more on Leah's laptop that could help the case.

Leah's father paused and looked away. 'Leah would hate anyone looking through her things like that. We weren't even allowed in her room without an invite.'

'I know it feels like you're invading her privacy but if it helps us to catch her killer, then maybe she wouldn't mind if she was here.' Gina stood and brushed the dust and Leah's stray hairs from her trousers.

'Okay, but we all know it will be that perv. He's your man. If getting that photo enhanced proves that, then, yes, take it.'

'Thank you. I'll get it back to you as soon as we've finished.'

'How long are you going to be?'

'We're nearly done.'

The man turned and went back down the stairs. Gina took the opportunity to open a couple of drawers and she spotted a new opened pack of socks with one pair missing. 'The watermelon socks.' She nudged them back in and closed the drawer. 'I can't help thinking that Leah's friends did something to her. What if it was some game or dare that went too far? I don't trust them.

I don't trust any of them and I don't believe that Caro gave the party a miss because of a hangover.'

Her phone beeped. It was a message from O'Connor.

There's another body, guv. From the description given, it could be one of the other kids that were camping out on Saturday night. Will you and Jacob head over to the river now or shall Wyre and I go? By the way, it's by the car park off Acton Road. Forensics have been called and should be nearly there.

'What was that?' Jacob could tell that something big had happened from her open-mouthed stare at the text.

'Another body. We have to go.'

As they headed out to the car, Gina's phone rang. It was Briggs. 'I have to take this. Get in, I'll be with you in a moment.' Jacob did as asked. 'You okay?'

'No, I don't know. Have you seen the tweet chain, the one linking the article to Meegan that Jim Berry posted?'

'Not yet.'

'It just says, *Murder is where the harte is* with three broken red hearts after it.'

'Who posted it?' She turned, trying to hide her shaking hands from Jacob as he looked out of the car window.

'It's not a proper name, it's just a series of numbers.'

'They're not going away.' She wanted to curl up into a ball and cry. Those messages were just the beginning now and Gina wondered if the whole world would see what she saw in that message or would they just see a typo?

'Just play it calm. We'll figure something out.'

She doubted it was going to be that easy.

Jacob opened the window. 'You coming, guv?'

'Got to go.' She turned and smiled when all she wanted to do was cry. 'Coming.'

CHAPTER THIRTY-THREE

As something hit my bedroom window, my eyes were stark. I glanced at the clock, it was now ten in the morning. I'd only managed to get to sleep at five and still Frank hadn't come home. Thank goodness that the television turned itself off in the night.

Another stone hits my window, then someone shouts. I could peel the curtain back for a peek but I daren't. I know exactly what's happening out there, especially when the word nonce is called out. There's a knock at the front door, then I hear the letter box open. 'Mr Meegan; Mrs Meegan; it's Pete Bloxwich from the *Warwickshire Herald*. I'd like to speak to you both, give you the chance to get your side of the story in before we publish our article.'

I ignore him, hoping that he'll go away.

'We both know your husband is a stinking rotten sex offender. Get your story out, Mrs Meegan.' He pauses again. 'Do you both get off on hurting kids? I have kids you know.' It sounds like he kicked the door.

'Go away. Leave me alone.' I know he can hear me shout as Frank can hear me when he's in the hall.

'Has Mr Meegan left you all alone to deal with the big bad wolf?'

He's scaring me now. First with the outright accusation, now with his sinister comments and I am alone. What do I say? No one knows that Frank is out. Sometimes his car is parked around the back, other times at the front. 'Leave me alone or I'm calling the police.'

'The police have already driven by twice and they haven't stopped. They don't care about kid killers. In fact, they hope that one of us will take the law into our own hands.'

I swallow knowing that I have no means to call the police and he's right. The police are parents, have families. Everyone hates me.

'Just open the door and let me in. It's better for you both if you speak to me, otherwise this crowd will draw their own conclusions and who knows what will happen to you. Poor Mrs Meegan, stuck in her chair, in her bed with no escape…' He says that in a voice like he's talking to a baby. 'You know it makes sense.'

Gasping for breath, I let out an uncontrollable sob. 'Just go away.' I cry like I'm a baby, uncontrollable wet sobs that won't stop. I can't stop them. I've been abandoned with all these problems once again, only this time I can't get up and run away. I'm stuck, in my bed with no food and nothing to drink; not that I could keep anything down. I need the loo and the tremor in my hand won't ease up. *How could you do this to me, Frank?*

Shouts of, *Our children aren't safe. Arrest him* or *I'll kill him myself. Disgusting paedo.* Frank never went anywhere near children. What they were saying was wrong but that didn't matter to the crowd. He was a paedophile as far as they were all concerned. I shiver at what he might be hiding. Have I got it wrong? Did he slide out the back and into the night on Sunday morning and hurt that girl? I can't think with the chanting and the insults. I don't know what's real or not anymore, then there's one voice I recognise. *Bastards. Disgusting animals.* My friend, Lara. A moment ago, I wanted my phone again; now, I'm not so sure. I lift the curtain up slightly and Lara's stare meets mine. I want to drop the curtain but I can't. I see her red face, full of rage. She grabs another stone and throws it towards my face with only the window saving me. 'Kid killers!' That insult hurts so much. The rest of the crowd now sees what Lara sees, me looking pathetic and hiding away. They point and stare and I see them all gossiping but can't quite hear what they're saying. Lara stares at me again shaking her head slowly and the others begin to chant. *Child killers, child killers, child killers.* I drop the curtain.

I've already lied enough. I'm not going down with Frank, especially as I haven't hurt anyone. The reporter shouts again through the letter box, making me jump. 'This isn't going away. I'm not going away. This crowd isn't going away.' I go to answer but the letter box drops as something hits the mat, then the garden gate squeaks. Too late.

I flinch as I hear the back door sliding open. They're coming for me. The angry mob have found a way in and I bet Frank left it unlocked on purpose so they could get me. He's now on the run and has left me in this mess. I hear step after step. They're going to kill me, I know it. The chants outside continue and they're louder. To them, I'm an effigy of hate. I just needed more time to find out the truth for myself. If Frank had left my wheelchair in the room, I could have got to the outside of the kitchen door in the night, shuffled to the cupboards and searched through everything but, as usual, everything conspired against me. Even my bedroom door is shut and I know I heard him slide the sideboard against the other side before he left. He has me trapped.

I shiver as the hall door opens then there's the heavy footsteps on the wooden floor. I'm dead, I know it. Now the crowd have decided that Frank is a paedophile child killer, they'll take it out on me. Whoever is out there, slides the sideboard out of the way. The handle to my bedroom door comes down and I pull the sheet over my head, knowing that a sheet offers no protection but I don't want to see my end coming. Swallowing, I wait to die.

CHAPTER THIRTY-FOUR

Gina pulled up in the Acton Road car park opposite the ambulance and police cars that were lined up; that tweet swimming through her head. A text came through from Briggs.

Whoever published that tweet has now deleted it. I'll keep an eye on Twitter, see if anymore messages come through.

She exhaled slowly. Whoever published that message had removed the evidence, giving her just enough time to see it or for it to be logged as a part of the investigation. She wondered for a moment if the team would see it as something personal against her or as just someone publishing a tweet with a typo.

'Well, I didn't expect this to happen.' Jacob got out and they both began to walk towards PC Kapoor who was tying some police tape around a tree.

Gina bit the inside of her mouth as she surveyed the area. 'Nor me. First Leah, now this. Maybe we're jumping to conclusions and it was nothing more than an accident but no.' She shook her head. 'That's too much of a coincidence. Leah was murdered in the early hours of Sunday morning, now someone matching Jordan Rolph's description has turned up dead.'

'We best go and see him for ourselves. Hear what Bernard has to say.'

'Morning, Jhanvi.' PC Jhanvi Kapoor smiled.

'Alright, guv. It's shaping up to be a busy week. Are you coming to pool night on Friday?'

Gina had taken to joining Wyre and Kapoor for the occasional pub night but this Friday, she was going to be doing nothing more than panicking over what Hannah had to say. Kapoor had taken to talking non-stop on these nights about her ambitions in the police and her family, which Gina always loved to hear.

'I think I have something on this week but next Friday, definitely.' That's if she wasn't herself in custody for allowing Terry to die. She gulped.

'Great, can't wait. If you keep going past me, follow the dirt path and take a right where it forks off, you'll then get to the top of the steps that lead down to the river. That's where they all are. I've just got word that the witnesses are on their way back up. PC Smith is bringing them. They found the body and one of the ladies did a pulse check too, so we'll get what we need from them first seeing as they got so close and touched the body.'

'I'd like to speak to them when I've caught up with Bernard. Could you please make sure they stay with an officer once they've been checked out?'

A woman emerged from the trees. She had a short grey bob and was wearing walking boots. A camera was swinging around her neck and she held binoculars in one hand. 'I might be in my seventies but I don't need any help with walking yet.'

'Okay, Mrs Sullivan.' PC Smith followed her through.

'Gillian, please.'

The other woman trailed behind, catching up a moment later.

PC Smith led them both towards the ambulance where the women started to protest against being checked over, saying that they felt fine. That they weren't in shock and they hadn't hurt themselves.

'Right, that's our cue to check out the scene.' Jacob stepped past PC Kapoor.

They did as instructed, following the dirt path. Gina placed an arm out, pushing the overgrown stingers out of the way. Thorny branches had entwined around the branches and her shoes caught in the long grass, dragging a trail behind her. She shook it away. 'It's wild out here.'

'I know. I just got stung.' Jacob shook his arm as if that would alleviate the irritation.

After a battle with branches, they finally reached the steps. With no railings, they were a hazard. The river trickled ahead and she heard the quacking of ducks and birds tweeting in the trees above. She glanced up at a tall tree trunk and saw a woodpecker tapping away. As they reached the curve in the steps, the spectacular view hit Gina. After living in Warwickshire for so many years, she'd never once taken this walk. She wasn't sure she'd want to now after what had happened. She swallowed, wondering if she'd ever get to see Gracie again given that Hannah was building up to something. The sinister messages that Briggs was receiving pushed to the front of her mind. What did they know? Then, a whooshing rush of blood to the head almost knocked Gina sideways. Seeing the body at the bottom of the steps took her right back to the night she pushed Terry down their own stairs to his death. It was like the universe was conspiring against her this week. She felt herself wobble a little, then she bumped into Jacob, gripping the arm of his shirt for dear life.

'Watch it, guv. Could do without you being carted off in that ambulance.'

'Sorry, lost my footing.' She hadn't trodden on the moss but Jacob put a thumb up and carried on as she removed her grip from his arm. She had to push all those thoughts of Terry out of her mind, for now. Easier said than done when all she could see was him lying dead at the bottom of the steps. That night flooded back into her mind. Him coming home drunk, pinning her against the wall; losing his footing and her delivering just enough pressure to make sure he went down. The look in his eyes as he fell backwards to his eventual death. His body lying at the bottom of the stairs and the pulse he still had. She waited until it was too late for him and only then called the ambulance. She may have acted instinctively when she nudged him but to leave him there dying and making sure he was dead, was something else. It showed intent. Good old 'mens rea', the guilty mind element that is needed to prove a murder conviction. She killed him. If she had delivered first aid and called an ambulance immediately like any non-murderous human being would have, he probably would have lived. It hit her again. Whoever was messaging Briggs somehow knew this already and they were coming for her.

Gina watched as Bernard and a crime scene assistant were finishing laying down the stepping plates. 'Don't come any closer and step to the far right of each of the remaining steps. We could be treading on evidence. Put these on.' He threw two forensics suits at them along with gloves, boots, face masks and hair coverings.

Catching them, Jacob passed a pack to Gina and she shakily took it from him. Each of them balancing on an uneven step, steep enough to give a person vertigo, eventually managed to dress for the crime scene. With quivering fingers, Gina zipped the suit up and followed Jacob down. At the bottom, they stood on the metal plates that were placed back a little, giving Bernard and the assistant a little room to move. The splashing of the river as it hit the rocks made it hard to hear what was being said.

Jennifer appeared from the riverside with a camera.

'Hi, Jen,' Jacob said with a smile.

She gave him a little wave.

Gina glanced down, her eyes fixated on the body close to the bottom of the steps. She shook her head, forcing that image of Terry from her mind. There would be plenty of time later to think about that. 'So, what do we have? Any evidence to suggest that it wasn't an accident?'

'Oh yes.' Bernard pointed to the orange hoodie on the back of the corpse. 'See that line of dirt on his back. That is a shoe or boot mark, just the one side and it's not complete.' He adjusted his face mask, re-tucking his beard in.

'He may have been kicked down the steps.' Gina's voice crackled and she gulped. Clearing her throat, she continued, 'It's definitely Jordan Rolph.' She recognised him from the camp and from his photo that was pinned up in the incident room. There was no mistaking his identity. His red hair was matted and blood had seeped from his cracked head onto a pile of jagged rocks. Body facing down; face to the side half smashed. She looked away.

'Rigor mortis has set in too which is going to make him difficult to move. We have to hurry though, a storm has been forecast for later today.' Bernard hunched over, above her as he spoke, blocking out a shaft of sunlight. When he moved again, the blinding light made her flinch.

With the boy's limbs sprawled out, Gina could see what Bernard was saying. 'Any estimate on the time of death?'

'Between two and four this morning but I'll let you know if I find out more later. The Home Office Pathologist is booked to do the post-mortem but it will probably be tomorrow morning now.'

'Similar time to when Leah Fenmore was murdered,' Jacob said.

'Can you tell us anything about the shoe mark? Size, maybe?' Gina asked.

'No, not right now. It's a partial. I may know more later when I've had a chance to assess it properly. From the shape, it looks like the contact was made with the right foot. See the way it curves right there.' He pointed.

Gina felt her heart rate increasing. Another day when a parent would have to be told that their child had been murdered. Kicked to their death down a flight of steps, head smashed on a rock. Things weren't getting any easier, they were getting harder and did this mean that the other kids were in danger or was one of the other kids his murderer? Her mind flashed to the others. Elsa's tweets; although she hadn't tweeted any more since being asked not to. Oscar, the boy with two personalities, the '*yes, sir, no, sir*' persona he put on for his father and the mildly deviant one his teacher described. Naomi, the girl who found Leah's body. Nothing was standing out about Naomi at the moment. The group of teens were all holding something back but at what cost? Would their secrets cost them their lives? The kids were up there as suspects, along with Meegan. She turned to Jacob who was making a few notes. 'We need to get some sort of protection for the others. Call the FLO, Ellyn. We need someone from her team to spend time with each of the parents. It's for their security but I also want them to report back with anything suspicious. Actually, we can utilise Kapoor here. I'd like her to stay with Oscar and his father. She's got a good eye and has started showing an interest in family liaison. I also don't trust Oscar as far as I could throw him. And ask uniform to visit Jordan's parents first, then I want Ellyn to be with them.'

'Yes, guv.' Jacob stepped away from the scene on the riverbank and began making the call.

She stared at the body. Two teens dead; one boy and one girl, and another three in the group who were still alive.

Jacob ended his call and headed back to Gina. 'Kapoor is waiting for a replacement for car park duty and Ellyn is sorting the other out now. An officer is on their way to Jordan's home to break the news.'

'Thank you. We'll speak to the two women who found the body, then head back to the station. After we've caught up, I want to head to the Meegans' cottage. I know officers have been driving past to keep a lookout but I want to be the one to speak to Mr Meegan again. I want to know that he was home last night. Apparently, the reporters have landed at their doorstep, along with a mob of locals with banners. I want it noted that Mrs Meegan is a vulnerable person in the sense that she's extremely dependant on Mr Meegan. I got a sense that something was wrong in that household and that she is possibly scared of him too and that worries me. Seeing reporters along with a mob forming outside is going to scare her.'

'Noted.'

'How far geographically do you think we are from everyone involved in this case?'

Jacob pursed his lips and cocked his head. 'The kids all live close by except Oscar who lives up the posh end. Naomi and Elsa live about two miles from here so it's walkable. Oscar, about a mile in the other direction, so a lot closer. The Meegans. I guess if you walk along the river, Mr Meegan could have got here in about forty minutes but he also has a car too. Again, the Waterside Café is a similar distance away from the Meegans' cottage.'

'We need to find out who was doing the drive-bys and if they saw Mr Meegan's car parked up. Hang on.' Gina paused to think. 'When we were there, there was a car parked around the back of the cottage, outside his back gate. He doesn't park on the front. They wouldn't have seen his car. Damn.'

'Maybe one of the neighbours did.'

'I fear that the neighbours might say anything now that his past is out of the bag but we'll ask them nonetheless. I definitely need him brought in for further questioning. Mrs Meegan is holding something back about that night which makes his alibi shaky.' She knew that would cause more stress for Mrs Meegan but it had to be done. 'We need to offer some support to his wife. She might want someone to sit with her while he's gone. I know from speaking with her that she depends on him for a lot. Maybe she'll talk to someone else. She clammed up with me.'

Another CSI brushed past with a crime scene tent, ready to erect.

'I guess we'd better get out of the way.'

Jennifer nodded and Bernard glanced up. 'I'll call when I know more.'

'Thanks, Bernard.'

A CSI hurried up to Bernard. 'We have something.'

'What is it?' He glanced over at the suited-up man.

'A torn piece of material on one of the brambles. It looks like a piece of black cotton.' The young man held it up in the evidence bag.

'Brilliant. Keep me informed. We may be looking for someone with torn black clothing. I'll add that to the boards.' Gina began walking back up the steps, not looking back at the body. It was all getting too much and her racing heart was making her nauseous. She needed to speak to Briggs before she lost her mind.

CHAPTER THIRTY-FIVE

My heart is still hammering from Frank's return. I contain my body into the corner of the bed against the wall, cowering as I don't know what he's going to do to me. That's what it's like living with Frank. He can be docile for ages, then he can flip for no reason but at the moment, tension fills the room, which makes our situation rife for him lashing out. My racing heart feels as though it might choke me. I'm hot and prickly, sickly even but I'm also relieved. I thought one of the angry mob had got in. 'I thought you were one of them. I thought I was going to die.'

'Bleedin' hell, Sandy. The sliding doors were locked. They're not coming in. Besides, it's gone a bit quieter. Some of them must have got bored and left.' He peered through the tiniest gap in the curtains. 'There are just a couple of idiots standing out there with placards; one of them is your lovely so-called friend. Soon, they'll get bored and go home.' He unfolded the piece of paper in his hand. He must have picked it up from the doormat. 'Bloody reporters.'

I don't know what came over me but I blurt my question out. 'Where were you in the early hours of Sunday morning and how did you get your scratches? I want the truth.'

'Not you as well. You sound like the police.'

He sat on the bed, making it dip a little and I can't help but be forced closer to him. He's trying to deflect what I asked. I might be scared but I'm not going to drop it. 'I heard the sliding doors open and then close on Sunday morning, in the early hours and

I lied to the police. I hear things you know and I'm not stupid, despite what you might think.' I flinch as he leans in and his nose touches mine. His breath smells sour like off food. There's a hint of beer on his breath too.

'You say anything to the police and I swear I will kill you. You know how easy it would be to slam you off this bed head first into something sharp and say you fell. I could make it look like an accident. Clumsy Sandy, trying to get out of bed without help or her wheelchair in place. She does it a lot. I told her she'd cause herself an injury one day.'

My bottom lip trembles because I know he means it. He has it all worked out. I know he could do it too. There's a coldness in his eyes. He was never what I'd call ultra-loving. He'd tell me he loved me but it always sounded mechanical. Love never reached his eyes.

'I didn't kill her.' He grins. His voice tells me one thing but all I see in him is a murderer.

Tears stream down my face. He's just threatened to kill me and I'm supposed to believe what he says. I know he's lying now. He has to be, otherwise why would he be so angry about me asking him that question? I'm not going to back down in my pursuit for the truth and if he hurts me, then so be it. 'What were you doing out?' He grabs my hair and seethes in my face. I feel his hot breath on my cheek.

'Don't you dare question me. I do everything for you. Everything. You're pathetic, you know that? You always were needy but the accident, it made you even needier. Pathetic little Sandy. You don't try to do anything for yourself, always relying on me. I'm sick of it.' He lifts up my curtain and peers out. 'Last woman standing. Lara hates you now. She hates us. You brought this on us by talking to her in the shop. I shouldn't have taken you with me.'

I want to say, *she doesn't hate me, she hates you*, but I don't. I cry. She sees Frank and I as one so, yes, she does hate me. He's right this time. I can't catch my breath between sobs. I'm trapped and I want some air. My bottom lip shakes, which I know annoys Frank. He's told me it's ugly on more than one occasion.

'Look, stop with this stupid grizzling. It's the last thing I need right now.' He pauses and leans away from me. 'Do you want a drink? Will that shut you up?'

I nod. What I want is for him to leave the room so that I can breathe. He's suffocating me in every way. 'Can I please have my phone?'

'You don't need it. If you see what they're all saying, you'll get even more upset and I don't want that. See, I do care. The things I do for you are out of love, even though you don't understand.' He walks back and kisses my cheek. I don't get him at all. 'Don't flinch like that. I mean, do I look like a killer?'

I stare at him. What does a killer look like? I know Frank is capable of recording women while they're in public toilets or in their own homes while they're getting changed. I know he's done that and he promised me that he would never do it again but I don't trust him. Do people like him really change or do they get worse, seeking thrill after thrill, finding each time less satisfying so they up the ante? I reach into my pocket and feel for the detective's card. What I need to do is find out once and for all what Frank is keeping from me in that damn kitchen and then I need my phone. His phone rings and he walks out of my room. I hear him moaning about having to go somewhere but agreeing to be there later this afternoon. He's going out.

He lets out a roaring scream and I think he's kicking one of the dining table chairs, then glass smashes on the floor. He's losing it.

Stomping back in, he stands in the doorway. 'I have to go to the police station in a bit. They want to talk to me again. I'm going out to clear my head.' He kicks my bedroom door and pulls his car keys from his pocket.

'Can I have my wheelchair?'

'Just stay there. I won't be long.'

'But, Frank. I don't want to stay here—'

'Whatever. Oh, you can stop worrying. A few drops of rain have sent the angry mob away; it's just your pathetic friend there, on her own. At least you can calm down a bit now. Have a nap or something.'

'All I do is bloody nap. I'm sleeping my life away—' He walks off.

The brightness of the day has gone and my bedroom now feels dark. I know we are due a storm this week as I heard it on the weather. It's been too humid and now a few blasts of thunder would clear the air.

The back doors are slid open and I hear him step out into the back garden. I don't hear the car in the distance. I expect he's left it in another road so that he didn't have to drive past the mob that had been at the front of the house. A smile emerges from my lips. He's left my bedroom door open and I can't waste this opportunity. I throw myself onto the floor and yelp as my elbow hits the wood. It's going to be a long day but it might also finally be the day where I get my answers.

CHAPTER THIRTY-SIX

The incident room buzzed with life. O'Connor and Wyre were seating everyone. Several uniformed officers were present and Annie from corporate communications was sipping what smelled like ginger tea. Gina checked the time. She had ten minutes before they started so she hurried along to Briggs's office and knocked.

'Come in.'

Her breaths came thick and fast as a dizziness swept through her.

'Here, sit down.' Briggs came over and helped her into a chair.

Trembling, she took a few deep breaths bent over with her head between her legs. After she'd calmed down, she sat back up. 'Sorry about that. I had to get out and I need to speak to you because I think I'm going crazy with what's happening.'

'Have you managed to speak to Hannah?'

She shook her head. 'I've tried to call her several times but she's not picking up. All I know is she wants to speak in person on Sunday. I'm scared. I mean, who's messaging us and who published that damn tweet? Besides, I don't even know who would have your phone number.'

'I've received another. It just says, *confess*. We need to find out who's behind this before it brings us both down, especially as our tormentor is going public now.'

'What do we do?'

'Nothing. There's nothing we can do.' He began to pace before standing in front of the window. 'I'm guessing that this person needs me or us to confess because they can't prove anything. I can't see how they can.' He began clenching his teeth. 'We sit tight.'

'I know what I did and you know what I did. No one else knows but why does it feel like they do? You haven't said anything to anyone?'

He turned and grimaced. 'Really, you're actually asking me that question. Why would I do that? My career is on the line as much as yours. If anyone finds out that I knew all along, I'm in for the high jump too.'

'My liberty is on the line and you know what they do to the likes of us in prison. I often wonder how much longer I can live with what I've done. It gets harder every day.' She bit her lip and flinched as the metallic taste of blood reached her tongue.

He walked over and kneeled in front of her, stroking her cheek. 'We will get through this, I promise.'

With a throbbing head, she flinched as a flash of lightning lit up the room and a distant rumble came almost straight after. 'If I was superstitious, I'd say this was a sign.'

'But you're not. It's not a sign and there are no such things. Put your logical head on, Harte.'

He was right but it didn't make the thunder sound any less threatening. A flash of Terry pinning her to the top of the stairs filled her mind. The sound of thunder boomed through the house, that and her baby daughter's piercing cries.

Gina gasped as Briggs placed a gentle hand under her chin and gazed at her, bringing her back to the moment. The past was exactly that; the past. His gaze met hers, the kind crinkles in the corners of his eyes warming her slightly as he calmly spoke. 'We're in this together and we'll get through this together. Right now, we have a murderer to catch. I'll keep an eye on Twitter and deal with the press. Get back out there and do what you're good at. We'll sort this, I promise.' What he was saying did not match his expression. She knew he was as worried about the messages as she was.

Someone banged on Briggs's office door. He stood and stepped back. Gina rubbed her eyes and sat up straight as he opened the door. 'Wyre, we're on our way.'

'Great, we're all ready.'

Gina glanced over her shoulder and saw Wyre looking at her. She smiled and stood, giving nothing away. That was the story of her life. Live a lie and keep it up. Briggs had received yet another message. She'd been targeted on Twitter. Things were looking bad and he was in denial if he thought nothing would come of it. Gina could feel it in her sinking stomach and her trembling limbs. Her day of reckoning was on its way.

CHAPTER THIRTY-SEVEN

Gina followed Briggs into the incident room. Standing in front of the boards, she glared at the map with all the pins marking out the various locations. Leah's and Jordan's bodies were discovered quite close to each other. And everyone that had come to light in the investigation was close enough to have opportunity, which didn't help to narrow down their list. Another crash of thunder shook the room and the strip light dipped. O'Connor's computer screen flickered off then it began to reboot. He swivelled in his chair and swore under his breath about losing some updates.

Gina swallowed the lump in her throat and stood tall. 'Okay, thank you for getting back so soon. Jacob and I have not long arrived back from the river where we can without doubt say that the body found is that of Jordan Rolph.'

Wyre grabbed a marker ready to write the updates under Jordan's photo on the new board that had been placed next to Leah's.

'It's early days for forensics but I've spoken to Bernard and it's clear that there is a partial footprint on the boy's back. There could be two reasons for this. He was standing high up on the steps and was kicked from behind, sending him plunging head first into the rocks below. The steps are steep and his skull has cracked so there was a lot of force, but the height alone could have caused that to happen. Secondly, someone could have placed a foot on his body as he lay dead or dying after he fell. We will know more after the post-mortem.' She gulped as Terry's body flashed through her mind again. This particular murder was too close to home. Turning, she grabbed the water jug in the centre of the table and poured a glass, taking a sip before continuing. 'While I was with Bernard earlier, one of the assistants found some torn black cotton on one of the bushes. It looked like it came from some black clothing. The sample will obviously be analysed for trace evidence. We might get lucky with some hair or skin cells. Bernard will keep us updated in real time.'

'Do we know what time frame the murder could have taken place in?' Wyre waited for an answer as she held the pen.

'We do. Between two and four this morning. We will need to re-interview everyone that has been flagged up in this case. Keep the kids at the forefront of your mind. We need to break down their wall. We need to know where they all were last night and pay special attention to anyone without an alibi or with an unreliable alibi. I put Sandra Meegan into that category. When Frank Meegan arrives in a bit for his interview, I'm going to head over to speak to her again. I feel she is in a vulnerable position because of her husband's past, which is why I want a panic alarm set up in her home. That is something I'll speak to her about. I don't have anything concrete here, but she may be at risk with Frank. When I spoke to her, I felt as though she wanted to tell me more but she clammed up. She also kept flinching as she touched her head. Maybe she hurt it on a shelf like she said or maybe tensions are running high and her husband hurt her. Jacob, would you and O'Connor interview Frank?'

They nodded.

'Kapoor?'

'Yes, guv.' The tiny PC leaned forward over the table and bit the bottom of her pen. The end of her shiny black ponytail flicked the table.

'How did you get on with Oscar's father? We need someone to report back but be sympathetic to any concerns that they may have. I particularly want Oscar to be observed.'

'I called and he said they'd be in this evening. He said he could protect his own son and didn't need our help but he confirmed that I could come over to see him if I had to.'

'Great. In that case, Wyre, can you attend with Kapoor and lead the interview? We're spreading ourselves thin but we can do this. As for Oscar's father, if he's not going to accept you being there, we may as well at least get that interview in. Look for everything and anything while you're in that house. If something seems off, no matter how small, note it down. Keep bearing in mind that Oscar is a different person when in the company of his father. Try to read between any lines if you can.'

Wyre and Kapoor nodded.

'Jacob, what did Ellyn say?'

He sipped his drink and placed the cup down. 'She has arranged for someone to be with Elsa's family and Naomi's this evening; both have accepted, so that was good. As for Jordan's mother, she didn't want anyone with her. She said that her sister was coming over and she wanted to be alone. I know the press have already got wind of the fact that Jordan is the latest victim and they have been hounding her for a statement.'

'I'll speak to her in the morning but in the meantime, I know budgets are tight and this is pushing us to our limits, but can we schedule in some drive-bys. I want to know she is safe from the press too. O'Connor, can you organise that? Also, please liaise with Ellyn and her team to collate any information that comes through.'

'Got it, guv.'

'Caro and Anthony, the two teens that didn't go to that particular party. At the moment, I don't think we need to offer them any protection. We can definitely rule Anthony out as he was out of town with his parents for a family funeral. Caro's family have confirmed that they were all at home that evening and overnight. But Caro, there is something I can't put my finger on. Bear her in mind and Anthony too. I'm convinced that they still know more than they're letting on. Maybe something happened at the last party and they're holding back.'

The room silenced and rain began to thrash at the window. Gina undid her top button. The storm wasn't clearing the stuffiness from the air. A stickiness was building in her armpits and her face felt clammy. Maybe it was the heat or the stress of what she and Briggs were hiding. 'Lastly, one for you, Smith. I know we've stretched uniform to the limit this week, especially as you've been busy too, but I need some more door-to-doors. There are two quiet estates that have entry points to that part of the river. If our culprit was on foot, they could have taken either.' Gina pointed to them on the map. 'We need to speak to the residents, collect CCTV and ask them if they saw anyone out of place passing through or hanging around.'

'I'll get on to that, guv.' The other uniformed officer nodded.

'Right, don't let me keep you another minute. Let's plough on. I don't want any more dead teenagers turning up.'

Annie stood. 'What about the press? They've been on the phone all day since we released that there was a body by the river. We gave them a holding statement but they're hounding us for more.'

Gina swallowed. 'I have more for them. Somehow we need them to stop harassing our witnesses at their homes. A few of the parents have complained that a new reporter called Pete Bloxwich keeps hounding them and he's quite pushy.' She sighed. That wouldn't go down well because they needed the press right now. 'DCI Briggs might have a more diplomatic approach in mind.'

Gina sat down and Briggs moved to the front of the room. 'The holding statement is enough for now as far as information goes. No details should be given such as the shoe print on the back of the victim's back but what we do need to put out is an appeal for witnesses. I'll prepare a press release in a minute and I'll speak at say…' he looked at his watch, '… four this afternoon.

It will be a basic appeal for any witnesses to come forward with time frames and expressing our condolences to the friends and family of Jordan Rolph.'

Annie finished scrawling a few notes as she twisted one of her blonde curls around her finger. 'Great. I'll get that arranged.'

The silence was soon filled with chatter as everyone in the room discussed what they were doing next. Slowly the room began to empty. Gina followed Briggs back to his office and closed the door behind them. 'Thanks.'

'What for?'

'Just being there.' He was right, neither of them had told anyone a thing. It was some chancer trying to play mind games with them.

'I'm always here, you know I am.' He stroked her hair and smiled. 'Now, go and catch that murderer.'

'I'll call you later.' She checked her watch. Mr Meegan was due in an hour. That gave her time to stare at the board and browse the system to look for links while she grabbed a sandwich. Then, she'd head off to speak to Mrs Meegan.

The anonymous messages to Briggs, and Hannah wanting to talk then refusing to answer her calls, was a coincidence; that was all. Hannah surely couldn't be the messenger. She wanted to shake her head and tear at her hair because she didn't believe that for one second. The more she thought about it, the less she believed it.

CHAPTER THIRTY-EIGHT

Caro began to dish up the pizza that her mother had left out for her and Jake. She phoned her dad again but his answerphone clicked on. He was meant to be home by now but no, he was late as usual and she was stuck looking after her little brother when she wanted nothing more than to curl up in bed.

'I don't like onions.' He scrunched his button nose up as she slid the pizza from the baking tray onto the chopping board.

'You ate onions last week.'

'Yeah, and I didn't like them. They were disgusting.' He pulled a face.

'Just pull them off.'

He picked up a slice and dropped it back on the board. 'It's yuck! Not eatin' it.'

'Whatever.' She wasn't in the mood to battle with him when all she could think about were the messages and the person following her. Her mother would have threatened to send him to bed or maybe taken his favourite toy if he didn't at least try to eat his dinner but Caro really didn't care. He stared up at her from the stool at the worktop gripping a plastic dragon in one hand, his little shoulders hunched over. 'Fine. Mum and Dad aren't here and I don't care if you die of malnutrition or all your teeth drop out.' She turned to the freezer and pulled a huge tub of chocolate ice cream out and gave it to him with a spoon.

His face lit up. 'Love you, sis. Can I eat it in front of the TV?'

'Go.' She smiled at him.

He didn't need telling twice. Before she'd even picked up a slice of pizza and pushed it into her mouth, he'd left the kitchen. She checked her phone again and tried her mother this time. Again, no answer. She jumped as it rang in her hand. 'Ant. What's up?'

'Have you seen Facebook?'

'No, not this afternoon. I've been trying to entertain my stupid little brother all day while my mother has decided to join a protest against some paedo. I'm stuck in and bored and I hate everything and everyone. What have I missed?'

'Body down by the river. Jordan's mum rang me early this morning askin' if he was with me. Well he weren't so I told her that, then I called back just to see if he was around as I couldn't get him on his phone and she said it's him, the body. Jordan is the body. He's dead.'

'Shit! No way.' Caro dropped the pizza and licked her greasy fingers. 'Did they say how?'

'No, not yet. It might be on the news in a bit. That's all I know. What if everyone else in the group is in danger? What if we're next?'

'But we weren't at the party. Leah and Jordan were both there on Saturday night. We were nowhere near it so I'd say we were fine.' She felt her throat closing a little as she thought about the messages.

'So! We were at the last party. It's one of them. It has to be Oscar. He can be horrible at the best of times.'

Caro glanced out of the kitchen window, wondering if her stalker was watching from afar. She focused on each small gap in the back fence but couldn't see anything out of place, then she shivered as she thought of the figure she'd seen when leaving the field. 'Do you seriously think someone is after us all?'

Anthony paused. 'Just be really careful. 'Kay?'

'Okay.'

'Look, I've got to go. Things to do.'

He hung up before she could answer.

Jake ran back in with the ice cream. 'Had enough now. Can I have some crisps?' Caro passed him a family bag of cheese and onion then gently pushed him back towards the living room. If he had a bad stomach later, it would be her mum and dad's fault for leaving her alone with him all day long. Besides, she had a lot on her mind and she didn't need the aggro from Jake.

As she thought about Jordan, her heart started to pound. She ran upstairs and looked out of all the windows in turn and finally, she entered her parents' room. She pushed one of the two home-made banners aside. *Save our children from paedos.* Her mother really was on one. She opened the laptop on the dressing table and waited for it to boot up and there was a picture of the man her mother was targeting with her protest. She thought back to the night she saw a figure lurking at the last party. Was it him? Maybe, but she couldn't be sure. Voyeurism? She read a bit more, not quite understanding what that term meant. There was no claim in the article that he was a paedophile but she shivered when she read that he'd been secretly filming people in public loos. 'Sicko.' She closed the lid on the laptop. Maybe he did deserve her mother's wrath.

Sitting on her parents' bed, she tried calling her mother again, then finally, an answer.

'Not now, Caro. Can't talk. I'll call you back.' That was all her mother said before she cut her off. Caro threw her phone onto her mother's side of the bed and lay back, closing her eyes until a moment flashed through her head.

Jerking up, she couldn't breathe. A flash so brief, it barely made sense. A naked body, Oscar's body. She'd seen Oscar naked on the night of the party. Clenching her hands, she jerked up and took a couple of deep breaths. She'd trusted Oscar totally and he let her down. Everything that had happened at the party had been his idea. The police knew she was hiding something, and she now was. First it was the missing memories of the evening, now it was the fact that Oscar and Jordan roofied her. Then they all drew on her and did things to her for a laugh, some of it she had no recollection of. She saw something else there; that had been as clear as anything but she wasn't going to think about that, let alone speak of it. No, the time wasn't right. She needed the police off their backs, after which she could have it out with Oscar when they were alone. Her phone beeped with a Snapchat message. It was from the anonymous messenger.

> *There are things you need to know. You have to meet me, alone. Time and place will be sent later. Tell anyone and you die. Don't turn up and you die. Your choice.*

The message vanished and Caro stared at the wall, trembling. Dangerous? Yes. But she had to know who was doing this to her.

CHAPTER THIRTY-NINE

Sweat droplets cloud my vision. A few moments had passed since Lara had shouted through the letter box. *I can't believe we were ever friends. You disgust me.* I think she's gone now. I shuffle a bit further along the floor then I finally make it to my destination with burning arm muscles. My wheelchair is next to the lounge chair. I need to pull my body up, then I can struggle my way into the chair. I didn't think this through very well, there's just nothing I can properly grip and I don't have the strength needed to get off the floor. After several failed attempts, my breathing is rapid and I'm exhausted to the point where I'm ready to give up. I just can't do it. Failed again and if I can't find my way out of this one, I'll suffer whatever Frank wants to dish out when he comes home.

Maybe I can get to the kitchen. My phone has to be in there as it's not in here. I drag and shuffle, taking short breathers along the way and, finally, I am at the entrance to the kitchen. I spot my phone on the worktop, way out of reach. I'll need something to hit it with. Maybe I can flick it down with something in the cupboard. A low rumble of thunder makes my heart skip a beat. Maybe once the storm has passed the humidity will too. This weather is giving me a thick head and the fact that it's swollen with so many thoughts isn't helping.

I shuffle along the crumby floor tiles. When Frank is mooching around in here having alone time, I hear him getting something out of a cupboard or drawer. He's not in here cooking, cleaning, or making a drink at these times. He's in here for another reason and I'm determined to find out why. When you've been with a person as long as I have with Frank, you know when they're hiding something and I'm going to find out what, even if it kills me.

As I reach the cupboards, I displace a pile of dust and crumbs that Frank must have swept and not picked up. Opening the corner cupboard, I see nothing but pots, pans and plates. Then I shift a little further until I can open the cupboard under the sink. Again there's nothing there but cleaning fluids and old cloths. There's the drawers, maybe I should check those. I pull open the bottom drawer and see an old tin box, one that I remember being in the shed of our old house. I assumed that Frank kept screws in it or something equally as boring. I strain to reach up, my arms jellied and weak from all the stress I've put on them. With a bit of effort, I roar as I grab it and drop it on the floor. It flies open, spilling its contents all over the kitchen tiles. I shift onto my side as my bottom is numb, keeping my right hand free to pick up the items. Photos of women and teenagers. The teens in the woods are squatting to pee; getting dressed; skinny-dipping in the river and making out. He has photos of the girls and the boys. I feel acid burning my throat. I want to vomit or scream with rage. I trusted him and he's betrayed me in the worst possible way.

My phone. What can I use to get hold of it? I still have that detective's number in my pocket and I'm going to call her. Frank went out on the night of the girl's murder and I have to tell the truth now that I have all the evidence I need. Tears flood my face. I don't know what will become of me. I can't manage on my own in this house and the thought of receiving home care makes me feel useless but this can't carry on. Doing the right thing is what I need to do and I have to do it now before he hurts someone else. I'm convinced he killed that girl.

I lift up some of the photos and my gaze rests on a memory stick. That and a few photos go in my pocket with the detective's card. If Frank comes back, he'll know I've seen his dirty secret unless… I place the box back in the drawer. This might buy me some time.

Grabbing an old spatula from another drawer, I reach up, trying to hook it behind my phone but it's not long enough. Tea towel. Reaching for the towel hooked in the cooker door handle, I manage to grasp it. Attempt after attempt at flicking the phone off the worktop exhaust me. I'm seeing dots and I'm so hot, so very hot and stuffy. I want to curl up and cry. That would be the easy thing to do. Cry, wait and accept whatever Frank will do to me when he sees what I've been up to.

I half-heartedly try one more time and it flicks the phone. I do it again and it lands on the side of my face. As I get my phone into position, I go to turn it on but it stays blank. It's out of charge. The lounge window smashes and I hear a whooshing sound. Fire crackling. I'm stuck. My life flashes before my eyes. Both me and the evidence I have secreted in my pocket are about to go up in flames. I've never sobbed so hard. What else can I do but let out a loud hopeless cry? Will the neighbours save me if they hear or will they sit out there and watch with smug grins on their faces? I imagine Lara laughing as the house burns to soot. It's over. He will get away with his crimes and I'm going to… I can't think about my end right now. I close my eyes and just lie here hoping that it will be over quickly. I hear flames licking the living room furniture and I wonder how long I have before it spreads to me.

CHAPTER FORTY

With Frank due for his interview at the station at any minute, Gina knew it was safe to visit the Meegans' cottage to speak to Sandra, alone. The wipers scraped another torrent of rain from the car window as she pulled up. Gutters were gurgling and there was no one crowding around the house anymore. No reporters and no protesters. The street was deserted due to bad weather. Drains filled as a stream of water gathered against the pavement, flowing downwards where it had started to settle on the waterlogged green.

Leaving the car, Gina made a run down the garden path and hurried to the canopy over the front door then she knocked. The acrid smell caught her nostrils. Smoke. She lifted the letter box up and peered through and saw a burst of orange. The cottage was on fire. She snatched her phone from her pocket. 'This is DI Gina Harte. Ambulance, fire service and police backup at thirteen Oak Tree Walk.' As she filled the operator in, she lifted the letter box again; the smell of accelerant thick in the air. 'Hello. Mrs Meegan?'

A murmur came from the kitchen. She was in there. Gina slammed her body against the door but it wouldn't budge. She stepped onto the grass and peered through the smoky kitchen window and banged. Rain trickled down her face and almost immediately drenched her hair. She saw the tip of a tea towel flick up. Mrs Meegan was on the floor. That was a signal if ever there was one. Gina grabbed a plant pot and smashed it through the kitchen window, knocking out all the excess glass from around the edges. Removing her raincoat, she used it to brush away the glass and line the bottom of the ledge with it before hoisting her body up. Slithering head first onto the kitchen sink, she grabbed the tap and managed to drag her body in further until she could get a knee through the window. She almost choked on the thickness of the smoke. There wasn't much time. She rolled and fell onto the stone tiled floor, knocking the wind out of her lungs. Gasping, she reached around in the smoke until she could feel an arm. Now was not the time to slow down.

Eyes stinging, she grappled around, grabbing the cooker handle to help her up but instead the cooker opened, sending her stumbling back to the floor. Getting onto all fours first, she managed to stand. Pain flashed through her side where she'd landed and she felt a trickle of wetness coming from her cheek. That's when she saw Mrs Meegan's outline. Although coughing, she managed to shout the woman's name but there was no response. 'Mrs Meegan? Sandra?' Still no answer.

Gina grabbed the woman under the arms and tried to pull her along the floor towards the hall. The easiest way would be to get out the front door but flames were licking the walls, devouring everything along the way. Gina filled the jug on the draining board with cold water and poured it over Mrs Meegan. Anything to deter the flames from catching her clothes. The cracking and crunching of fire reached for the bannister as Gina dragged the woman further, narrowly missing the fire's smouldering fingers that reached for them. A sickness passed through her as she inhaled another lungful of smoke. Dry heaving and retching, she finally reached the front door and flung it open, falling out. That's when she took the hand that was held out. 'I'm fine, help Mrs Meegan.'

Jim Berry stared at the woman as if he hated her but he got a little closer and grabbed one of her arms before trying to drag her over the threshold. Gina leaned into the hall on her knees to help him while Jim grabbed the woman's other arm. As they got her to safety on the garden path, a crackling bang filled the kitchen and a lick of a flame almost reached the front door. Dragging Mrs Meegan along the rain-drenched path, Gina knew they were safely far enough away. She lay the woman down and felt for a pulse.

'Here, take this.' Jim passed his anorak to Gina, which she placed over the woman. That's when she heard sirens in the background. Help was on its way.

'Could you look out for the fire engine and ambulance and wave them down?' Jim nodded and walked to the edge of the path, looking out.

'I have it…' Mrs Meegan's face contorted in pain. Her voice barely coming out as she spoke.

'What do you have?' Gina placed her ear close to Sandra's mouth.

The woman was trying to wriggle but Gina could see her hand reaching for her pocket. 'Take it.'

Gina reached in and pulled out the photos and a memory stick that were safely nestled in the woman's pocket as she wiped the blood from her face. Sitting in the rain, she coughed and coughed until she could cough no more. 'Mrs Meegan,' she spluttered. The woman didn't answer and her head flopped to the side. As the ambulance and fire truck pulled up, she beckoned them over and lay back in the rain, exhausted but relieved that they finally had something to arrest Frank Meegan on. A sadness washed over her. Mrs Meegan had suffered enough with her accident and being married to Frank, now this. She shook her head and stood, feeling slightly wobbly. A paramedic ran over and began holding something to her cut. 'It's just a scratch. I'm fine.' And she was. There was no way she was going to hospital or anywhere for a check-up. She had photographic evidence in her hand and yet another crime scene to deal with. She stared up at the cottage as a firefighter began to spray water at the flames.

PC Smith got out of his car and ran over. 'What happened here?'

'Arson. That's what happened. When I arrived, I could smell accelerant. The fire started at the back of the house. It was coming from the lounge when I arrived. The garden and the route to it will need sealing off and Bernard will need to be called.' A coughing fit took over and she dry heaved.

'You okay? Shall I get a paramedic?'

She waved her arm. 'No, I'm good. I need to get back to the station right now while they have Frank Meegan there.' She grabbed her phone and called in the evidence she had, taking photos on her phone and sending them through straight away. Frank Meegan was not leaving tonight. 'Have you got an evidence bag?'

PC Smith ran to the police car and opened the boot before returning with a bag. 'Here you go.'

She placed the memory stick inside and sealed it. 'I need to see what's on this now. Wait here for Bernard and keep me updated. There might just be enough evidence on this to send Meegan down for a long time.'

CHAPTER FORTY-ONE

Gina removed her shirt and grabbed an old blouse that hung on the back of her office door. The smell of smoke was making her icky. There was a knock at her door. 'Gina.' Briggs burst in. She didn't even try to cover up her bra. He'd seen it all before. Instead, she reached for her deodorant and rolled the stick under her arms.

'Sir.' She smiled. 'Any news on Sandra Meegan?'

'She's suffering from smoke inhalation and has had a sedative but she's alive because of you.'

'Sedative, typical. I wanted to speak to her. I guess it will have to wait until tomorrow but she's okay. That's good news.' She coughed into a tissue then pulled her clean blouse on. 'That's better. I know I stink but I'm not leaving until I've seen what's on that memory stick. Has Frank been arrested?'

'Jacob read him his rights as soon as you got that message over to us. He's not going anywhere tonight. One of the photos you sent us was of all of the teens dancing around and it just happens that they were wearing the same clothes in that photo as when they came in and had their interviews the next morning. That photo was of the Saturday night or early Sunday morning. Meegan didn't even try to deny it. It's just a shame that his house has gone up in flames. We might never know the true extent of what he's been up to.'

'We can thank Mrs Meegan for what we do have. She'd dragged herself into the kitchen and found the photos and memory stick and she passed them to me outside the house, knowing that they would help us. Right, now that we have Meegan in custody, let's see what's on that stick. The photos are great but I want more before we present the case to the CPS.'

There was no way she was going to risk the Crown Prosecution Service not pressing ahead with a charge if they got all the evidence in order. The only thing that would add the cherry on top would be a full confession.

'Did you get checked over?'

'I'm fine. It was just a bit of smoke. I feel much better now I've had some fresh air. I really wasn't in the house that long.'

'I'm not on about the smoke, I'm on about that cut on your cheek and the other one on your arm.'

She shrugged. 'They're not that deep. I must have scratched myself when I smashed the window and climbed in.' She glanced at the mirror again. Blood had seeped out of the plaster she had put on. 'I'll grab a new plaster from first aid. It'll be fine.'

'Okay.'

New plaster on wounds and drink in hand, Gina hurried to the incident room where Briggs was sitting in front of a computer. 'Let's do this, then I want you to go home, have a shower and rest up until tomorrow.'

She grabbed a biscuit from an open pack and crunched away hoping it would take the burning taste away from her throat.

'I mean it. You're under a lot of stress with the case and the messages. We both are and I need you fresh on it again in the morning. Do you want me to bring some food over later? I know you, you'll eat a chunk of cheese and a few crisps and call that dinner.'

She stared at him for a minute as she crunched away. 'Yes. Come over, bring a takeaway and we'll work. Another set of eyes might just be what's needed.' She stared into the corner of the room.

'What?'

'I can't stop thinking about what Hannah has to say and those messages… I don't want to be alone tonight. If I'm going down—'

'Shh.' He placed his finger on her lips. 'No one is going down,' he said in a whisper as he looked around to make sure they were alone.

She continued her sentence. 'Let me finish. If I'm going down, I want to spend my last few days with you.' A tear began to spring down her cheek as reality sunk in. Warmth radiated between them. She wanted to grip him hard and sob, and she knew he wanted to hold her too, but that wasn't going to happen right now.

'Later.' He placed what would have looked like a friendly hand on her arm to anyone entering.

She smiled and wiped her eye as they glanced at the screen. He opened the first file on the memory stick, not one of them was named. 'Bingo.'

'This is sick.' After letting the video run for a few seconds, Gina looked away. She did not want to see Jordan and Naomi having sex. 'Next one.'

'That's Leah.'

They watched as Leah stared into the bushes almost like she was staring into the camera. 'Who's there?' the girl slurred as she stumbled while struggling to pull her knickers up. 'Oscar, stop being a dick and come out. If you're spying on me, I'll kill you.'

'She looks docile, like she's struggling to walk. She was on something. Either that or she's absolutely hammered. Look, she's losing her balance.' Leah stumbled to the ground.

The camera moved in closer until it was almost upon her. 'Who are you?' Then it flicks off and that is the end of the clip.

Gina looked away. 'Looks like he's our new number one suspect. I just wish that his wife hadn't covered for him in the first place, we might have saved Jordan.' She felt a rage building up inside her. Clenching her fist, she banged it down on the desk. 'He should still be alive and we let this man slip through on the word of his wife.'

'You didn't have enough evidence to bring him in.'

'We should have done something. Set up surveillance, I don't know. Anything. I've stuffed up. The press are going to be all over us.'

'There's one way to make things a bit better.'

'Really.' She rolled her eyes. 'I don't see how.'

'Let's get the case in order. Collate all the evidence and go through everything again to be certain. Speak to Mrs Meegan again in the morning and get a watertight case together to present to the CPS, all before tomorrow evening. We can do this.'

She smiled. 'We will do this.' If this was her last case, she was going out on a high. 'Bring a Chinese takeaway tonight, okay?'

'Yes. Consider it done.' Her gaze remained on his until Jacob and O'Connor entered.

O'Connor pushed the end of a pasty into his mouth and placed a tray of them on the table. 'Something from Mrs O. She thought we'd need some sustenance.'

'Not for me, Harry,' Gina said as she patted her stomach. The last thing she wanted to do was ruin her evening with Briggs by filling up on a pasty. 'Watching my figure.'

He shrugged. 'More for the rest of us. Great result.'

'It's not in the bag yet. Wait. Do you see what I see?'

'What is it?' Briggs leaned in a little closer and O'Connor stood behind her.

'In this video, Leah's top is slouching over her shoulder. See the side of her breast? The faint bite mark is there. Whoever killed her didn't bite her and we know she had sex, but with who? We need Meegan's DNA tested against the sample. Maybe something happened earlier in the evening too?' Gina carefully removed the memory stick from the computer and held it up. 'It may look like it's in the bag but I know there's more to this case and I'm going to unearth what those kids are hiding.'

CHAPTER FORTY-TWO

Hair dripping wet, Gina went into her room and sat on the edge of her bed. Having a shower had made her feel a little more human again but the smell still lingered up her nose, like it was ingrained in her. The cut on her cheek was raw and burned. She wondered if an infection was building up. The angry red outline stood out on her pale skin, pale from the shock of what the day had brought. She tilted the mirror away, not wanting to look any closer. She dabbed at her sores again with a tissue.

Her phone began to ring and Hannah's name flashed up. 'Hannah.'

'Mum, I get home from work and I have like twenty missed calls. What the hell?'

'I need to speak to you.'

'I said we'd speak on Sunday when I come and see you. I can't talk to you on the phone and Greg's just pulled up.'

'Why, Hannah? Why on earth can't you just tell me what's going on? I'm beside myself with worry.'

Hannah paused.

'Hannah?'

An uncomfortable silence passed between them.

'I'm worried.'

'So am I, Mum. Really frigging worried.'

'Please talk to me. Do you know anything about messages that have been sent to one of my colleagues?'

Hannah paused far too long to be convincing if she said no. 'What?'

Gina's brow furrowed and she heard Gracie yelling in the background as Greg walked in and mumbled something to his daughter.

'Have to go,' came Hannah's chirpy answer before the call ended. Whatever Hannah had to say, Greg wasn't privy to it and it was so serious Hannah couldn't speak about it on the phone. Someone knows what Gina did and they have told Hannah, now Hannah wants to have it out with her. Gina's mind whirled. It had to be Terry's misogynist brother, Stephen, or maybe his deluded mother, Hetty, who had no idea how violent and abusive her precious Terry was. But... how on earth would either of them get hold of Briggs's number? She threw her phone onto the pillow and grabbed her hair, pulling a few strands out as she roared in frustration. Her days as a free woman were seriously numbered. Lying to everyone around her was one thing, but her daughter. If Hannah were to come out and ask what happened on the night her father died, could Gina stick with the same story she'd shared over the years? Everything would come out and Gina didn't know if she had the strength to deny it any longer. Keeping secrets is mentally exhausting and it eats away at you, bit by bit, until you no longer recognise who you are. Gina turned the mirror to face her again and stared long and hard. Who was she?

She pressed the Twitter app and looked at the chain of tweets that contained the last menacing tweet. An account made up of random numbers had just made a post. Three broken hearts. She refreshed and then it vanished.

A car pulled up on her drive. She ran down the stairs knowing what little time she may have left needed to be used wisely and there was something she needed right now, more than anything. Opening the door, Briggs greeted her with a takeaway bag. She dropped it on the floor and dragged him in by his collar, pressing her lips hard onto his in the hallway as she pushed the door closed.

He went to speak but she held her hand over his mouth. She didn't want to hear a single thing that would take this moment away. 'Don't say a word,' she whispered in his ear.

They made their way into the lounge, leaving a trail of clothes behind them, desperately grabbing each other, stopping at nothing.

When you can't see a future, you take what you have right now. That is exactly what she was doing and she was going to enjoy every moment before her world came crashing down.

CHAPTER FORTY-THREE

Wednesday, 4 August

Caro checked her phone again. It was now two in the morning. She listened to her father's snores in the far bedroom.

Slipping out of bed, she pulled her jeans up her legs and threw on a T-shirt and hoodie. With shaking hands, she took the long metal nail file from her bedside table and popped it in her backpack. She wasn't going to meet some unknown person in the middle of the night without some form of defence but she had to know who was messaging her and, most of all, they had something to tell her and she had to know exactly what that was. She pressed her lips together and swallowed. She wondered if she could actually hurt someone with a nail file if it came to her having to defend herself from being murdered. The thought of pushing metal through someone's skin almost made her gag. Time to go.

Step by step she soon reached her bedroom door, avoiding the squeaky floorboard next to her wardrobe. If that rattled, then so would her wardrobe and her mum was a light sleeper. Caro would then be rumbled. Gently, she pushed the door handle and eased it open before stepping out. She exhaled as her dad's snores continued.

'Caught you.' Jake turned on his torch as he stood outside the bathroom door, the torch he used for going to the loo in the night. He laughed and lit up his face under his chin.

She kneeled down and almost pressed her lips against his ear to whisper back. 'Jake, I need you to not say a thing, okay?'

He whispered back. 'Three bags of Haribo?' That was his price.

Caro put a thumb up and he watched her go. One step at a time, she reached the bottom of the stairs and saw right through the kitchen window. The handlebars of her bike glinted in the moonlight. It was exactly where she'd left it, propped up against the fence. It would take too long to walk to her meeting point. Turning the lock in the back door, she flinched as it clicked open. Heading out into the garden, she grabbed her bike and started cycling down the path, through the estates in the direction of the woodland. As she listened out for the river in the background, an owl hooted from the tall trees above. Flinching, she stopped just before the thicket and stared into what was pitch-black night as a fox darted across the path only to vanish behind a tree. A branch snapped and her phone lit up with a Snapchat message.

Follow the sounds.

It wasn't an owl. It was a person hooting. She leaned her bike against the thick bark of an ancient oak tree, her heart racing as she waited for another signal. It never came. Pulling the nail file from her rucksack, she took a step into the darkness. Mouth watering and stomach flipping, she stopped, knowing that continuing was a dangerous move but the need to know was a powerful lure.

Why are you stopping? Just a bit further. Come on or are you chickenshit scared?

She was scared. Her messenger had that right. She was scared of being attacked. She was scared that Jake would tell and she feared her mother's reaction. The message vanished off the screen. With sweaty hands, she held out the nail file and inched forward.

A rustling of leaves culminated in a dark figure emerging from the bushes, setting Caro's senses on full alert. Her heart boomed as adrenalin raced through her body. She brought the nail file round and pierced the person's skin then ran. There was no way she was ending up like Jordan or Leah. The figure went to grab her but she pushed so hard, the person toppled giving her the advantage she needed. Blood thumped through her body and her head went light. If she passed out here and now, this person could do who knows what to her just like that night at the party. They all did things to her and still she couldn't remember everything. She ran on her shaky legs, pushing through every branch until she reached her bike. Without glancing back, she rode away, needing to get home and back into bed.

As she reached her back gate, her phone lit up again.

You shouldn't have done that!!!!! Bitch. You're dead!

Then, the message disappeared. Caro knew no more than she had earlier and now, with an uncontrollable tremble, she entered the kitchen and locked the door before leaning back on it and hyperventilating. A shuffle came from the hallway and a dark figure entered.

Tears spilled down her cheeks. 'Go away.'

Jake stepped forward. 'Did you get my Haribo?'

She pulled her little brother close and hugged him, knowing but not caring that he'd feel her banging heart against the side of his head. 'Tomorrow. We need to both go back to bed quietly. Don't wake Mum and Dad.'

'Okay.' She held his hand and guided him back up the stairs in the dark and still her dad snored. Relief and fear washed over her. When she got into her room, she turned on her bedside lamp, that's when she saw the blood trail down her hand. She had stabbed a person. She popped the nail file under her bed, hiding it away for now. The one thing she still lacked was answers but she now knew that she was looking for someone with an injured leg. Did she stab him hard enough? Who knows? *Bitch. You're dead!* Who was trying to kill her? She shivered, cleaned the blood from her fingers with one of her make-up wipes and slipped back into bed but she knew she wouldn't sleep. Someone out there wanted her dead; she knew that for definite now. Listening to the rustling trees outside, she wondered if he was there, watching; and even angrier now that she'd hurt him.

CHAPTER FORTY-FOUR

The sun was coming up over Cleevesford General. The rain had cleared leaving a cloudless blue sky. Gina spotted Jacob's car and gave him a wave. After a shaky start, Briggs had helped to calm her down and now, she had to focus. Nailing Meegan was everything and tonight, just maybe, she'd have a chance to really rest up or maybe she'd finally get Hannah to talk to her. She felt her heart humming away. *Forget Hannah, for now.*

'Alright, guv.' Jacob waved.

'All good.' She jogged a little to catch up with him and they headed through the entrance door into the long corridor that led to the wards. A cleaner was mopping ahead, the smell of disinfectant catching Gina's nostrils. 'I hate the clinical smell of hospitals.'

'Me too, guv. Talking about hospitals, did you get your cuts looked at?'

She scrunched her nose. 'No.'

'That one on your cheek still looks a bit red.'

'It'll be fine. I only did it yesterday so it will look red.'

He shrugged. 'It looks like it's becoming infected. You might need some antibiotics.'

'Will it make you happy if I book an appointment with my doctor when we get out of here?'

'Yes. You need to before it goes gungy and green and it starts to eat away at your face and you have no cheek—'

She jokingly tapped his arm. 'You've made your point. Shut up now or you'll put me off breakfast.'

As they reached the ward Mrs Meegan was in, Gina pressed the buzzer and stared through the glass window.

A nurse buzzed them in. 'No visiting on this ward until ten thirty.'

They held up their IDs and Gina smiled. 'We're here to see Sandra Meegan. She was brought in yesterday after a fire at her house.'

'I see.' The nurse picked up a clipboard, her nurses fob watch brushing the page as she leaned over. 'She's in bed four which is in a side room. I think one of your PCs asked that she be put in one for a bit of privacy, ready for when you came to speak with her.' The nurse pointed. 'It's that one there. Knock and wait for her to call you in. She's a little sleepy as she asked for sleeping tablets last night after the sedative and she slept like a log.'

'Thank you.' Jacob followed Gina over. She knocked on the window and glanced through to the room. Sandra lay facing the window, not turning to acknowledge the knock. Gina pushed the door open. 'Mrs Meegan? It's DI Harte and DS Driscoll. May we come in?'

A few sobs came from Sandra and she pulled the sheet up to her chin, using it to wipe her eyes. 'I've lost everything.' Sandra paused. 'I knew you'd want to speak to me.'

'I'm so sorry.' Gina sat on the plastic chair next to the bed and tilted her head so that Sandra had to look at her. 'Mrs Meegan?'

'Can you call me Sandy?' The woman began to hack and cough. 'The smoke, it's on my chest.'

'Sandy, what you did yesterday was nothing short of heroic. You must have really struggled to get those photos and the memory stick but you did the right thing in giving those to me.'

'The right thing for who? I have no home now, no husband, nothing. It's all gone. Do you know who burnt my house down?'

'Sorry. Forensics have been and I'm hoping to speak to them later. Uniform would have interviewed your neighbours. There's nothing for me to inform you of yet but as soon as I know something, I will let you know. I promise. Would you mind me asking you a few questions about your husband and the fire?'

She sniffed and shook her head. 'I need to sit up? I'm all crunched over.'

'Do you need any assistance?'

'No thanks.' She rolled onto her back and used her arms to hoist herself into place, then she grabbed a tissue and blew her nose.

'Can we start with your husband?'

'Yes, I do have some things to share with you. That night, when the girl was murdered, I heard Frank go out of the sliding doors in the lounge in the early hours of Sunday morning. I'm really sorry I didn't tell you.' She paused and gripped the sheet. 'He was angry when I asked him about it and I didn't want to make him any angrier. He made out that he was really upset that I was basically accusing him of murder just because of a stupid mistake years ago. I knew there was more to it and my wheelchair won't fit through the doors of the kitchen, which is why I was on the floor. I knew he was hiding something in there and I had to find out what. And I kept your card in my pocket. If I found anything I was going to call you, I just wanted proof.' She swallowed and another tear slid down her cheek.

'You're doing really well.'

'I really wanted to call you before but he takes my phone off me all the time and leaves it in the kitchen where I can't get to it. It's like a control thing. He won't let me have friends and I barely leave the house. I don't want to live like this anymore.' She sobbed.

'It's okay, Sandy. You don't have to.'

'Really? Where am I going to go after all this? My family don't want to know me because I stood by Frank after his conviction. I have a sister but she always hated Frank. She thought he was a creepy sleaze and I guess she was right all along. I gave up everyone for him. What a big mistake.'

'I'll contact the council. Someone will be able to discuss temporary accommodation with you. You will need somewhere safe to go when you're discharged.'

'Thank you.'

'Did you know that another boy was murdered in the early hours of Tuesday morning?'

Sandra shook her head. 'No.'

'It was a boy who was also at the party on the night Leah Fenmore was murdered. I know you had reporters outside the front of your house and there were a few protesters. What was Frank doing that night?'

Shaking, Sandra reached for her cup of water and sipped. 'He slipped out the back and left me on my own all night.'

Jacob scribbled away, making notes.

'Can you remember when he left and when he got home?'

'He left around teatime on Monday evening and didn't come back until about ten in the morning, the next day.'

'Did he say where he'd been all that time?'

'He said he needed to be alone, to clear his head.' Her voice got croakier with each sentence until some of the words she spoke were being eaten up by the frog in her throat.

Gina knew that gave him opportunity. Maybe Jordan saw him on the night of Leah's murder so Frank needed to shut him up. It was possible that Jordan was blackmailing him. There was no evidence of that on Jordan's phone. Gina had seen all his messages. Most were smutty jokes and arrangements for parties and outings. He did however have the Snapchat app and those messages would have disappeared.

'Did your husband say anything else that you think might help us?'

She shook her head.

'You know that him withholding your phone and leaving you trapped like that is a form of abuse. Does it happen often?'

She nodded, her bottom lip trembling. 'He's always nasty to me. Says I ruined his life with my injury and I always feel guilty. I did ruin his life. I chose to jump off a cliff when I'd been drinking. I'd been arguing with Frank over what he'd put me through with his conviction and I saw the locals diving in. He told me not to be stupid and that I was drunk but I didn't listen, feeling for once that I was in charge of what I did and he couldn't tell me what to do. I knew straight away, as soon as my legs hit the rocks beneath the sea. It was as though I'd been struck by lightning. The next thing I remember was waking up in hospital. The locals had pulled me out. Frank took the news that my legs would never work again. To begin with, he promised to be there for me. Now I think about it, he was always an abusive angry person. I wasn't really allowed friends and he pushed me around a little, mostly when he was drunk. I was never good enough for him and now I know why. He got his kicks by spying on unknowing people. I was just his normal life cover-up story and now this has happened. Two dead kids. It's all my fault. I should have said something when you asked before. Maybe it would have stopped at one dead kid. That second one is on me and I have to live with that forever.'

Gina swallowed a lump in her throat. Living with extreme guilt was the absolute pits.

'I just want to die.'

Gina scrunched her brow and swallowed. 'None of this is your fault. It's Mr Meegan's fault. We're going to make sure you get the help you need to move forward from this.'

'Won't there be a trial at which I'll have to relive all this again?'

Gina nodded. 'I'm so sorry. Unless he pleads guilty you would be called to give evidence if he's charged.'

'I will do it and I really want to do the right thing now. I owe it to the families of those kids. I have to do the best I can.'

'You're doing really well but I'd like to talk about the fire too. Can you tell me about the run up to it?'

She took a deep breath. 'The protesters had been around in the morning but the heavens opened up and they left. It was tipping it down and I was stuck in my bed, as usual.'

'Can you identify the protesters?'

'Not all of them. I've given the police officer that was here earlier a list of the neighbours who were there and, thinking about it, I didn't mention Lara Blakely who I went to school with. I met up with her again this week in the supermarket and we spoke. It all changed when the news about Frank's past came out. She went from friendly to total hate and pitched up outside chanting hate with the mob.'

'Blakely, I recognise that name.' Gina glanced up at Jacob who flicked through his notes.

'The mother of one of the kids we spoke to, guv.'

'She said she had a daughter and a little boy.'

Gina made a mental note to speak to Lara Blakely in connection with the fire. 'Okay, so what happened after that?'

'They were shouting things like paedophile and I just wanted to hide away. Like I said, when the rain came, they went away. The noise had quietened down so I lifted the curtains up and couldn't see anyone. I saw Jim Berry leaving his house. He got into his car and drove off. Not long after, Frank came back then he got a call from you and said he had to leave again. Only this time, he left the bedroom door open.' Sandy shook her head. 'Last night, he shut me in and pulled the sideboard against the other side of my bedroom door to make sure I couldn't get out. When he left, he forgot. That's when I decided to get to the kitchen. Once there, I searched the bottom cupboards and drawers. That's when I found the photos. I laid them out on the floor before putting some of them and the memory stick into my pocket. Then, I heard the sound of a window smashing from the living room and I got a hit of chemical smell. I think it was petrol but it could have been something else. I knew what was going to happen. I began to shuffle in the direction of the hall but the smoke filled the place quicker than the fire did. I'm sure I heard it taking the armchair and the settee. I… that was it. I thought I was dead.' She swallowed and closed her eyes for a second. 'Then you came in and pulled me out. I half remember hearing Jim Berry at the door so he must have come back from wherever he was.'

Gina wondered if the man had popped to the petrol station to fill up a can before setting fire to the Meegans' cottage. But then, Lara Blakely was angry enough to protest outside all morning. 'Did you see or hear anyone else at the time the fire was started?'

Sandra shook her head and leaned back. 'No. I just know that someone wants to kill me and the worst thing is, I get it. They think I'm a threat to their children, just like Frank is. From now on, I will always be that child murderer's wife, the one who might have known. The one who might have been in on it.'

'That's not true. You found evidence and came forward.'

'Try telling that to the angry mob.'

Gina inwardly agreed with her. Sandra wasn't in the best of places.

'There's something else.'

'Okay?' Gina waited for Sandy to answer.

'A reporter, someone called Pete, I think. He was being really horrible to me, shouting through the letter box. He asked if I got off on hurting kids before telling me that he had kids. He sounded really angry.'

A few tears escaped and Sandra wiped her eyes. 'The worst thing is, I wouldn't hurt anyone, let alone kids. I haven't got it in me and I hated what Frank did in the past. I hated it but I also loved him, I needed him… I'm such a fool. I should have got out then and come back here on my own to start a new life. We would never have gone on that holiday. I could have changed my name, met someone else. Life could have been so different.

Stupid, stupid, stupid…' Sandra slammed her knuckles into the bedside cabinet over and over again until Gina grabbed them.

'Please, you're hurting yourself.'

'I. Don't. Care. I deserve to be hurt.' She carried on banging until her fists were bleeding, then she yelled and screamed.

A nurse ran in. 'I'm going to have to ask you to leave. Now.'

'Sandra, I'm sorry. I'll pop by to see you again.'

The woman sobbed and slumped back as the nurse came by her side. 'Please just get Frank out of my life. He's a murderer. He hurt those kids. I didn't know.'

Gina felt a shiver around her neck. Seeing Mrs Meegan break down like that had set her heart pounding. All she saw was a desperate woman, controlled and manipulated by Meegan, who had lost everything over the past few days. The nurse held her hand up, gesturing for Gina and Jacob to hurry up out of the way.

As they reached the hospital entrance, Gina leaned against the wall where the smokers were standing and took a few deep breaths.

'That was intense.' Jacob ran his hand across the top of his head.

'Some people just go around ruining other people's lives regardless of the consequences. We have all we need to charge Meegan. One more interview and we'll do just that. Can you organise for Lara Blakely to come in? We can't drop the ball when it comes to the arson attack. Sandra Meegan could have died and we'd be looking for another murderer. Another thing, I want our reporter, Pete Bloxwich, brought in to be questioned over the arson. I don't like the way he's conducting himself with the parents and Mrs Meegan. He sounds a bit of a creep.'

Gina grabbed her phone and called the station. O'Connor answered. 'Hi. We're on our way back. Can you ask Ellyn to be there, see if the family liaison officers have anything to report from last night? Also, Wyre and Kapoor spoke to Oscar Spalding again. We need a briefing before we continue.' She ended the call and turned to Jacob. 'My visit to the doc's will have to wait. I can't sit by and wait for another one of the teens to be murdered so charging Frank Meegan is a must. There's no way he's walking this afternoon. I'll meet you back at the station.'

'See you there.'

Gina's mind flashed back to the interview with Caro Blakely, her mother in attendance. Lara Blakely clearly stated that if anyone hurt her daughter, she'd kill them. Gina had dismissed it as throwaway at the time. She'd heard a lot of parents whose children had been hurt say that very thing but Lara had been at the Meegans' cottage all morning. Had she stuck around thinking that Frank Meegan was in and taken the opportunity to set fire to their property? Maybe the reporter had taken matters into his own hands. The whole case stunk like a great big burnt-out house. She needed to clear the air to see the truth.

CHAPTER FORTY-FIVE

'Right, team. Gather round.' Gina stood at the head of the table quenching her dry throat with a glass of cold water. 'Quick catch up then I'm going in there. The evidence is now stacked against Meegan for the murders of Leah and Jordan. The only cherry on the top would be some forensic evidence but so far we have none. That doesn't mean that none will turn up, it's just that there is so much to analyse from the scene which Bernard and the team are working through. What we have now is Mrs Meegan. She claims that her husband slipped out on the night of Leah's murder and he wasn't with her at the time Jordan was murdered either. That now makes him our prime suspect.'

Ellyn pulled a seat up but stayed near the back of the room as she played with the ends of her hair. She squinted as a shaft of sunlight caught her eye.

Wyre tucked her chair in and began eating a banana. 'He's refusing to say anymore until his solicitor arrives, which should be anytime now. The press have already convicted him if you check out what is being reported on their social media. This thing is about to explode.'

Gina brought the briefing back on track. Trying to ignore the media for now was her plan. The last thing she needed was for them and their sensationalist stories to interfere with her trains of thought. 'Okay, how did it go with Oscar Spalding? Did his father let you get a word in?'

PC Kapoor rolled her eyes and O'Connor leaned back.

Wyre continued. 'Kapoor and I went over last night and I spoke to him about Jordan. Mr Spalding clearly didn't want his son to speak. We were almost shoved out of the door.'

'That rings true. It wasn't much different when Jacob and I spoke to him.'

'He said that he and his son had the best security alarm system going and that no one would be able to get in or out if they didn't have the right fobs or weren't buzzed in. I felt that Oscar wanted to say something but his father shut him down at every opportunity. He seemed upset about Jordan's murder. We offered to have a panic button installed in their home but Mr Spalding turned that down too.'

'Did you look around?'

'We were led into the first lounge and that was as far as we ventured. There was something.'

'Okay?'

'Oscar seemed to flinch when he sat, like he was in some sort of pain but I couldn't see any injury. He rubbed his leg but that could be anything. I asked him if he was okay.'

'And.' Gina dabbed the cut on her cheek with a tissue. The seeping had stopped, for now.

'He started saying that he knocked into the patio furniture but his father told him to shut up and that what I was asking wasn't relevant to the case. He said his son wouldn't speak again without a solicitor present and that we had to leave immediately.'

'Leg injury? We'll bear that in mind.' Gina ringed Oscar's name on the board. 'Ellyn, thank you for collating all the information from the FLOs. Can you update us on that? Please, tuck in a bit. You're one of the team.'

O'Connor shifted his chair to the side, making room at the end of the table. He offered her a biscuit but she smiled and shook her head.

Ellyn pressed her glossed lips together before starting. 'Naomi Carpenter and Elsa James's families were much more receptive to our presence than Oscar's by the sound of it. Elsa's family were genuinely scared and took up the offer of a panic button. My colleague stayed until around eleven and had nothing unusual to report. There were tears and fear that Elsa or one of the others could be next.'

'Did she speak about the night of Leah's murder?'

'She didn't say much other than what is already in the file. She also hasn't posted on social media since the day of Leah's murder. The family seemed supportive of each other. The FLO did report that she overheard a phone call between Elsa and another person where Elsa had reiterated that she hadn't said anything about the weed, but that was all.'

'Not much more to go on then. How about Naomi Carpenter?'

'I was with them until about midnight before the family finally decided that they were going to bed. I offered to get someone to stay but they felt they'd be safe in their home. They didn't want a panic button but were happy about the drive-bys. I don't know what it was about Naomi, I kept catching her staring at me, like she was analysing me. I noticed she was tapping on her phone all night. I tried to joke with her about the tapping in the hope that she'd find it funny and open up a little but she just left the room and went upstairs. Later on, I went to the toilet and heard her speaking on the phone, referring to some argument and that she wished she'd never said certain things to Leah.'

'We know something caused Leah to want to leave the party and go home. Did she elaborate or do you know who she was speaking to?'

'No but her voice was raised. She told the other person on the call that they couldn't say anything. Then the call ended.'

'Did you see her after that?'

'I tapped on her door and asked if she was okay as I'd heard her shouting. She said it was nothing and she was just joking around on the phone with a friend. I tried to get her to elaborate but she said she was tired and upset about Jordan and she wanted to go to sleep. Her mother came up and took over. I tried to say that if she knew something or that someone was upsetting her that we could help but she said that no one was upsetting her and that she was fine. Her mother ushered me out at that point. That's when I left the house, just after that. I did notice a tissue on her bedside that looked like it had dabs of dried-up blood on it. She said she always had nosebleeds when she was stressed and hearing the news about Jordan and Leah had brought one on.'

'What is your instinct, from being there?'

'Something happened that night and they're keeping tight-lipped. Whether it caused or led to Leah being murdered, I don't know.'

Gina sighed. 'I feel like we're getting nowhere but then again, given that we have so much on Frank Meegan, what they are hiding possibly has nothing to do with Leah's and Jordan's murders. I need to interview Frank. It's time to put everything to him. Can you please check whether his solicitor has arrived?' Gina glanced at O'Connor.

He picked his phone up and called Nick, the desk sergeant, and nodded. 'Just coming through the door. She wants to talk with him first then he can be interviewed. He said he'll see her to interview room four.'

Gina exhaled. 'Great. Just to update you, Jacob and I saw Sandra Meegan this morning. She has confirmed that Frank Meegan left the house on the night of Leah's murder and was gone all night when Jordan was murdered. I need you all looking into the arson case on the Meegans' property as I'm not ruling out that the incidents are all related. I've briefly updated the system and as you know I want Jim Berry and Lara Blakely interviewed. Jacob and I will take Lara. Wyre and O'Connor, can you take Jim? There's someone else I want to interview too, a reporter for the *Warwickshire Herald*, Pete Bloxwich. He was giving Mrs Meegan a hard time. She said that he was shouting through her letter box, asking her if she got off on hurting kids and telling her that he had kids. She said that he sounded really angry. This is going beyond a reporter trying to get a story and the fact that he came across as threatening makes him a suspect too.' Gina stood up straight and smiled. 'Right, let's keep this momentum going with Meegan. We may just have solved the murder case.'

Gina swallowed as everyone went about their business. Frank Meegan was the obvious choice. He had opportunity and a past, which might suggest he got caught watching Leah and decided that he wasn't going down again. It would benefit him if she was dead. It's possible that Jordan saw him there that night and could have identified him. That would be a motive for Meegan to take him out of the equation too. But why would Jordan turn up in the middle of the night to meet Meegan? Blackmail? Deception – did he think he was meeting someone else? Was it all too tidy that Meegan did it? Gina was about to find out. She gulped down her water and headed to her office in preparation for the interview, the one that could nail Meegan.

CHAPTER FORTY-SIX

Caro yawned as she turned in bed, bright sunshine beating through her curtains. She glanced at the time. It was gone eleven in the morning. Tormented by dreams of someone creeping up behind her, coming from nowhere, had woken her several times; rendering her exhausted. Her mystery messenger still had no face. Was he a harbinger of death? Some creepy night-time beast trying to lure her to her own murder. She reached under her bed. The nail file was still there but the blood had dried up. She'd stabbed someone and that someone was going to attack her again – she knew it. The more she thought about how she met up with this mystery person, the more stupid she felt. She'd put herself at risk; big time. They told her where and when to meet them and they were waiting.

Her phone flashed. She gulped, hoping it wasn't another mystery Snapchat message but it was just Anthony.

I'm sorry about not doing more when they roofied you. Friends?

His message vanished, the same as the menacing messages she'd been receiving. It was so obvious that she'd been drugged. The missing pieces, the mega hangover, the nausea, the half-remembered bits of the night. Anthony and Jordan fighting. She trusted them but they abused her trust. She'd never have agreed to drug them. A moment passed through her thoughts. She remembered stumbling into the next tent and being pushed out. Words were said and that's the bit she was really struggling to recall. She knew who was in there and what was happening but the last piece was still missing.

Jake burst through the door and dived on her bed, hurting her arm. 'Mum wants you downstairs now and if you don't get my sweets, I'll tell her you went out last night.'

'I'll get them later, I promise.' On an ordinary day, she'd march him out the door and tell him where to go but he now had leverage. Instead, she shifted her squashed arm from underneath his wriggling body, turning away from his sour morning breath. Her mother could never know that she'd left the house to meet someone unknown. She'd go berserk and ground her, not to mention lecture her on the dangers. She was sick of being lectured and she was sick of being grounded by her parents for the smallest of things.

Grabbing her phone, Jake began pressing buttons and grinned as he took a selfie.

'Give that back.'

'I was just going to play a game.'

'Go and play with your own things.'

'Caro.' Her mother's voice boomed up the stairs.

She dragged herself out of the bed, stretching as she opened her curtains.

'Caro!'

'Coming.' She and Jake hurried down. 'I'm not even dressed yet.'

Her mother scrunched her brow and stared. 'Your pyjama top is on the wrong way.'

A consequence of dressing in the dark while shaken up. She shrugged, hoping that her mother would say no more about it.

'I have to go out in a bit and I need you to look after your brother. Your dad's at work and can't get back to sit with him.'

'Do I have to? What's so urgent?'

'Yes you do, he's your brother and he isn't booked in with the childminder today. I have to go to the police station. They want to talk to me.'

The sun shone through her mother's hair, giving the dry ends a salmon pink twinge. Caro gulped. 'Why?' Blood thrummed through her head. She rubbed her temples, willing her anxiety to not give her away.

'I don't know yet but they've insisted. So you and Jake can do something fun, like bake some cupcakes.'

The last thing Caro wanted to do on a sweltering day was bake cupcakes with her annoying little brother. She wanted to go back to bed and sleep until the afternoon. She paused. Her mum looked at her without saying a word for about a minute and it felt weird. Was her mum being called about the last party that Caro had attended? The police were closing in and they would all end up in trouble. Had someone seen her sneaking out last night? One of the other's had blabbed. Maybe Anthony was so consumed by the guilt of letting her get roofied, he told the police. But he would have called her to warn her. They were close enough as friends to not allow surprises like that to happen. One of the others has said something. That must be it. But who? Elsa couldn't keep off social media when the body was found and she gossiped about everyone at school. It had to be her. She normally thrived on drama. Besides, it was she who dared Jordan to smash a few side mirrors off the parked cars in the village area. That's it, the police must know about the fighting and the dares, and all those bad things they did. They were in big trouble. She forced a smile. 'Okay, cupcakes it is.' It would take more than a batch of buttercreamed cakes to diffuse her mum's anger when the full story came out but it was worth a try.

'Yeah!' Jake ran around the kitchen screaming with joy as Caro stared at her bike, out of the window. She'd left the gate unlocked after coming back in the night. That's something her mother would notice.

Lara went towards the sink with her glass. 'I'll get you some water, Mum. You've got a lot on today.' Caro beamed a wide smile.

'Thank you.' Her mother eyed her with suspicion.

Caro filled the glass and passed it back to her.

'Right, I best get ready. Can't turn up in my nightshirt.'

As soon as her mother left the room, Caro hurried out and bolted the gate before her mother reached her bedroom window. At least that secret was safe, pending the three bags of sweets she still owed Jake. He stared at her and smiled as he pointed to his mouth and made a zipping motion. A Snapchat message flashed up on her phone and her fingers quivered as she opened it.

U r gonna pay for what u did! Slag.

'What is it?' Jake asked as Caro sharply inhaled.

'Nothing. Just check to see if we have any icing sugar. We can make a list of what we need from the shop.' She glanced out of the window, trying to peer through the gaps in the fence. Someone wearing a dark top hurried away and Caro's heart felt like it had stopped for a few seconds.

CHAPTER FORTY-SEVEN

Before entering interview room four, Gina knocked and entered the viewing room next to it. 'I'm going in now.'

Briggs smiled as he watched through the one-way glass. Meegan was sitting rigidly and biting his nails, his hairy stomach on show where his T-shirt was too short. Tiny beads of sweat glistened on his forehead and nose.

Gina entered, followed by Jacob. Both sat without saying a word until Jacob started rolling the tape and introducing everyone; notepad coming out. 'It's now thirteen forty-five.'

'Mr Meegan, we have some developments in the case.' Gina kept the brown file in front of her closed for now. His stare fell onto it.

'I want to know how my wife is or I'm not speaking.'

The solicitor cleared her throat. Black jacket despite the boiling hot weather and hair in a neat grey bun with lipstick so red it felt like it was filling the usually gloomy room with a burst of colour. 'My client is worried about his wife and has the right to an update before we continue. Not only is she injured, he's lost his home.'

Gina placed her hand on the table. 'I saw Mrs Meegan this morning and apart from a bad chest and cough from the smoke inhalation, she was fine. She spoke to me and sat up. We are working with the council to help find some suitable temporary accommodation for her to go to once she is discharged.'

He glanced to the side and then back. 'So she wasn't hurt at all?'

'No, thankfully I was on my way over to speak to her before the fire reached her.'

'But the house is burnt down?'

'I'm afraid there has been substantial damage to your house.'

Mr Meegan exhaled and Jacob made a couple of notes. His solicitor whispered in his ear and he cleared his throat. He barely looked as concerned as he was making out.

'So moving on, I went to speak to Mrs Meegan this morning, I'm going to put some questions to you.'

Again the solicitor whispered, her long, thin fingers hiding her mouth from the mirror behind Gina and Jacob.

'Okay. I just want to help clear all this up as I didn't hurt or kill anyone.'

'Did you leave your house at all between midnight and two on the morning of Sunday the first of August?'

'No. My wife already said that I was in with her all night. I had no reason to go out.'

Gina bit her bottom lip, wanting to smile but holding back. Mrs Meegan had already dismantled his use of her as an alibi. Now onto Jordan's murder. 'Did you leave your house at all between one and four in the morning on Tuesday the third of August?'

'No, I was at home. You'd interviewed me and the bloody residents were protesting on the path outside my house all day, making a right nuisance of themselves. I paid for my crime all those years ago and I never once murdered any one and I'm not a paedophile, but that doesn't matter to scum like them, does it? So much for your drive-bys keeping us safe. The moment I leave to come here, to help you as requested, my wife is almost set on fire. That's how safe we are. Those protesting bastards tried to kill us both.'

'This morning, Mrs Meegan made a statement that you were out of the house at both of those times I just asked you about and that you told her not to say anything.'

'No! That's not true. She's making it up. My wife loves a bit of drama. I have this problem with her all the time. Since her accident, she craves attention and she was angry with me for not charging her phone. We had a row, that's all.'

'The problem with your claim here, Mr Meegan, is that Mrs Meegan actually presented us with irrefutable evidence. Do you understand the charge of perverting the course of justice?'

He nodded, a tremor forming at his fingers. Quickly burying his hands in his lap, he let out a huff sound.

'For the tape, Mr Meegan nodded. He's aware that not telling the truth or misleading us could have serious consequences.' His solicitor tensed her shoulders and leaned in to whisper to him again, taking a few notes after. 'I'm going to show you some photos and you're going to explain how you got them.' Gina opened the file and pulled out a photo of all the kids at the camp and the other one of Leah on her own. 'See this photo, the one of the kids all together, they are all wearing the same clothes that they were wearing on Sunday morning. What a coincidence.'

'What, these? I found them.'

'I will now add that we have a memory stick with recordings of the same teens and many others, at different times and during different parties.'

He slumped back and sighed. 'That stupid cow.' Gina knew he was referring to Mrs Meegan.

'At one point, we hear your voice over the top of the film, whispering to yourself, telling one of the girls to turn around. Leah Fenmore saw you and knowing you'd go straight back to prison with a longer sentence this time had you thinking, didn't it? With the poor girl being drunk, possibly even having taken drugs and separated from her friends, you seized your opportunity and strangled her to death. It was easy, wasn't it? In her state, she didn't fight back.' Gina leaned in and stared directly into Meegan's eyes.

'No, that didn't happen. I just took photos, that's all.'

'And you filmed, and then you killed Leah.'

'I took the films but I didn't kill her. Happy now!' He stood and slammed his hands on the table. As he exhaled, beads of sweat dribbled past his brow.

Gina passed him the box of tissues. 'Sit down, Mr Meegan.' She stared at him for a few seconds. 'The thing is, one of the other kids saw you. Jordan Rolph.' Gina slid a photo of Jordan wearing a rugby top. 'You lured him to this area on the night of his murder.' Gina pulled out a map and pointed out the location on the map. 'An area of outstanding natural beauty, apparently. Once there, you took him by surprise and kicked him down the steps, resulting in him receiving a cracked skull that killed him. All that to cover your tracks.'

'Ha, I can prove I didn't do it. I wasn't there.' He prodded the map. 'Yes, I left my wife alone and I'm sorry I lied but I knew how it was going to go. You lot hate me already.'

'Mr Meegan, we just want the truth.'

'I drove way out of the area where no one knows me and I checked into a hotel for the night. It all got too much and I needed to be away from all the people outside. I thought they'd kill me and that my wife would be safer on her own. They don't hate her. I'm the real target.'

'Okay, so where were you?'

'The Splendid Hotel in Worcester. There were security cameras in the car park and I parked at the front. I checked in after driving around for a while and I stayed there all night. You have to call them.'

'Don't worry, we will.' Gina slammed the file shut and the solicitor began once again gesturing and whispering with Meegan. If CCTV could prove he was at that hotel all night, then her theory would be blown out of the water. 'In the meantime, we'll be bringing charges against you for the recordings and photos.'

'As you can see, my client is innocent of murder.'

'That has yet to be verified but I'll let you know when we've been in touch with the hotel and received the recordings.'

'When they come through, I'd like to request bail for my client.' She tapped her long red nails on the desk and smiled.

'I'll keep you informed.'

'Thank you.'

'What if I can help you?' Meegan was clutching at straws, Gina could see desperation all over his face.

'You saw something while you were there, didn't you?' That was the next line of enquiry and she'd humour him for now even though she hadn't spoken to the hotel as yet.

'Can you put a word in for me, if I help you? I didn't hurt anyone after all.'

Gina furrowed her brow. 'I beg to differ. Filming people doing private things does hurt them. How about you help me because a sixteen-year-old girl was strangled to death and a boy was kicked down some steps to his death. Their parents and friends will never see them again and they are devastated, as you can imagine. There is a very dangerous person out there and they might kill again. Do the right thing, Mr Meegan.'

'I have to think about myself too, damn it!'

'I'll mention that you were cooperative to the CPS. That's all I can do.'

The solicitor nodded to him.

'Okay, I didn't see anything but I heard something. Someone else was shuffling around behind me but they were too far away and the foliage was thick. Not to mention it was the middle of the night. They must have stayed hidden. I caught a flash of what could have been black or grey material, maybe a T-shirt or knitwear but, as I say, it was night. The stars and moon don't give much light in that part of the woods, what with all the tall trees. That spooked me so I left and went home. I thought one of the kids had seen me and I just wanted to get away. I hurried back, locked the patio doors and went straight to bed.'

A description of the black material found at the scene of Jordan's murder was springing to the forefront of her mind. First things first, she had to properly eliminate Meegan. 'Do you wear dentures or have any missing teeth?'

He scrunched up his nose. 'Yeah, all my wisdom teeth gave me trouble and they're gone and three from the bottom row.' He opened his mouth and pulled out his false three, spit stringing from the plastic plate.

They were the wrong teeth to match the bite mark on Leah's breast and she wanted him to hurry and put them back in before she heaved. 'Okay, thank you. Interview terminated at fourteen twenty-five.' She glanced at the man as he and his solicitor began to talk about Mrs Meegan and his house. He turned to her and stared for a second too long, then looked away quickly. There were still layers to peel back when it came to Meegan. She checked her watch, Lara Blakely would be waiting and she didn't want to keep the woman any longer than she had to.

As they left Meegan and his solicitor talking, Briggs came out of the side room. 'Damn, we may be back at square one. I can tell there's more.' Jacob nodded in agreement.

'And me, sir. I just need to work out what that is. Do you know if forensics have scoured his cottage yet? I know it was in a mess and drenched last time I asked.'

'They've been there all day but we have safety issues. Part of the hall ceiling and the stairs have been burnt through which is why it's going to take longer. I've asked them to update us as soon as they find anything. They confirm that an accelerant was used and they found a bright green petrol can that had been thrown in the bushes out the back. It looks like our arsonist left something behind. I just hope we can get a fingerprint or something else that might help.'

'That sounds like good work. I'll speak to Lara Blakely now, see what she has to say.'

'Great, but first, get someone to check his alibi with the hotel. They may be able to email the CCTV files. There is a chance that Meegan is lying about ever being there, which again would put him straight back in the prime suspect frame.'

Gina hoped that would be the case, otherwise it was back to the board. Two murders, no suspects. Her head began to throb. The fear of another murder was real.

Gina looked up and saw Nick, the desk sergeant, leading Pete Bloxwich through. 'I got a call saying you lot wanted to speak to me about the case and as I was lurking about in your car park waiting for the next press release, thought I'd pop in. Got some juicy information about the case? The public are dying to know more. They lap this kind of thing up.' He grinned.

Gina checked her watch and turned to Nick. 'Can you tell Lara that we'll be with her soon? Apologise for keeping her waiting.' She led Pete down the corridor. 'This way, Mr Bloxwich.'

CHAPTER FORTY-EIGHT

The man sat on the plastic chair, slapping his lips as he chewed gum. The mint scent filled the tiny hot room. His cool blue shirt fell over his jeans. 'So, what have you got for me?'

'Mr Bloxwich—'

'Call me Pete.'

'Pete. This is a voluntary interview which means you can leave at any time.'

'What? I thought you wanted to talk about the Meegans?'

'We do, that is correct.'

'Well, what's that got to do with me?'

Jacob began recording and introduced everyone in the room, stating the time too.

'Why are you interviewing me about the Meegans?' His smile had now gone and he rubbed a hand over his stubbly chin.

'You were seen at the scene not long before an arson attack was committed on the Meegans' cottage so we need you to tell us about your moves yesterday.'

'You think I did it!'

'We also have a report that you were harassing Mrs Meegan, shouting through her letter box not long before the attack.'

'I dropped my card through her door. Said it was best if she told her story so that the public didn't draw their own conclusions, then I left.'

Gina leaned in. 'She said that you accused her of getting off on hurting kids. I mean you of all people should know what it means, brandishing those sort of accusations without any evidence. You can see how it looks. Within a couple of hours, someone has set her house alight. She could have died.'

'But it wasn't me.'

'So tell me how your day panned out, times and everything.' Gina leaned back and folded her arms.

Pete checked his watch and huffed. 'I was hanging around until it started raining, you know, I was talking to the protesters. There was a woman, really angry she was. Blakely, I think her name was. She gave me a quote. Something on the lines of not wanting paedophiles living amongst our children and I agreed with her. Who wants these people in our neighbourhoods?'

'Isn't your reporting meant to be objective?'

He shrugged. 'Well, Mrs Meegan didn't want to talk so I guess it was always going to be one-sided. I can't make people tell their story.'

'What time was this?'

He shrugged. 'Don't know. When it rained, I followed them to the community centre where we carried on talking.'

'Did you go back to the Meegans' cottage?'

'No… I mean, I went to get my car and went back to the office.'

'What time was this?'

'I don't know. Maybe one.'

Gina watched as Jacob noted that down.

'I didn't do this. Yes, I was angry, who wouldn't be? I mean the man spies on women. I have a wife and daughter. People like him sicken me but I'm not the only one who thinks like this. I must say, the Blakely woman was going for it large. If she wasn't firing stones at the windows and shouting, she was telling me how much this type of person should die. You should speak to her. Now, do you have any updates for me to report as I have to get back to the office? If that's it and you're not arresting me, I'm going.'

Gina sat up and sighed. She didn't have enough on him but she did urgently need to speak to Lara Blakely who was waiting. Knowing that she had been so active outside Mrs Meegan's cottage definitely put her in the frame. 'Thank you for coming.'

'That's it! Thank you. What do I tell the public?'

'Come back for the press conference later with all the other reporters.'

As he got up, his chair fell over and he stormed out of the interview room.

Jacob shrugged as he spoke to the tape. Gina followed the reporter along the corridor, making sure that he left. He went through to reception without looking back.

CHAPTER FORTY-NINE

A quick gulp of water and Gina stepped straight into interview room one where Lara Blakely was waiting. The woman's messy curls fell gently over her porcelain skin. 'Sorry to keep you waiting, Mrs Blakely.'

Jacob shuffled in and sat beside Gina.

'Why am I here?'

'You're a potential witness to a crime and we thank you for taking time out of your day to speak to us.' Gina observed the woman, wondering if she might be capable of arson.

'Really? I said on the phone that I didn't see anything. I'm sorry to hear about the fire.'

'We are just going to ask you a few questions. This is a voluntary interview which means that you're here of your own accord and you can leave at any time.'

She nodded and linked her fingers. Her white cotton summer dress fell over her knees.

'Yesterday, there was a house fire on Oak Tree Walk which resulted in one of the residents ending up seriously ill in hospital. We know that you were there most of the morning. We need to know what happened and who you saw.'

'Is Sandy okay?'

'She's being treated at the moment, but she has lost her home and most of the contents. We have evidence to believe that the fire was started deliberately. We also know that there was a mob of people protesting outside this house and one of them was you.'

Lara gulped. 'Her husband, he'd been done for spying on and recording people. I was speaking to the other residents and it seemed obvious that it was her husband who murdered Leah, and then Jordan. She was married to him, which means she had to be in on it. Why would anyone stay with a man like that? I mean he's a convicted perv and now a murderer. We wanted him arrested so decided to protest and get the media involved.'

'What time did you leave the scene?'

'Wait, am I being accused of burning their house down?'

'No, Mrs Blakely, but we are interviewing everyone who was protesting. We know that emotions run high at times like this but that doesn't excuse people taking the law into their own hands and nearly killing an innocent woman.'

'She had to know it was him who murdered those kids.'

'What makes you say that?'

'She lives with him. She knows he's already a convicted perv and she stayed with him.' Lara swallowed and looked into her lap. 'I'm sorry. I shouldn't have said that but I'm angry that two kids have been murdered. I do feel sorry for her, totally. She's lost so much.' She paused. 'Sandy and I used to be friends at school and I saw her again this week at the supermarket. She was with him, her husband, and I guess, if I'm honest with myself, he didn't seem like the nicest of people. I can't remember how the conversation went but I gathered that he just wanted me to leave Sandy alone. She sneaked my card into her pocket as if she didn't want him to see.' Lara swallowed. 'Then I found out on Twitter about his past and I blamed her too. I shouldn't have done that…'

'Have you ever seen Mr Meegan before?'

'I wasn't sure that I had but then I think I remember seeing a profile with his photo on it, but not the same name. He tried to friend me on Facebook but as I didn't know him, I rejected the request. He knew who I was and that's creepy. I also saw that he'd liked one of my daughter's photos on Instagram. He's a total weirdo. He's been tracking those kids online, I'm sure… well, I think I am.'

'Going back to the afternoon of the arson attack. Can you tell me who you saw in the area?'

She shrugged. 'I don't really know all their names. Most were just neighbours but I remember one man, Jim, as he introduced himself. There were several others and a reporter called Pete from the *Warwickshire Herald*. When it started raining, we all headed over to the community centre for a hot drink as we were all soaked through, then I left. I really can't remember the time, early afternoon I'd say.'

'Did Pete, the reporter, leave before you?'

'Yeah, maybe ten, twenty minutes before.' Gina scrunched her brow. Her story was now matching with the reporter's.

'Where was your car parked?'

'Just opposite where the Meegans live. I got into my car, waited for the mist to clear from the windscreen and met my husband with his lunch. That's it, I would have been with him at one thirty because that's when he has his break.'

'Where does your husband work?'

'Cleevesford Plastics, he's the logistics manager. You're going to check with him, aren't you?'

'We wouldn't be doing our job if we didn't. A woman was nearly killed so we have to be thorough. Do you remember seeing anything or anyone at that point?'

'Oh my… yes. I saw a flash of green plastic through the rain. A person was carrying it and heading around the back. It could have been a petrol can.'

'Can you tell me how tall this person was, build and features?'

'Only that they were wearing a dark jacket, navy blue, I think. The rest was a very fast blur. I just remember the colour green as it stood out. I drove off then.'

Gina watched as Jacob caught up with the notes. She wondered if Pete, the reporter, had hung around and not noticed Lara in her car.

'Where is Sandy going to end up?'

'I really don't know, Mrs Blakely.'

After the interview, Gina headed out into the corridor, leaving Jacob to finish up.

'Guv?' Wyre's plait swished from side to side as she jogged towards Gina. 'We have a fingerprint match on the petrol can. You need to come, quick.'

CHAPTER FIFTY

'Pick up, pick up, pick up,' Caro said as she gripped her phone.

'What is it? I'm helping my dad at work. If he sees I'm slacking, he'll have a frenzy.' Anthony sniffed.

'I needed to speak to someone. My mum has been called into the police station for another interview or something and I don't know why. I don't know what to do.' She peered around the door to see Jake sitting in front of the oven staring at the cakes rising behind the glass.

'Why would they want to speak to her again? It's not like she's the killer. Idiots. It's probably nothing.'

'Easy for you to say. Have you heard any more from the police?'

'Nah.'

'Have you spoken to any of the others? Oscar, Elsa or Naomi?'

'I've called them all. Oscar said to just shut up and say nothing. He literally threatened to pound my head if I spoke about the party we were at and, after last time, I know he would. I had a go back about him drugging you but he kept saying that he hardly gave you any and I needed to chill.'

'What if he drugged the others though? What if he drugged Leah? He's so good at putting on a butter-wouldn't-melt act. When the police interviewed him and his dad in their big house, they'd have looked perfect, not like the rest of us.'

'It was weird. Both Elsa and Naomi have had a cop each spending most of their time at their houses, saying that they could be in danger. Naomi is losing her shit but she's sitting tight. I don't know what to do for the best. Shit's gettin' serious. Maybe we should say something.'

Caro leaned against the wall and Jake shuffled past and went into the downstairs toilet where he sang as he peed. 'We can't say anything. We all agreed. We did things we could be charged with. There's the damage to cars, the graffiti. Why did we let Oscar talk us into doing such stupid things?'

'Whatever. We did stupid things but Leah was killed. D'ya really think they'll care about some graffiti?'

'And the weed? The roofies they spiked me with. There was more, I saw something on the night of the last party and I need to have it out with the person before anything is said.' Caro tapped her fingernails on the worktop, her mind turning everything over.

'First, cops have got bigger things to deal with than a bit of stupid weed, second, what the hell 'aven't you told me?'

The fire alarm began to sound. 'Got to go.'

Jake finished washing his hands and ran out of the toilet.

'I told you to watch the cakes, now look at them.' The edges were blackened.

'But I was going to pee myself.'

She pushed him out of the way and pulled the cakes from the oven, placing the tin on a trivet. 'Mum's going to go ape.'

As Lara ran through the door, she began wafting at the fire alarm with her handbag. 'What the hell? I leave you for an hour or so and this happens. Caro? You should have been supervising. You could have burnt the house down.'

'Sorry, Mum.'

Lara looked at each of them in turn and grabbed them both, hugging them closely.

'Sorry about the cakes, Mummy. We can make them again,' Jake said.

She bent down and kissed his forehead. 'We'll do them together.' She glanced back at Caro. 'Sorry for shouting like that.'

'What did the police want?' Caro noticed that her mum didn't seem angry. In fact, she looked worried when she smelled the smoke in the kitchen.

'A fire occurred close to where I was yesterday and they wanted to ask if I saw anyone around. When I came home and heard the alarm going off, I panicked. I'm just so glad both of my babies are safe.'

Caro indulged her mother in her over the top hugging, relieved that was all her mother had been asked. Her phone beeped again. She gently let go of her mother's hand, leaving her fussing over Jake and she gulped.

One, two; coming for you.

CHAPTER FIFTY-ONE

'Right, what have we got?' Gina followed Wyre into the incident room.

'We have fresh prints all over the can that match up to someone already on our database.'

'That is brilliant.'

O'Connor turned away from his computer screen and grabbed a Chelsea bun.

'Who is our arsonist?'

'It's Frank Meegan.'

Gina burst into laughter and stepped further into the room. 'I guess our slimy reporter is in the clear. I knew Frank Meegan was holding back. Just before coming to the station as I was leaving here, he must have started that fire. The evidence that Mrs Meegan gave us. He wanted to burn it all away.' Gina's laugh turned into a frown. 'He knew that his wife was virtually stuck in that house. We're looking at arson with intent to endanger life and that carries a hefty sentence. He was prepared to kill her to bury every last bit of evidence against him. I'll get onto the CPS in a minute to discuss charges further. We need more. He'll probably say that it's his petrol can, which is why his prints were on it. Have the team searched the rest of the grounds yet?'

Wyre opened an email on one of the computers. 'They've sent these photos so far.'

Gina flicked through each one in turn. They ranged from cigarette ends to discarded rubbish. Then came the shed. 'That's a navy-blue jacket hanging up on the shed wall.'

Wyre nodded. 'It was still damp in the creases too.'

Gina quickly scanned through the notes. 'I've just spoken to Lara Blakely, one of the protesters and mother to one of the kids that didn't go to this particular party, but went to the last one. She said she saw someone in a navy jacket holding what looked like a green petrol can scooting around the back of the house. He must have parked in another street after leaving just in case anyone saw him, then hurried back in the rain feeling safe that no one would be around, then whoosh. He set fire to the house. He has opportunity, he matches our witness description, the timings fit and he has a strong motive. We just need to know if he's lying about staying at the Splendid Hotel in Worcester. After all, he's proven that he's capable of killing if he tried to burn his wife to death.'

Jacob hurried in. 'The hotel are about to send the footage but it's bad news. They say that his car never left the hotel all night. And another thing. There is footage of him in the hotel bar until one in the morning. He never left. It shows him falling all over the place after drinking too much whisky. The staff said they almost had to carry him to his room where he vomited on their carpet and fell asleep face down before they'd even left him. This made him totally unforgettable to everyone on shift that night. He wasn't in any fit state to kill Jordan Rolfe.'

Gina threw her pen to the table and grabbed her hair. 'Damn! What are we missing? First things first. We discuss with the CPS charging Meegan with the following; arson with intent to endanger the life of Mrs Meegan and for voyeurism by installing equipment with the purpose of obtaining sexual gratification and the possession of indecent images of children for the filming and photographing of the teens. He's not going anywhere but that still leaves us with a double murderer on the loose. Go back to the teens with everything we have, especially Oscar. His father is going way over the top to keep us away. Look everyone over again and get back to me. I want to look further at John Tallis, the Waterside Café owner. I don't have a motive in mind as yet for him but we have to start with the leads that have been left dangling. Jacob, can you handle the call to the CPS? I'm going to speak to DCI Briggs, then I best be the one to break the news to Mrs Meegan before she hears it through the media.'

'Of course, guv. It will be my pleasure.' He smiled and left the room. O'Connor and Wyre turned back to their computers as Gina headed out to Briggs's office, knocking then pushing the door open.

'He's not our murderer, sir. I was so sure.'

'I think we all were. Now you have to find out who is.'

'Two out of five kids murdered. We have to stop this before we have a number three.'

Gina's phone beeped and Briggs peered up. Gina swallowed. 'It's three broken heart emojis from the same anonymous number, just like on the tweets.' She exhaled slowly with her eyes shut. 'I can't deal with all this.' Her phone beeped again. 'It's Hannah double confirming that she'll see me Sunday and not to keep calling.'

Briggs stood and placed a hand on each of her shoulders, making eye contact. 'You can and you will. We'll get through this.'

His phone beeped. He let go of her shoulder and picked it up.

The truth is coming out and you are both going down.

'Is your daughter doing all her messaging at once? The timing is a bit coincidental.'

He thrust the phone in her hand and she held back the urge to throw a chair at the window and scream.

'It has to be her.'

Why, Hannah? Why?

CHAPTER FIFTY-TWO

They've given me something to help me relax, at my request of course. I just want to forget Frank and forget everything that has happened. I hope the council find me somewhere to be discharged to soon. I hardly have any money in my account and I don't know what will happen with the cottage. Maybe the insurance will come through soon and I can be checked into a hotel or get a suitable rental until it is fixed up and sold or… I feel my throat choke up, the cottage might be a complete write off. Still, I'm not going back there, ever. The time has come for me to start living and Frank is only bringing me down. I need to leave here and get out of Cleevesford once and for all.

Was that a knock or did I imagine it? I really don't care. Heaving myself up a little I squint and look down, light-headedness keeping me still for a moment. I close my eyes and it's like I'm moving on an escalator that never reaches its destination. As I open my eyes, I'm staring at the woman. Who is it? Detective something. I see a red beating heart at the forefront of my mind's eye. Boom, boom, boom, just like the blood that is coursing through my body as I freak out. Harte. That's it. DI Harte. I have her card in my pocket. I feel for it but I'm not wearing my cardigan.

'Mrs Meegan? Sandra. Sorry to disturb you.'

You're not disturbing me. I want someone to talk to. Maybe we can make tea and sit in the garden. 'Hello.' That's all I can manage. I want to say so much more. The cloud is lifting a little. I'm speaking nonsense. *Get a grip.* I have to buck up before they deem me not fit to leave this place and I want to get out.

I'm in hospital. My house was set on fire and Frank is at the police station. Get a grip, Sandy.

'Are you okay to talk, only I have something to tell you?'

That doesn't sound good. It's the way she said it, the inflections in her voice and her downturned lips. That look of sympathy that I'm so used to seeing off everyone. Pity for the woman who's paralysed. I'm sick of pity. I'm going to show everyone that I'm a strong and capable human being. 'Just get on with it.'

'Can I get you anything?'

I need a drink but my arms are too weak to reach the water and the drifting in and out of weird dreams has distracted me. 'Water.'

The detective woman pours a glass from the water jug and passes it to me but I'm lying awkwardly on one arm. Pushing and twisting my torso, I'm back onto my bottom, grimacing as I pull myself into an upright position. I take the plastic cup but my grip says no and it almost spills. It's okay though, DI Harte still has the other side so she pours a bit through my lips.

The water is refreshing and the clouds are lifting a little more. I squeeze my eyes closed a few times hoping that the fuzzy filter will go away and it does a little. I see the detective's slight lines around her eyes and now she is smiling, I can see that it's a kind smile. Her brown hair has fallen from her bobble, framing the edge of her heart-shaped face.

'Are you okay to talk? I can come back if you're not feeling up to it.'

I reach out with my shaky fingers and place them on her clammy arm. 'Please stay.' I don't want to be alone all day and no one will come to visit me. She's all I have at this moment. The nurses have no time to talk and neither do the cleaners. I wonder if they all hate me because they know who Frank is and what he's done. *It's the wife of the child killer.* I can hear their whispers in my head. I'm scared they'll poison me or suffocate me when I sleep, after all, the angry mob tried to cook me alive. I just want to tell them all that I didn't know and I certainly didn't help him do all those wicked things.

'Sandra?'

'Sorry, I was just thinking. My mind is all over the place. It keeps racing and I…' I maybe slurring a little or stretching my words but I'm okay. I know my mind is back in the room. 'I asked them for something strong and that's what I got.' I wipe a string of dribble from the corner of my mouth.

'I'll try to make this as simple as I can.'

'Have you come to tell me you've arrested Frank for murdering those kids?'

'No, quite the opposite. Frank has an alibi for the second murder and, at present, we're linking the two, but there is something I have to tell you and it is that he's been arrested.'

'For the videos and the photos. I really thought he'd changed.'

'It's more than that.'

Now I'm alert. It's as if the drugs are wearing off fast. 'What? I have to know?'

'We have arrested him for attempted murder. I'm so sorry to tell you that it looks like your husband set fire to your house. We have a witness and forensic evidence to place him there at the time.'

I shake my head a little too fast and the room spins a little, sending me into a flurry of panic. 'That can't be right. You're saying that Frank tried to kill me?' I grip the bed rail to ground myself. I know I'm not really spinning but it's reassuring to know I'm still, even though my head is trying to deceive me.

'I'm afraid so.'

I can't help the flood of tears that begin to fall. Fat plopping tears that slither down my face, gathering in the crease of my sticky chin. He's not a child killer. Maybe, just maybe people will give me a break now. But wait, he tried to kill me. 'He wanted me dead.' My sobs fill the room. It's been a long time since I had any love for Frank but to know he tried to murder me is something else. I don't have words for this feeling. I grip the DI's arm, my nails digging in as I tense uncontrollably.

'I thought I should be the first to tell you before the media get wind of it. His arrest will be announced later today.'

'Thank you for being here.'

'I'm just so sorry I came with such bad news. Is there anyone you want me to call? You shouldn't be alone.'

I shake my head. 'I don't have anyone. Frank made sure my family would never be a part of my life. I see it now, I see it all.' I can't stop now I've started. The words flow out of me with ease. All that pent-up hurt needs to escape. 'In the early days before my accident, he wanted me all to himself… When he started doing…' I turn slightly in shame, '… bad things, I was nothing more than a front, an alibi. Why didn't I see it? I stayed with him. He convinced me he was ill and needed me to stick by him; that he'd change.' I pause, trying to find the next few words. 'He'd buy me flowers and tell me how much he loved me for sticking by him but he soon turned weird again. Then that holiday came and I was so angry with him and his mood swings, I jumped in the sea on a whim and ruined my life. Then he had me right where he wanted – trapped.' Another flood of tears come and she passes me a tissue.

'Men like Frank are cruel. I can help you access the right help when you're ready. You can manage on your own in the right property. There is support out there. You can look for work, start a course or join some community groups. What do you like doing?'

I smile. I used to like making clothes. 'Dressmaking.'

'I'm sure there is a whole load of courses or groups that meet up. You deserve better but you need to give yourself permission to take it.'

I still have my hand on her arm. 'Thank you.' I know the solution to everything sounds easy in her mind but what she's saying isn't impossible. I've dreamed about going back to work. I can get an adapted car giving me my freedom back. I have so much to offer and I want to be around people again. I was really good in the world of finance.

'One step at a time. Is there anything else I can get for you while I'm here?'

I shake my head and blow my nose. 'Make sure he doesn't get away with it, any of it. The photos, the videos, I'll help in any way I can. I'll stand up in court and tell everyone what I know. He needs to pay for what he's done.'

'I'll do everything within my power to do that and I'll keep you updated all the way.'

'Who killed those teenagers?'

'I'm afraid we don't have an answer to that question yet but we're hoping to soon.'

She swallows. I can tell she doesn't believe what she's just said. Maybe they're not close to catching the killer. My eyelids begin to close. That short outburst has exhausted me.

'Thank you for speaking with me. I can tell that you're tired so I'll leave you alone to rest.'

She goes to stand. 'Wait. Can you tell the staff here that my husband didn't kill those kids and that he tried to kill me? I don't want them to hate me. I really do care what people think. They don't care that I haven't done anything and I don't want them to poison my food.'

'Of course, although the nurse I spoke to before coming in said you were a nice lady so I don't think you have anything to worry about. Nobody here will be poisoning your food. You're safe now.'

'Will you come and see me again?'

I can see her stalling to answer. She's here doing her job, visiting me again in this state isn't the top of her list and maybe even crossing a boundary for her but I always think, if you don't ask, you don't get. She's the only person who properly listens and doesn't treat me like I'm dirt on their shoe. And, maybe, I'll share with her just how cruel Frank has been in the past, when I can think straight. He should pay for the things he did to me too but I suppose trying to kill me would be the ultimate crime against me that he could pay for.

'Of course I will. It may be in a few days but it will be lovely to catch up with you when you've had a chance to fully recover.'

'Thank you. See you soon.' She smiles and leaves. I know she's not my friend, I'm not that naïve but I look forward to her visit.

Everything begins to sink in. Frank has been arrested. He's finally out of my life.

CHAPTER FIFTY-THREE

Gina grabbed her laptop bag and placed it on the incident room table. 'Right, I'm heading home which is where I'll be working through the evening. I want everyone back here for an eight in the morning briefing. Spend the evening going over everything again ready to start again tomorrow.' O'Connor, Jacob and Wyre had a defeated look about them. Frank Meegan's alibi had set them all back.

Wyre glanced at her notes. 'I've spoken to the families of the kids and we can see them all tomorrow in turn, except Oscar. His father said he's had enough and doesn't want us coming around.'

Gina folded her arms. 'Hmm. I don't like the fact that Mr Spalding is trying to keep us out. We really need something that will get us through the door or get Oscar into this station. He knows something and with our other suspects eliminated, each one of those kids has to be at the top of the list now. It's still too early to get all the forensics results back too and that includes toxicology. We're working mostly on our detective skills here. Spend some time looking into Oscar and his father. They're putting up too much of an obstruction. I believe the devil is in the detail. Look at everything. Read the notes on the system until you can reel them off as easy as you can when someone asks for your date of birth. Look at every photo, every little detail in the background. The answer is there, somewhere. Analyse every interview. Replay them. I know it's a lot to ask but I saw the latest headline. We are being branded as incompetent. Three days, two murders. They keep asking who's next. Regardless of what anyone asked for or wants – even Oscar's father – I want drive-bys on all the kids' houses overnight. If anyone leaves, put an alert out and we need to monitor their movements.'

'Do you really think it could be one of them?' Jacob stared blankly and let out a half yawn.

'I hope it isn't but what I hope doesn't matter. They were all there. They had opportunity and any one of them could have overpowered Leah in the state that she was in. If Frank Meegan is to be believed, he stated that on the night of Leah's murder he wasn't alone in watching her. That doesn't totally implicate the kids either. For now, we have to theorise as to who that person might have been and, as it stands, it could have been any of the others at the camp or an outsider. Also, who bit Leah? What was all that about? Not one of the teens has mentioned having any type of relationship with her so who did it and why?'

Wyre scrunched her brow.

'Have you got an idea?'

'I don't know. There's just so much going through my head right now.' Wyre pressed her lips together.

'Like I said, go through the files again and again. If you get a light-bulb moment, call me any time. Right, head home and get some food. It's late and I need you all here with your best game faces on tomorrow. Don't speak to the press either. That is an order from above.' Gina nodded and they all stood, talking as they began to disperse.

Wyre came over to the boards, brows furrowed as she scanned everything.

'Go home and clear your head.'

'Okay. See you first thing.' Wyre packed up her belongings.

'See you tomorrow.' Gina watched as they all left.

Briggs entered. 'Bloody journalists. They just don't stop. This new one, Pete, is being a right nuisance. At least he's stopped calling every five minutes since his interview. Have you looked out of the window?'

Gina walked over and glanced down at the car park. 'When did that lot arrive? There were only three of them last I looked. There must be twenty now including the nationals.'

'They're branding the murderer, the camp killer. Making it sound like some eighties B-movie. They've also mentioned the other kids. *Headline – Two down, three to go.* It's scaring everyone. We've had callers galore. If a kid is more than five minutes late home or doesn't answer their phone, the parents think they've been killed. I suppose it will pay for everyone to be cautious given that we don't know what's happening next, but that doesn't help us. The team taking the calls are stretched to their limits. They've had to bring in people who are off today.'

Gina swallowed. 'First murder, early hours Sunday morning; second murder, early hours Monday morning. This morning, no murder and no reports of anything untoward happening in the night. This killer barely left a gap between the first and the second murder. Can we make sure those drive-bys are every fifteen minutes?'

'Yes, it's going to inconvenience uniform but we can't risk another teenager turning up dead.'

'Great.'

'Do you want company tonight?'

Gina shook her head. 'Thank you but my mind is all over the place. I also can't keep thinking about Hannah and I know that's all we'll talk about. I'll call you though, keep you posted.' Gina grabbed her bag, smiled and left with a churning stomach.

As she pushed through the sea of journalists and photographers, Pete Bloxwich stared across at her as she nudged through. His grin almost made time feel as though it had stopped. 'Lyndsey Saunders sends her regards. If you have any fresh info, you should let me in.' He placed a card in her hand. 'The *Herald*. Local paper for local people. Lyndsey said you were really helpful in the past so maybe you and I can work together. I can help… I answered your questions, didn't I?'

'Mr Bloxwich, no. You will be informed of any updates along with anyone else. Harassing me outside my workplace won't do you any favours, neither will harassing witnesses to give stories. Look what happened to Lyndsey. Carry on like this and you will end up like she did. Please step out of my way!' He frowned and stepped aside. Gina hurried back to her car, her breaths shortening. The messages to Briggs and Hannah wanting to speak, was it all down to the rogue reporter trying to rebuild her almost failed career. The very mention of Lyndsey Saunders's name filled Gina with both fear and rage. Lyndsey spent her last moments trying to bring Gina down in a previous case and the journalist had been suspended for how she'd acted and now she'd simply passed the baton on. Gina loosened her top button then dropped her car keys from her sweaty hands. Fumbling, she gripped them tight and turned back to see that the reporter was staring right at her grinning. Between him and the messages, she felt like she was suffocating.

CHAPTER FIFTY-FOUR

Thursday, 5 August

The rustling of a fox at the back of Oscar's long garden sent Caro's heart banging in her chest. Now all she could hear was the thumping of blood as it pumped through her head. She'd sent Oscar the message a couple of hours ago and he'd messaged back, agreeing that they had to see each other. He was going to tell her everything. She trusted him. Oscar had hurt a lot of people. Beating them up if he didn't get what he wanted. She knew Anthony didn't really want any more to do with him after the fight and she could understand that. Caro and Oscar had been friend's forever and best friends on and off. He'd never hurt her. She gulped, wondering if just because he hadn't hurt her yet, he couldn't hurt her now. She shook her head as a hint of doubt crept in. No, she trusted him. He was going to fill in those final gaps and with the police monitoring his house, it had to be in the middle of the night. He knew she'd come and vice versa.

She felt along the back of the fence in the moonlight for the gap she and Oscar made years ago. Oscar's father had never found it. Caro knew this was how Oscar sneaked out to all those parties he was never allowed to attend in the past, but now he'd simply lie and say he was staying with friends like they all did. His father was the strictest. Ruled their household like he was still in the military and since Oscar's mum had died, he'd been obscssively holding on to Oscar like he was still a little kid.

There, she felt the gap and dropped her rucksack on the ground. As she crept through, she caught her leg on a piece of sharp wood and felt a trickle of blood slide down to her ankle. Then it stung. 'Oscar,' she called in a loud whisper as she crept around the back of the summer house, breathing in as the gap was so tight. She lit up her phone and it flashed off just as she caught the time. Five past one in the morning. She was late and he still wasn't ready. She squeezed out into the bottom of the garden and sat on the decking. She wiped the blood from her calf, flinching as she pulled out a splinter. Where was he?

She stared up at the huge garden with the sectioned off areas and veggie patch that was bigger than ten gardens on her row of houses. The main house was elevated with a huge patio area and sofa style seating everywhere. Glancing up towards Oscar's bedroom window she wondered if he'd forgotten about their meet up and fallen asleep. She grabbed her phone but it wouldn't come back on. The battery had completely gone. If he wasn't out in five minutes, she was going back home and calling it a night.

She almost screamed as she stood and took a few steps back and felt a hand on her shoulder. That's when she saw Oscar's grinning face lit up with his own phone. With all that was going on, he was trying to scare her like this was all a Halloween trick.

'Got ya!' He laughed and turned the light off his phone.

'You idiot.' She hit his arm as she tried to calm down her breathing. 'What the hell took you so long? I've been waiting forever.'

'The police have just passed. They come every fifteen minutes, on the dot.'

'Really?'

'I've been watching them from the landing with my dad's binoculars. They probably wouldn't have noticed me leaving out the back but I didn't want to risk anything. I waited until PC Plod had passed and then hurried to the back, then I remembered the security light and the CCTV. I had to quickly disable both.

My dad's a light sleeper so I had to escape like my life depended on it.' He grinned.

'Good for you. My dad was snoring the house down when I left, so I'm okay for a few hours but I need to get back before it gets light.'

'Let's go.'

She followed Oscar behind the summer house and through the gap in the fence, grabbing her rucksack on the way. They both half ran until they were far from Oscar's house. Caro went to turn right onto a path that led to the golf course. 'Not that way.' Oscar pulled her by the arm.

She shook him off. 'Where are we going?'

'You'll see.'

She stopped under a street light. 'I'm not following you without knowing where we're going.'

He stopped and sighed. 'You always want to know everything. Nothing is ever a surprise with you. Boring.' He made a yawning motion and laughed. 'We're going to our hang-out.'

'Isn't it closed?'

'Has that ever stopped us getting in?'

Caro scrunched up her nose. 'I guess not.'

'Come on, let's hurry, then I will tell you everything you want to know.'

'Can't you tell me here?'

Oscar looked both ways and laughed. 'No. Either come to the hang-out or buzz off back home. Since when did you become such a scaredy-cat?'

'Since I was attacked the other night and I found out you roofied me at the last party.' She folded her arms and stood still.

'I can explain and I will. All will be revealed at the hang-out. Who attacked you?'

She shrugged. 'I had a message to meet someone in the woods and they came from behind. I stabbed them with my nail file.'

Oscar stared at her, his smile dropping. 'That's awful, babe.' He stepped closer and gave her a friendly hug.

'Yeah, almost as awful as being roofied. Why should I trust you?'

He let go and his gaze met hers. 'Because it's always been you and me against the world. We stick together, like we always have done through school. Come on before we get caught and someone calls the police and reports us for loitering. I could do without my dad on my back right now.' He walked away with a slight limp.

'What happened to your leg?' She swallowed the mass in her throat.

'Oh, it's nothing.'

'So you didn't attack me?'

'What is this? I thought we were friends. Why would I attack you? If you must know, my dad did this.' He pointed to his leg.

Her shoulders slumped and she began to play with the end of her hoodie. 'Things still hard at home?'

'The bastard kicked me in the leg earlier. He's still angry that I brought the police to *his* door. Big bloody bruise, an all. I don't even feel like it's my home. I hate him and I hate that house.'

'I'm so sorry.' She knew Oscar had endured a few beatings from his dad and this was just another. She'd spent years dismissing his weird behaviours because of what he'd suffered since his mum's death but Oscar always said his mother was in a better place. She held his hand. 'Let's go to the hang-out but you have to promise that you'll tell me everything.'

'You know I will. I trust you. Do you trust me?'

She stopped dead. Refusing to take another step. 'I want to see your leg.'

Oscar stared right at her, standing rigid. All friendliness in his tone now gone. She'd seen his sudden change in mood many a time but it had never occurred because of something she said. He reached out and grabbed her by the arm, pulling her to the ground. 'You had to go and ruin it, bitch.'

CHAPTER FIFTY-FIVE

Still half asleep Gina's dream continued. She saw Hannah's long blonde hair waving in the wind as her daughter was about to push her off a bridge in the same way that Gina had pushed her father down the stairs all those years ago. As she toppled back, eyes wide, hands windmilling, knowing that she was about to crash into the rocks that stuck out of the shallow river but she didn't fall into water, she fell into a seat in a courtroom and the judge's voice boomed out. 'How do you plead?' *Guilty, guilty, guilty.* Those words kept repeating over and over as Judge Peter Bloxwich stared at her.

Gasping for breath, Gina jolted up in her bed, drenched with sweat as her phone buzzed on the bedside table. Ebony purred before stretching on the end of her bed. Grabbing her phone, she answered. It was Briggs. 'Gina, we have another missing teen on our hands. Everyone's been called in. Hurry.'

'On my way, sir. Who is it?'

'Oscar Spalding. His father just called to say that his CCTV and security lights had been tampered with. No sign of a break-in and the doors were locked. It looks like the boy left of his own accord. His phone is turned off too.'

'We need the dogs out in the woods covering the area of the two other bodies and beyond.' Gina touched her throat and swallowed.

'Already sorted.'

'I just hope we don't find another body.'

'Me neither.'

'I'll call Ellyn, see if she'll be able organise for someone to be with Mr Spalding if he's amenable to having a FLO at hand. Given that his son is missing, I suspect he'll want someone with him this time. What happened with the drive-bys?'

Briggs took a sip of something and cleared his throat. 'They all went ahead as planned. Every fifteen minutes without fail. The same PC drove past all three of the kids' houses constantly. During his breaks, another officer took over. They didn't see any activity coming from the house. As Mr Spalding refused any help, that's all we could do to protect his son. What we couldn't do is walk around the house all night. His father did find something when he went out to explore in the back garden.'

'What?' Gina grabbed a tissue and dabbed her damp forehead. Six thirty in the morning and the sun was already beating through her thin curtains.

'He found a trail of blood by his summer house and followed it. Behind the outbuilding there is a cut in the fence. That's how his son must have got out without using the main security gate.'

'We need to know if it's his blood.'

'His father said the trail starts at the summer house and ends where there is a shard of wood sticking out.'

'That's where the injury occurred then, at the shard of wood. It must be. Someone came into the garden that night through the hole in the fence, heading to the summer house, and Oscar left with them. That's a starting theory. Are forensics on their way?'

'Yes and Mr Spalding is cooperating. They'll be able to take a sample of the blood and something with Oscar's DNA on it. We'll soon know if it's a match to Oscar or if we have a match on the system. We need to find him before all this blows up in the news.'

Gina's mind flashed back to the weird dreams she'd had. She opened her mouth to share them with Briggs hoping to alleviate her anxiety a little, but changed her mind. There were more pressing things to deal with. Right now, they had to find the missing boy and hope that he was alive. 'I'll meet you at the station in half an hour.'

'Great. See you soon.' She heard his front door slam before he ended their call. Five minutes to grab a shower. Five minutes to dress and then the drive into work with damp hair. She shot out of bed knowing that this boy's life might depend on them getting a move on. That was now three out of five. She could see the next report in the *Herald* – Cleevesford police team fail again and another kid is murdered. She swallowed as her breath quickened.

CHAPTER FIFTY-SIX

As Gina pushed through the crowd of shouting journalists she gripped her laptop bag and phone.

'DI Harte, what are you doing to find the killer?'

'Why are Cleevesford Police so incompetent?'

'What has Frank Meegan been charged with?'

'The public have a right to know more. Two kids have been murdered. Who's next? People are rightfully scared.'

'Five went into the woods, four came out. Another one killed in the woods. What are you all doing?'

The questions continued until she reached reception and passed Nick on the desk. He wafted a piece of paper in front of his glistening face, his cheeks a rosy red colour. 'They never stop. I've had to escort more than five of them out when they've come in to try their luck. A couple of them have helped themselves to our water cooler. The cheek of it.'

'They're a bloody nuisance. If they just left us to do our job instead of getting in the way, maybe we'd have found the killer by now. It's not like we haven't done a press release every day.' She exhaled and continued through to the incident room where a tray of coffees greeted her. 'Thank you to whoever made the coffee.'

O'Connor frowned. 'Thought we could all do with it today.'

Wyre, Jacob, Briggs, Smith, Kapoor and several more uniformed officers all crowded around the table.

Briggs stood. 'Right, we have no time to waste. As we all know, we have a missing teenager. Oscar Spalding's father called in to say that his son wasn't home this morning at six. That is the time he usually wakes his son and he said his bed wasn't even slept in. It looks like Oscar disabled the CCTV and alarm system too. What concerns us most is the blood at the back of the garden. I've had word that forensics are now in attendance along with uniform, who are cordoning off the area. As this is the case of a missing minor, the DNA tests will be absolutely prioritised so we should know soon if the blood on site is Oscar's. A FLO has arrived at the Spalding residence and is sitting with the father. If she finds anything out, she will report back immediately but from what she can tell, it looks like Oscar left in the night of his own accord. His laptop is on its way to the tech team at the station as are his other devices, including the ones he uses for online gaming. There is also a search going on that Smith and Kapoor have set up, thank you for that.'

Kapoor nodded and smiled.

'Dogs are being used to see if they can track Oscar down. We hope we don't find that this boy has ended up like Leah and Jordan. Any news or updates, let Harte and me know immediately.'

'Yes, sir,' Kapoor said.

'Over to you, Harte.'

Gina stood beside him, glancing back at the board. 'You know what we have to do. Jacob and I will head over to Naomi's house and speak to her family again before heading over to the Spaldings'. We have to get to the bottom of what's going on. Wyre, you and O'Connor head over to Elsa's and question her again. They are the only two of the party left and, as far as I'm concerned, they're either dangerous or in danger. One of them knows something and we're not treading too lightly this time. Just bear in mind that another one of their friends is missing but don't be afraid to push them a little more, either.'

Wyre and O'Connor nodded just as a member of despatch came through; a young man with a moustache that curled at the ends. 'Sorry to interrupt but I was just heading in through reception.'

'That's okay,' Gina replied.

'There's a Lara Blakely in reception and she's in a state. Her daughter is missing.'

Gina glanced around the room. That had come as a shock. 'Bring her through to an interview room. I'll see her immediately.'

The man left. She added Caro Blakely's name to the list on the board. 'The kids that didn't go to the party. There was another one.' She searched for the name on the boards. 'Anthony. Wyre, you go to Elsa's as planned but with Smith. O'Connor, you go with Kapoor to Anthony's. Why didn't we put in the same levels of help for those kids, the ones that went to the previous party?'

She grabbed her notes and nodded in Jacob's direction. 'Let's go see Mrs Blakely. Two kids are missing and we need to find them before it's too late.'

CHAPTER FIFTY-SEVEN

The shaking woman's hair frizzed, framing her face. 'You have to help me find her,' Lara Blakely screamed, tears slipping down her cheeks.

'We have a team searching the woodland and the whole area.' Gina knew that was of little comfort to the woman in front of her who already thought of her daughter as the next camp killer's victim. Jacob jotted down her name and the time.

'You're looking for a body?'

'We're hoping that we find Caro safe and well. It would really help if you told me what happened as you remember it.'

Lara pulled a tissue from the box and blew her nose. 'With all the chaos that's been going on lately, I forgot I had an appointment to meet a client at their hotel, then I saw my iPad flash up. I was meant to be there for eleven this morning. I rushed up and got ready then knocked on Caro's door. This was about nine this morning. There was no answer…' Lara's voice began to break into little whimpers.

'You're doing really well.'

'I went in and then I saw that she wasn't there. I ran into Jake's room and he said that she left the house in the night, that he'd heard her go but didn't know what time. I asked why he didn't say anything and he said that his sister sneaked out in the early hours of Tuesday morning too and she made him promise not to tell. He said she seemed really upset and shaky when she returned.'

Gina made a mental note that Tuesday morning wasn't the morning Jordan was murdered.

'This morning, I noticed that the back gate was unlocked as was the back door. That's how she went. I swear, I was so angry that Jake didn't come and wake me, I shouted at him…' Her bottom lip began to tremble. 'And now he hates me.'

'I'm sure he can see how upset you are and he must be worried about his sister too. Can you tell me a bit about Caro? How has she been lately?'

'Not herself. She's been emotional, quiet and a little sad looking here and there. I'm struggling a little with work and the kids. I feel as though I haven't been there for either of them. Then I spent most of my time off the other day protesting outside that horrible man's house.' Gina knew she meant Frank Meegan. 'My daughter's two friends had just been murdered and she needed me but I left her alone to deal with that. I should have cancelled everything to be there for her. What kind of mother am I?'

'One who cares. This is not your fault.' Gina knew how hard it was to balance a career with one child, she couldn't imagine having two. 'Did you try to call her?'

'Over and over again. It's as if her phone has died or been turned off. I had a quick look around her room to see if she'd left it but she'd definitely taken it with her. She never leaves her phone for a second and it's out of character for her to not answer.'

'Does she often sneak out?'

'No, never. She's more likely to tell me she's staying with a friend so that she can sneak around, which is what happened when she went to the previous party that you know about. This is so out of character. Now that I think about things, I've caught her with a few worried looks on her face, like she has something on her mind but she's not a talker. I've found if I push her, she gives me the silent treatment. I just don't know what I'm meant to do. No one ever prepares you for being a parent.'

'How well do Caro and Oscar know each other?'

Lara let out a smirk through her tears and shook her head. 'That boy has been the cause of many tears in our household.' She paused and cocked her head. 'Is this something to do with him?'

'He is currently missing also which is why I asked. Could they be together somewhere?'

'No. That boy is trouble.'

'Can you please tell me why?' Gina leaned in a little.

'He'd always get her into trouble with his stupid dares. I've had to beg shop security not to report Caro for shoplifting. It's his fault, each and every time. He gets her into trouble. Like at school, they used to sneak out together when they were meant to be in lessons, then the school would call me up to moan. It's stupid things but I wasn't happy about him hanging around with her but I couldn't stop them. I thought they'd calmed down a lot over the past year. He's been in a fair few fights. I think he starts most of them. He's a bully and others seem to follow him blindly. I wouldn't be surprised if he hurt those kids.'

'You mean Leah and Jordan?'

'Yes.'

'Why would you say that?'

'Because he has this look, one he saves for when his father isn't around. You can see the menace in his eyes. It's like he screams dominance and control. When he's in the room, it's as if Caro needs permission to move and not only that, she seems to be happy about it; they all do. He gives me the shivers. I don't like him. He's behind all this and he'll kill her too. You have to find my daughter. She can't defend herself against a bully like him.' The woman wiped her nose again.

'Do you know of any places where they might go?'

'No.' The woman started sobbing again.

'Mrs Blakely, I'm going to get an officer to go home with you where I want you to wait. If Caro tries to contact you, she might call you on the home phone or she might come home.'

'Okay.'

'Just to reiterate, our teams are out there searching. Also, in a short while, I'd like to come over too and take a look at Caro's bedroom. Would that be okay? There may be a clue in there as to where she's gone.'

'Anything. I just want my baby back home.' The room filled with Lara's primal screams, the pain of her missing daughter evident in her whole body. Gina could only imagine what she was going through right now. It wasn't looking good.

CHAPTER FIFTY-EIGHT

Gina pulled up outside Lara Blakely's house. Terraced but large. Beautifully manicured shrubs at the front with two bay trees standing guard, one each side of the door.

'I hate this, guv. The team have been searching the woodland for two hours now and nothing has led them to Oscar or Caro.' Jacob scratched his chin.

'Something has to give in this damn case. If one or both of those kids are dead…' She swallowed and closed her eyes.

'We can't think like that, guv. It's good that we haven't found a body. They could have just run away together.'

'I'd like to hope that they have, that it's some teen romance and they'll be home when they run out of food or money but we both know that's not it. Let's go.'

They hurried to the door and went to knock but Lara had already opened it. Her eyes stinging red and glassy, she led them both through to the kitchen where her husband was pacing in a suit. Gina knew the exact same was happening over at Oscar's right now. Someone knocked at the door and Gina hoped it was PC Kapoor. She'd been reassigned to sit with the Blakelys all day.

'It could be her.' Lara ran to the door.

Mr Blakely pressed his temples. 'It's not, she has her own front door key.'

That's when Gina heard Kapoor's voice. At least they had someone to sit with them and Kapoor was observant. She'd take mental notes, listen and sympathise. No one was to be ruled out of the investigation. Gina glanced up at Mr Blakely. Maybe he hated that his daughter was knocking around with Oscar and has finished him off for good. She shook her head. She could see he was distraught and had no reason to think that.

'Hiya, guv; DS Driscoll.' Kapoor sidled in, fanning her uniformed body with her hand. With all the bodies crammed into the kitchen, it was sweltering.

'Where's your son, Jake, is it?' Gina hadn't seen the boy.

'Oh, one of my neighbours is watching him. I don't want him upset so he's playing with her little boy.'

'I know this is hard but can we take a look at Caro's room, now?'

'I'll show you up.' Lara led the way.

Gina and Jacob followed her up the stairs. They passed what looked like an office. Sample pads everywhere, mood boards, colour wheels. Material and a sewing machine. Then Lara stopped outside the second bedroom door. 'This is Caro's room. She'd hate anyone being in it but we don't have a choice, do we?'

'She'd want you to do this. We need to find her and if the clue to her whereabouts is in here, we will find her.' Gina gave her a sympathetic smile.

Lara pushed the door open. 'I'll wait downstairs. Please take care with her things.' Lara picked a fleecy blanket up from the floor, smelled it and hugged it before leaving with it clutched in her arms.

As soon as Lara was down the stairs, Gina hurried in. 'Time is against us and we have to get to Naomi's. Get looking.'

Gina took the end of the room by the drawers and wardrobe while Jacob took the bed. They slipped on a pair of blue latex gloves and started rummaging.

Within minutes, Gina had been through the wardrobe. 'Nothing here.' She moved over to the drawers and the dressing table, taking in all the photos that were stuck around the edges of her mirror. Teens looking happy, pulling funny faces, posing like models in clothes shops. All normal stuff. Jacob was now down on all fours, pulling things out from under the bed then he huffed. 'Found something, guv.'

'What?' she asked as she pulled a notebook from the bottom drawer of the bedside table.

'There's a long metal nail file here and it looks like there are traces of dried-up blood on it and there's a smear on the carpet too.'

'Good find. Bag it. We'll need forensics here to take samples. We need to find out whose blood that is.' As Jacob began bagging up the item, Gina placed the notebook on the dressing table and bagged up Caro's hairbrush. 'We need these sent to the lab immediately.' She picked up the notebook again and began flicking through the doodle pages, the lists of homework assignments, a game of hangman until she stopped at a few pages of scrawled notes marked up; the things I can remember and what I've found out.

'What's that?' Jacob finished with the evidence bag.

Gina gulped as she read. 'I think we may have just found out what happened at the last party and it's not at all pretty. Poor Caro. We need to find this girl and quick.'

CHAPTER FIFTY-NINE

Caro opened her eyes and her head ached like mad. The sun's rays filtered through the picture window that ran high up across the back wall. The heavy pain in her arm and torso reminded her of how bad things had got. The grit in her eyes was itching and the wound on her leg was still stinging. It didn't matter anymore. Nothing mattered. 'It's over, isn't it?' A tear slid down her cheek.

Oscar's stare felt heavy on hers. His livid, angry outburst just waiting to escape. She looked away, not wanting to antagonise him. He didn't answer her question. In fact, he didn't say a word and that was worse.

A scurrying sound came from behind the stack of hockey sticks. That's when the rodent appeared.

She'd miss Jake, even though he was always a nuisance; and her mother who always tried to do her best – Caro knew that. If she'd confided in her mother, maybe things wouldn't have led to this. It was time to say goodbye to them all. Another tear slid down her cheek and mingled with the dirt that had stuck to her face during the struggle.

Blinded by the sun, she leaned back and stared at the water-stained ceiling. 'Oscar, please say something.'

Again, no answer from Oscar. He shifted slightly and gave her that sinister laugh where the one side of his mouth upturned. She should have known better than to think it was always him and her, that they were the only people that mattered. She didn't matter to him anymore. No one mattered to Oscar, except Oscar.

Caro shivered knowing the end was coming. Pain, so much pain, especially her split lip. 'I guess this really is the end.'

CHAPTER SIXTY

'Update me quickly.' As Gina stood outside Naomi's house with Jacob, she waited for Wyre to give her a summary of what was happening at the Spalding residence over the phone. 'Have you been able to access Oscar's bedroom and gadgets?'

'Yes, guv.' Gina nodded to include Jacob on that answer. Wyre continued. 'We've found something worrying; a wad of bloody dressings and bandages in his bedroom bin. I knew when I saw him he was walking with a limp but the amount of blood looks like he'd sustained quite an injury. Forensics are taking samples at the moment. The blood is going straight to the lab to run against the blood by the summer house. It's being prioritised over everything else.'

'Jacob and I found a bloodied nail file in Caro Blakely's bedroom too. We need the blood results to make full sense of who hurt who and the question is why. Anything else?'

'Yes, a sachet of powder that looks like it could be Rohypnol. Oscar kept it in a plastic box under his bed.'

'Does Mr Spalding know anything about this and how is he?'

'His father says he knows nothing about the powder and he seems vacant. He keeps staring out of the window. He's in a real panic over where his son might be and he keeps muttering about him being out of control. When I try to ask him more, he walks out of the room. It's like he's having some sort of breakdown.'

'Keep pressing as best you can and try to access any tech that Oscar had access to. We need to know where Oscar and Caro might head to.' Gina swallowed. 'We can't rule out that someone else is involved which is why I'm here now, at Naomi's house.'

'If we crack the tech, I'll call you straight away. I'm also heading straight over to the James's residence. There's a FLO with Elsa at the moment so hopefully we might have some more information to work with soon.'

Time was slipping away from them. They were dealing with a double murderer who had killed with no hesitation each time.

'More blood, I gather?' Jacob followed Gina up the garden path.

'Sadly, yes.' Gina knocked loudly and heard scuffling behind the door.

Dina Carpenter answered. Her pale skin was more a shade of grey today with red rimmed baggy eyes. Her white blonde hair tied up in a messy stack was threatening to fall into a matted entanglement. 'Come in. Sorry about this. I didn't sleep. We've been so worried. Naomi has been up half the night and we keep thinking about what's happening.' She pulled the door open and stepped aside. 'Your family liaison person arrived a short while ago too. Come through.'

'We're sorry to have to question Naomi again but as you are aware, two of her friends are now missing.'

'Who's killing our kids?' Her lip quivered.

Gina stepped into the long narrow kitchen with a view of the small but well decked out garden. Several trimmed conifers hid the back fence. She nodded at Ellyn who was spooning instant coffee into a row of cups. 'We urgently need to speak to Naomi.'

'She's just taken the dog for a walk around the block. I didn't want her to go but she said I was being suffocating. So much for being a parent who cares.' The woman looked at her watch. 'She's been gone a while so she shouldn't be more than a couple of minutes.'

They all turned to look through the window into the garden as they heard a dog barking, but Naomi didn't come through the back gate.

'That's probably her now.'

Only Naomi still didn't open the back gate and come into the garden. The dog's barks got louder and more frequent. Then came the yelping. 'Is he okay?'

'He doesn't normally make that sound.'

Dina went to open the back door but Gina nodded and went out first. Ellyn came to her side. 'It's okay, I'll check on the dog.' Something was wrong. Gina could tell and the confused look on Dina's face showed that she thought the same. The woman moved aside for Jacob to follow and she began to visibly quiver.

Opening the back gate, Gina turned quickly to see a large St Bernard tied up to a stump in the grass. Abandoned and pleased to see her, it wagged its tail. The dog slobbered and licked her hand as she untied it and walked it back through the garden. 'Your dog was tied up outside.'

Dina almost crumpled and leaned against the worktop. 'They've taken her too.' Her tears came out like blubbering sobs as the shock sunk in. 'I shouldn't have let her walk the dog.'

Ellyn led Dina to a chair and sat her at the table.

That's when Gina spotted the Fixodent tooth glue on the side. 'Who uses this?'

'What? My daughter is missing and you're asking me about this?' She picked up the half-used tube and dropped it on the table.

'I'm sorry, Mrs Carpenter. I wouldn't ask if it wasn't important.'

'Naomi. She uses it. She has a missing tooth and uses it to fix her denture.'

'Which tooth?'

The woman slapped her hand on the table. 'Why are you going on about the bloody denture? You need to get out there now and find our missing kids.'

'Please, it's important.'

'Top right.' Dina began to count and closed her eyes. 'Third one along from the meat-eating tooth.'

'What was she wearing when she left?'

'I don't know.' Mrs Carpenter looked around. 'Her short-sleeved yellow hoodie.'

Gina nodded to Jacob. 'I need to make a call.' She hurried towards the front door.

'What's going on?' the woman shouted.

Gina went out the front and phoned Briggs immediately. 'Naomi has to be considered a suspect in this too. She made up some story about needing to get out with the dog, then left it neatly tied up. She's now gone or maybe she's been taken, blackmailed. I don't know yet but I know this isn't good.'

'Harte, slow down a little.'

'Sir, that's three missing kids now. Naomi Carpenter isn't at home and get this, she has a missing tooth, third from the canine, top right; that could make her Leah's biter.'

'I'll make sure everyone knows. The techies have all the laptops and gadgets that the kids own and they're trying to work through the info and crack passwords. Wait, I have an email.'

'What is it?'

Briggs went silent for a few seconds. 'The lab rushed the blood testing through, the blood at the back of the Spalding's fence. It doesn't belong to Oscar but it does match up to Caro Blakely's. What's more is that the samples that you delivered straight to the team a short while ago from Caro Blakely's bedroom matches that of Oscar Spalding.'

'Are we saying that Caro stabbed Oscar with that nail file?'

'That's what the evidence shows.'

'Opening night, Leah's murder. Second night, Jordan's murder. Third night, possibly, Oscar is stabbed with a nail file. Was he trying to kill Caro so she attacked him with her nail file or was she trying to kill him? And where is Naomi and, based on a very possible working theory, why did she bite Leah? What's going on with these kids?' Gina paused and smiled at the postie as he walked past. 'Have you read the contents of the notebook which I also dropped off, the one we found in Caro's bedroom?'

'I have. At least we know why Caro didn't want to go to another camp out party given what happened to her.'

'They drugged her with Rohypnol. That's sinister. And something that looks like Rohypnol has just been found in Oscar's bedroom. Call me as soon as you have any updates on the tech. We need someone to report on that fast. Lives depend on it.'

'Wait, there's someone knocking.'

Gina listened as Briggs spoke in his office.

'They've cracked Oscar's laptop and I'm going through it now. I'll call you back.' Briggs hung up and Gina swore at her phone before dropping it back into her pocket.

Jacob hurried out of the Carpenters' house and ran down the path. 'Mrs Carpenter said that there was a hang-out that the kids used to go to but Naomi never said where it was. She remembers overhearing a conversation between Naomi and a friend. They complained about the dust and a leaky roof. She doesn't know any more, but she gave me this.' Jacob held up a tablet. 'A team is also on the way. Mrs Carpenter has also agreed that Naomi's room can be searched.'

'As soon as the team arrives, we need to get over to Elsa James's house. She might be the missing piece to all this. I'll call ahead so that she's not let out of sight until either we or Wyre gets there. We can't afford for her to go missing.' Gina grabbed her phone again to make the call.

CHAPTER SIXTY-ONE

Wasting no time, Gina turned off the ignition. Jacob followed her up the path to the house where Elsa James and her parents lived. Banging loudly, she waited and Wyre answered. 'Please tell me that Elsa is here.' The beating midday sun was now almost at its peak and there was no breeze to speak of. A humming of insects flew around the overflowing bin that turned Gina's stomach as she inhaled.

'She's safe and sound in the living room, guv. It's a bit crowded in there. One of Ellyn's team is here too.'

'Before I go in, do we know any more from Elsa?'

'No, guv. She's upset and agitated, as expected. None of her friends are answering their phones or the messages she's been trying to send to them. We've managed to keep her off social media, which is good.' Wyre gave a half smile.

'Okay, with Naomi now missing, she's all we've got.'

'Naomi's missing?' Wyre's brow furrowed. 'Since when?'

'Over the last hour. She went out to walk the family dog and left it tied to a post outside the back gate and is now nowhere to be seen.'

'Not good.'

Gina and Jacob stepped into the crammed hall, knocking several coats off the coat hook. Jacob nudged them into a neat pile against the wall along with the stack of shoes. A terrier bounded over, wagging its tail.

'Buster, get back now. Sorry about the dog.' Mrs James stood there, still in her dressing gown.

'That's okay.' Gina patted the yappy dog and it kept running in front of her feet as she headed to the living room. Elsa was sitting in the chair by the window, head in hands, staring at her blank phone as if waiting for news.

'Mr James, Mrs James. I know we met on Sunday morning but I'm DI Harte and this is DS Driscoll. I don't have time to explain everything but what I can say is that right now we have three missing teenagers who are all part of Elsa's group of friends. We are deeply concerned for their safety and just want them brought home.'

'Three, I thought there were two?' Mr James stepped forward as he scratched his beard.

'There were but now another has gone missing.'

'Who is it?' Mrs James asked, worry lines spread across her forehead.

'Naomi Carpenter.'

'Not Naomi! She's Elsa's best friend. She stays with us all the time. Her mother must be distraught. I should call her—' Mrs James went to grab her phone.

Gina held her hand up. 'Please, someone is looking after her at present and we urgently need to speak to Elsa. May we use your kitchen?'

The woman dropped her arm, clutching her phone against her side and nodded. 'Elsa, love. The detectives need a word with you. It's about Naomi.'

Elsa tightened up her high ponytail and stood, pushing her phone into the pocket of her jeans. 'I was waiting for her to message me back but she hasn't.'

As they entered the kitchen, Gina and Jacob left the FLO and Wyre with Mr James in the living room, where Wyre was filling him in on the updates with Naomi.

'Elsa, can you tell me why Naomi was messaging you today?'

The girl glanced back and forth between her mother, Gina and Jacob. She began to pick a spot on her head, lifting the thick coat of foundation away. 'Err… she said she couldn't get hold of Oscar and she was worried. I said it was probably nothing and that he was probably having a lie-in but we've been checking in with each other every morning since what happened to Jordan. We were scared.'

'And?'

'Oscar didn't message Naomi and she was panicked so she said she was going to look for him. Now she's offline and I can't get hold of her, see.' Elsa held her phone up on Facebook Messenger and the conversation was just as she had described.

'May I read the whole message chain?' Gina reached over to take the phone but Elsa snatched it away.

'It's private.' She began to gnaw at her knuckle.

'Elsa, we believe that Naomi, Oscar and Caro are in immediate danger. Two of your friends have been murdered. I want to bring them home safely and you can help me.'

The girl's face began to redden and her eyes watered up. 'I'm sorry, Mum. We were just being stupid and it all went too far.' She handed the phone to Gina. Mrs James hugged her daughter.

Gina scrolled through the messages. Before Saturday night, they were just about who Naomi and Elsa fancied, what A-levels they were taking and what was on at the cinema. Then the night in question came. They talked about the meetup at the woods and all the alcohol each of them would be bringing. Then came the check in messages between Elsa and Naomi. It was like bits of the conversation were missing. The roofie was mentioned and both girls swore that they wouldn't say a word as they'd all be in huge trouble. Then came the source of Elsa's worry, where she told Naomi that Leah had sex with Oscar. 'Do you carry on these conversations on other platforms?'

'We use Snapchat.' Gina knew those messages vanished after the recipient had read them. Not her favourite kind when it came to a murder investigation.

'Tell me about the relationship between Oscar and Leah.'

The girl shook her head rapidly. 'I can't.'

Something was holding Elsa back. 'Why not?'

'He said not to tell or something bad would happen.'

Gina leaned in. 'Something bad has already happened and it could get worse. Three of your friends are missing and I'm truly scared that someone will get hurt.'

'I swear I didn't know on the night and neither did Naomi. Caro Snapchatted me the other day and told me something that Anthony had told her. That at the last party, Anthony had been fighting with Oscar over it. I know he had a funeral to go to but Ant then said he wanted nothing more to do with us and the parties.'

'What is it you're trying to tell me?'

'Oscar roofied Caro's drink at the last party and the one last week, he did it again with Leah.'

'Thank you for being honest with me.' Gina already new about Caro's drugging from the notebook entries.

'I've been getting these threatening messages saying that if I tell anyone, I'll die. They were on Snapchat too. Naomi received a few and we've been panicking which is why we didn't say anything. We know it was Oscar even though the sender was anonymous. It had to be him. Someone has also been following me about here and there and I know that was Oscar too. I caught him looking up at my bedroom window. He's been following Caro too. She was so distraught, trying to piece together what happened to her but then she had a go at me too.'

'Why was that?'

'Does my mum have to be here?'

'It's okay, love. I'm not angry. Just tell the truth.' Mrs James gripped her daughter's shaky hand.

'I slept with Oscar on the night Caro was drugged. I was so wasted, I don't know why but I did. She sort of came around and stumbled into the tent we were in but Oscar shooed her back out and she got into such a weird state. Shouting incoherently. She was barely standing though.'

'Were you drugged?'

'No, I thought he liked me and I liked him but after, he ignored me.'

'I hope you used protection.' Mrs James rolled her eyes.

'Mum! Neither of us wanted to become parents. We're not stupid.' A wash of relief filled Mrs James's face. 'Please don't tell Dad.'

Her mother pursed her lips.

'Why did Oscar drug Caro?'

'It wasn't what you think.'

Jacob scribbled away and Gina tilted her head a little and looked sympathetic. 'So tell me in your own words.'

'It was a joke. Nothing more than that.'

'Drugging people is dangerous and it's definitely not a joke,' Mrs James said.

'I didn't do it, Mum. I didn't know Caro had been drugged until I saw Oscar and Ant scrapping over it. It was too late as she was already slurring her words and looking a bit odd.'

'What happened then?'

'They just did silly things like drew on her with a pen, like a moustache, things like that, then Caro started waking and getting really agitated. It was like… she was having anxiety attacks or seeing things. Oscar said it was a bad reaction and that shouldn't happen, that she was just meant to be a bit chilled out. Eventually they managed to calm her down and put her to bed in her tent. We carried on with the party and just thought she'd sleep it off.'

Gina frowned. 'But then Oscar drugged Leah at the second party? Did he rape her?'

'He'd already slept with her earlier. We all knew that the drugging was wrong which is why he's been threatening us if we said anything. I'm scared of what he might do and I don't think Caro knows that he's been sending the horrible messages to her to try to scare her into staying silent.'

'But you'd all been checking in with each other every day, Oscar included?'

'Oscar said we had too. I think it was more about him controlling us. Making sure that we hadn't spoken. Naomi went looking for him. She Snapchatted me. I told her not to bother after how he'd been with us but she said we'd all done things we were ashamed of and that we needed to stick together so that our secrets remained just so. That's why she went. We've all done things we're not proud of.'

If Oscar thought Caro or Naomi would say something, then they were both in immediate danger. 'I'd like to talk more about this later but could you tell me where they might be? Is there a hang-out that you meet at?'

'There are a few.'

'Okay.'

Jacob waited, ready to note them down.

'There's an empty house on Guild End. Right at the bottom. It's been boarded up for years. That's one of them. Then there's Ant's dad's allotment shed but we haven't hung out there for months. That's on Pickering Green.'

'You've been really helpful, thank you, Elsa.'

Gina hurried out of the house and relayed those two locations to Briggs. 'We'll head to the Guild End house, send a team to Pickering Green where Wyre will head to now.'

CHAPTER SIXTY-TWO

'Hey, guys, are you here?' Naomi slipped through the opening and landed hard on the stone floor, twisting her ankle slightly. She yelped as she rubbed the area where the lightning bolt of pain had struck, just as she heard the sickening crunch. She imagined that her mum had found the dog by now as Butch had been whining non-stop as she ran away from the back of the house. The dog's sad stare followed her as she ran around the corner, leaving him.

She checked her phone again. It was definitely switched off. The police could trace anyone to anywhere. She'd seen how they worked on the TV. She checked the other pocket of her jeans. Her SIM card was still there, far apart from her phone. Possibly paranoid but she didn't care.

As Oscar hadn't answered any of her messages, she had to at least eliminate that he might be at one of their hang-outs. With the police on their way to her home for yet another talk, she needed to know what to say and with Oscar taking the lead role in all this, he needed to be the one to guide them. After all, if he ended up in trouble they would be in it too. She swallowed as she carried on rubbing her ankle, listening in silence for any sign of life. She'd definitely have bruising and tenderness for a few weeks.

Outside she could hear the sound of the birds chirping from the treetops in the afternoon sun. She swallowed as she thought of all the things she was guilty of and it wasn't a pretty thought. If the truth came out it would shock everyone, that's why she'd do or say absolutely anything to protect their secrets. She wasn't proud of her part in it but it was time to work through this and start again with a story that worked for all of them.

She frowned. All had been fine until Caro got involved. Why did she have to discuss everything with Anthony? The mystery messages that Oscar had ordered Naomi to send to Caro were simply meant to shut her up, just act as a warning but then she went and stabbed Oscar in the leg. All he was going to do was freak her out enough to keep her quiet. Caro had gone too far this time and she was going to pay. Stabbing Oscar was the final straw and now she was paying.

Naomi was sick of their little weird friendship. How Caro would follow Oscar around like a sad puppy, that's why it had been easy to laugh away the night at the last party when Caro was drugged up so they could humiliate her. She should have learned her lesson to not be such a saddo, but no, that sad little puppy would always chase Oscar around.

Naomi grabbed hold of an old battered chair and stood, allowing a bit of her weight to bear down on her ankle. She wasn't getting anywhere sitting around. It wasn't as bad as it looked. One step after another, the pain began to ease. She pushed through the piles of junk and dusty old equipment until she reached the rusty door. Pushing it gently, she caught the sound of a squeak as someone rattled around.

They were here. Time to shut Caro up. If one of them spoke, they'd all go down. As she burst through, a ray of intense sunshine blinded her as a thick dusty old blanket came over her head before someone wrestled her to the ground. 'Oscar, it's me,' she tried to blurt, but instead, she inhaled a lungful of dust and felt the suffocating weight of heavy material being pushed into her face. She rolled around, disorientated in the dark, trying to hit out and kick but to no avail. Heart battering against her chest, she couldn't breathe as nausea began to kick in and she was hot; so hot, and gasping; hyperventilating. Kicking again, her feet met nothing but air as her attacker held an arm to her neck. Strength almost gone, she could see dots upon dots through her closed eyes, and they were getting bigger. *Can't breathe.*

The last thing she heard was the manic laughter. 'Welcome to the party.'

CHAPTER SIXTY-THREE

Gina drove the car alongside the gates of the derelict house on Guild End Road. She glanced through the barbed wire fence that was padlocked shut and rattled it to test how secure it was. 'They didn't get in through the front.'

Jacob waved at the police car that had just turned, then he headed along. He shook the perimeter fence as he followed it around. At the end of a row and quite a way from any other houses, this one had sat in a state for years; known as the project that ran out of money. The owner had gone to live abroad, abandoning it. It was nothing more than a blemish on a small rural road that the other residents preferred to forget. Gina knew of its presence. It had been the target for illegal raves in the past. Before it had been fenced off, the land had been occupied by travellers for a while but since then, she'd heard of no issues with anyone hanging around but this is where Elsa said that the kids met. But how did they get in? She couldn't see any material trapped in the barbed wire. She nodded to the uniformed officers to stand guard at the front of the gate while she followed Jacob.

'I don't want to alarm them if they're here, so whatever you do, don't make any loud noises. I'd prefer the element of surprise so we can swoop in quickly and take control of the situation. We must remember that two teens have been murdered. Whoever did that is dangerous and I don't want a hostage situation.' Gina followed Jacob around the perimeter, pushing through an entanglement of brambles and bushes. As they emerged through a tree, Jacob flinched and almost fell back as a wasps' nest hummed away and the pesky creatures began to angrily buzz around them. First there were a couple, then a few more and then a whole swarm came at them.

Gina and Jacob ploughed through. She felt a sting piercing her arm. 'Bloody thing.' She slapped the wasp away.

Both waving their hands, they eventually escaped the wasps and reached the edge of the back of the house but the fence was on the floor as if it had been trampled down. Stepping over it, Gina kept close to Jacob as they got nearer to the back. Three windows to the first floor, two to the bottom, either side of a back door. All were boarded up except for the one on the top left. The board looked as though it had been pulled away. She walked up to the downstairs boards and began to pull but they were nailed firmly in place. Gina gulped. 'I'm going to have to climb onto the canopy to get in.'

'It looks too dangerous, guv. This place is a death trap. We should wait for backup then we can get in through the door.'

'That would alarm them. I don't want them to know we're coming in.' She turned to him as she inhaled. 'Keeping quiet could be a matter of life and death. I'm not risking a kid's life.' The cuts to her face and arms were probably going to feel like nothing by the end of this. She imagined ceilings crashing in and floors disappearing. She pushed everything out of her mind. Now wasn't the time to overthink anything.

'I should go in.' Jacob stepped ahead.

She pulled him back. 'No. I'm lighter and smaller than you. That opening is tiny. There's also less of a chance of all this coming down if I go. You're going to have to help me onto the canopy.'

He frowned.

'What are you waiting for?' She stretched her arms out a couple of times and took a few deep breaths as she stood poised underneath, hoping that the even ledge would hold her weight.

'I want it noted that I don't like any of this.'

'Noted, now give me a lift up.'

He linked his hands and she stepped into them. He lifted her as high as he could. She reached the top of the canopy and gritted her teeth together as she used all her strength to pull up her own body weight. The wood cracked and crunched, threatening to come loose and fling her onto the stingers and brambles below. Muscles shaking, she wondered if she would be able to do this. Her upper body strength wasn't what it used to be and her underarms were more bingo wings than toned, but she did it. Sweat dripping down her forehead, she slid along the canopy on her belly until her knees passed the edge. She kneeled and wiped her brow, taking a moment to catch her breath. She hadn't even got into the house and she was already exhausted. She thought of Caro, Oscar and Naomi and she knew she had to get to the bottom of everything. She gulped as she stood, knowing that what she might find was another body or maybe two. She shook her head.

She peered through the bottom of the window and saw that half of the roof had collapsed, allowing in shafts of sunlight. Pulling her body up once again, the canopy crashed to the ground just as she tipped her body through the window. After a struggle, she landed on a pile of dusty old blankets that coated her nostrils with a musty smell. That of mouldy dampness and possibly excrement. Standing, she glanced back, and put her thumb up to Jacob who had now been joined by another officer. Everyone would now be in place. One word from Gina and the battering rams would have the whole place opened up.

As she stepped forward, the creaky floorboard crunched beneath, setting off falling debris underneath. Pigeons flapped and flew away through the roof. She shook the woodlouse off her hand and carried on forward, testing each bit of wooden floor as she went. In the hallway, the bannister was missing and the stench of urine hit her.

Standing in silence, she listened for any movement, anything at all but she couldn't hear a thing. She went to open the first bedroom door but it crashed into the room. A stained mattress had been pushed against the back wall and was surrounded by beer cans and a couple of used condoms. The next room was just an empty bedroom with a view of the living room below where the floor had fallen through. Then lastly, the bathroom. She pushed the door, which resisted a little and she could see that it was nothing but an empty shell, all bathroom furniture stripped. A bucket sat in the corner. She'd found the source of the urine smell.

Time to tackle the stairs. She knew the living room was clear but what about the kitchen? There had to be another reception room too. Her foot plunged through a wooden step, piercing the skin on her ankle. Blood trickled into her shoe. She either wanted to kick the step or cry. Everything hurt and the intense heat was making her feel sick.

As she reached the bottom step, she heard a scrape behind the reception room door. Placing her ear against it, she listened for voices; movement; anything. The scrape came again. She gently pressed the rusty door handle, took a deep breath and pushed as quietly as she could, then she fell back and shouted out as a dark mass charged towards her.

CHAPTER SIXTY-FOUR

The battering ram followed and the ragged-looking crow fought its way out, flapping against Jacob and the three officers. 'Move to the side, guv.'

With the protection of body armour, the officers pushed in and called out police as they entered the room. There was no point though, the house was empty of people. The only living thing had been the crow and the rat that just scurried away. 'They're not here,' she said in a broken voice.

'They've all been here, though.' Jacob stepped through and gazed at the board. Photos were pinned everywhere. All the teens with drinks in hand looking like they were having a party in this very room. Items of clothing had been left and even a few cans of pop that hadn't been opened. Nub ends of roll-up cigarettes that Gina suspected could have been marijuana.

'Where are they?' Gina paced back and forth to calm her banging heart down. Her fists clenched with frustration, she could feel failure running through her veins. It felt like weakness, sickness, shaking tension that was ready to explode. All that effort for nothing. There were still three missing kids. 'Look for clues, any clues. There must be something here that might help.' They all put gloves on and began to rummage. Gina focused on the photos. Some were taken at shopping centres, others at school. Caro had a huge smile as she duck pouted for the camera with one strap of her skinny top hanging off her shoulder. Elsa and Naomi were pecking each other's lips, bottles of beer in hand.

Oscar posed with Jordan, baseball caps on back to front. Anthony simply smiled, looking a little more reserved. Leah was in a clinch with Oscar as Jordan and Caro sat in a corner staring at her phone. The photos continued. They were either taken in public places, out in the woodland or in the house. Gina's phone rang. 'Wyre, what you got?'

'Nothing, guv. The allotment is clear. We've also checked through the windows of all the surrounding sheds and buildings. We spoke to some of the gardeners here and none of them seem to recall seeing any kids hanging around lately. There is no sign of them.'

'Damn. This location is clear too. They've been hanging out here, but they're not here now.'

Gina's gaze stopped on another photo. Caro was sitting on a stack of folded material, arranged into yellow, red, blue and green piles. 'Paula, I'll call you back.' She ended the call. 'Where could this be?' She pointed.

Jacob leaned over her and scrunched his brow. 'Stacks of material and a concrete wall. Who knows?'

She pointed to another photo. 'Here, there's another photo of Leah and Jordan smoking.' Leah's large pupils stared into the camera, a huge beaming smile on her face. 'Is that a pile of yoga mats?'

'I think so but bigger. Crash mats, maybe? It could be the leisure centre or a gym.'

'Those are hockey sticks too. It's obvious!'

Gina's phone rang again. It was Briggs.

'Sir.'

'You need to get to the school now. We've cracked Oscar's computer and we've got into his Facebook and Messenger app. The kids used to hang around in the PE equipment storage unit that is next to the main school building. I'm sending backup now.'

'There are photos here of a room full of PE equipment and it definitely looks like they could have been taken at the school.

We're leaving now. We'll get this house sealed off in the meantime until forensics can get here.'

'Go now before it's too late.'

She hung up. 'I'll need two uniformed officers to stay behind and seal the house off. Jacob, we need to get to Cleevesford High. It looks like this photo could well have been taken in the sports storage unit.' As she turned to leave, Gina saw a short-sleeved yellow hoodie hanging on a picture hook. 'Naomi's been here today. That looks like the hoodie her mother described, the one she was wearing when she went out with the dog.' Gina shifted the hoodie slightly and saw a note stuck to the wall.

Oscar, if you come here, find me. I'm heading to the unit.
We have to end all of this once and for all.

She pointed. 'I think that just confirmed it. We know where they are. Let's hurry, before it's too late.'

CHAPTER SIXTY-FIVE

Gina hurried out of her car, Jacob close behind and they met with the officers and Wyre in the middle of the car park. The tall three-storey building stood quietly, like any school that was closed up for the holidays. The car park was empty except for their cars. She spotted an ambulance pulling in, all precautionary in case one of the teens was injured. 'Quick briefing.' She adjusted her stab vest and called them over into the shade from the building as she spoke. 'The gym storage unit is just behind this main building, at the back of the sports hall. Hello.' She waved at the man in shorts who was approaching.

'I'm Stu, the caretaker. I was told to be here when you arrived.' The man smiled.

'Thank you. Yes, we have reason to believe that some of the kids may have broken into the gym storage unit.'

'And you need all these officers to deal with a couple of kids. Things like this can happen now and again, we normally just call the police and they get a slap on the wrists and we re-board or glaze the broken entry point.'

'There's a bit more to it this time. I need you to keep away. Do you have a key for the building?'

He gulped, rubbed his stubble then passed her a huge bunch of keys. 'It's this one.' He passed them to her, giving her the exact key to hold on to. The bunch jangled. 'What's going on?'

'We'll explain all to you in a while. As I said, keep back. Please wait over there by the police cars.' As he went to turn, she called him back. 'Hey. Have you seen anyone around today?'

'I was tidying some of the shrubs and I thought I saw a girl on the field but that's it. I wasn't out here the whole time.'

'Do you have CCTV on the storage unit?'

'Nah. We did have but it kept getting vandalised. I think the kids kept throwing things at the camera until it smashed. We only have the ones on the front, now.'

Gina gave him a half smile and he carried on towards the police car. 'Right, team. As before, search the perimeter first. We are not going to burst in and alarm any one. If you see anyone, come to me as quietly as you can.'

Wyre and Jacob nodded.

'Let's go.' She scuttled across the grass and over a wall before heading around the building. The huge field went on forever. Perfectly green and cut with a cricket pavilion up the one end and fenced off tennis courts at the other. A track was painted out in the grass. Then she saw the ugly grey unit. She waved everyone across, placing her finger over her lips as she did. They stuck close to the back of the main building where she hoped they'd all blend in a little should someone be peering out of the unit.

Gina stared at Wyre and two officers and pointed to the far side of the building, keys still in her other hand. They nodded and broke away. Gina looked at Jacob and the remaining officers and motioned for them to follow her. Slowly, she crept up to the large unit. The windows were quite high up. She stood on tiptoes to peer through the first one but all she could see was a large room, over stacked with gym equipment. Tennis rackets spilling onto the floor, large nets of balls.

She jumped as Wyre crept up behind her and tapped her on the shoulder. 'Guv, I think we have the entry point but I can't see through the windows on the other side because of the blinds,' she whispered. Gina followed her around the building, staying under the other window as they hurried to the back. Gina put her thumb up to Wyre.

A large crate had been placed on the floor and a wooden box had been stood on top of it. That's when she spotted the broken window; clean out as if the glass had been missing for ages. Gina carefully stepped up onto the crate, then the box and peered through. That's when she heard a pained cry.

'Help.'

She jumped down. 'We're going in.'

Sprinting to the front of the unit, she placed the key in the lock and heard it click on the turn. She handed the bunch to one of the officers and stepped into the musty cramped room and saw the door ahead.

'Ahhh.' Another yelp coming from behind the door.

'Ready?' Gina waved her hand for everyone to get into position. If the killer was there holding the victim, there was a chance they could be taken hostage. Her mind flickered back and forth. Was it Naomi, the biter, or Oscar, the one who seemed to be controlling everything? Was Caro out for revenge after she was drugged? Too many possibilities. She placed her hand on the door and gently pushed. She recoiled, there was so much blood.

CHAPTER SIXTY-SIX

Gina ignored the boy tied to the wooden chair and headed straight to the body under the blanket. His charges for the druggings would come later. She pulled it away from the head of the girl and felt for a pulse. 'Call a paramedic.' The boy carried on yelping in pain. There was no pulse at all. She turned Naomi onto her back and pushed her finger around the girl's mouth, pulling out her loose false tooth before beginning CPR. She breathed into her, then started chest compressions.

'Clear the way.' A paramedic ran in and took over.

Gina remained on her knees, getting her breath back as she watched Jacob and Wyre untying the boy. Another paramedic ran over and began to try to stop the blood that was coming from his head. More blood seeped through his jeans.

'Oscar, you're safe now.'

It was as if the boy couldn't see her. He shouted and yelled, dribble running down his chin. 'She drugged me...'

'Oscar?' Gina stood right in front of him as the paramedics carried on helping him. 'Where's Caro?'

He began to hyperventilate and shake. 'She's gone... she's gone.'

'Gone where? Please, Oscar, we need to find her.'

'She did this. She killed the others.'

A shiver ran down Gina's spine. That teenage girl looked like she wasn't capable of killing anyone. Her mind whirred into action. Leah had been either really drunk or drugged. That would have made her an easy target for Caro. Jordan had been standing at the top of a flight of concrete steps. She'd simply come up from behind and kicked him over the edge. Gina's mind flashed back to how Terry had fallen down their stairs to his death. It was so easy to do that even a girl as petite as Caro could manage it. Then Oscar, he claimed to have been drugged, was that Caro's revenge. Naomi had come in search of them and Caro had simply taken her by surprise as she had Oscar bound to a chair and now… Caro was nowhere to be seen.

Gina bent over again. 'Oscar, please. Where is Caro?'

'She left. She had a bag and some money. She said she was leaving for good.' He began screaming in pain as the paramedic tended to the stab wound on the top of his arm. 'She left me here to die, said I'd bleed to death and the maggots would eat me before school started again.'

'Did she say where she was going?'

Oscar went white and heaved as he turned, throwing up on the paramedic's foot. His body began to shake and his eyes were closing.

'He's lost a lot of blood and he's going into shock. You're going to have to leave so that we can get him out.'

Gina and the team stepped back and watched on as the other paramedic declared Naomi dead. Gina's stomach dropped and she hurried out, gasping as she left the building. She kicked the wall and roared. 'How could we let her die?'

Jacob and Wyre joined her, both looking as dejected as Gina felt. They had been too slow and Naomi Carpenter's parents were going to receive the news that their daughter, who was out walking their dog that morning, had been murdered. She turned around. 'Right, let's all pull it together. We have a fugitive on the loose. Get all units up to date. She's dangerous and we need Caro Blakely caught now. There's only so far a girl of her age can get.'

Gina's phone rang. 'Sir.'

After giving Briggs the fastest summary ever, he continued. 'Mrs Blakely called. She's reported that a tin of money she kept in the food cupboard has been emptied, best part of five hundred pounds. She also noticed some of her daughter's clothes were missing. It's looking like we have ourselves a teenager on the run.'

Gina leaned back against the wall as she watched Oscar coming out on a stretcher. Eyes closed and paramedics hurrying with him to the ambulance.

'Can you put an alert out for Caro Blakely with the rail and bus services? We need officers showing her photo to everyone who works there. Call me back if you have anything.'

'I'm on it now. Search the vicinity. You might find something that tells us where she was heading. Does the boy know?'

'He's in shock and now unconscious. We'll need to catch up with him later. He's in a bad way. I'm going to check out the unit here and then I'll head over to Mrs Blakely's. She has to have some idea of where her daughter might go.'

Briggs paused for a moment. 'O'Connor has just checked in. I'll get him over there immediately and you can join him when you can. In the meantime, if we get any tip-offs this end, I'll call you straight away. Good with that, Harte?'

'Yes, all good.' He ended the call and Gina stepped back into the unit one last time. Through the second door, she swallowed as all she could see were the tips of Naomi's feet. Her body now left for the crime scene investigators to deal with. She put on some gloves and entered, taking in the wasted life that lay on the floor, searching for anything.

Her phone rang again. 'O'Connor, what's up?'

'It's Anthony. He was meant to be in his bedroom but it looks like he jumped onto the porch and he's gone. He left a note.'

CHAPTER SIXTY-SEVEN

The bus trundled past the Woodrow Centre shops, an estate in Redditch. She was ever closer to Redditch town centre. As soon as she got on that train and into Birmingham, the sooner she'd be heading up north. Maybe Edinburgh. Caro had always fancied Scotland. She had enough money to get her there and then maybe she'd find some cash work in a café or on a market. Shaking, she gripped her bag. She'd done it. She'd made them pay and now she had to get away. Having a head start, she'd be well out of the area before anyone found Oscar and Naomi's bodies. She glanced at her new phone, only one number programmed into it and smiled at the adventure that was about to start.

She pressed that number and waited until her call was answered. 'Are you on your way…?' She listened as he spoke. 'I know, I can't wait. We're going to have such an adventure.' She ended the call. He was waiting right where she'd told him to and they were both using their new phones.

As the bus continued down the bumpy bus route, she glanced out of the window, trying to ignore the other passengers. One of them stared at her split lip so she turned away. *Don't look anyone in the eye. Stay invisible.*

Her clothes were plain. Jeans and a black T-shirt. Her pumps grey too. Flat, definitely flat in case she needed to run. She gripped her rucksack, knowing that it contained everything she'd need for a while. The world was waiting for her and she was excited to see what it had to offer. How did she feel? High; that's how she felt.

A woman on the opposite seat caught her smiling. Caro looked away. It would all be over soon.

As the bus trundled down the hill and into Redditch Bus Station, she hurried up to the front, ready to disembark. The train was due in ten minutes and there was one more thing to take care of. One more person who should have done more to help her but didn't. Now it was his turn to die. Just a little shove in front of the train as it pulled in and it would all be over.

She hurried off the bus leaving the Kingfisher Shopping Centre behind her and waited for the traffic lights to turn red before running across the road. She hurried down the slope, bought her ticket and there he was at the end of the platform. She glanced back at where the tracks reached a tunnel, still there back from the times that the track used to run right through. This stop however was the end of the line. It was also the end of the line for Anthony.

He smiled and waved as he stood there with his rucksack ready to go with her on their adventure. He'd been easy to persuade. The promise of drinking, fun, sex; he'd fallen for it easily. Had even promised not to mention it to his parents and just to leave a note saying he'd be back in a few days. He smiled and for a moment, she liked his smile and she wanted to lean up and kiss him.

The train began to trundle in so she ran, making it to him before the train got too close. *Goodbye, Ant!*

CHAPTER SIXTY-EIGHT

Lara Blakely sobbed into her hands as Gina relayed everything she knew. Mr Blakely stood with his back to her and Jacob as he stood over the sink. Jake, their little boy, cried as he came out of the living room after what felt like the tenth time. Lara called him over and hugged him closely. 'Mummy loves you but please can you go and watch your programmes so that I can talk to the lady for a minute?'

Mr Blakely turned and picked the little boy up, taking him out of the room without so much as glancing at Gina.

'Is there anything we can do for you or maybe there's someone we can call to be with you all? I know this has been a shock. An officer will be here soon to stay with you through this.' Gina paused. 'I'll also need to take a formal statement from you down at the station.'

Lara grabbed her keys. 'I'm ready.' She began to shake and fell against a kitchen stool, grabbing it to steady herself. 'Why us, why my daughter?'

Gina couldn't answer that question.

'I thought we were good parents. We love our children, care for them and give them everything. Only a few years ago, we had nothing and were almost homeless but we turned it all around. What went so wrong? We're good people. Do what we're meant to do. Work hard.' Tears began to spill down Lara's blotchy face.

'Are you sure you don't know where Caro might have headed to? We are worried about her and the state she might be in.' The thought of a young wasted life that would now be spent behind bars saddened Gina.

'I wish I did.' Lara paused. 'It's only a matter of time, isn't it?'

Gina frowned.

'Until the protesters turn up at our door. Until people chant for us to get out because it must be our fault.' Lara walked over to the banner she had been holding while parading with the protest group outside the Meegans' house. 'Parents are always to blame when their child kills, aren't they? If this was happening to anyone else, I'd be out there screaming in the streets, getting angry; shouting my mouth off while waving banners. Our lives are ruined.' The woman paused. 'Where does this leave my little boy? He'll be a target for bullies at school. People will smash our windows, set our home on fire.' She began to sob.

'We will do our best to help you through this, Mrs Blakely. I know it will be hard but it's not your fault.' She nodded to Jacob to pass her some tissues.

He picked up a kitchen roll from the side and passed it over. 'Here you go.'

Gina pulled a couple of sheets and passed them to Lara.

'I've been outside Sandy's house shouting murderer and paedo… What have I done?' She wiped her eyes. 'I need Caro found. I need to ask her why? I know you said that group of bullies drugged her but she should have come to me. We could have reported what happened together and faced them together or as a family. To do this… to murder them over some stupid pranks and dares, it's insane. I feel like I don't know my own child and I can't put into words how much that hurts. How did I not see this?'

'We don't know all that happened but when we find Caro we hope to find out more. She'll need you more than ever.' Gina knew that to be true and she knew how conflicted Lara must be feeling.

The woman made a deep guttural sound as she cried while hyperventilating. Gina wanted nothing more than to be able to tell her that everything would be okay, but it wouldn't. Her phone rang. 'Sorry, I need to take this.' She stepped into the garden, leaving Jacob with Lara and answered Briggs's call. 'What have you got?'

'Railway ticket office at Redditch Station have confirmed a sighting of her and there's been an incident. We've also released her photo to the media. It's going to be on social media and everywhere in no time at all. Get the family out now because the shit is about to hit the fan.'

Gina ended the call and gripped her phone to her chest, dreading sharing the latest news.

CHAPTER SIXTY-NINE

Caro ran behind Ant, up past the Custard Factory, an older part of Digbeth that had become trendy to set up a shop or an art studio. Panting heavily, she couldn't go on like this for much longer.

Ant was pulling away from her. 'Slow down,' she called.

'No way, that security guard is catching up. Whatever you do, don't slow down or I'll get arrested for punching his friend.' How did Ant manage to run so fast and not look exhausted?

Caro had come that close to pushing him in front of the train but as it rolled in, people were looking and for a second she imagined that it would be better to run away as a pair. They'd have each other's backs on the journey and Ant wasn't a fugitive. He'd be able to get work and look after them both. It made so much sense at that very moment. That's why she'd stopped short of placing her hands on his back and nudging him under the train. She'd made the right decision. He'd defended her against the guard that was about to pull her aside and then he'd made a run for it with her.

As they turned down a side road, Caro crashed head-on into an elderly lady pushing a shopping trolley and bumped into the wall of a pub.

'Get up!' Ant yelled as he reached the end of the road. He pulled his phone from his pocket, reading something on the screen as he ran. Then he stopped, turned and stared at Caro.

As she leaned against the wall, she took a few breaths and wiped the beads of perspiration from the beating sun from her forehead with the edge of her black T-shirt.

'Watch where you're going, you stupid cow,' the old woman said as she picked her trolley up off the floor.

'Piss off, Grandma.' She had no time for a lecture.

Ant was still. 'Why aren't you running? Hurry.' Something was wrong.

'You're wanted for murder. It's all over Twitter.' He grabbed his hair and began to seethe.

She was on her own now. It was all out there and the whole country would be looking for her. As she went to run, she flung back into the security guard's chest. He had a hold of her T-shirt from the back of her neck. She tried to wriggle and turn to make him release her but it was no good.

Caro watched as a PCSO ran up behind Anthony and brought him down to the ground. He didn't even try to get away. It was over. She was over. A tear slipped down her cheek. She knew what was coming next. With flailing arms, she tried her best to lose the guard but it was no good. He was too strong.

'It's easier and less painful if you stop waving your arms.' He smiled at her with his crooked teeth on display. It was the man that Ant had punched, the red mark on his cheek the only giveaway of the assault. 'It's over.'

A police officer ran up behind him, calling all units as he took over and handcuffed Caro. 'Right, let's get you back to Cleevesford Station.'

A tear rolled down her cheek as he read her her rights. Arrested on suspicion of three murders and the attempted murder of another. She collapsed to the ground as she thought of her mother's face and what her father would say. All her friends at school would know and they'd hate her.

He drove her to it… Oscar! She'd make sure the world knew he was to blame.

CHAPTER SEVENTY

Gina answered her ringing phone as she stood outside the ward that Oscar was recovering in at the Cleevesford Hospital. She listened, nodded, bit her bottom lip and smiled before ending the call.

Jacob gave her a long stare. 'What?'

'Caro's been caught after Anthony punched a security guard at New Street Station. Security was about to pull them over as he recognised the photo that we'd sent over. The kids made a run for it but security gave chase, catching up with them on a side street past the Custard Factory. They'll both be transported back soon. That leaves us just enough time to speak to Oscar before heading back to the station.'

'Yes! Get in there.' Jacob punched the air.

'It's over.' Gina glanced through the ward and saw the boy sitting up in bed with his father beside him in a chair.

'It's hard to believe she managed to kill three of her peers. Such a dainty little dot. I don't think I've ever been more surprised by an outcome.' Jacob scrunched his nose and mopped his hairline with a tissue.

'It's easy when someone is standing on the edge, at height and it's easy when someone is drugged or drunk. It's also easy when someone is caught unaware.' All three were true of how Gina managed to help Terry to his death. He was drunk, teetering on the edge and totally unaware of what was coming. It had all been too easy even though Gina had been not much more than a nervous wreck of a waif at the time. She knew exactly how someone perceived as the underdog could win this one.

Jacob looked into her eyes, pausing for a few seconds before nodding slowly. 'You're so right.'

'Let's go and see what Oscar has to say, that's if his father will let us get a word in before shooing us out of the way.' Gina walked past the other bay where a man was snoring heavily and they stopped at the end of Oscar's bed. 'Hello, Oscar. Sorry to disturb you but we really need to speak with you about yesterday.'

'No probs,' he said, flinching as he tried to shuffle up the bed further, holding on to the thick dressing that covered his stab wound.

'Look, my son has been through a lot and I'd appreciate it if you just—'

'Dad, sir, please. I nearly got killed yesterday and I'm not proud of some of the things I've done. I want to talk, so just sit down and shut up.'

Oscar's face reddened and Gina wondered if that was the first time ever the boy had managed to stand up to his father. Maybe he'd taken out all his pent-up frustrations on his peers.

Mr Spalding slowly sat, keeping his gaze on Gina as he did. 'If that's what you want but you should have a solicitor present.'

'She tried to kill me. I don't need a solicitor and I'm sick of everything. I don't want to be this person any more. It's because of you, Dad, and this is where it ends. I've had enough. I've done a lot of growing up over this past twenty-four hours.'

Gina smiled sympathetically. She knew there were things she'd have to question Oscar about, mostly his use of Rohypnol, but her main focus was on his attempted murder. 'Thank you. We know you're in a lot of pain so we'll try not to keep you too long. When you get out of hospital, we'll need you to come down to the station to make a formal statement.'

'Course. The docs say I'll be in a couple of days so we'll come then, won't we?' Oscar turned to his dad.

The man leaned back, suspiciously eyeing Gina and Jacob up. 'It's getting late and he needs plenty of rest so if you get on with it, we'd be grateful.'

'Thank you. Oscar, I'll start with the forensics that we found. We found your blood on a nail file in Caro Blakely's bedroom. Can you explain that?'

'Yeah. I did something stupid and I think I scared her. I'd been sending her anonymous messages saying that I knew what had happened to her at the first party and that if she met me, I'd tell her everything. Naomi sent some of these messages too. We needed her to shut up but she was freaked out, a liability I guess.'

'Please carry on.'

'Yeah, I sent a message asking her to meet me in the woods. I was going to jump out and tell her it was just a joke, all part of the dares that we were joking around with. I hoped that I could persuade her to keep quiet and that it made sense as we all did things we weren't proud of now. That was the plan. I hoped she'd see that we all had something to hide, including her, and that she wouldn't tell. I didn't get the chance though because she half turned in the dark, stabbed me in the leg and ran off, so that backfired. I know scaring her like that was stupid after what had happened to Leah and Jordan. I had no idea at the time that it was Caro who killed them. I mean, she could have killed me for that stupid prank.'

'What did you want her and the others to keep quiet about?'

'It wasn't just me. None of us wanted our secrets to come out. Will I get into trouble if I say?' He scratched his nose.

'We'll have to look at the severity of everything but this case is a huge one. It will go to Crown Court and witnesses, including yourself, will be called. If you cooperate now, it will benefit you in the future.'

Mr Spalding sighed and nodded.

'The things we did were stupid. They'd start with drinking games, things like streaking through the woods and dancing naked and filming it so that no one would talk. But it was done for laughs. We got worse the more we drunk. We'd smash wing mirrors off cars, spray obscenities on peoples' garden walls and steal from the lorry drivers when we were drunk. We'd post dog mess through letter boxes. Dare each other to sleep with and kiss some of the others even though we might not fancy them. That's it. That's what we did.'

'How about the Rohypnol?'

Oscar sighed. 'Jordan said he got it from a dealer.'

'Did you drug Caro Blakely?'

'I was being egged on by Jordan but I only gave her a sprinkle and pocketed the rest. I didn't really want to hurt her.'

'What happened?'

'When it began to take effect, we drew on her. That's how stupid it got. We didn't rape anyone if that's what you think? It was all done for jokes and pranks. But Caro was scared and went a bit mad. I felt bad about it so we settled her in a tent and carried on. Anyway, I hooked up with Elsa at the first party, then Caro stumbled in while we were…' He looked at his dad. 'We were having sex and she called Elsa by Leah's name. She looked livid. I know she likes me, she always has done to the point of obsession and it got too much. I was glad she caught me and Elsa. I thought then that she'd get the hint that we would never be a thing. Anyway, it must have been about three in the morning, I felt really guilty and I was so drunk. I felt bad about hurting her feelings so I went into her tent. She was woozy and tried to talk but I told her to just rest and we'd talk the next day. I just lay on the ground in her tent and fell asleep. I swear I didn't touch her. That's all it was. The next morning, she was sick and hung-over and really angry at all the drawing on her body which I helped her clean off. It sounds immature now but when we were drunk, it seemed so funny. She couldn't look at me after that and she'd started to give Leah horrible stares as she still thought I'd slept with Leah.'

'And the most recent party on Saturday?'

'We invited Caro but she didn't even answer. We just assumed we'd upset her and she wasn't coming.'

'And what happened to Leah that night?'

'We were going to do the same, joke around and get something embarrassing on Leah so we did give her a bit of roofie.'

'But you had sex with her.'

'Yeah, but that was earlier in the evening, before the roofie. I don't need to drug girls into being with me. It was to joke around. Everyone was in on it, not just me. We were going to draw on her face and hope she didn't notice in the morning as we all thought it was so funny when we did it to Caro. She'd sort of drifted a little and we had this joke going that Naomi would give her a love bite for a laugh thinking that her mother might see. We pulled down her T-shirt to the top of her breast and Naomi actually bit her and we all burst out laughing but she was hammered. It was nothing more than a stupid prank that went too far. That really brought Leah round and she went wild and got really angry with us even though she was struggling to stand and walk. After ranting around the fire for a few minutes, she staggered off into the woods. We all ran after her, told her we were sorry and that we'd look after her, that was near the clearing but she told us she hated us and that she'd trusted me and I'd let her down. I did let her down…' Oscar ran his hand over his head. 'It's my fault she died. I did let her down. Earlier she was saying how much she liked me and I felt bad as for me it was just sex. Anyway, she was going at us, shouting and telling us to shove off so we left her behind and headed back to the camp. I said she was just attention-seeking and that she'd come back when she finished sulking.' He paused. 'We left her.'

'So you drugged her and left her alone thinking she'd make her way back to you?'

Mr Spalding stood. 'Don't say another word, son. My son is the victim here and here you are trying to blame him for all this.'

'Sit down!' Oscar trembled and stared at his father. 'This needs to come out. I'm so ashamed of what I did. If I'd treated Caro better, she'd have never have had a jealous fit on Leah and come over that night to kill her. The worse thing about it is…'

'Go on.'

'I thought I saw her lurking around that evening, watching us but I was high, I thought I'd half imagined it. I could have said something earlier and Jordan would still be here. It's all my fault.' Oscar began to link his fingers and twiddled them. 'I deserve to be punished.'

'You were punished, son. That bitch nearly killed you.'

'Mr Spalding, I'd appreciate it if you let Oscar speak.' Calling anyone a bitch wasn't sitting well with Gina especially after all the mean things that had happened. Jacob continued making notes.

'She's not a bitch, Dad. Caro has problems and she needs help. I'm as much to blame.'

Mr Spalding sighed and shook his head.

'Can you take me through what happened earlier today?'

'Yeah. Caro messaged me and said we had to talk. This was in the early hours. She came to meet me by the back of the summer house and she asked me to walk with her. We decided to go to the school gym unit, which is where we used to hang out. I knew we'd left a few cans of pop and it was comfortable sitting on the crash mats. When we got there, she opened me a can of pop and we started talking. A few minutes later, I was out of it. She got me back and drugged me, probably with one of her dad's sleeping tablets. How's that for revenge? As I was going under, she kept saying that I would now know how it felt, that Anthony told her that I'd drugged her and now I was going to pay. There was a manic look in her eyes and she said that I had it coming to me, just like Leah and Jordan did. Then she started crying, saying that we were best friends and that I'd abandoned her for the slut, that's what she called Leah. Then I was gone.'

'What do you remember next?' The man's snores in the next bed got louder, making it harder for Gina to hear.

'I woke up with a stiff neck, feeling spaced out. I was tied to an old chair with the ropes used for skipping. She laughed like some crazy person as she said I snored like a pig. That's when I saw the body on the floor. I didn't know it was Naomi at the time, all I saw was a pair of legs sticking out of the blanket and I knew then she was going to kill me. I shouted at her and called her lots of names I'm not proud of using and then she pulled out what looked like a little chopping knife and screamed so loud as she stabbed me, I thought my eardrum was going to burst.'

'And?'

'It was like reality hit her. She kept looking between me and Naomi's body on the floor, half tearing her hair out and crying. I played unconscious in the hope that she'd also think I was dying or dead. Then her phone pinged and she split. I was just relieved she hadn't killed me. I thought I was going to die. However much I tried to wriggle free and loosen the ropes I couldn't get out and I was bleeding. It was as if my hands weren't working or they were shaking too much. The sun was blinding me through that little strip of a window near the roof. It was confusing and disorientating. They said I was dehydrated when I came in.' He paused. 'Am I in big trouble?'

Mr Spalding stood again. 'Son, I'm not taking no for an answer this time. He's had enough now. We'll come to the station with a solicitor when he's discharged but that's it for now. Please leave my son to recover. He's been through a lot.'

'Thank you for all that, Oscar. You've been really helpful.' Gina nodded to Jacob and he closed his pad. Gina checked her phone and a message had come through. Caro Blakely was now at the station and ready to speak. It was time to get the full story.

CHAPTER SEVENTY-ONE

Caro sat at the table, the appropriate adult sent by Children's Services on one side and a solicitor on the other side. The woman from Children's Services popped her glasses on. The short round solicitor loosened his tie and mopped his brow with the end of it. Jacob leaned over and turned the fan on before taking a deep breath and exhaling slowly. Evening had come and it wasn't getting any cooler. The girl was wearing standard issue track bottoms and a grey T-shirt after her snagged black T-shirt had been entered into evidence. The material had appeared to match that of the torn material found at the scene of Jordan's murder and Caro had worn it again all day. 'Caro, you're going to have to speak to us eventually.'

The girl placed her head in her hands and sobbed. 'They drugged me, they deserved it. I just wanted Oscar to love me but he humiliated me after I've been such a good friend to him all these years.'

'Caro, please tell me what happened on the night of Leah's murder.' Gina leaned back, listening to the recording device hum in the background.

'I knew they'd be there so I sneaked out. It was easy getting out of the house as my dad was always taking sleeping tablets and my mum couldn't hear me moving around over his snoring. I couldn't let them get away with what they did to me. I wasn't going to kill her. I just wanted to hurt them, maybe have a go at them and ruin their party but I watched and waited, not knowing what to do, then they all left Leah in the clearing. As I did, I saw that perv from Oak Tree Walk lurking but he ran off when I caught him. I knew he wouldn't say anything as he wasn't meant to be there. Oscar slept with her…' Caro sniffed. 'I loved him, I always did. I did everything for him, everything he ever asked me to do, and he promised that we'd be together forever but I saw him go into his tent with Leah again, earlier that night. The others had chanted and joked about them outside but I got angrier. I remembered him having sex with Leah at the last party. It was meant to be me.' Gina didn't correct Caro on the fact that Oscar said he'd slept with Elsa on the first night. 'He was meant to want me. Leah spotted me, her pupils were all big and she just laughed at me and called me a loser as she swayed about the place. I pushed her and she fell back. She didn't even try to fight me off, she didn't have the strength and I don't even remember strangling her but my hands were around her neck and she'd gone. I got on my bike, which I'd hidden way back and hurried home. At first I thought she'd wake up and all would be fine then the news broke on Facebook and I knew she was definitely dead.'

The woman from Children's Services tilted her head as she watched on and Caro turned to her. 'Can you tell my mum I'm sorry. I didn't mean to kill her, I just wanted to make her say sorry.'

'Caro, can you tell me what happened to Jordan Rolph?'

She sobbed a couple of times and wiped her eyes. 'He sent me a Snapchat saying that he'd seen me lurking on the night of Leah's murder. He said he was going to tell the others that I'd been watching them that night. I told him I saw who killed Leah and that I'd tell him if he met me in person. He called me straight back and said that he knew it was me and he's not an idiot.' The girl tittered which Gina found a little disturbing. 'He said if I had sex with him, he'd conveniently forget. We both sneaked out. When I got there, he was standing at the top of the steps with his hands in his pockets and I was shaking, petrified that he would tell. I didn't know what else to do and I wasn't about to have sex with him…'

'What did you do?'

Caro shook her head and wiped her nose.

'Caro, what happened next?'

'I kicked him hard and he fell. I didn't mean to kill him but when I checked on him at the bottom of the steps, I could see from the light of my phone that he'd cracked his head and he didn't seem to be breathing.'

'So you left him?' Gina gulped. Gina had left Terry dying at the bottom of those stairs for ages.

Caro nodded.

'Moving on to today and Oscar.'

The girl yelled out and began to wail like a trapped cat. 'I loved him.' She stood and slammed her fists into the wall until they bled.

'I'm sorry, for the safety of my client, I'm going to have to request that we end this interview.'

Gina nodded and swallowed. It wasn't going to give her any pleasure to charge the sixteen-year-old with triple murder and one attempted murder but it had to be done. 'We'll prepare the charge sheet. Interview ended at twenty past nineteen hundred hours.'

Gina left the room with Jacob and the solicitor, then she caught Lara's eye as she sat waiting in the family room. Gina opened the door.

'What will happen to my daughter?'

'She'll be charged and will await trial. We'll know more later. In the meantime, I'll get someone to come and speak to you if you'll just wait here in the family room.'

'I can't believe this is happening to us.' Lara broke down.

'I'm so sorry, Mrs Blakely.'

Wyre came in with a hot drink.

'Thanks, Paula.' She left the two of them together and stood in the corridor, clearing her head of the chaos that was swirling around.

'That was intense, guv.' Jacob led the way back to the incident room.

'It was. Why don't I feel like we have a victory?'

'A kid murdered three kids, it's sad all round. I just can't process it.'

Gina shook her head. 'It's going to be a long night.' She swallowed, knowing that she still had to deal with Hannah this coming weekend. Caro Blakely was now going to pay for all that she'd done. Was Gina going to pay for her wrongs now?

Her phone beeped. It was another message from the anonymous number.

I know you killed my Terry!

She called Briggs. 'There's something I have to do before I interview Caro Blakely again.'

'What's happened?'

'I know who's sending the messages.'

'Who is it? I need to know—' Gina ended the call before he made his way across the station and to her. Pushing her way through the journalists, she saw Briggs coming out of the main door but he stood no chance of catching her up as the mob swarmed around him for some news. Pulling away, her hands shook and her stomach sunk. This was going to be a showdown.

CHAPTER SEVENTY-TWO

Gina's ex-mother-in-law's straggly grey hair fell in all directions. She held up her phone to Hetty. The woman retied her dressing gown and leaned against the doorpost.

'I banked on you coming.'

Gina held back, not wanting to shout and yell on the doorstep of the woman's house. 'How dare you send me these messages, and to my colleague too.'

'Police, my arse. I know what you did to Terry and I know what your colleague did to our Stephen. You must be a good shag for him to go that far to help you out of the shit.'

Gina seriously wanted to slap the woman right now. Respect in Hetty's household had never existed in any context.

'Your so-called colleague threatened to set poor Stephen up with a murder charge or plant some evidence.'

That was true but there was no way Gina would ever admit to that. Not to Hetty, not to anyone. The need to speak had been overridden with the need to preserve oneself and she didn't trust Hetty at all.

'You killed Terry, didn't you? He didn't fall down those stairs. I've seen the way you looked every time it was mentioned; the emotionless statue that you were at his funeral and that service that Hannah planned a few years ago. A person only has to look at you to know. You ooze guilt from every pore. I hope you never know how it feels to lose a child. What happened, Gina?'

With shaking hands, Gina turned away and paced back towards the gate before almost running back up to the door, her nose touching Hetty's ear. Hetty flinched. 'Here's what happened…'

The woman stared open-mouthed as Gina continued to whisper.

'Your son broke my bones. Your son raped me, repeatedly. Your son locked me in a shed. Your son used to shout so loud at his baby daughter I was scared he would kill her. Your son was a monster. You made that monster. That is exactly what happened. You could see that, Hetty, couldn't you?'

The woman pushed Gina away and shook her head.

In a low voice Gina continued, 'You saw the marks on me and the pain I was in and you turned a blind eye, just like you did with your husband all those years ago. You made a monster called Terry. That is what happened and you have the nerve to turn all this around onto me! Your son was a drunk and he fell. I won't let you bully and intimidate me like he did all those years ago just because he's dead.' Gina felt her face burning.

'No, you killed him and my husband never hurt me.'

'We all know, Hetty. Everyone knows. Your family, your friends, your neighbours – they heard the shouting too. I heard them gossiping. Stephen and Terry used to laugh when they used to talk about how he gave you the belt when you "nagged him about his drinking". Your own children laughed at their father abusing you.' Gina moved in so close, she could smell the bacon that Hetty had just eaten oozing from her skin. She whispered so quietly that Hetty would just about hear. 'You created two monsters, make sure your other monster doesn't turn and get his comeuppance. If he does, that's on you too. If anyone killed Terry, you did. You sat by and did nothing to correct his behaviour, to shape that nasty little boy into a good man.'

'But…' Tears began to spill from the woman's eyes. No one had ever said anything like this to the mighty Hetty but now the mighty had fallen.

Gina pushed the door open and saw exactly what she'd expected to see, a phone running on record. She grabbed it and spoke into it. 'I repeat, your son beat me, raped me and mentally abused me. For the tape, he came home drunk one night and fell down the stairs. I called an ambulance and the police but they couldn't save him. There was no evidence of any crime at the scene.' Gina paused. 'Even after all he did to me, Hetty, he was my husband and the father of my child and I loved him. He died, so please stop harassing me or I'll be forced to take action and I don't want to do that. Let's not air our dirty linen. It won't do either of us any good.'

The woman's bones cracked and creaked as she crumpled to the doorstep.

'How did you get my and my colleague's numbers?'

Hetty shrugged her shoulders. 'I'm not saying another word. I never want to see you again.' She sobbed, anger and bitterness still present in her face.

Gina deleted the recording, the phone numbers and messages between her, Briggs and Hetty before dropping the phone into Hetty's lap. Although she'd confessed nothing, she wanted Hetty to know that she'd gained nothing by her stunt.

The woman remained there as Gina drove away. Not one element of their exchange had been satisfying. In normal circumstances, Gina would like nothing more than to be able to help a woman who was just coming to terms with her own abuse after all these years but she couldn't be there for Hetty, not after everything that she'd done. Gina pulled over in the car down the road and yelled and cried. Her phone rang and she answered. 'I'm on my way back, sir.'

'Are you crying, Gina?'

'Yes.'

Briggs went silent. 'What's happened? I need to know. I feel sick to the stomach.'

'It's over. I'll fill you in when I get back.' She wiped her face. 'I'm on my way now. Be there soon. Sorry I left like that, it just couldn't wait.' She pulled back onto the road and headed back to the station, ready for a long night of finalising everything with the CPS. It had been an intense few days and all she wanted to do was go home, catch up on some sleep and wait for her daughter to turn up on Sunday. Only after that could she finally rest.

CHAPTER SEVENTY-THREE

Saturday, 7 August

DI Harte did come back to see me in hospital and I feel so much more positive after our chat. For the first time ever, I managed to open up about how Frank had been treating me and it's helped. She also helped me see that there is so much I can achieve. I refuse to let my mistakes in life stand in my way anymore. I had a social worker visit earlier and there's a place for me, a downstairs temporary apartment that is equipped for my needs. I can stay there until I've sorted my life out. That might take a while but she said there was no rush. I still don't know what's happening with my burnt-out cottage and the insurance. Nevertheless, I'm looking forward to getting my discharge papers and leaving this room.

I jump as I hear a knock on the door. It's Lara. The last time I saw her, she was shouting paedo at me from the kerb outside my cottage. My stomach begins to jitter and nausea begins to swell. I can't even escape them in hospital. I grip the emergency buzzer.

'Hi.' She smiles at a nurse before entering.

'Lara.'

I can't work out why she sounds like she's trying to be nice. 'It's good to see you looking so well and dressed.'

'I'm leaving any minute now. The cough has gone and my chest is a lot better. Just waiting for the docs to let me go.' She moves closer to me and I swallow.

'Look, I'm sorry about the way I was, at your house. What your husband did, it wasn't your fault.'

I look up, my gaze meeting hers and I see fear in her eyes. 'Thank you.' I feel a tear welling up in the corner of my eye. 'I heard about your daughter. How is she?'

Lara shook her head and looked away. 'I don't know. She's not saying anything to me or anyone really. I don't know her anymore. To do all those things—'

Only now did Lara really understand what it was like to be the object of blame for someone else's wrongs. I know there are no winners here, just enlightenment. 'They're terrible things that she did but you're her mother. She's going to need you.' At least I can walk away from Frank. She has it worse than me.

The woman nodded as a few tears slid down her cheeks. 'Remember that stupid pinkie promise we did at school? What were we, ten, maybe?'

I smile. Too much has happened for me to be angry forever. I remember back to when we were kids and I know I have to reach out. I may be too soft but I care, I really do. 'Yes, I said if I told people that you stole Charlotte's pens they'd blame me too as we were friends. You know something, Lara, I'm still your friend now. We're friends and whatever might come, we'll face together.'

Lara began to sob. 'How can you want to be friends with me? I stood outside your house shouting my mouth off, blaming you. How can you be so forgiving?'

'Because, Lara, I could use a friend right now too. I know how you feel and I know what you're going through to a certain degree. We can help each other through this just like we helped each other as kids. I know we weren't best friends for long as you went to a different senior school but I always missed what we had. Besides, things are going to get tougher for both of us, it'll be nice to have someone who understands.'

Lara stepped in and put her arms around me and, for a moment, I felt like we were ten again. Life will never be the same for either of us but it was ultimately tragedy that brought us back together as friends and I intend to be a good friend in all this. Having friends is all I wanted and now I can be there for Lara. She's as much of a victim in all of this as I am. I nearly lost my life and she's lost her daughter and I know what it's like when the angry mob call. I'll be there for her every step of the way.

EPILOGUE

Hannah played with the ends of her long plait as she sipped the coffee that Gina had placed before her. Ebony jumped through the cat flap and began eating her food.

'So, what's going on, Hannah?' Gina knew that Hetty had got hold of her number but she didn't know how. What she did know is that Hannah had the answers.

Her daughter's cheeks reddened and blotches formed at her neck. 'I did something really stupid, Mum, and I'm so, so, sorry.'

'Okay.'

'When I visited last, I went through your phone.' Hannah paused and gulped down more of the drink.

'Why were you going through my phone?'

'Nanny Hetty asked me to. She said she wanted to get the number of your boss and I knew who she meant when she said the man in his fifties. You've mentioned your DCI, Chris Briggs, before. I saw the messages on your phone and I read them. I know you're both in some sort of on/off relationship. I didn't want to give Nan the number but she kept going on, saying that this Briggs threatened to plant some evidence on Uncle Stephen once and she said she was going to take care of it, once and for all.'

'That's an absurd accusation. So you gave her his number without speaking to me?'

Hannah nodded. 'I'm not proud of my part in this but I owe you the truth. I couldn't say anything when you called as Greg was there and I didn't know if talking on the phone would incriminate anyone. I didn't want anyone to get in any trouble.' She shrugged and began to play with the handle on the cup. 'Anyway, after I gave her your number, it got more sinister.'

'Sinister.' Gina felt her hands tremble with anger in her lap. Her daughter had ended up in the middle of all this and now she hated her ex-mother-in-law more than ever. Her mind flashed to the woman crumpled and crying on the doorstep.

'I don't know. I think they're going a bit mad, if I'm honest. I overheard Stephen and Nan talking. They're convinced that you must have had something to do with Dad's death, but that's just stupid. We all know it was an accident. The way they talk about you...'

'It's okay. I know the sort of things they say.'

'It's not on. I don't know why they hate you so much and I don't believe for one minute you would have had anything to do with Dad's death. I know he was drunk and he fell down the stairs.' Gina gulped, hoping that Hannah couldn't see her guilt. 'I think I need to distance myself from them. Nan has been good to Gracie but she's not good for me anymore and I don't want my child to grow up around them with the way that they speak. Stephen hates women, I can tell by the way he calls them names and treats them. I don't know how his girlfriend stands to be around him. Nan doesn't put him right either and I can't forgive that. I have a daughter and being around them is toxic so I'm cutting myself off from them. I'm sorry I chose them over you in the past and I'm sorry I gave Nan the phone numbers.'

Gina reached over and hugged her daughter. At last, there was a break in the tension between them. 'It's okay. You know I'm always here for you.'

'Thanks, Mum. About the messages, just tell your colleague to tell her to get lost and I'm sure she'll go away.'

Hannah had no idea that Gina had already sorted this problem. Since facing Hetty, there had been no more messages or communications of any kind.

'Nan is just full of ridiculous ideas and needs putting in her place. If he tells her to stop harassing him and that he knows who she is, I'm sure she'll stop. I'll tell her too when I call her next. I'm not bothered if she has a go at me anymore.'

A ray of sunlight reached the far wall of Gina's kitchen. 'I'll pass the message on to him.' She smiled, not giving anything away.

'I'm going to ask you a question and I don't want you to lie to me. I sense things, like the way you were at Dad's memorial a few years ago and the way you stiffen when I talk about him. I want the truth, Mum. What was he really like?'

This was the conversation Gina had been dreading. However bad her ex-husband was to her, telling her daughter about the beatings, the rapes and the control wasn't going to be easy but if their relationship was to move forward, the truth had to come out. The time had come. 'I hope you've got nothing else on today.'

Hannah shook her head. 'I'm here all day. In fact, I told Greg that I'd be staying over so take your time. I just need the truth.'

A tear slid down Gina's cheek and Hannah hugged her mother. 'It's okay, Mum. Take your time.'

Some truths should never come out but others should. It was time to face the monster of the past who'd done nothing but divide them. It was time to rebuild things with her daughter.

A LETTER FROM CARLA

Dear Reader,

I'm truly grateful that you chose to read *One Left Behind*. The support from the crime reading community always makes me feel welcome as a reader and an author, and for that I'm thankful. I also hope you enjoyed the ninth instalment of the DI Gina Harte series as I thoroughly enjoyed writing it.

If you enjoyed *One Left Behind* and want to keep up to date with all my latest releases, just sign up at the following link. Your email address will never be shared and you can unsubscribe at any time.

www.bookouture.com/carla-kovach

As with my previous books, the subject matter is dark. I specifically chose teenagers to focus on in this book as I feel those years spent battling hormones and seeking acceptance makes them vulnerable and susceptible to doing things that they wouldn't normally do. I certainly wouldn't like to be that age again, navigating my way through the demon that is peer pressure while not knowing if I wanted to laugh or cry on any given day. I also felt I had to tell Sandra's story in this book. Not only did she have mobility problems, she was trapped in an abusive relationship where she couldn't see a way out of her situation. I also wanted to play with the idea that people who stand in judgement of others might just get the tables turned on them. It's so easy to angrily throw blame without proof of a person's involvement. I appreciate that we're innocent until proven guilty.

Whether you are a reader, a tweeter, a blogger, Facebooker or a reviewer, I really am appreciative of everything you do and as a writer, this is where I hope you'll leave me a review. They not only help me, they help other readers.

Again, thank you so much. I'm an avid social media user so please feel free to contact me on Twitter, Instagram or through my Facebook page.

Thank you,
Carla Kovach

CarlaKovachAuthor

CKovachAuthor

carla_kovach

ACKNOWLEDGEMENTS

I'm super thankful to the team behind the book. I might write a draft but so many people are a massive part of the package as a whole and I couldn't do this without them.

Massive thanks to my editor, Helen Jenner. As always, I'm grateful for all the work that you do. You see things I don't notice and come up with the best notes that really polish my work. I love working with you and hope to continue being a part of team Helen for many books to come. I also love the covers that you and the designer work so hard on. They look stunning and make my books stand out like shiny diamonds on a shelf.

Covers mean so much which is why I want to say thank you to cover designer, Lisa Brewster. I absolutely adore it!

Huge thank you to Peta Nightingale too. It's always a joy to hear from you about contracts and how my books in the Netherlands are doing.

Kim Nash, Noelle Holten and Sarah Hardy; you are all superstars in the world of publicity. You work above and beyond, creating a fanfare for our books. Thank you so much for all that you do.

I'd like to share a huge thank you to all the brilliant bloggers for giving up their time, I appreciate everything you do and it's lovely to read your blogs too. I'm touched that you chose my book to read and review. It means a lot. And I need to mention the Fiction Café Book Club, a group on Facebook of which I'm a member. I'm grateful of all the mentions and positivity that comes my way.

I need to mention the other Bookouture authors. The amount of support given makes me feel as though I'm part of a big happy family. It's wonderful to have this sense of belonging and I'd never take that for granted.

Derek Coleman, Su Biela, Brooke Venables, Anna Wallace and Vanessa Morgan, thank you so much for beta reading my work. Getting those first reads before my books are published always makes me feel less nervous on publication day. Your input and support remains invaluable to me. Thank you for your friendship too.

DS Bruce Irving, you help me when it comes to the real world of policing; the bits I've never seen except on TV dramas. I know we have some gruesome conversations, each valuable in bringing my plots to life – hehe. Ginormous thanks for that and long we may continue to have our discussions.

Finally, I have to thank my fabulous husband, Nigel Buckley. I'm grateful for the cups of coffee, the encouragement and the support you give me. You help me when I'm stressed and having a bad day and you're always there to celebrate my achievements too.

Printed in Great Britain
by Amazon